TALLAH

TALLAH

BOOK ONE

C. M. Antal

Podium

Cover design by Baconstrap
Map by Daniël Hasenbos

ISBN: 979-8-3470-0101-9

Published in 2026 by Podium Publishing
www.podiumentertainment.com

Podium

THE FROZEN EXPANSE
Aztroa Magnor
Great Watch
Drak's Perch
Garet
Marestra
THE CRAGS
Bastra
Valen
Drack
Solstice
Inner Sea
of Vas
Hepius School
of Healing
SALMEK'S
RUINS
Ria
Bisery River
The Twins
Mourning
Sea
Calabran
Old Forge
River Calis
THE GREAT DIVIDE
Neant
THE GREAT DIVIDE
Amaranth
Hoarfrost
Academy
VAS
Humanity's Bastion

TALLAH

CHAPTER ONE

Blood and Fire

Vermen stank. Their stench filled the narrow tunnel and masked the burnt hair and meat smell of the three guards Tallah had just smeared across the walls.

In the enclosed space of the cavern, they sat clustered around smoking fires or lay in their own filth and droppings. The rank odor escaping into the wider network of passages made Tallah's eyes water beneath her mask.

She counted two scores of the creatures. There could have been maybe twice that. Well armed and well fed, by the looks of things. All shapes and sizes had gathered to this nest. Some were heads taller than she was, while some barely reached her knees. All affronted her.

Two wargged humans snapped at one another, leashed to a pole just far enough away that they couldn't properly fight. A group of the vermen were gathered around them, poking and prodding the two into frothing fury before unleashing them on one another. Jeers and snarls egged on the fight.

There was a shaman by the largest fire, dressed in stained robes and adorned with bone fetishes. It looked to be painstakingly instructing two of the others to do . . . something. She couldn't make it out for the distance even if she lifted the mask for a better look.

Realization dawned when one of the largest vermen raised a spear. A body was tied to it, limbless and naked, vaguely female. For a brief moment, Tallah hoped it was a corpse.

Corpses don't scream when set to cook above the fire. The girl made a horrible noise as they began rotating her over the flames.

Tallah wove illum into a firefly and sent it out towards the wretch. It floated as a mote of dust on the soft draft until it was near enough to the flame. A flick of her fingers sped it up to impact soundlessly against the girl's exposed shoulder. A silent command and the firefly burst inside her chest cavity, pulping her heart. The vermen hissed in confusion as the screams cut out with a gurgle. They'd been tormenting the poor thing for quite some time, by the look of things.

"There's one above the fire," Sil whispered in her ear, finally caught up. "See him? In the smoke?"

She did.

One more prisoner hung in a cage above the lick of the fire, slowly rotating in the updraft of hot air, clear sight of him obstructed by the smoke.

Tallah had to squint to be sure it was even a person. "Alive? Are you sure?"

"Seems to be." Sil's eyes glowed a faint lime green as she studied the scene. "He's malnourished to the bone, but there's a heartbeat. I can't see more from this far." She let out a soft squeak as she stepped into the offal of one of the dead verman guards.

To answer her questions, the wretched man screamed, jerked his limbs in the throes of some fit, and then was still, head wedged between the bars.

"That's the sound I heard." Sil snapped her fingers. "I told you I heard screaming. Ha!"

More vermen dropped whatever they'd been doing to gather around the fire and study the limp corpse roasting there, its cooking stench finally enough to overpower their musk.

Disgusting beasts, barely worth the time to kill. Tallah scrunched up her nose at the prospect of dirtying her hands on these blight-carriers.

But after so long exploring the tunnels with no result in sight, this seemed as likely a path forward as any other. And it afforded her a rare chance to work out some frustration.

How many days already spent beneath the mountain? She'd asked Bianca to stop keeping count, as it served to annoy her. Sil would likely complain soon enough, denied late-wither sun and fresh air for so long on this insane quest. And she'd be right to be upset. A couple more galleries explored to no result and even Tallah would accept they'd failed.

"Don't kill the one in the cage. I need him alive." Sil pointed to the fighting wargs. "Those two you should destroy. Too far gone."

"Do you need him in one piece?" Tallah donned the silver mask and had another glance around the cave for any hidden cantrip enchantments. Nothing.

"Human-shaped, preferably. Just make sure he's alive when you're done. I'll only need him for a couple of heartbeats."

"Right. Stay put. Make sure none of them get out. Shouldn't take long."

Vermen hadn't come to check on their missing guards. Intelligent enough to form a horde, not enough to ensure safety, even if this particular nest looked to be better organized than most. No females in sight so the young were kept somewhere else. Weapons on racks. Food stacked in sacks and crates. This was a small raiding army, and she could bet some wild honey that it wasn't the shaman who'd organized things.

No matter. It wasn't the first oddity they'd found since coming down into the Valen-Drack Passage. If she spent time wondering on each, she'd never get anything done.

As she stepped out of the tunnel mouth and saw Sil's weave in the air, barriers blocking the exits they could see, the wretch in the cage looked up at her. It wasn't an errant glance. He'd turned his head towards her and raised his hands in a decrepit gesture of warding.

Is he warning me off? That's precious. She would've winked at him if not for the mask. She settled for a smile.

The vermen bristled at her approach, dozens of beady black eyes turning in stupid silence to regard the intruder. Her heels clicked on the filth-encrusted stone floor, no effort made for stealth.

They hissed and swarmed like the rats they were, clubs and swords raised high. Some, two brain cells richer than the rest, cocked crossbows and took aim.

Her fireflies flitted out in a storm. With finger snaps, she launched them outward to bury into fur, scraps of armor, eyeballs even. The imbeciles didn't even flinch to avoid her volley.

With another snap, they detonated. Five vermen burst apart like overripe fruit, the concussive bangs of detonation echoing in the cavern. They fell in bits and showered her in offal and blood.

Bugger! She'd been too close, allowed them one too many steps.

Twin fireballs turned the beasts with crossbows into burnt-out grease stains on the wall. Air burned out of them in screeches of agony.

The wargged humans rushed her, their chains loosed. Poor wretches. A few days earlier and they might have been spared. As they were, she cut them down with heat lances, turned them into smoking effigies that screamed more than any human should rightly be able to.

Some of the screaming came from the imprisoned human above the fire. His cage swayed in the shock wave of her explosions, but she hadn't hit the thing. Why was he screaming?

A fresh wreath of fireflies turned the next line of vermen into splattered gore.

The rest was simple cleanup. The shaman had tried to raise a staff and channel some crude effect. Laughable. A fireball burned the meat off its bones and turned the staff to ashes.

One rat died clawing against Sil's barrier after discarding its weapon to try to make a run for it. She blasted out its spine and left it squealing in the muck.

The foodstuffs caught fire, the smoke tasting acrid. A hand gesture signaled Sil to drop the barriers so some of it could rush out through the tunnels. Whatever filtered out through the rock gaps above would be visible for miles around the mountain if anyone had a care to look.

Ash rose on the sudden updraft of hot air. It stuck to her clothes like fine powder and made her sneeze, the worst the rats had managed against her. She did feel better, though. A bit of exercise had done her good.

One final firefly drifted up to the cage and blasted apart its chain. The awful bone gibbet crashed down to the scattered embers beneath, right atop the charred corpse. The man inside screamed himself into keening cries, ran out of air, loudly inhaled, and screamed some more. She considered killing him for the quiet while she paced through the room, stamping out any whimpering survivor.

"Blood of the Goddess, what thistle got in your knickers?" Sil asked as she picked her way over the gore-strewn room. "I get you're frustrated, but this is just deranged. Ugh."

Tallah spat black ash and cleansed her mouth with water from the canteen. "The man's alive. Shush."

All the vermen lay dead or still smoldering. No other traps that she could see. Maybe some guards farther out in the tunnels had escaped her purge, but she wasn't about to run after them. Why even bother?

She dragged the cage from the fire, heedless of how the bugger inside squealed. One of his legs was bent at an odd angle, bone pushing out against leather-like skin. "Touch him and we can move on. There's another tunnel on the other side of the cave. We may as well keep going."

"Get him out of there. I don't want to touch that thing. Those are human bones."

Tallah sighed and bent to the task, ripping apart the wreckage to extract the sorry sod. Not a man at all but a boy, at most twenty summers if she were any judge. Patchy stubble covered his cheeks, white as snow, wherever he wasn't blistered or covered in sores. Starved right down to skin and bone.

How'd that happen?

A vague weave hung on him, like a poorly made enchantment. Was he blessed? She turned him over for better inspection.

"Ah, here it is."

He had one of Anatol's idiotic blessings tattooed on the back of his neck.

Slow death through divine regeneration. One had to be either inexperienced or an utter imbecile to have that thing tattooed. Likely wouldn't have lasted much longer even without her intervention.

At some point he'd begun laughing. Sounded like a toothless saw blade trying to cut ironwood.

"All yours, your prissiness." Tallah kicked him over so he'd be looking up at them. "Be quick about it."

"Yes, yes, I don't want to be in here any more than you do. See if there's anything worth picking up. Food's running low."

"I'm not eating anything from here."

Even without it being disgusting on a conceptual level, the whole place stank of rot, rat droppings, and who knew what other kinds of filth. How a creature could live like this and still be somewhat intelligent was beyond her imagining.

Sil knelt next to the man and placed the tips of her fingers on his forehead. "I'd ask for your consent, but I feel you're not in the best state of mind to give it. My apologies. *I require touching this mind.*"

Lightning cracked and the cave exploded in red light. In a heartbeat, Sil was blasted from her feet. She impacted against the far wall, almost ten yards away, with a wet crunch and the sickening sound of bones snapping.

Tallah's feet moved before the rest of her had time to react. With her heart thundering in her throat, she found the healer in a pile, one arm bent awkwardly beneath her, blood dripping by the corner of her mouth.

She trained a fireball on the still laughing man—

"N-No," Sil croaked from the floor, choking. "Don't . . ."

With a glance to confirm he was still on the floor and not somehow attacking, Tallah knelt and extracted a vial of accelerant from the thigh pouch Sil wore for emergencies. It had cracked but was usable.

It was a struggle to get Sil to drink the mixture.

"I . . ." Sil choked on blood as it was forced out of her lungs by the healing draft. Tallah helped move her palm to her chest while she coughed and struggled to form words between gasps of pain. "*I require . . . this one . . . be mended.*"

The draft stabilized her condition, but the prayer got her back to her feet in a burst of healing light.

"Bones of my sisters, that hurt," she complained as the healing incantation completed its work. "Nearly cracked my skull open." She ran a hand through her hair and grimaced when her fingers came away bloody. "Did crack my skull open."

Unassisted, she stumbled forward to where her staff lay. "Put that away. He's not dangerous. Give me some space to find my wits."

Tallah put out the fireball she'd kept floating just above their heads. Whatever the bastard had done, she was ready to send him to an ashen grave.

Sil had other plans.

"How are you alive?" She approached the bugger and poked him with the butt of her staff. "Why are you even here?"

He howled with laughter punctured by cries of anguish whenever his blessing fired off. Now that Tallah looked at him more closely, she could see the exact moment when it activated.

"What happened?" she asked.

"Well . . . you won't believe this." Sil poked him again. "This blighter's an Other."

Tallah stared at her, and then at the man. She must've misheard. "You can't be serious."

"Happens that I am." Sil shrugged. "Either he's an Other, or he's gone so far over to the mad side that he's conjured up stuff the theaters of Aztroa would pay fortunes for. He's not from Edana."

"Maybe you've hit your head too hard? Heal again?"

Sil gave her a level, steady glare and pointed the staff's blue jewel at her. "Maybe I'll whack you once over the head, and you can tell me if it makes more sense to you then. Guy's alien. And to top it off, he's enchanted too. Got a strange mesh in his head protecting something. I touched it and you saw the rest. Not aelir or human made."

A man, locked in a cage, half-dead, who was an Other and touched by the divine?

It stank of destiny malarkey. For a heartbeat, Tallah considered burning him to ash and forgetting she'd ever laid eyes on the wretch.

"Interesting Other?" she asked instead.

"I don't understand most of what I've seen in his head from his life. From the more recent, however . . ." She turned in place and studied the walls. "There's a secret door over there. People were brought in, taken through, and never brought back out. May be of interest."

Now the temptation to burn him became overpowering. Christina rose to the surface of her thoughts, the ghost tempering her fire with her own infectious curiosity. 'Don't be rash, Tallah. Might be he's useful to us.'

"Can you heal him?"

Sil barely considered the question before answering. "No. Maybe the Sisters could. But look at him. He's got both feet in the grave. I can't heal malnutrition, dehydration, and whatever flavor of crazy's gripping him."

Tallah scrunched up her nose and regarded him, a thought forming. If she ignored the stubble and the overgrown hair, now that she really considered the man, he couldn't have been more than . . . fourteen summers? Sixteen? A boy that had gone in over his head likely and ended up in an impossible situation.

She slit open a rend and dug her hand inside.

"Have you gone daft?!" Sil gaped at the helmet she pulled out. "Keep that thing away from me."

"It's not for you. It's for him. I need a siphon to power it."

"No!"

"Yes."

"It's inhumane!"

"He'll live and he'll be mobile. What else would you want? If we can't find what I'm looking for in this secret passage you mentioned, then we portal out and we get him to the Sisters." She rolled the bi-horned helmet in her hands thoughtfully. "You got a name from him?"

"Vergil. And it's still no guarantee the helmet's going to help. You know what it did last time." Sil eyed the thing with a lovely mixture of loathing and distrust. "Best leave the bugger. He'll expire soon enough."

"I'm taking him. And I hope the ghost remembers what it got the last time it acted out. Heal the boy so I can stick this on his head. Think I broke every bone he's got when I pulled him out."

Tallah could feel Sil's disapproving glare on the back of her neck as she stuffed the helmet over the boy's head. A snug fit, though—she had to pack in his ears or risk clipping them off.

"You stay between us. I don't want to get thrown again," the healer said, sidling up behind her.

"Just get it over with. I want to see this secret tunnel."

Sil invoked her prayer over Tallah's shoulder, and together they watched the boy spasming as the goddess's grace healed whatever ailed him. Anatol's blessing was a stupid stopgap that barely did much healing at all, aside from scrapes, bruises, or light internal bleeding. And even for those, it was wholly unreliable. Pretty much like the god Anatol himself.

Next came the tether. Sil tied her to the helmet via a thin illum thread that transferred her reserve to the artifact. For some heartbeats, nothing happened.

The boy—Vergil—screamed and jerked on the floor. He rolled onto his stomach with some difficulty, then brought up his hands under him. After several false starts, he managed finding his feet to stand up.

"Did I also manifest that?" Sil peeked out at the result.

"No. You were dressed at the time. Possibly just contextual. We never did study this thing properly. Someone got skittish about handling it."

A translucent set of plate armor covered the desiccated half-corpse.

"Interesting enchantment. Does pull a lot of illum."

That ridiculous helmet housed an insane spirit—or echo of one, Tallah wasn't entirely sure on the details. Fueled by illum, it could take over whatever host wore the stupid thing as Sil had learned on her own when they'd found it.

Vergil banged fists against his armored chest, screaming at the top of his lungs. If that was the ghost's madness, or his own, Tallah preferred not knowing.

"I hope you're happy. You've let that thing run loose again." Sil kept Tallah between herself and the boy. She'd first worn the helmet and suffered its possession.

At least this time the possessing ghost didn't seem inclined to challenge Tallah. It instead rushed some half-burned verman corpse and attacked it with fists and armored feet, mulching it into a paste of organ meat and shattered bones.

"Oy, bugger," she called. It turned slowly in place. Only the whites of the boy's eyes were visible through the T-shaped visor of the helmet. He growled, the language as alien as Sil claimed he was. She thumbed in the direction of the wall. "There's a door somewhere over there. See if you can find it."

Had it actually understood her? Maybe. It turned away, stomped over a couple more rat corpses, then bolted for the wall.

Straight for the bloody thing. And through it with a deafening crash.

"He's found the door," Sil pointed.

"Certainly one way to do it."

Sounds of a struggle echoed from the dark chamber beyond. The ghost howled. Something answered it and then screamed out in pain.

"Draws out quite a lot of illum. A staggering drain if it fights."

They passed through the gap opened up by Vergil and, a short way forward by the light of a sprite, they found the boy mashing a strange corpse underfoot. It would've been twice as tall as a man, maybe just as wide, and had the head of a beast grafted atop a corded mass of muscle.

"Chimera," Tallah noticed. "Well, this is finally promising."

Three more similar creatures tried barring their way. Two died to her fire. One collided headfirst with the horned helmet and did not walk away. Four guards to oversee a short corridor of barely twenty paces that ended at a cylindrical unlit pit. It bore down into the mountain with signs of some mechanism available for . . . something.

"I can't see a way to activate this." Sil studied the walls around the pit for the usual secret lever. The Valen-Drack Passage was lousy with secrets and lairs.

"There's illum woven in here. Like the old platforms in Hoarfrost." Tallah looked into the depths and sniffed in annoyance. "If I were hiding beneath a mountain, I would be paranoid enough to make sure I controlled the way down. I'll bet you that if there's some clockwork here, it's locked at the bottom. We'll jump it."

'I'm here.' Bianca swapped places with Christina and offered her ability. 'You need to practice with me, so I will not be holding your hand on this. You can manage a simple controlled descent.'

Sil scrunched up her nose as Tallah rose in the air. Vergil growled low, prowling the edge of the pit. He'd picked up a nicked sword from one of the guards and was testing it against imaginary foes.

"Be. Gentle! At least this time." Sil complained when Tallah lifted her in the air. "Last time you bruised me black and blue, in very unpleasant places, I might add. I may return the favor if you do it again."

Vergil struggled against her invisible grip, kicked out and flailed his arms about like an animal caught in a snare. She considered smashing him against a wall to quiet him, but expected the living boy within the magic armor may not survive the violence. Shaking him up and down a few times, though? That did the trick.

It took the better part of a bell to reach the bottom of the shaft in slow, steady descent. Here and there small windows had been cut in the rock like vents, too narrow and low for any of them to fit through. It only left the descent and the unnerving silence. Even after almost half of wither spent beneath the Valen-Drack mountain range, the eerie underground silence still managed to get under Tallah's skin.

Air felt somehow thicker the more they descended. It stank. Blood. Offal. Like an abattoir in midsummer. Sil gagged loudly.

"Right path," Tallah said.

"I'm going to regret this, aren't I?"

"Only if you breathe through your mouth."

The mask's sight showed power woven beneath. Not just the natural flow of illum, but something stagnating, shaped and set into stone. She could recognize a sanctum's overall shape easily enough even from that. Yes, definitely the right path and the right place. This was a Vitalis's domain. Old one. Powerful even from afar.

They touched down at the bottom uncontested. A single wide door led them out.

"Blood of the Goddess!" Sil exclaimed.

Tallah removed the mask and got a real look at the scene stretching away from their sprite light.

Flesh on the walls. Flesh on the ceiling. Skinless. Shivering. Undulating. Moving and crawling, extending feelers to them. In the Ikosmenia's sight it was all woven power, illum stored in networks of sinew and nerves. In real-sight, a fever dream.

"Not even the weirdest type of sanctum." She stalked forward, hardly keeping the giddy joy from her voice. The floor squelched underfoot and tried to suck down on her boots as she walked. "Don't tarry. Keep your sprite close."

A mouth grew atop a meaty stalk and tried to bite through her boot's heel. She stepped on it and tiny teeth crunched.

Vergil grumbled and swung his sword at some of the larger fleshy growths to little effect. They pulled back into the wall and grew sneering faces. Some mirrored their own.

Incredible how the helmet kept the boy animate and moving, she thought. A testament to the skill of whoever had made and enchanted it, for whatever inane purpose something like that would have served.

"Save your strength, ghost," she suggested. "You'll get enough to fight later."

Sil's sprite illuminated more of the horrors ahead. Bodies were hung from hooks and embedded into walls. Drooping, wax-like corpses extended feeble hands towards them. She burned some but elicited barely more than hisses of pain.

"Why?" Sil asked.

"Why what?"

"Just . . . why?"

"A Vitalis needs biomass. Blood especially. Best way to store blood is in living tissue. Best way to build a self-defending sanctum is, well, you see it. There's a reason Catharina burned most of the Vitalises at the dawn of the empire."

Sil sneered at this. "She's missed one."

"More than. Most surviving ones have laid down old practices. This one looks to be a fundamentalist."

It got noisy when the tunnel opened up into a large, barely lit cavern. Bodies covered the walls—were the walls—and they all spoke in a cacophony of mimicked languages. Vestigial reactions, likely. Most had been remade in some fashion, broken down, sewn back up, explored and then emptied of whatever made them valuable.

Standard practice for a Vitalis and their unceasing quest for understanding the leverages of life. This one looked to have gone far off the shores of sanity.

Eyeballs of various shapes and sizes provided strange luminescence, a yellowish light that made everything beyond the sprite all the more grotesque.

"Hello," Tallah called out. "I'm looking for the master of this place." Theatrics. Chances of anyone actively listening were nearly null.

One of the corpses ripped itself out of the wall and charged them, exposed viscera clinging to bones too mismatched to be all its own. It was a self-defense reaction to intruders in the domain.

She allowed it to cover half the distance separating them before she turned it into a bonfire. It stumbled with the impact of the first fireball, took a few more steps forward, and finally collapsed. It screeched as it burned to ashes.

And others answered it.

"Best be ready. They'll come from all sides. Keep your barriers up."

She didn't need to check that Sil obeyed her instruction. Vergil, however, rushed forward, sword out, to meet the first of the assaulting creatures. Should have probably stuck him in one of Sil's protective cages. Would be a shame to waste him in here.

In one strike, he bisected the leading chimera, neck to groin, his sword cutting all the way down to the rock with a dull clang.

Tallah whistled in appreciation.

'Well, that was definitely something,' Christina echoed her amazement in the back of Tallah's mind. They knew the ghost in the helmet was strong, but this was far above expectation. She watched the boy swoop under the scything strike of another beast, flash his sword in a bloody arc, and cut two of the monsters in half at the waist.

The illum draw he enacted on her was nearly painful. *Well, best not let him fight alone, then.*

Twin heat lances burst apart several of the chimeras crowding ahead. They came from the walls, ripping out of their meaty cocoons to trail flapping muscles and thick sinews like a puppeteer's strings. Most were only armed with jutting spears of bone, their own limbs fashioned into weapons.

She snapped her fingers, and a constellation of fireflies appeared to orbit her head. Another snap and they all loosed to pop wherever they could dig into the advancing corpses. Less effective than with the rats. Small explosions ripped throats and ribs apart but did little to deter the advance.

"Behind you!" Sil called out from the mouth of the tunnel where she'd hunkered down.

Tallah turned and launched a fireball at a creature that had come out straight from the floor itself. The blast turned its upper half into cinders, but its feet kept carrying it forward, screeching as it burned and flailed its deadly limbs at her. She had to hit it again, harder, to finally see it fall.

More encircled her. Vergil fought a cluster of them, stepping over pieces he chopped off, kicking, punching, slashing at everything that came within his range. Impressive as he was, he'd be overrun soon. Bodies crowded in the background, spilling out of side passages, climbing one over the other in a mad rush to die.

It was getting hard to focus now that they were within her killing range. Rot. Burning hair and charring meat. Keening cries of pain, all too human in their suffering. She closed herself up to them or risk faltering in her determination.

This close up, she needed to defend with both sword and flame, constantly moving back towards the tunnel. Their sheer numbers were enough to overrun her and the boy.

'A bit of an overreaction to only three people wandering in,' Christina suggested with amusement. 'I'm swapping back with Bianca until you find the master of the place. You don't seem to need my help that badly.'

'I'm ready,' Bianca confirmed.

Tallah reached out a tether and yanked Vergil back from the fray, sending him sailing above the mass of bodies. Even before he landed, she heaved forward with a kinetic push. Her back burned with the effort as Bianca took over for a heartbeat to handle the complex calculations of force that she needed.

'Brace,' the ghost whispered. 'It will hurt.'

It did. A second heave of power felt like being ripped in two by the colliding forces she commanded, while at the same time being stretched out and compressed as Bianca wove her tethers and fulcrums.

"Barriers up!" Tallah called back as she prepared a real hit.

In a moment, Sil's barriers separated them from the advancing horde, wedged into the gap Bianca's efforts had created. They'd been pushed against the wall, cornered into the small cone of light the sprite offered.

Bastard things, she complained. The ghost ignored this as she took over again for the complicated equations.

Bianca pushed out beyond the barriers. The monsters did not stop advancing, instead crushing the ones in front between the mass behind and the invisible walls. Cracks began forming, and Sil yelped with the effort of maintaining the separation.

This had clustered the beasts together enough.

Tallah wove a line of flame orbs above their heads, putting as much strength into each as she dared without burning all the air from the room. Each new layer of fire compacted the one beneath, made the flames burn brighter. Hotter.

The air sizzled with the heat. The wall behind them fried and screeched.

"Drop the barrier," she ordered.

Sil did and the flames shot outward, guided by Tallah's hands, at the speed of her thoughts. They cut straight through corpses, melted flesh off bones, disintegrated heads and limbs.

At first a fanning strike to gain space. The first line of horrors died without screams as the fire melted them down to blackened stumps. She brought the orbs around, replenished their heat, and scythed through those that followed. A deep breath of acrid, overheated air. Whatever escaped her flames was brought down by Vergil as he stalked behind her line of devastation to kill whatever she missed. If he was bothered by the heat, it didn't show.

Ten heartbeats. Twenty. Thirty. She let out the breath, gasped for a second and choked on the noxious fumes.

Smoldering corpses littered the cavern floor. Those farthest back retreated into the tunnel mouths, running and screaming. Vergil chased and cut down some of them.

Sil rushed to her side and handed over a vial of aerum. The serum acted quickly to replace the air she couldn't draw in.

On the far side of the room, Vergil collapsed, the enchantment's strength waning.

Burnout, Tallah realized with a jolt. Barely able to move, she signaled for Sil to take the siphon from her. The healer obliged and staggered with the draw. It felt like a boulder shifting off her own shoulders. Vergil straightened and trotted back to them.

With some help from Sil, they moved out into one of the tunnels and away from the still-burning pyres of corpses, where the smoke was thinnest.

"That wasn't fun," Sil quipped and let out a tired sigh. "So many bodies. How?"

Tallah huffed and pitched forward, hands on knees, trying to regain some semblance of coherence. She'd burned herself out. Used too much illum. Her limiters had flashed hot and at least a couple of them had cracked into uselessness. Channeling would be less controllable for now, but in here she felt that might be of help.

'I had fun,' Bianca said, and radiated her pleasure. 'Should do that more often.'

Get buggered.

Before she could ask for nettle dust, Sil already had a bag in hand and offered it up. She accepted it gratefully.

One inhalation of the fine powder cleared up the dizziness accompanying a near-total illum depletion. A second lungful opened her up to more power and strength steadily returned as they cowered behind two layers of protective barriers.

"Better?" Sil asked.

"Much. Thank you. Had to exert myself."

Sil grumbled, her eyes following the path forward. "There's something waiting ahead. Voices."

"Hardly. They're moaning, not speaking."

"Clearer than the others so far. More chimeras?"

Tallah shook her head.

"Vitalises are loath to waste biomass. I've just burned away some hundred ready-made bodies, and crippled a lot more. Whoever's master of this place won't want to throw more meat at us unless they're certain they'll kill me. Moving forward, I'd worry about poison. Or walls closing in to suffocate us." She grimaced and gestured to the curious stalks wriggling on the wall. "All of this is the Vitalis. They know we're here." She pointed to a baleful yellow eye on a wall. "They know exactly where we are."

"So . . . why not kill us?" Sil dipped a hand into a rend and pulled out some purgers and stored the vials in her satchel.

"Wounded ego, I'd guess. If I make more of a nuisance of myself, they'll want to deal with me personally." She straightened and grinned. "Let's see what else I can break in here."

She fixed the mask over her eyes.

The way forward was guarded beyond the first bend in the tunnel. Two large chimeras loomed ahead, and died to Vergil's sword. Tallah took the time to restore her illum reserves while the boy made himself useful.

At the end they emerged into a circular room, well lit by captive sprites. Maybe thirty paces across. Terrifying.

Sil took one look at the content, turned around, and was violently sick outside the threshold.

Rows upon rows of bodies. Living. Female. Maimed to *fit*.

"A breeding room," Tallah surmised on a single look. Aelir. Elend. Humans. Mostly humans, of various ages.

All pregnant in some stage. Cradles of bone held each limbless body with a myriad of horrid tubes dug into the flesh. Some were headless. Most may as well have been, under the mass of feeding tubes attached to their faces. Only terrified eyes stared out, unseeing.

"This is precisely why Catharina had them all burned. They run out of easy-to-access bodies so they start breeding their own." She spat and shook her head. A fundamentalist for certain. Either extremely old or stupidly powerful to flaunt their strength like this.

Vergil paced the room, and the ghost possessing him quieted down to a low, angry growl. Even that mad thing couldn't accept this atrocity.

Sil took another shaking look inside, shivered violently with revulsion, and looked to her.

"I aim to kill them," Tallah said before the healer found her voice. "Any objection?"

A nervous shake of the head answered her. "I don't . . ." Sil swallowed the lump in her throat, dry heaved and turned around. "I don't know how they could be healed. Best put them out of this misery."

If this wouldn't bring out the master of the place, nothing would. A breeding room took years to create, set up, and especially to populate. Losing one was a blow no Vitalis would accept sanguinely.

She stepped into its center and prodded Christina for aid.

'What do you need?'

A Titan's Punishment would kill everything in the room without suffering. She could burn them, but there was already too much pain in here. In the mask's sight, the illum of the room was bloodred, stagnating in its sickness, already past the threshold of decay.

"Get out," she growled.

The boy retreated out the door, not even looking back. He didn't want to be in there anymore than Sil did.

She would've preferred keeping the Titan as an available weapon for dealing with whoever it was that controlled the place, but this needed it more. A breeding room in this day and age, and a well-stocked one too?

The ugly things that grew where nobody ever dares look.

Desperate eyes stared at her as she took position in the center of the room, right beneath the surgical white light of the sprite globes. Some of the victims raised feeble stumps. In warding or in salute, she could never know.

Not only a well-stocked one, but also spectacularly cruel. What diseased mind the Vitalis needed to even dream up something like that?

'I'm ready,' Christina offered. She radiated her own displeasure.

"You got their attention. More are coming," Sil called from the hallway. "Boy's holding them off. Be quick. He won't last."

Tallah raised a hand and surrendered control to Christina. A Titan's Punishment was a complicated devourer, and she didn't trust herself enough with the power to cast it on her own. Lightning discharged off her body, concentric lines of power spreading out from her feet, scorching the living floor. Electricity buzzed in her chest, the charge steadily building, louder and louder in her ears. Her teeth vibrated.

Christina unleashed it without warning, a blinding white bolt of lightning that struck the ceiling a heartbeat later. Without control, it would have punched right up through the rock. Instead, the ghost curved the power, sent it spilling back down the walls to spear every body as it raced back to her, the grounding anchor. She allowed it in and guided it back out to make sure everything in the room was dead.

It lasted for shorter than a breath. When she dispelled the weave, nothing was left of the monstrosity but burnt-out corpses, shattered cradles, and bare, scorched rock. Darkness crashed in when her glow disappeared.

Outside, Vergil perched atop a mound of corpses, breaking one apart with his hands. In the narrow corridor leading in, they couldn't corner him, so he held the passage. Sil's nose bled with the effort of feeding him illum.

"I think that's the last," the healer said as she dropped her barrier. "May the Goddess guide these souls away from here."

"May she do just that. Come. We're going to keep on breaking things until we get our host's full attention."

"The wall was screeching while you were in there. I think you have it all."

"Good. I'll break some things just for my enjoyment, then."

Sil blew her bloody nose on the hem of her dress and then inhaled nettle dust for strength. The draw of the helmet was hard on Tallah herself, let alone on a healer, but Sil seemed to manage it well enough.

"I can take the siphon back now," she said, feeling much better.

"No need. I can handle him."

"Suit yourself."

She cut a bloody path through the sanctum. The place beggared the imagination with its size and cruelty. Laboratories with pristine glass instruments, used for unspeakable things. Holding cells. Real, bloody torture rooms.

'They're well connected,' Christina mused. 'I don't see a Vitalis leaving this place to go shopping in Valen. Must have some thralls doing the dirty work.'

"What did you say you got out of the boy's head? About this place, I mean," Tallah asked as she set another room aflame. She had to shout over the screeching of the walls and the dying wailing of creatures burning to death inside.

"He saw people coming and going. Someone brought prisoners to the vermen and handed them over. There's a whole operation in here."

"Fancy that. Vermen being paid. If I were still in the Guard, I'd make it a personal mission to find whoever was doing the selling."

Holding cages, empty and filled, all burned to ash.

Whatever glass she found, she turned to slag. Glass remained bloody expensive south of Aztroa. Let them try to find more to replace the expensive apparatus.

Some sort of shrine dedicated to Ort and his reaping. She took special pleasure in destroying it.

In a few bells' time, she must've ruined decades of work for the master of the place. Now she began finding passages sealed tight against her intrusion, grown bone and meat barring her way.

"And here's our invitation," she crooned as they were led down the only unsealed passage.

"Into a trap, you mean."

She shrugged. "I doubt they want to throw more bodies at me. So far I've destroyed the harvest of a few years, and salted the fields."

Vergil was crimson and stank at her side. Blood and other, grosser, fluids stained his conjured-up glass armor. He'd been fighting ceaselessly since they came down, and nothing seemed to even faze the mad ghost of the helmet. He'd picked up some severed arm from somewhere, fashioned it into a bone sword, and carried it like some gruesome sickle.

For now, he was proving his worth and Tallah did not like it one bit. Her teeth itched at the good fortune that had brought him in her path. Later, if she survived the upcoming meeting, she would give him due consideration.

They descended a narrow flight of stairs going deeper still underground. The air down there was cooler than it had been atop, but the stench of death was worse.

A throne atop a central dais dominated the room that the stairs led into. Human bones, of course, for ambience. Old Vitalis, and full of themselves.

The room was operation theater and display case bundled up in one. Most of the horrors to here, aside from the laboratories, had been afterthoughts, a sanctum overgrown and overfed. In here, there was deliberate design for cruelty raised to a form of art. Splayed-out bodies covered the walls, skin and muscle pulled back to reveal wet, writhing organs. The victims were still alive and in terrible pain.

Tallah would need to purge the room.

"I did wonder who had gotten lost in my home," a sweet, feminine voice whispered, "scaring my children and trampling my work."

Someone sat atop the throne, and Tallah couldn't contain her glee. She grinned ear to ear as she gazed upon the sanctum mistress, revealed at last. No wonder she hadn't come up to meet her assault.

A reunion between old adversaries demanded proper setup.

Naked as the day she'd been born, Anna Theala sat among the jutting bones, regarding Tallah with cold, yellow eyes. The fury on her face was poetry.

Finally!

She hadn't allowed herself the hope that this was indeed Anna's sanctum, but here her quarry was, as pristine and young as on their graduating day at Hoarfrost.

"Hello, Anna." She approached the throne, ignoring the chimeras creeping in from other passages. "It's been entirely too long."

Anna looked like she hadn't aged a day. Tallah lifted her mask a fraction just to get a better look. Yes, it was the same petite woman from the Academy, pale as a ghost, drawn-faced, with a nose slightly too sharp to look attractive. Her eyes were different, catlike, yellow and wider than they should be.

The flesh doll occupying the throne was a near-perfect replica of Tallah's old clique-mate. Tallah cast a glance around the room.

"I know that's not the real you. Theatrics were never your strongest trait, Anna. Come out and greet me properly."

She got a sneer in reply and, rising from the floor, two more dolls flanked the first.

"What have you done to yourself, girl?" one of them asked, smiling as those yellow eyes seemed to measure and weigh her all at once.

Sil yelped as another doll rose right next to her and circled her, eyes distended in curious pleasure. "Lovely work, yes. But I can see right through it." She leaned in and stage whispered, "I could make you into this, child. Would be no trouble at all. No need to hide under petty glamours."

Vergil interposed himself between the doll and Sil, and growled in threat. The doll slid out a forked tongue as it joined the others.

"I'm not here to reminisce with you, Anna," Tallah said.

"Such a pity. I couldn't imagine what other business the whore of the Academy would have with me and mine."

Lovely attempt at an old insult. Anna would be close even if she hid. Close enough, at least, that it wouldn't matter for what happened next.

Tallah reached into an inner pocket and brought out the real reason she'd done all this, why they'd been searching for so long beneath Valen's mountains. The black gem buzzed in her hand as she held it between thumb and middle finger, showing it to the doll.

"I claim you, Anna Theala, born of mother Viostra Theala and father Logovich Eilan," she whispered to the crystal. It melted away from her hand and puffed to black smoke. "Does that answer your question?"

Oh yes, it did! The doll was on her feet, shaking with anger.

"How dare you?! Have you taken leave of your senses?"

Anger was the first thing the enchantment stoked. If it would have failed to latch onto something, it would've just gone inert and reverted back to its crystal shape. Anna was indeed close. It didn't matter that she hid behind her toys. A soul trap, once active, wouldn't be easily tricked.

"As clearheaded as you've ever known me," Tallah teased.

The challenge was issued. She could see on the doll's face the first reactions to the trap's effects. The call of the music rising. The unnerving echoes of things being dug out from the depths of memory. Soon, Anna would start feeling the hooks digging into her essence and yanking out whatever she thought hidden and inviolable.

She couldn't help but smile at the reaction. The monster was faced with something more monstrous than she, something that didn't care for her strength or the protection of her sanctum.

"A century since we've seen one another, and this is how you greet me . . . What has the outside world come to?" the doll asked, voice just slightly shaken.

'She's blustering. Good,' Christina commented. 'For all she sees, she can't see me. We hold the advantage.'

The doll moved down from the dais with slithering movements, away from Tallah. Anna had never been a thing of beauty, and her doll only exaggerated her lack of grace.

Chimeras gathered around the throne into a wide, agitated circle of gaping maws and misshapen bone weapons.

She won't dare unleash on me. Tallah took stock of the surrounding beasts. *She knows the old rules.*

Unleash the children to kill her, and Anna would be trapped with that thing in her until it got everything it wanted. If it didn't, it would drive her insane with its insistence. There was only one way out: Fight the one that activated the trap and sacrifice their soul to its thirst. Tallah watched the equation play out on the doll's face as she regarded her creatures, wondering if their connection to her was strong enough to fool the enchantment.

It could be. But at the moment of activation, the mind was addled and confused. Fear ran high. Given time, Anna would see the loopholes. Tallah wasn't going to allow her that time.

"Old witch Zakovia always said that it's folly to fight another channeler in their sanctum. I've always wanted to try it." Tallah cast a slow gaze across the room. "Can't say I'm terribly impressed by what you've done here."

Was Anna even pursuing anything anymore? Or had she just become another obsessed Vitalis, digging deeper into depravity for depravity's sake? Ripping her away from the work would be doing her a favor, though she'd likely not see it as such. Anna could carry a grudge ten times her size.

The doll smiled and showed rows of perfect needle teeth. "I'm going to rip your heart out and keep it beating forever somewhere in my sanctum. Maybe where my children piss and shit."

'Cute. Worthless as a threat, but cute try,' Christina chuckled. 'She's never been very creative.'

"Let's get this farce over with." Anna brandished her wand and invited the start of the duel.

Tallah turned slightly and showed off the silver wand clasped to her belt.

She didn't reach for it. Instead she cracked her knuckles and drew her sword. A calculated insult. She'd thrown down the literal gauntlet and now refused to use her wand for the duel.

Anna's face was enraged to the point of parody.

She swung the wand and blood erupted from the floor and walls. It surrounded her in a tide, moving unnaturally through the air to form thick red needles. Excellent control, as expected. More monstrous replicas of Anna rose from the surrounding mass. Longer, more feral limbs. Clawed hands. Distended jaws filled with too many needle teeth.

Sil had already moved back and gotten barriers up. Vergil was at her side, a growling beast that paced the limits of the invisible wall.

"Protect Sil," Tallah ordered. She ignited a fireball and wove two more in waiting.

She faced a small army leering in the surgical light. Whatever beauty Anna mimicked was gone now as the dolls spread out to advance on her. Only the pretend one remained on the steps of the dais, blood flowing like a living creature around her trembling form.

The first salvo of fireballs blasted two dolls to blood mist. Broken limiters funneled too much illum into the effect, but one couldn't argue with explosive results.

They rushed her in pairs. One heartbeat to make her fireflies, another to let loose. Dolls were already on her, claws swiping, fangs bared for her throat.

Tallah exploded heads and chests, ripped limbs off, and turned one construct to a bloody smear of gristle and hanging chunks of flesh. It was the only one to fall.

The rest, in tatters but undeterred, ganged up and tore at her. Her sword met claws and the impact lanced pain up to her elbow. Their weight pushed her down to the floor, maws snapping at her arms and shoulders, trying to get to the throat.

A heat lance ripped one in two and gained her enough room to cut the throat of a second. Enough time to blast them off with Bianca's kinetic push. The ghosts cycled inside her.

Another push, backward, got her back to her feet. A gesture erected a flame wall two steps away, catching one doll full-on in the inferno. Too close to breathe, but it bought her space to think.

Sil screamed somewhere behind and to the side. No time to worry about her. She'd need to manage with only the boy for support.

"Only that? You issue a challenge as ill-prepared as this, Tallah?"

Anna laughed. Blood rushed through the air, the needles only visible in the mask's sight. She raised fire walls to arrest their advance.

A heat lance counterattack failed to penetrate the flowing barrier swirling around her opponent. A fireball blasted it open wide enough for a follow-up shot to take the arm holding the wand.

Another flesh doll rose from the organ mass of the floor and grabbed the thin thing before it even had a chance to clatter to the ground. A swing and needles flew in an arc.

No time to raise another wall. They hit Tallah as she turned away. Pain flared in a line across her chest, then burned worse than her fire. She choked on blood but swallowed it down rather than spill it.

Anna could do terrible things with a drop of blood. And in here, a drop anywhere was too many.

Christina cycled to the fore as Tallah backed away for space. More flesh dolls rose to harry her.

'Careful. She's close. Won't hide too far from her wand. She was always overly reliant on her focus.' Christina offered her memories of dueling Anna in their younger days.

Little help at the moment. The more dolls Tallah killed, the more Anna made, each new construct uglier than the last, barely even looking human. She faced a myriad of malicious yellow eyes, keenly aware that she was being pushed back. Soon there would be nowhere to retreat to.

"Girl, see reason." Anna's voice spoke out of too many mouths, like thunder in the cavern. "If I just kill you now, you won't have to see what I'll do to your friend. Annoy me further, and I may keep your head alive just so you can watch."

Bluster. They both knew she couldn't be allowed to live for Anna to have any chance of besting the soul trap. Good. The curse continued to plan, doing its ugly work.

Christina provided her strength. A ball of lightning flashed forward from the tips of her fingers to hit the closest doll. Its scream distorted into echoes. Tallah swung her arm around and tracked the next doll. And the next. Lightning arched between the creatures and sent them scattering.

More screams mixed with the echoes. Sil's. Vergil's. The upper half of some shattered creature, trailing tangled entrails, rolled across their arena to trip up a flesh doll.

Tallah used the momentary distraction, wove a volley of fireballs, and fired them off in quick succession. More blood misted. She aimed always for the source of the weave, chasing the wand's illum around its trajectory. Each doll that grabbed it allowed her an opening.

"That does not hurt me, Tallah."

She didn't hear the rest of Anna's threat but followed up with lances in a wide arc. No more time for subtlety. Claws raked across her back, one creature too close. Its claws snagged in Tallah's under-armor, the leather carapace holding strong. She pulled away and swung the sword around. It caught the creature clean through the throat, beheading it.

Softer now. Not as defined. Not as hard to kill.

Realization distracted her for a heartbeat too long.

Something slammed into her and a long spear of bone thrust through her abdomen to explode out of her back. The pain nearly blinded her. It had erupted straight from the floor, right at her feet, masked by the chaos of illum conflagrations. One sweep of the sword cut off the half-formed arms holding the spear, another cut the shaft so she could stagger away. Anna was speaking, but Tallah barely heard anything over the onrush of her own heartbeat threatening to burst out of her chest.

Her blood ran down her leg and onto the floor. Tongues licked it.

A barrage of needles caught her attention. She deflected with a wall of flame, moving awkwardly, stumbling over the thing impaling her. Something punched through the wall and straight into her shoulder. Bone. Sharp and barbed. It poked out the other side and staggered her. It pulled her forward, barbs digging into flesh, rending bone and muscle.

Too much pain! She screamed in suffering and frustration.

So bloody powerful! Anna was a beast and, in the center of her sanctum, a goddess. Christina swapped with Bianca inside her, and she nearly blacked out when Bianca ripped out the spears in a burst of kinesis.

'Follow the wand. I've got you.' Bianca threaded power through Tallah's flesh and pulled the wounds tightly closed. Pain was razor-sharp and tasted of iron and bile. Her feet were dead weights attached to the ends of her legs.

Her eyes darted past the flitting illum of the dolls crowding her. The wand wasn't with them anymore, its trail a bloodred comet in the noise. She swung in place just in time to meet a doll's claw swipe. The parry sent fresh agony through her bloodied side, but illum still burned in the furnace of her chest. A lance burst the doll apart.

Then she saw it.

At the far edge of the room, illum twisted. It revealed the coward as she prepared something complex.

"There you are," she screamed in elated triumph, even as she could no longer feel most of herself.

No time to think. No time to look for Sil and make sure she was still alive. No time to make sure her companions were out of the bloody way. All of her reserves poured into a single Disintegration blast.

Darkness lit up with blinding, glorious light.

The air ignited.

All of her screamed in protest as she barely contained the devourer and aimed it at the wand's position. If she missed, they'd all be dead and none of this would've mattered.

Her effort was rewarded by an anguished cry. The sanctum itself screamed, its many voices turned to echoing, crashing thunder. Earth shook with the impact of the blast.

And Anna's dolls were no more.

Only Anna herself remained, a ruined carcass embedded in a throne of nightmares, revealed at last for a heartbeat before darkness overwhelmed the throne room. She spoke but Tallah couldn't hear her. Blood sloshed in her ears. The slowing beat of her heart. The ringing of the blast.

She needed to finish the job before she collapsed.

Already her vision frayed at the edges and her breathing wheezed in her chest. Every step forward was agony and triumph of will.

Anna kept speaking. What of . . . who knew? Who cared? Tallah was only aware of the weight of the sword in her hand and the gaping emptiness in her. All of her illum had gone into the devourer. She was spent and burned out. Nothing but the waning strength of her arm to defend her if attacked now. Maybe not even that.

She stumbled. Steadied herself on the sword. Pushed forward the final few steps.

"I'm sorry," she mumbled the words as she met the burned-out hollows of Anna's eyes. "For what it's worth, I'm sorry." She was. Truly. Not for killing the creature that her old rival had become, but for what came next.

Her strength failed halfway through cutting Anna's throat, and darkness crushed her.

CHAPTER TWO

Good Folk

"Must you, really?"

One of her daughters burst apart and was cooked to ashes before Anna had a chance to reabsorb the bloody mess. No matter. She had enough mass to make a thousand more if need be. But so much shared pain began to climb to distracting levels, so she shut it out.

The music flooding into her was harder to ignore, try as she might to seal her senses off to it. It sang in her veins, along the leagues of her spread nerves, clawing its way through her many conjoined brain stems.

"Girl, see reason." She spoke through ten mouths just to drown out the siren song. "If I just kill you now, you won't have to see what I'll do to your friend. Annoy me further and I may keep your head alive just so you can watch."

In reality, it would be years before she'd let her old "friend" expire, now that she'd allowed her presence in the heart of her sanctum. The nerve of the harpy! Coming into her home, destroying her work, setting her efforts back by a full decade. In the outside world, manners must have gone to pot.

Then again, calling for reason had never worked on this particular ill-tempered sorceress. A hundred summers passed by, and she remained just as obstinate, obtuse, and difficult. Her sister must've finally given up on trying to wring something worthwhile out of her—

Odd thought, that. The Amni sisters, let alone the youngest, hadn't crossed any of her minds in decades. So why now?

With twenty more daughters raised from the meat of her wombs to occupy the flames of her assailant, Anna turned her attention inwards and studied the firing of her neurons. Or, to her mounting horror, their death.

Interesting. *Tallah Amni.* She injected the thought among the electric storm of her mind and watched it spiraling through vast stores of memory, activating synapses and connections she'd not touched in decades. Something caught its scent and chased it like wildfire.

Ah, there it was. The corruption that ate her thoughts and crushed every barrier she set in its wake. An evil, malevolent cancer spreading through her mind, gorging itself on her . . . leaving nothing behind. Cell death chased the path of its touch.

Ugly thing. But then again, what else could she expect from an ash eater like Tallah?

Invite an old friend into your home, watch them trample your work, offer the chance to explain their actions, and ultimately get cursed for it. So much for gratitude among equals. She wouldn't be doing anything of the sort ever again. Now to clean up the mess and start undoing the damage done.

"That does not hurt me, Tallah," she said as she drew out of herself and saw the ruination of her children. Flames scorched her precious sanctuary. She doused them in blood. "Do you think I would allow you to walk out of here alive after all this? Your theatrics do not impress. And I've dealt already with your tawdry little trick. Lie down and die, please. It saves us both the time."

A bit of bluster in that. It normally took her weeks to grow a fresh body and imprint on it. Her own physiognomy was far more complex than the daughters she threw into the fight, and copying her synaptic map was a long, gentle process that she couldn't dare rush. But still, a body was being grown in her own displaced womb and would be ready for imprinting soon. She'd probably not need it, once she force-fed Tallah her own entrails and ended the curse, but it paid to have contingencies.

Maybe she would preserve the head, so she could scoop out the brain and divine what the dreadful thing afflicting her actually was. Soul magic, for sure. But what particular form of it?

Tallah was proving herself more resilient than a bloody cockroach. They'd never stacked well against one another. Fire was, after all, anathema to life. She'd taken plenty of pyromancers into herself, but few had been as fiercely determined as this one. If she'd had more time and wasn't chased by the soul-devouring beast within, she might give her old friend's desperation some more considerate thought.

For now, she needed her dead, as much as she'd like to protract the punishment. Maybe end the life, allow for a few moments of brain death to ensure the cancellation of the threat, and then reanimate whatever remained? Barely enough satisfaction for the damage wrought, but one took what one could get.

Her many-eyed gaze settled on the other two. The male was fodder.

Beneath the enchantment he wore, there was nothing even worth vivisecting. A skeletal husk wrapped in a conjured piece of armor. Disgusting. Whichever child cut his throat could eat the corpse, for all she cared.

The healer, however . . . Young enough. Strong. Still fertile. Yes, good for breeding stock. A squirt of aerosolized pheromones marked her for safe capture and preparation. She let the children deal with that without her supervision.

A fresh wave of pain scythed through her carefully arrayed defenses. Two daughters dying. Not dead. The ash eater learned as she fought, leaving the daughters in agonized suffering rather than ending them outright. Hard to avoid all the ways in which pain fed back into her. With as many paths as nerves, the art of her craft turned against her. And was Tallah throwing lightning bolts at her? How?

"You tire, whore," she crooned as she grew tongues and licked the blood off the floor and walls. "I have your taste. You remember what I can do with just a taste, right?" Her wand, lent out to the daughters for use, made its way back into her hands. Exposing herself would be a risk, but to fashion an answer to this whole indignity, she needed her focus. She'd make a poison fit like a glove for her noble-born old friend, something for a deservedly screaming death.

"There you are." Tallah, wounded and bleeding from a hundred wounds, grinned and dropped the half-corpse of a careless daughter. What followed from her was so much more than fire.

Anna's world went white. Shadows, children, and daughters were all cremated to ashes. She screamed, the sound burning out of her real throat in peeling sheets of agony. Her skin blistered and burned away. Nerves shrieked. Blood, her own and her sanctum's, boiled to vapor. A blow to her real self! It opened her up like an explosion from within, and the beast in her devoured with impunity.

When the pain burned itself out, the body she inhabited was beyond ruin, the spare nowhere near ready to receive. For the first time in her life, she panicked, even as coherence slipped away from her. Survive! She must survive.

Her killer approached on unsteady feet, barely in better shape than she. No more fire. Now she brandished a sword, its edge glistening bloody in the final burning embers of her home.

One last gambit before it would all be too late. One last daughter had survived. If she had but a few more moments . . .

"I'm sorry," Tallah whispered, the words a gurgling effort. "For what it's worth, I'm sorry."

And she slit what remained of Anna's throat.

* * *

The sanctum whimpered, seemed to gather its remaining strength, and screamed—Anna's children were coming.

Sil crawled in the dark until her fingers wrapped around the shaft of her staff. She breathed out a sigh of relief, gathered her courage, and summoned a light sprite to face the horrors that had survived.

The boy was nowhere to be seen in the small sphere of light, but she felt him tug on her for strength. Whatever he faced, now that Tallah had likely failed, it would tear him limb from limb. She was keenly aware of every effort he made to buy them moments of life.

Her nose bled, and the illum siphon was a physical ache now. It projected the beats of her heart into her ears. In a few more minutes, she would be spent, and they'd all be dead.

With considerable effort, she moved the sprite around. Shadows leapt and squirmed out of its light.

Tallah was in a corner, collapsed to her knees among a throng of flesh dolls. Looming above her, Anna was revealed at last—a near-corpse embedded into a cradle in the wall, kept alive by a nightmare myriad of tubes and flesh tendrils, mother of the monsters leering at the edge of the light. Wisps of shadow clung to her exposed viscera like a tattered mantle.

Sil found the strength to pick herself up and stumble forward. If not for the staff, she would have crawled.

Tallah's unleashed devourer seemed to have hit Anna full-on. It had also consumed every light in the room, shattered the glow-globes and the lit eyes, and plunged them into the suffocating underground dark that Sil's sprite was no match for.

Vergil flew in from somewhere and crashed against the wall a pace away from her, tossed like a doll by something she dreaded to imagine. He bounced back to his feet, twisted his horned helmet back in place, and rushed back into battle wielding a broken sword and howling his inhuman war cries. Sil gasped with the tide of illum he demanded of her.

She obliged. If he fell . . .

"After all that," Anna's ragged voice said, each word a gurgle of effort, "I'm still alive, whore. You've failed." It whispered from the mouths of the dead and the dying.

Anna laughed bitterly, and her head rose with shuddering effort, her face a flayed mask of bloody horror that tried in vain to knit itself back together. Tallah did not meet its yellow gaze.

"You've slain so many of my children, but more come. I'll—" She forced herself to draw a spluttering breath. The flesh dolls around her dangling feet jerked but did not rise. "I'll still claim the day."

Tallah's sword lay by her side, discarded in a spreading puddle of red. A dark gash trailed off halfway across Anna's throat and bled black. Blood bubbled and gurgled out of the wound as the monster kept forcing herself to speak.

"I will have . . ."

Anna's head slumped forward, and she breathed out her last sputtering exhalation. A jagged black gemstone erupted out of her chest and dropped to the floor with a dull splash, finally sated and filled to bursting. It crackled with power as the sorceress's soul settled inside.

The sanctum wailed as its mother was ripped from it. Deafening echoes of its wordless cries mixed with the braying of beasts in horrendous cacophony, each heartbeat bringing it closer.

Sil slipped on the blood, fell, and crawled to Tallah's side. She set two fingers to her friend's throat, praying for a pulse. A moment passed.

Another.

Was the soul in the gem Tallah's?

No, no, no, no, no. Sil shifted her fingers, praying through gritted teeth.

The sorceress's heart still beat. It was faint and slow, but it was there, pumping out her life through the penetrating wounds in her chest and side.

Set up barriers, drop the siphon to conserve illum, and let the boy be torn apart? Or do I risk a healing spell so you can fight again? Can you still fight? Why do you do this to me?

She dug through her satchel. Two of her vials had shattered when the boy pushed her out of danger earlier, and the last one was half-empty. It would have to do.

A hulking beast rushed out of the dark, howling in mindless fury. She put up a barrier in panic, and the effort left her head spinning. Claws raked at the wall. More of the creatures stepped into the light, finally past Vergil's last stand. Was he dead?

The boy came leaping at them out of the dark and body-slammed the decaying creatures into her wall. He fought tooth and nail, gauntlets and boots against blades and spikes of bone, but he was losing. More arrived from the furthest reaches of the sanctum. They all howled, barked, and brayed their bloodlust, still so bloody many.

Skinless masks of suffering glared balefully as Vergil set himself between the tide and the cracking invisible barrier. He growled in answer to their calls, crushed a skull beneath his ghostly armor, and raised his fists to meet the charge.

Sil tipped Tallah's head back and forced her clenched jaw open.

"Drink, you mule," she whispered in urgent frustration.

The sorceress was in the throes of illum burnout, the second since they'd descended into Anna's domain. She didn't react to the words, and Sil had to hold Tallah's mouth open as she poured the healing draft down her throat. The thought that Anna might have poisoned her was too terrible to consider, so she prayed instead.

For now, the bleeding stopped. Tallah's coat and armor hung off her in ribbons, but no more blood seeped from under them. Sil touched the fresh scars and breathed out a wordless thanks to the Goddess.

"Come back," she called to Vergil as he threw down a creature and stomped it into a bloody pulp. "I need help." She corralled the beasts just an arm's span away from his reach, and her wall immediately began to buck and crack under the weight of bodies.

Vergil growled as he retreated to her side. Only the mad whites of his eyes showed through the visor, looking at the inert sorceress with hatred so pure that Sil trembled in spite of the heat. If he turned on them . . .

No. She squashed the traitorous thought and fought to keep the fear out of her voice. "Pick her up and be ready to run when the portal opens. No—"

The wall shattered, and the mass was upon them. Vergil's punch flew out like lightning and smacked the first horror in the mouth. Its head nearly snapped off its mismatched shoulders. Its claws raked his pale armor in a dying spasm.

Sil put up as many barriers as she dared. The toll climbed into blackout exhaustion. Lightheaded and nearly giddy with terror and illum consumption, she struggled to focus and find the way back to Valen. A moment of carelessness could see her as insensate as the sorceress. She teetered on the very edge of that precipice.

Something angry slammed into her walls when Vergil picked up Tallah on his shoulder. More, ever more of Anna's children came and encircled their small pocket of safety. Far from the throngs they had fought on their way down, but too many to handle in their depleted state.

She held up her staff, and white light pulsed around the blue jewel on its top. Time crawled by, and barriers started failing with deafening crashes. She couldn't reinforce them while attempting the connection. Blades and drooling maws stuffed with fangs glinted beyond her flickering sprite. A riot of malign limbs reached for them like a thicket of skinless red flesh and glittering white bone.

Another barrier shattered under the weight of bodies. She still couldn't reach Valen's illum hearth. Panic convulsed in her chest. Blood flowed into her mouth, thick with the taste of iron. It dripped off her chin and under her shirt, sticking her clothes to her chest.

A white gateway opened in the air just as cracks began forming in her last line of defense.

Vergil ran through without waiting to be told.

After a moment's hesitation, Sil rushed to Anna's corpse and stooped to pick up the soul gem. Revulsion wracked her at its touch, but she gripped it tight in numbing fingers. It would all have been for naught if she left the dreadful thing behind.

The final barrier shattered. Four paces and a forest of claws, scythes, spears, and swords of bone separated her from the portal.

She swung her staff at the first chimera that rushed her and brained it. Its skull shattered like an egg, and dregs of brain hung down the ruin of its face. It kept coming, a mountain of overgrown muscles that barely even resembled a man anymore. Old training came back to her as she twisted in place with her staff and lashed out at two more enemies, knocking them back. The jewel atop her weapon stained from blue to purple.

Three paces to the portal. The wall at her back. Her entire world reduced to that pocket of failing light. Just enough room to swing the staff but not to push ahead.

Another of the Anna's brood, some perversion of an aelir, wrapped clawed fingers around the haft of her staff and pushed her into the wall with strength that beggared belief. With a cry of anger and terror, she forced the staff between the jaws of its maw and kneed it in the groin. It did nothing but send pain lancing up her leg.

White human eyes speckled with blood bore into hers, mad with fear and anguish. Arms fashioned into a pair of bone spears reached from the crowd to impale her. Hands pawed her from the dark, grabbing clothes and hair, pulling with inhuman strength she could not match.

I don't want to die like this, she thought in a panic as she gagged on the decaying stench of so many bodies crammed around her.

The boy stumbled back through the portal, howled as he regained strength, and smashed into her assailants. The one on her stumbled sideways and nearly dragged her down with it. Vergil caught her arm and wrenched her back. Hair and clothes ripped painfully as he pushed her to the white gateway. His attention was already on another foe as he readied to pounce.

"No," she said. "Go through. I need to be last." It would close otherwise.

She marveled at this impulse as she swung her staff in time with his fists. Tears stung her eyes and half-blinded her as she rallied one last effort. She should have gone through and left the wretch to the monsters, but she didn't. He had come back for her. The will needed to cross a portal backward was titanic; she knew from bad experience.

Vergil grabbed a beast's scythed arm and ripped it off to use as a makeshift blade. He fought like nothing she'd ever seen before, a howling mad tempest of violence on her side.

She made a final effort of will and put up one last barrier in the small space his efforts gained them.

Vergil ran through the portal, and Sil followed right behind.

It was near impossible to know where Valen's illum hearth would direct their portal. Sil would take any place as long as it was out of the blasted caves.

She stumbled out and turned on her heels. They were following. She swung at the first head that poked through the gateway and smashed it right in the eyes. Vergil kicked it back.

Limbs were already crowding through, grabbing for the edges of the portal to drag themselves through.

With what last dregs of illum she could draw in, she forced a barrier in their wake. They pounded on it so hard that she feared it wouldn't last the heartbeat. Bellows, howls, and cries of daemons echoed into the night as the portal fizzed out and dispersed. Arms fell twitching in the mud.

Sil spat a glob of blood and blew her nose in her hand. Her teeth chattered with the adrenaline rush of their hair-thin escape. They had survived.

It was difficult to accept.

"Where are we?" she mumbled to herself as she looked around. Her sprite had been left behind, and she lacked the reserves to make another. Keeping the boy lit up already pushed her limits.

It was nighttime in the outside world. Her eyes, used to the underground dark for only the Goddess knew how long, started picking up details in the vague light.

Vergil was lifting Tallah back up on his shoulder from where he had left her against some wooden fencing.

Vague, dark shapes resolved into a tight cluster of hovels.

The jagged curve of Valen's mountains loomed black against an overcast sky.

A slow icy drizzle, mixed in with early winter sleet, greeted their arrival. Dogs barked madly somewhere, rattling their chains. The howls of Anna's monsters echoed and were swallowed by the night.

"What's this now?"

"Who's there?"

"Ammie, get my crossbow! Keep Georgie in bed."

A cacophony of voices echoed from the small cottages. Yellow light flared through cracks in wooden shutters.

A gang of burly men dressed in furs rushed out, armed and ready for a fight. They brandished crossbows and handheld oil lamps, only to be met by a soaking wet, bloodstained, shivering healer that barely held herself propped up on her staff. She couldn't imagine what she'd do against five armed men, but Vergil tensed for another fight.

"S-Sorry. We didn't mean to wake anyone up," she stammered, trying to march her wits into line.

A farmer, barely taller than her chest, lifted his lamp to her face, blinding her with its light.

"Adventurers," he announced, and there was a groan of dismay from the rest of the men.

They turned and fanned out in a circle around them, checking the surroundings.

"What did you bring down on us, girl?" the leader asked and pointed his crossbow straight at Sil's chest.

"Nothing. We-we-we came by portal." She stamped down on an arm still squirming at her feet. "It's closed now. Nothing else came through."

The man peered past her at Vergil, but she moved with the light. With her free hand, she gestured for the boy to stay calm and not aggravate the heavily armed men. His growls did not bode well.

A long quiet settled among the men flanking them.

"Bog, ye stand guard. Yer going out at first light with the goats, anyway," the leader called out. One of the men groaned, and the others, satisfied that nothing came out of the dark at them, reluctantly returned to their homes.

"Come with me," the leader said, addressing Sil, and turned on his heels.

She obeyed and gestured for Vergil to follow.

The man led them to a small barn at the back of his homestead, where he drew aside the heavy wooden beam barring the double doors.

"I gather that your friend there needs a healer's ministrations." The white-haired man beckoned at them to enter and set his lamp down on a short three-legged stool. "Will you be needing I fetch Buzz, our healer?"

Sil was at a momentary loss for words. After the greeting, hospitality was the last thing she expected.

"N-No. No, I think I'll manage," she said, panic rising that someone might get a good look at them. She kept herself between the light and Tallah, shielding her in the cast shadow. "Thank you so much."

"Don't be mentioning it. We's good people here, if a bit gruff." His scowl melted into a gap-toothed grin. "Not the first group to stumble into our little corner of the world. Make yerselves comfortable. Don't mind Cricket. She's friendly enough."

He walked out and down a muddy path, back to his cottage. "Knock if ye need anything," he called back. "The missus will come round in the morning wi' some cheese and bread."

Vergil set the sorceress down against a bale of hay and backed away from her, mumbling with each step. He went out into the sleet rather than stay near. Sil could hear him talking to himself in his odd language but didn't have the energy to decide if that was something to worry about.

She sat down heavily on the hay and breathed out a long sigh of weariness. A goat peered around the wall to a stall, thoughtfully chewing.

We almost botched that so bad, Sil thought as she studied her friend. It had been such a close contest of skill and power between Tallah and Anna. The black gem in her hand buzzed like an annoyed wasp when she studied it. Ultimately, it went into the bottom of her stained and ruined satchel.

Before she could deal with Tallah's afflictions, she needed to handle herself first. The illum siphon that kept Vergil upright had almost sucked her dry. She blew her bloodied nose against the hem of her skirt and then dug in the small pouch she had belted to her calf. That had survived unmolested at least.

She pulled out one of her last remaining bags of powdered ink nettle and inhaled a lungful. It cleared her dizziness and opened her up to more power. It would keep her going for a few bells more, and the boy would stay possessed. If she dropped dead, so would he, but that didn't bear thinking about just now.

A shudder tightened her shoulders when she thought back on how she had almost convinced Tallah to leave the wretch as they found him, starved and nearly dead in the gibbet. Without him, they would've been cut to ribbons thrice over.

So bloody close. So bloody stupid . . .

Tallah, at some point in the battle with Anna, had taken off her silver mask. Now she had a death's grip on it, fingers locked rigidly as Sil tried to pry it away.

No stirring.

Sil knelt by her and cupped her face with both hands. Tallah's gray eyes were bloodshot and trembling slightly. Pink lines of scarring crowded around the left socket, along with crusts of dried blood. Anna had almost claimed that one. The healing draft had saved it, for now.

There was one sure way to get someone out of that kind of stupor, at least without something pungent enough on hand.

Sil held Tallah's head up by her chin and struck her as hard as she could. Vergil cracked open the door and peered in.

"Ow." Tallah's lips moved, and she blinked in response.

For good measure, Sil slapped her again.

"Ow!"

Tallah's eyes snapped angrily on Sil's, turning a sudden, razor-sharp focus on her.

"Oh, goody, you're still with us." Sil allowed acid to drip into her words, though she couldn't mask the relief she felt.

Tallah blinked again and looked around. "I can't see out of my left eye," she immediately complained as she frowned at their surroundings and tried to rub feeling back into her face. "Where are we?"

"Don't paw at it," Sil ordered, and swatted her hand away. "Lie back. Sit still. What's your name?"

She got glared at. "Tallah Amni," came the rote answer. "You're Silestra Adana. I can feel and move all my fingers and toes. We should be in Valen's vicinity, continent of Vas. I still can't *see*."

Sil nodded and was satisfied.

Now . . . Now she could focus. Not relax, not yet, but focus. Anna's dying domain was hundreds of yards beneath them. The rational side of her doubted that the mindless hordes could find their way out of the labyrinthine depths of the dying sanctum, let alone out of the tunnels leading to it.

To work would take her mind off the inevitable what-if.

With Tallah conscious again, she willed herself to stop expecting eyes peering out of every shadowy nook, allowed the smell of hay and goat to cover the stench of blood, and turned her attention to her ministrations.

Her satchel was ruined. Most of her drafts were lost, her precious vials shattered, and the stowed herbs polluted beyond use. Her tools, encased in small ebony boxes, had survived, along with some of the medicine stowed in sturdier, painfully expensive bottles.

She donned a monocle and inspected the blinded eye.

"Can't promise you won't need to visit Aliana when we get back, but we'll see in the morning," she commented.

Tallah frowned at her.

"It wasn't a bad joke," Sil lied.

She made a compress from a clean cloth drenched in a foul-smelling tincture and applied it over the stricken eye. The sorceress obeyed her instructions without question while Sil pulled off her tattered coat, trousers, and leather armor.

"Where are we?" Tallah asked again as she was made to lift her arms.

Sil had to drag, pull, and cuss at the ruined vest of an armored carapace that the sorceress wore on her back. It had begrudgingly survived the mauling of the chimeras, but their claws had dug through in too many places. Drying blood held it stuck fast to Tallah's back.

"I'll tell you soon. I need to check your ghosts," she said as she got to Tallah's bare skin.

"They're both berating my 'thoughtless actions.' I'd dare say they're fine."

Sil pressed Tallah's head forward, chin to her chest, so she could have a better look at her back and the scars there.

"If it's all the same to you, mighty sorceress, I'd rather I checked."

Months of work, pain, and horror to gain a sorceress's soul. Sil would accept no risk to the other two, regardless of their host's protesting.

One of Anna's bone spears had gone straight through Tallah's shoulder. It was a hair's breadth away from ripping through the sutured pattern of soul thread on her back.

The twin bindings were still pristine, albeit blood-spattered, two octagons of crisscrossing, multicolored threads that Sil had painstakingly sewn through the skin of Tallah's back.

The left one, the one that contained Bianca, was still raw and healing. The right, Christina, had almost finished incorporating into Tallah's flesh, so much so that it mostly resembled a pattern of old scars now. Maybe damage would no longer impact its use, but they weren't ready to test that theory.

"It was close," she said, tracing a finger over the bindings. So delicate and so risk-laden. "Carapace did its work."

The sorceress shuddered at the touch and giggled. It sounded forced.

Her lower wound, which had gone through her abdomen, had missed Bianca's suture entirely. Sil allowed herself a breath of relief.

"You threw out a lot of power in there. Did you expose yourself?"

"I did not expose myself, no. We were careful."

"Not careful enough."

Soft pink scar tissue covered the entry and exit holes, and a line of pink went across her torso. Sil whistled through her teeth as she traced the path of the healed cut. Anna had tried to eviscerate Tallah in battle with the crude efficiency of a war surgeon. The scarring was bunched across her belly and stomach, a mess of lines that must've hurt terribly when fresh.

"Bianca did what she could. Kept my innards where they should be."

"I can see that. You're lucky she's not as headstrong as you."

Too close a call by any reasoning.

The healing potion had done all it could in the caves. Barely sufficient.

"To answer your question, we're somewhere in the right arse cheek of nowhere, as far as I can tell," she said. "Some small village in . . . I have no idea. It's dark. High in the hills, I think."

"Anyone get a look at us when we transferred in?" Tallah continued, switching hands on her compress.

"A bit, but the weather's shit, and they only had oil lamps. We scared some farmers out of bed. Not that I think they'd recognize you, way out wherever this is. I kept you out of lamplight."

She applied an ointment to reduce the scarring. A thorough inspection and a wash with a damp cloth revealed a tapestry of more angry welts and freshly healed cuts. Tallah looked to have gone through one end of a meat grinder and out the other.

Sil proffered a small bottle with a grayish green liquid sloshing inside. "Drink this."

Tallah stuck out her tongue.

"Yes, you need to. No, I don't care that you don't want to. I don't know what your old friend stuck you with, so drink up."

Tallah's color almost matched the liquid as she downed the vile thing and grimaced afterwards. Sil took away her compress and inspected the eye again, pressing with her fingers around it.

"Any pain?"

"No."

"See anything out of it?" She moved her finger in front of Tallah's face while keeping the good eye covered up.

"I see the vague outline of a rude gesture."

"Good. You won't have to regrow the eye, but it will need some tending." She bandaged a soaked eye patch over it. "Twice in a day. I'm amazed you're not completely blind yet."

Few things annoyed a healer more than an illum burnout. The self-inflicted magical damage produced when the sorceress pushed herself this hard was damn near impossible to heal with any sort of reliability. Tallah's eyesight only kept getting worse with each excess, as if to spite Sil's efforts, alchemy, and even healing prayers.

"How's your illum flow?" Tallah asked, noticing Vergil pacing outside. He was arguing with himself. It sounded like he was losing.

"Steady. Got a few bags of ink nettle left, so I think I'm good until we get to Valen with the bucket-head over there."

Tallah tried to get up, but Sil pressed her firmly back down.

"I'm not done with you. Chin up. I want to look at your limiters."

"Give me the illum tether, then," Tallah insisted while Sil stashed away her supplies.

"Don't be stupid."

She checked on the silver choker around Tallah's neck, applied ointments where the skin had blistered, and then checked on the three bands on each arm.

"You've managed to crack every single one. I just remade all of them. Why do I bother?"

"They're still in one piece," Tallah insisted. "You need to strengthen them even more."

"There's no alloy strong enough to deal with your unicorn stubbornness. Do you know how long it took me to make these? Do you know how hard it is to get good quality electrum?" She sighed and sat opposite her friend. "Just get us our clothes."

"If it makes you feel any better, these are . . . were your best yet. They've worked well. I managed to aim the devourer this time."

Tallah chuckled as she tried to open a rend. She had her arm raised and made a grimace as her brow furrowed in something that looked like agony.

"What's the matter?" Sil asked.

Tallah grunted and shut her good eye tight, her grimace darkening.

"It hurts. Give me a moment."

Sil had never experienced illum burnout. Healing magic was too efficient for that, and she'd never needed to use her other abilities extensively enough to crack under the strain. Tallah's pyromancy was a different matter altogether.

"You don't need to do it right away. We can wait. It won't be dawn for a couple hours more."

Even in the meager, flickering lamplight, Sil could see the tears in Tallah's eye as she pushed through the pain and forced open a small black portal that hung in the air. Normally it should have been as tall as Sil. Now it barely fit a hand through.

"See?" She breathed a sigh of relief and dropped her arm on her lap. "I'm fine." The tremor in her voice separated the truth from her lie.

Sil slapped her across the back of the head.

"Stop. Using. That stupid devourer. It'll kill you one of these days, and it won't be a pretty sight for anyone. I'll have to scrape you off of whatever you splatter against."

Tallah just cackled and pursed her lips in mockery, and Sil had to relent in the face of overwhelming disregard for her concerns. She dipped her arm up to her shoulder, into the portal, and rummaged about. After some choice muttered curses, she pulled out two bundles of clothes.

She took off her wet and fouled white outfit and looked at it mournfully before tucking it into a bag. She donned a much more modest gray woolen robe, with matching woolen travel trousers underneath, and sturdy boots. She needed the Goddess's own patience to find them both while groping blindly in the rend, and then some more to pull them out through the narrow opening.

"Can I get dressed now?" Tallah asked. Despite her bravado, she shivered in the chill of small hours. Never a good sign on a pyromancer.

"Blue lips complement your red hair well," Sil said, but she threw her the remaining bundle.

With a sigh, Tallah took out the low-cut, dark blue dress. It had sequins on the neckline.

"I hate this dress so bloody much," she whined to no one in particular as she drew it on with some difficulty. She looked like a bandaged scarecrow wearing something too short and too wide at the hips.

"Blame your entire caste for that," Sil commented. She pulled out a wide-brimmed hat from the portal and passed it over. "No proper sorceress would wear sensible clothes, right?"

"Anna didn't wear any at all. I'd follow her example in a heartbeat if Christina wouldn't gag every time we passed a mirror."

They shared a chuckle at that, tension bleeding out of them while the dark outside drifted into the diffuse light of morning. High, dense clouds put up a vain fight against the coming of the day.

Sil tucked away the ruined clothes, mask included, and with a voice echoing somewhere outside, called Vergil back in.

"What do we do about him?"

Tallah shrugged. "Nothing. We'll say he got cursed by something and we need to get him to the Sisters." She looked him over. Aside from some scratches, the boy was in no worse condition than when they'd found him. "Not that it's far from the truth, anyway. I doubt anyone here speaks whatever language this thing keeps spouting off."

It was true. He had been wearing the helmet for hours and rambled without pause. Nothing he said had made even a lick of sense to either of them.

"And what about the actual person under the helmet? What do we do about him? Do I report him when we get back?"

"Succumbed to starvation. Half eaten by a ratman. It doesn't matter, because I'm not giving him to the Guild."

Sil nodded. She took out a crumpled scroll from her satchel and made some notes on it.

"Fine then. You ready?"

"As I can be," the sorceress confirmed as she drew herself up to her full height. She became unbalanced with the effort.

Sil pulled her close by the waist and held her up, her staff held between them. She lifted it and thrust the butt of it hard into the ground. A flash of light traveled from it to them, up their bodies, and fizzed out into the air.

Vergil made a confused noise as the afterglow dissipated.

Tallah slipped easily into Tianna's skin. Red hair turned raven black, silver eyes midnight blue, and her dress fit properly now. It took a moment for her to stabilize in her form.

Sil almost failed to. She was tired and weary and struggled to stabilize into her tall aelir persona. Jumping species was always confusing and disorienting, but it had been a long time since she had difficulties keeping the shape coherent.

"Breathe, Sil. Nice and slow," Tallah whispered, keeping an arm around her middle. "You've done this a thousand times already. Let it happen."

She did, and she had. Heartbeats later, she felt herself settling into the disguise as she exhaled slowly.

Tallah readjusted her dress and had a few experimental turns to make sure she wouldn't trip over her own feet. Sil rubbed her palms for warmth and scratched a few choice places.

"I get that wool's cheap and all, but whoever decided initiate healers should wear it exclusively needs a beating."

"Are you dears all right in there?" An old woman's craggy head popped in through the half-opened door.

The crowing of a cockerel sounded moments later, as if almost embarrassed at being late to wake.

Their host was dressed in a simple white woolen dress with a sheepskin vest and walked in carrying a small wooden tray. Covered in melting sprinkles of snow, it held some fresh, steaming bread and a ball of white cheese.

"Simeon was telling me one of you was in a bad way. You need I fetch in Buzz, our healer?" she asked. She kept a pleasant smile while she blew out the spent lamp and packed it away up on a tool shelf.

"Uh, no, ma'am, thank you," Sil replied with a slight bow to the woman. "Thank you so much for allowing us to stay the night here. We did not know where we were or what time it was. We did not mean to startle people out of bed."

The woman blew a raspberry and roared with laughter.

"Now don't you be worrying yourself over that, sweet little thing. We look out for one another up in these hills. You never know how many friends you need when the drays come howling."

She noticed Vergil in clearer light now.

"Is that young man there . . . er, all right?" she asked in a low voice. "Should I bring him a coat? The poor lad's close to naked."

In the morning light, Vergil's conjured armor was translucent, like cloudy plates of interlocking glass. It left very little of him to the whims of imagination.

"Not exactly, no. He ran into some kind of curse while we were exploring an ancient ruin underground," Tallah replied. "We aim to get him to the Sisters of Mercy in Valen."

"Aw, the poor dear. Them's ugly things, curses," she muttered, wiping her hands on her apron. "Ah, but me manners. I's Ammie. Don't know if Simeon mentioned me."

"No, ma'am," Sil replied and took the woman's callused hand in hers. "My name is Silestra, and my partner here is Tianna. The naked one is Vergil. We were just out on our first sortie for the Guild." Sil gave her a sunburst smile that only ever worked on an aelir's ageless face, with an earnestness that made their host blush. "If you don't mind, could you tell us where we are?"

It had its intended effect as the woman's eyes focused solely on her.

"Well, dear, you're in Cliff's Edge. Valen is about two days away, northward me thinks, by cart."

"Ohhh," Sil mused. "We're somewhere out in the Ruffle, then? I was afraid we'd be further off from the city proper. Any chance there is some transport going there?"

"There is, yes. It should come round these parts by noon, but with the snow and rain, it may be a tad late."

Tallah was watching Vergil who, in turn, had stopped talking and was looking transfixed at their conversation. Nothing had stopped his incessant blathering since they'd put the helmet on him. The older woman fascinated him.

"Oh, thank the Goddess's mercy. I was afraid we'd have to walk all the way back. Is it a coach?"

"A cart, actually." Ammie smiled at her with the simple patience of country folk. "We're too far away and high in the hills for such luxuries as a *coach*. But you can talk to Amus when he comes 'round, and he'll give you a ride on his cheese delivery. I'll talk to 'im and let you folk know when he's about."

"Thank you so much again, Ms. Ammie." Sil kept her smile warm in spite of the bone-deep weariness she felt. "Allow us to repay for your hospitality." She reached for her satchel, but Ammie's tough hands pressed on hers.

"None of that. You just tell people down in the city there's good folk up here, and that they ought to buy our cheese." She winked at them and made to leave, stopping just shy of the door. "Though you could help by splitting some logs for the fire. If that's not too much trouble?"

She hadn't even finished speaking when Vergil was already running down the path to a pyramid of logs stacked behind one of the houses. He picked up a wood-handled axe leaning against the pile and began quartering logs with a fury. His enthusiasm left the three women watching him speechless for a time.

"That is not your wood, is it?" Tallah pointed to a different house. "Your tracks lead to that one." There was an identical pyramid of logs next to the fresh path.

"Aye, that be Miriam's lot. All the same, she'll be happy for the help. I'll bring him a coat and some trousers." Ammie nodded her farewells and headed off, leaving the two in the barn doorway watching Vergil working.

They shrugged, pulled the door closed against the cold, and sat on the hay, eating their breakfast. Cricket finally came out of her stall and stared at them with an animal's mindless interest.

"Tallah?"

"Yes?"

"Can you please shoo the goat away? It's chewing on my dress."

By noontime, Sil had to use another bag of ink nettle to replenish herself. Vergil worked the entire morning, and his efforts dragged on her. She strained under the sapping effects of the cursed helmet but still refused to pass it over to Tallah. With good weather, they'd probably be in Valen before she succumbed to nettle sickness.

Vergil had chopped his way through the entire pile of wood at Miriam's, the neighbor's, and, at Sil's instructions, also worked his way through most of Ammie's stockpile. He drew some odd stares, but people seemed used to adventurers passing through their little hamlet.

Getting him to wear the sheepskin coat and trousers had been an exercise in frustration and much cussing on Tallah's part. Either the possessing ghost despised clothes, or it was being willful out of pure spite. Threats of immolation were made, promptly ignored, and then attempted to be put into practice.

"She wasn't kidding," Sil said, shivering in a midday light snowfall. The world shimmered white as winter rolled implacably down the mountains. She leaned on her staff, now wrapped in a thick woolen covering purchased with some difficulty from Ammie. The woman had kept insisting on gifting it away.

Ambling up the dirt road was a shambling mule-drawn cart. Its wooden wheels creaked and rattled, and metal jugs in the open bed jingled under their canvas. The driver had a cover draped over his shoulders, his breath steaming in the crisp air.

"I feel as if I'm visiting a bad museum piece. I sometimes forget these places still exist. I used to get rides down into Solstice in one of these when I was a girl," Tallah reminisced. "Never liked the smell of horse."

Cliff's Edge was a small community of scattered homesteads. They reared livestock and sold the excess produce, and not much else happened there as far as Sil could gather. Sheep bleated in their enclosures and goats screamed in horrifying near-human voices. The rest was the eerie silence of the high hills.

How do they even stay sane out here? She did not voice the question. She tried to put the caves out of her mind. They remained far beneath them, hidden, unguarded. Open.

She took a few steps through the snow to warm up and hide restless nervousness. Looming above, the mountains were a constant reminder that she'd be all too glad to leave them behind.

Ammie came out to meet the cart with two large metal jugs. She talked to the would-be coachman and pointed to the two waiting by the muddy road. Amus nodded as she explained.

"My tits are freezing," Tallah groaned. She kept trying to scratch under her eye patch, despite Sil's protestations.

"At least you have the hat," Sil replied, shaking melting snow out of her hair. "Why, precisely, don't I have cold-weather gear?"

"Because we're idiots." Tallah blew into her hands. The temperature had dropped even more since morning.

Why she wasn't infusing herself to keep warm was worrying Sil more than she wanted to admit.

Watching the cart amble towards them felt like waiting for an iceberg to shift. It rattled up the road with the patience of millennia.

"No," Sil said with more than a little malice, "could it be because a certain someone ignored me when I asked for us to stop for necessities before we headed into the hills?"

Tallah shrugged.

"We had food. Don't blame this on me. It wasn't supposed to take up our entire wither. Leaves hadn't even turned color when we set out."

Sil did not even crack a smile.

"If you get frostbite anywhere nasty, I won't be treating it. Maybe next time you'll listen to me for once," she grumbled as the cart rattled to a stop in front of them.

"Good day, Your Graces," the cart's driver said, unmoving under his canvas. He pretended, with very little skill, not to have overheard the conversation.

"Good day, sir." Sil smiled at him, though her teeth chattered in the cold. "Would it be possible for us to accompany you back to Valen?"

"Aye, Ammie told me." The man in the cart pushed the cover off his shoulders and climbed off his perch with a nimbleness that belied his age. His beard hung down to his trousers. He rounded the cart and prepared two spots for them among his load of cheeses and milk jugs. Ammie came by and handed him a bundle of blankets.

"You dears take care now. If you's ever in these parts again, do come visit. Bring us some news of the big city, aye?"

She helped Amus set up a comfortable spot for them for the long, slow trek.

It wasn't the most dignified way of travel. It wasn't even quick or comfortable. But it beat walking or trying to transfer closer via portal. If Valen's illum hearth had sent them here, there would be very little chance that it would choose another destination if Sil tried again.

Well . . . bugger.

They settled in, got comfortable, and soon saw the last of Cliff's Edge's scattered thatch-roofed huts shrinking away as the road sloped down into the valleys.

Vergil walked. If he minded the chill, he didn't show it. The long trek gave the two channelers ample time to study and discuss him.

"I'm going to take apart that helmet after we drop off its contents at the Sisters," Sil mused, nestled against Tallah, talking in a low voice. "And Anna's wand. I'm looking forward to dissecting her enchantments. There were interesting things happening when you fought."

"You picked it up?" Tallah asked, eye closed against the bright snow-covered landscape.

"Grabbed it off the last doll you blasted. Nearly lost my head for it. Hope it was worth it."

Tallah yawned and nestled into Sil's side for warmth, Anna gone from her attention.

"Baaah!" she mock-bleated and chuckled. "We end our hunt in the back of a cart. Like sheep. You're even dressed like one." She dozed off, chuckling, before Sil had properly picked her expletives.

On the descent from the hills, grazing land turned into flat farmland, pockmarked by farmsteads among empty tilled fields. Snowfall from the mountains turned to sleet and soon to rain. Miasmas of burned straw and dung wafted up to them as they passed through the quiet countryside.

Tallah slept fitfully and woke often, even in her exhausted state. Sil held her so her sudden cries wouldn't spook the cart driver, though she was sure he feigned his ignorance.

Village after village rolled by in the relentless rain. Scatterings of homes across naked hills. Groves of hidden hovels in narrow gorges. Sil and Tallah huddled under the tarp as Amus's cart stopped and he picked up his deliveries from folk that, more often than not, didn't spare them a glance.

They spent the night in a dry and warm barn close to the road in a final village before the hills leveled out. The driver opted to sleep in the cart, under his tarp.

Sil switched the illum siphon to Tallah. Resting would be impossible with the constant draw of the helmet, and the sorceress could keep the effect going for much longer without help if she wasn't exerting herself. In her state, Tallah wouldn't use her abilities to their proper extent for a good long while. A passive draw was manageable. It only made her sleepy.

Closer to Valen, the dark held little of the terror it commanded in the mountains. Patrols passed by in the night. Boisterous adventurers on their sorties. Armed men astride from the Citadel, still on their routes in spite of the weather. Sil heard them in the depths of night, grumbling, sharing short barks of laughter or cusses.

Closer to Valen, ratmen and chimeric horrors seemed . . . well, distant nightmares that only clung on to the shadows of Sil's imagination.

Still, she slept little.

They returned to the road at first light. The cart rattled on, rain fell, Vergil splashed through the cold mud behind the cart, sullen but still muttering.

Tallah fell in and out of consciousness. Sil stroked her hair under the tarp and otherwise enjoyed the gray scenery as it crawled by.

She felt light, disassociated from reality, drifting back to herself as Valen's walls drew closer by the hour. Anna's caves and her monsters faded in winter's cold light.

CHAPTER THREE

Personal Care

Valen loomed against the horizon. Its high walls and spires flickered with pinpricks of light visible from half a day away. A pulse of light shot upward and punched through the cloud cover as the illum hearth vented excess energy.

They reached the Black Gate late that night, with the rain turning to sleet again. It was warmer near the city, but winter's icy fingers groped for its throat. The smell of rotted burnt wood and the cacophony of fresh masonry hit them way before the sight of the gate did. Familiarity shook Tallah out of another fitful bout with sleep and cleared the cobwebs in her head.

They said their goodbyes at the gate, reined in Vergil, and left Amus to his deliveries. They even bought a wheel of hard cheese off him, small enough to fit in Sil's rend.

"I'll sell the tunnel map and see if there's anyone looking for this guy," Sil said as they walked along the cobbled thoroughfare towards the central fortress of Valen, jostling among the throng of workers gathered for the rebuilding, at least until the first real snow would stop them. "I don't want any surprises on our hands later on."

"When you're done, come down to the Sisters." Tallah had her hand on Vergil's shoulder, holding him close as they walked across the busy street. She ignored the stares the boy gathered.

"Can you get up there on your own?" Sil had been mothering her incessantly for the past half-day, as if she'd been crippled in some way by her spat with Anna.

'I would be terribly impressed if you admitted you can barely walk.' Christina woke in the back of Tallah's mind and voiced her amusement, pushing forward the mental image of a mocking smile. She and Bianca had been mostly quiet since the village. That blissful peace of mind never lasted long.

"I'm perfectly capable of walking half the city on my own, thank you very much. I'll meet you there." Tallah's temper flared, but Christina's taunting kept it subdued. She wouldn't give the ghost such satisfaction, even with Sil giving her boast a mocking smile of her own.

"Sure you are, Your Ladyship. But just in case." She handed over a vial from her satchel. "If you get dizzy or feel nauseous on the ramps up, drink half of this, then a swig of water, then the rest. If you still feel sick, just sit down, and I'll find you eventually."

She walked off before Tallah could protest and offer to shove the vial where the suns normally didn't shine. Christina snickered again.

'And you say we are unbearable in our worries.'

Tallah ignored this.

Valen's night life was chaotic, especially now that they had nearly finished rebuilding the outer walls and the gates, and all work was slowly moving towards the heart of the city.

As a major hub for the Guild, and with one of the largest Halls outside of the empire, adventurers and travelers came and went at all hours. Aside from them, the city's more mundane industries employed at least half the population and worked all hours. Valen never slept, never slowed, could never stop. They even wrote it on billboards.

She watched Sil stop on a street corner and wait for a ride. It wasn't long before an illum-powered carriage came into view. It belonged to the Enginarium and had become a common sight in Valen. A metal box on metal wheels running on metal tracks. How anyone could get on one of those and not feel sick was beyond understanding.

Sil loved the bloody things. She packed herself in with the rest of the sweaty, stinking commuters and was away faster than a swallow.

Tallah missed the horse-drawn carriages. Their horrible smells less so. They were no longer allowed in the city proper, as Valen had relegated all transport to the Enginarium's engines. The city was cleaner for it, but it meant she had no choice but to walk everywhere.

Rain and sleet had washed Valen, scoured its streets and alleys of their many and intricate miasmas. Aside from the ever-present scent of ash always lingering on the air, the city smelled . . . not exactly clean, but pleasantly rural.

Tallah made no effort to step over muddied puddles and fresh banks of soot that washed out from the gutters and gathered on the roadside. The horrid dress was due a burning anyway.

At least the boy didn't seem to mind the long, slippery walk, as opposed to Sil's incessant whining every time they had to get anywhere on foot.

Vergil's strange look here, deeper into Valen, drew less attention even as he proved prone to shout and curse at passers-by. Tallah smiled her apologies at people and ushered the madman along, keeping a tight hold on his arm as he strained to reach out and punch anyone who made eye contact. Like an attack corallin on a leash almost.

It made for a slow, heaving trek up the many stairs that led up to their destination. One more lashing out from the boy and she may just have left him to plunge off the walls.

The Sisters of Mercy occupied a large, white-marbled, green-roofed building on the outskirts of the Medical Quarter of the Inner Plaza. Through the center of the dome's roof passed the ten-yard-wide trunk of a white-leafed tree. Its canopy offered shade for the hospital in the long summers, while its roots provided the raw sap that they refined into medicine.

The Sisters, druids of the Dryad, plied their healing arts for any and for all, regardless of species or allegiance. All were welcome, for a price, in the bosom of their capricious Goddess.

Tallah walked through the open archway, shaking melting snow off her hat. She marched past the line of people waiting in the atrium and tried to enter an ornate side door, just behind a green-clad priestess who was trying to sort through those for whom the coming of winter was proving dangerous.

The priestess grabbed her arm before she could wrap fingers on the door's handle.

"Where does the lady think she's going?" the woman asked with practiced patience.

"In. I'm expected."

"The lady is expected at the back of the line with the rest of the Dryad's many seeds."

Tallah tried to pull her arm away, but the woman's grip was like iron.

"I'm expected," she insisted, and planted her feet, defiant.

Vergil grumbled next to her. His hands balled up into fists, but he made no threat against the priestess barring their way. Rather, he was looking at the crowd, and they at him, the tension in the room starting to froth.

"Aliana is expecting me," Tallah insisted, forcing a smile.

"The high priestess is not expecting anyone at this hour. Please head to the back of the line, and you can ask for her when your turn arrives."

"What's the noise?"

A tall, heavyset woman opened the ornate door and walked out. She wore the same flowing green robe as the other priestesses bustling about, but hers also had white leaf embroidery that showed her rank.

One look from Aliana quieted the room and even had Vergil taking a step back. The high priestess of the Dryad wore her rank like war plate, and her glare was a spear.

"Finally. Aliana, tell your wench to let go of my arm."

"What's going on, Siphra?" the woman asked without even glancing at Tallah.

"This one is giving me cheek. She tried to jump the line." Siphra yanked Tallah forward and finally released her arm. "Her friend is agitating the others."

Aliana swept her dark gaze over the gathered crowd again. None met it.

"Line looks quiet to me. I'll deal with her," she said.

Tallah met her sneer with a grin and poked her tongue out at the priestess. "I did say I was expected, did I not?"

Aliana shoved her through the small door, and Vergil followed, as cowed as the others by the imposing olive-skinned high priestess.

"How dare you!" the woman bellowed when the door clicked shut.

For anyone who had only known Aliana of Tohman as the severe priestess of the Dryad, the blazing fury in her voice and eyes would have been cowing. Tallah, however, paid it no mind as she tried to find a place to set her hat. The office was small and tightly packed with books, salves, and medicine bottles. White leaves formed garlands that intertwined among the apparatus used to distill their valuable sap and lent the room some of their luminescence.

Herbs and other supplies were neatly stacked on shelves, each with its own label written in the Dryad's peculiar runes. Complex notes of herbs and antiseptics scented the air.

On the main desk, among the office scrolls and the many files on patients, was a bottle with a thimble glass next to it. Both were filled with an amber liquid.

"Calm your humors, Aliana. I bring you something that you're going to like." Greetings were a rare thing between Tallah and the priestess.

"Where's Silestra? I don't deal with you without her present." The older woman scowled at Tallah, giving her a sneer vile enough to curdle dairy. It would have worked on anyone else.

"She's busy. Today you deal with me." She picked up the bottle and took a swig from it. "I've always liked that you respect yourself enough to drink something expensive." She hiccuped. Whatever that was, it went down burning.

"Sil's at the Guild Hall, if you really must know, declaring the death of this guy and his friends." She gestured with the bottle towards the twitching Vergil, diverting Aliana's attention to him.

Vergil looked wretched in the white leaflight of the office. His clothes hung on him like dressings on a scarecrow, and his stench overpowered the smell of disinfectant. Aliana stiffened as she looked him over.

"Maybe *like* is a strong word." Tallah drank more and swished the burning liquid inside her mouth. "I need you to fix him. We found him in a ratman camp, caged and starved, in the Valen-Drack Passage. Pretty sure he's gone insane. The rats were eating his female companion alive. Or at least we assume it was his companion. Haven't gotten a coherent word out of him yet."

Aliana's demeanor changed as she turned her interest on Vergil. The boy stiffened and grumbled, backing up a step.

"How is he standing?" she asked, picking up her thimble and draining it. "Looks to me he should be dead."

Tallah pointed to the helmet.

"That bucket on his head houses some kind of ghost, or an echo of one. We're not terribly sure what it is. Its strength, however . . ." She shuddered and drank more. "To call it simply impressive would be lying. We've been feeding it illum for a few days now, and it kept the boy alive and going. Lad's also got one of those stupid blessing tattoos the paladins give to their fresh recruits. If I stop the illum siphon, I don't think he'd last the day."

Aliana raised an eyebrow. She drummed the tips of her fingers over her lips.

"I assume this was your idea. I couldn't imagine Silestra coming up with something so vile. What were you doing in the tunnels?"

"That is none of your business. Can you help me, or do I leave the corpse here?"

Aliana shrugged. "We were running low on fertilizer anyway. Take him back or leave him, it's no skin off my cheek."

'That worked well,' Christina whispered. 'We need her help, not her disinterest.'

Tallah shrugged.

"I'll have Sil take another crack at him, then. She said you'd be a better choice, but it seems you don't like a proper challenge after all, oh great High Priestess of the Twiggy One."

She snapped her fingers and pointed the boy to the door.

Aliana downed the rest of her spirit and set the glass on top of the bottle, pulling it away from Tallah's grasp, to Tallah's annoyance. She had planned to take the whole thing with her.

"Do you want him back on his feet or just lucid enough to answer whatever you need him to?"

When all else fails, appeal to Aliana's pride. Christi, this used to work perfectly, even with you. It was Tallah's turn to inwardly smirk at the ghost.

To Aliana, she said, "Walking, talking, and as sane as you can get him. Don't dig too deep in his head. There's some kind of enchantment in there, we think, which kicks like a unicorn if you bother it. Sil tried to mind-touch him, and it flung her away. Literally, I might add. Broke a rib or three when she hit the wall."

"How do we get him out of the armor he's wearing?"

"It's going to disappear on its own. It's a secondary effect of the helmet. Don't ask. You know how these southern relics work generally."

"I'm going to charge you an arm and a leg. And I'll double that because I need to deal with you instead of Silestra." The woman's tone did not soften, but she was curious. Tallah and Sil never failed to provide the challenges city life lacked.

"Add in this as well." Tallah leaned over the table, grabbed the bottle, and waggled it. "I haven't had a proper drink in weeks. Sil's kept me on tonics and water. No alcohol at all."

"Silestra being smart and responsible while out in rough places? I'm truly amazed." She clutched at invisible pearls around her neck. "It's a pity she still associates with you, brigand."

Aliana opened the door and shouted out for some girls. Three large women arrived at a trot, and she explained the situation to them in concise terms, quick and efficient. Two of them got a rough hold of Vergil's armpits. The third grabbed his helmet. He fussed a bit, looking confused from one to the other, grunting, uncertain of the hostility in their actions. He would have struggled, but Tallah glared at him.

"Ready," all three called in unison, and she dropped the illum siphon. It felt like a weight dropping off her shoulders. Vergil's legs buckled under him as he was led away. The third woman handed the helmet to Aliana.

"Why's there a big red willy painted on it?" she asked, studying the ugly horned thing.

"Ask Sil. She'll be more than happy to tell you all about it." Tallah grinned and drank.

"Now push off, sorceress. I'll send a runner to fetch you when we're done. You're still at that swanky place?"

Tallah didn't leave. Instead, she pulled off her eye patch. The eye, as if to spite Sil's ministrations, had gotten worse. It stung, and the pain had only numbed due to the alcohol. The scars, unseen now, itched like a bugger.

"Can you do something about this?" She pointed at the stricken organ. "I hate not being able to see your face in all its ugly glory."

"You've been giving Silestra a hard time again? I should leave you like that."

"But you won't."

Aliana gave an unpleasant little smile.

"Of course. That, I'll deal with personally. Wait right there while I fetch my tools. I'll make sure you remember this time why it's in your best interest not to end up back here."

Tallah felt ice climbing up her back, and she shivered despite the burning hearth. She wouldn't ever admit it, even to the voices in her head, but Aliana's ministrations frightened her.

When she saw the array of tools the old priestess brought back and the lack of any kind of pain-relief salve, she wished she hadn't asked for help. Two bells of screaming obscenities later, she would have preferred going blind.

Sil walked through the great ornate doors of the Guild Hall. Adventurers who flocked to Valen worked dawn to dawn, regardless of season. In them, the empire had a willing workforce onto which it could unload many of the more trivial jobs that the great machine could not be bothered to deal with.

She wasn't one of them, not really, but played the part for all the benefits she and Tallah reaped.

The sea of people carried her along towards the great kiosks that crowded the central pavilion of the Guild Hall. Sprite lamps had turned the cavernous insides of the smallest of fortresses into perpetual day, and the noise made all the great taverns of Valen seem quaint by comparison.

After weeks in and under the mountains, all of this made Sil feel faint.

"Good tidings, Miss Silestra Adana. You're a rare, pale sight for these sore eyes," the man behind the counter said. He bowed his head as she approached.

Lucian, a portly human of some sixty summers, manned one of the many kiosks that bought information off of whoever was willing to sell. His gray eyes always smiled whenever she visited, especially when alone. He wore the green-and-blue uniform of the Guild, with black buttons signaling his speciality.

"We haven't seen you and your mistress around for such a long time that I thought you may have returned to Calabran. I had hopes that you'd at least say your farewells."

Sil smiled back and touched two fingers to her lips, mimicking the real aelir greeting, *I shall tell you no lies.*

"Good tidings, Master Lucian. The mistress has kept us rather busy outside of Valen since last we met."

Information merchants such as Lucian had their own tents set up inside the Halls, guarded against prying ears by powerful enchantments and hidden blades.

"Did she? I don't remember seeing your names on any of the sorties we've sent out," he replied, and showed her to a cushioned seat.

Sil graciously accepted. She gestured an apology, hand over right breast, eyes closed.

"It wasn't on Guild duty, Master. We went out on Her Grace's behalf. She had a mind to explore more of Valen's beautiful countryside before winter came down on us."

Lucian's orderly poked his head in, summoned by some secret means, and brought in a tray of tea and sugar cubes. The aroma of rose filled the room. Lucian himself poured her a cup and added six sugar cubes to it.

"Then it must mean you've brought me quite the treasure trove today," he said as he served her.

Sil eyed the sugar, and he added another cube to her cup.

"That is certainly my hope, yes." They spoke in quiet voices, the lacquered wood desk between them, both sipping tea.

Lucian knew his business like few others and treated her with a courtesy that not many enjoyed. Sil knew there were now no other adventurers waiting to be led in to see the man, and keen ears would be listening in on all she had to say. So much attention for one little healer attending to one noble's wayward daughter.

Tianna of Aieni Holding was the daughter of one Fyodor of Aieni Holding, head of the Divide Expansion Trade Company of Calabran. He owned more than thirty ships at sea and nearly a third of the shipping routes between Calabran and Estuary, one of the few humans doing big business with the Aelir Dominion's great capital.

That the reclusive Fyodor was long dead and the real Tianna had been lost at sea wouldn't become common knowledge anytime soon if Sil and Tallah had their way.

"And, Master Lucian, it is my, and my mistress's, hope that you also have something of interest for her. I know it is terribly presumptuous, what with our absence, but I trust you have been as tenacious as ever in pursuing our request."

"That depends on what you trade with me today, Miss Silestra. You asked for something quite . . . difficult."

"Nothing for free" was his reminder to her.

Nothing for free, as always.

She opened her satchel and drew out several scrolls kept in black, oiled sheaths. One bore the seal of the Valen Library. The others were unmarked.

"I believe this will much interest you," she said as she opened the marked container and pulled out an old, battered map. She spread it across the table, and Lucian offered his inkwell to keep it from rolling back.

"The Valen-Drack Passage," Lucian said after a glance, a more genuine smile creeping under his moustache. "We rarely hear anything of those roads anymore."

"We are aware. They are old, treacherous, and abandoned by gentle folk. You already know this very well." She opened another of her containers and spread out the scroll inside. It was another map. "And here is what I aim to sell you."

Now his impeccably plucked eyebrows really went up. The map she presented was drawn over the skeleton of the old library one, and showed many side passages, caverns, and cuts across the tunnels. Cramped annotations accompanied the extended galleries. His expression grew even more impressed as she laid out the rest of the scrolls. These departed completely from the original.

"Mistress Tianna had a mind to practice her cartography skills," Sil lied, hiding it behind a sip of tea. She had drawn up the maps, and Tallah had written the annotations. They were of no more use to them now that Anna was dead but should still fetch a good price. Too few adventurers now braved the old tunnels and the gallery of creatures and rogues they housed.

Dozens of requests to the Guild went unanswered when they concerned those gods-forgotten places and the unfortunate people living close.

"That is a very dangerous place to explore for . . . practice." He wanted to reach for the maps. Sil saw it in him as she rolled them back up and slid them back into their cylinders. "Especially for two novice adventurers. I am delighted to see you safe and hale after such a journey. It must have been dangerous."

"It was, and it took a significant amount of cunning on the mistress's part to see us through."

She opened her last canister and showed him a scroll full of notes in a tiny, meticulous script.

"These are locations for some creatures that might interest the Guild, as well as some unfortunate victims of the tunnels that we ran across." She pushed the scroll across the table to him. "Mistress Tianna wishes to hand this over freely, a token of her gratitude for your meticulous services. You have been of great help to her since she has arrived in your wonderful city. I call it a token of our friendship."

Something changed in his face when he read the scroll and strained to decipher her horrid hand. It came and went in a flash, meaning that some information there might have been worth more than the maps. Bugger. She forced herself to keep smiling and chew the sugary slush at the bottom of her cup.

Lucian was quiet for a long while.

"I will buy the maps off you, Miss Silestra." When he spoke up, his features were carefully arranged into a mask of friendliness that strained to hide a predatory grin. "I will also reward you for some of the news here. Some people are interested in these things."

"That is very kind of you," she replied, matching his smile. "If you do not mind my asking, what got you so enthused?"

He leaned forward and spoke in a low whisper. Sil couldn't help but lean forward to participate in the charade.

"You see, you describe a verman pack on here. Unless I'm wrong, they were of some interest to the Storm Guard. They'll be keen to get news of their destruction."

Sil's heart boomed at the mention of the Storm Guard, but she resolved not to let it show.

She whispered, "What about the victims?"

"What?" He drew back and read the scroll again. "Oh, these. Human male, supposed paladin order, and female aelir, unknown. We have so many groups missing, Miss Silestra, that I couldn't guess if they were some of ours. And if I wrote a list of all missing persons for which we've posted queries, the stack of scrolls would be taller than yourself."

Sil checked the boy off her worry list. Now for the real reason she played this dainty charade with the most unscrupulous agent of the Guild.

"On behalf of Mistress Tianna, I accept what I'm sure will be fair compensation for our effort. I am certain she will be as pleased as I that we have aided the Storm Guard in some small measure."

She drummed her fingers on the lid of one of her containers. Lucian went back to one of his shelves and extracted a scroll from among many.

"I'm afraid your mistress will be terribly disappointed in me on this matter. This is all we could find and all we may share. But if you may indulge me, please tell why she needs this information. It's not something I normally get asked for."

He reached to pour her some more tea. She placed her palm over the cup and refused politely. If Lucian had his way, they'd be talking until morning, and she'd spill secrets without even realizing it.

"It is no great secret," she said. "Mistress Tianna had often heard of this rather exclusive clique of sorceresses when she was a student at Hoarfrost Academy. She would dearly like to meet some of them and learn from their vast experience. Her power grows . . ."

She left the implication hanging.

"Well, I'm afraid she'll be disappointed." He unfurled the scroll and cleared his throat.

"Christina Cythra, dead. Confirmed. Murder.

"Anna Theala, believed dead. Last seen in Drack. Date of sighting uncertain.

"Bianca Vel, dead. Confirmed. Details redacted by order of Her Imperial Majesty, Empress Catharina the First.

"Lucretia Saral, believed dead. No recorded movements in over five decades. Last seen in Drack.

"And Deidra Aratol, wanted for crimes against the Eternal Enlightened Empire. Sizeable reward available for any information on her whereabouts. No information available."

He handed her the scroll with an apologetic smile. "I'm afraid Mistress Aieni is too late to find or meet most of them. And she would be foolish to seek the one still kicking around."

They had left off one name from the list. Tallah Amni, traitor to the empire. Dead. Sil did not think it wise to mention the omission. She nodded and accepted the list.

"It was a fancy of hers. It is regrettable, but I believe it will only encourage her to surpass their legend by her own means."

Everything on the scroll was near worthless except for one thing. They knew that one more of the group was alive. If the empire pursued this Deidra Aratol, then she could be found. And she could be killed. A new hunt rose on the horizon with the winter sun.

It was more than enough to warrant stomaching Lucian's questions about their travels.

Sil found Tallah in the small hours of the morning, on the steps in front of the Sisters' great hospital. There was a near-empty bottle by her side. She was watching traffic pass by in the gloomy sprite light, looking comfortably numb to the cold, neatly hidden under the wide brim of her hat.

A thin layer of snow covered the walkways and hid the black ice beneath. The sorceress chuckled every time another passerby slipped and fell.

"I see Aliana's kicked you out in the cold," Sil said by way of greeting, taking a seat next to her on the wet marble steps. Tallah offered the bottle, some liquid still sloshing on the bottom.

"I walked out on my own. This time. Took her stuff." She slurred the words.

"Did she look at your eye?" Sil studied the liquid, holding it up to the nearest sprite-lamp. "No weird insects floating in this?"

Tallah turned to her and displayed her bright-pink eye.

"She did. Gave me a full course of her ministrations. Hurt like you wouldn't believe. I thought you bunch weren't supposed to enjoy hurting your patients." For all her griping, she didn't seem upset about the treatment.

Sil opened her satchel and pulled out a pair of round spectacles. She cleaned them and handed them over. "I assume I'll need to make a new lens for you," she said as Tallah looked around.

"Still in range. I'll let you know if I get a headache later."

Sil finished up the bottle and hiccuped.

"How does she drink this stuff? If there were any justice in the world, this would make you blind." She grimaced and leaned on Tallah, watching a stout aelir'sar take a nasty fall. Her instincts urged her to help, but her mind pointed out the hospital behind them. There was a still a trickle of people coming in, even at that strange hour.

"I got us about a hundred Valen griffons for our trouble." She yawned and shifted closer. "Your little prize is of no concern to anyone, so he's yours to keep."

"That's about double what I expected the maps to fetch. Was Lucian so happy to see you?"

Sil chuckled. "Hardly. He couldn't be greasier if they dipped him in lard. Do you remember killing a verman shaman?"

Tallah squeezed her eyes shut and made an effort to focus.

"Vaguely. All rats look the same."

"It was that one with the robe. You blew its spine out." She mimicked a minor explosion with her hand. "It was of interest to the Storm Guard, if you can imagine it. Lucian even offered an extra reward for killing the blighter. I smiled and accepted, though he now thinks the world of your abilities."

Tallah scrunched up her nose and grumbled. "Sometimes I forget the gap between myself and who Tianna's supposed to be. It's too early to get the Guard interested in her."

She closed her eyes and leaned her head on Sil's shoulder as they sat in the cold, silent for some time. Heat wafted off her. A fever, or just burning off some illum for warmth? It was hard to tell.

"What next?" Sil asked when she felt the cold bite at her toes.

"Next, I may be sick. Give me something for it."

Sil handed over a toxin purger in a glass vial, the last of her supply. She had it ready before the sorceress even asked.

"All at once, or you'll vomit it out," she instructed, but Tallah had already downed it.

The sorceress sighed in relief as the alcohol was purged out of her. Her breath misted in the frigid night air, blown away by a gathering wind. She shivered and was trying to hide it, the heat coming off her a fever.

"We're staying put and laying low, after Tianna's fashion," Tallah said, speaking clearly. "I'm itching to know what you got out of the boy's head."

She pushed herself up and stretched the stiffness from her joints. Sil followed suit, dusting the snow off her clothes.

"Don't blame me if stuff makes little sense. I have no reference points for most of it, and it's la-la, as far as I can reason it out. I've been trying to sort through it since we got out."

"If he's an Other, then I'll be quite disappointed if he turns out to be boring. I'll put him back in the caves myself." Tallah didn't sound like she was joking.

They walked abreast down the steps from the Upper City into the Lower, by the side of the Daylight Wall. About a hundred yards elevated the Upper City. They could have taken the Enginarium elevator down, but that also made Tallah sick.

That only left the stairs. Few people still used them. The wind had turned savage and howled outside the many small windows. Sil drew close against Tallah, the sound all too similar to the cries from the caves. Those would take long to sink below the surface of memory.

The Meadow had once been a watering hole on the edge of Valen, back when the city had been younger and wilder. Tallah, in her more pensive moments, talked about those days with uncharacteristic fondness. Now the once-quaint tavern offered the best accommodation that money could buy just shy of the Fortress itself. For someone like Tianna, making her name in the world while spending her father's significant fortune, it was the only possible lodging.

It hugged the great city wall at the end of a labyrinthine mess of alleyways and thoroughfares. Anyone unfamiliar with the dense cluster of the Lower City would never hope to stumble upon it, and for the regulars it was a point of pride to know the way by heart.

Even that early in the day, with cold Cares's light just kissing the lip of the Outer Wall, the Meadow was abuzz with activity.

They found the owner almost immediately in the chaos. Or rather, the other way around. She was with them when they stepped through the door, as if she'd come out of the woodwork itself to greet them.

"Welcome back, Your Ladyships." Tallah started at that too-cheerful tone for the hour, speaking right next to her ear. "I was not warned of your return. Shall I get your apartment ready?"

"Good morning to you too, Verti," Sil said and bowed to the woman. They allowed themselves to be led through the early-morning crowd. "Yes, please. We've just returned tonight."

Verti, an elendine with ash-gray hair, was the eldest, and matriarch, of the Bergama family. They had owned the tavern since the early days of the empire, mother to daughter, in a long, unbroken succession. For her to meet them in person was an honor.

"I feared something ill might have befallen you ladies," Verti said as she led them up the spiral inner stair. "It will take some time for heating and hot water to reach your room. We had a new Enginarium boiler and pump installed this week. The cold still lingers in some places. I hope you will pardon the discomfort."

"It's all right," Tallah said and yawned. "I just need food and drink."

"Will you be having breakfast? Or dinner?"

"Both. Either. I don't care, as long as it's proper food. I'm sick of dried meat and cheese."

Verti smiled as she unlocked the heavy master's lock to their apartment.

"I understand, Mistress Aieni. There will be neither of those."

A gaggle of workers came in moments later with fresh linen for the beds, flowers for the vases, and wood for the hearth. They worked under Verti's stern gaze with the efficiency of long practice.

"Food will come up shortly," she said as she walked out, satisfied with her staff's work. "As always, please enjoy your stay with us. I remain your servant."

Tallah undressed and took the first turn to soak in a hot bath. Sil inspected the room and belongings.

Their three large chests lay as they had left them, locked tight and warded against curious hands. She checked every enchantment. Nothing had been disturbed while they were gone. Verti would have probably set at least one guard, for propriety's sake.

She set her staff on a rack, tightened its covering, and then emptied her satchel on a table. Tallah's silver mask would need cleaning and disinfecting, but it could wait. Anna's bone wand exuded a cold, surly malice, and Sil was glad to have it off her person. Both items went into a locked compartment in the largest chest.

The black gem she stowed in the deepest, darkest part of their armored travel chest. Tallah would see to its storage when she recovered more of her strength. There wasn't enough acid in the world to burn away the feel of it from Sil's hands.

She undressed at long last and took out fresh clothes. "I'm going to burn you when we're done," she mumbled as she held out the rough, itchy dress for inspection. "I'm going to make an evening of it, with wine and a comfortable chair from which to watch you burn."

Dinner arrived just as they switched for the bath. Tallah met the two caterers at the door barely dressed, and Sil slipped into the bathroom as they babbled their way through presenting the meal.

The tub was copper, and large enough to fit four women of Sil's stature, while the bathroom itself could host a luncheon. A complex system of copper pipes protruded out of the ceiling to provide hot, cold, and fizzy water through three separate nozzles. The chill lingered—Tallah must've had a cold dip—and reminded her uncomfortably about all the rough living they'd been doing for weeks, memories of grisly mutations scratching at the surface of her thoughts.

She submerged under hot water, eyes closed, listening to the throbs of her heartbeat as all other sounds became muted.

It worked to drown out the memories of this last terrible week. Tallah could detach herself from the horrors that had tried to claw their innards out, but it wasn't as easy for Sil. She feared what her first sleep in a proper bed would conjure up to sour the night.

When she surfaced, Tallah was there on the edge of the bathtub, handing her a glass of rose petal wine.

"Tell me about the boy."

Sil raised an eyebrow and took the proffered drink.

"Are you serious? You couldn't let me enjoy the bath?"

The sorceress shrugged. "You take forever in a bath, and you like a glass of wine whenever you soak. Plus you're fond of this vintage. I don't see why we can't both get what we want."

All true.

Sil sighed and leaned back, the foot of the glass pressing on her chest.

"Fine. Wash my hair and I'll tell you about the blasted boy."

CHAPTER FOUR

Cinder

The smell.

By the Goddess's grace, this smell!

The foulness in the air had taste. It even had texture. Quistis could chew on it if she had a mind to, and a stomach made of weapon-grade steel.

"Yer telling me a rookie did this? With a straight face?"

Barlo wore, like her, one of the new Enginarium hazard masks, and his voice was muffled by the protecting layers. Even though they did nothing against the smell, these were supposed to protect against other airborne filth. Quistis needed more convincing.

By the light of a sprite, the cave looked like something scraped off the bottom of a nightmare. The rot had set in, and whatever was left of the ratmen that hadn't been originally incinerated or reduced to splattered gore was now decomposing into puddles of fluids speckled with bits of fur and armor.

It reeked. The damned smell overwhelmed her concentration. The way the mask chafed didn't help either.

"Are ye sure we're in the right place?"

Quistis checked the annotated map again and retraced, for the third time, their path coming in.

"Right place, Barlo. Shut it and just find the stinking corpse. I want us out of here as soon as Rumi and Vial get back."

"That side tunnel ain't on yer map, is all I'm saying," the large vanadal warrior commented as he turned half of a ratman over with the sheath of his sword. Rotten meat slid off festering bone with a wet thud.

He thumbed towards a passage marked by a man-shaped hole in the rock. Someone had smashed through to open some secret way. It wasn't noted on the map.

"What channeling bursts someone from within?" he asked, making a face at another corpse that seemed to have been quartered.

"A Vitalis mage's," Quistis replied. "But this wasn't a Vitalis mage in here. One wouldn't leave so much blood go to waste."

"Rare buggers. Never met one of them. Do we have any?"

"Couple. In Aztroa. Breed's dying out, if we're lucky."

Quistis tried not to take in every detail of the scene, but it was tremendously hard as she picked her way carefully among the refuse. She was glad for the thick-soled boots she wore.

Barlo griped, but he was more accustomed to this sort of scenery. He kept turning bodies over, making a trench through the gore in his search.

"If Lucian bought that rookie story, then he needs to retire. Poor humie's gone soft in the stone." He tapped his thick temple as he stepped over the remains of a tall ratman. That one had been cleaved in two at the waist. Its entrails had dissolved into stringy ribbons of congealed matter that spread away like garlands on a dress. "If I'm any expert, I'd reckon there was an entire cadre in here. A lone ash eater doesn't kill like this."

Quistis knew that Academy-trained channelers had to show at least a modicum of decency in their work. What she was seeing in the cave spoke of unhinged use of deadly force and very little discrimination.

But they were there more than eight days after the fact. At least eight days, by her calculations. Ratmen lived in abject filth as a rule, so the estimation was likely on the generous side.

"Well, we're in the right place," Barlo called from somewhere further ahead, out of her sprite light. "I found the aelir'rei. She ain't a pretty sight." He beckoned her forward with the torch.

Quistis made her way towards the paladin's voice, trying not to slip in the mess. Her light sprite showed the remains of an aelir, judging by whatever was left of her. The rot hadn't eaten her face yet, but the rest was just a bloated, leaking mess that made a good effort at turning her stomach. She sighed and turned away.

"They could have buried her."

"Hard to bury someone in solid rock, Captain," Barlo said, stone-faced. "Let's see if we find that damn shaman's corpse."

"I'm going to bite Lucian's face off when we get back. I don't know if I'll flog him before or after I spit him out."

Barlo chuckled as he turned over more bodies. Human remains. Old. Before the killing. Gnawed bones scattered by the violence.

"Lucian couldn't have known someone would stumble across our operation. Be happy he remembered yer interest in these critters."

The maps had shown many entryways that the Guard had never even suspected. Whoever had drawn them had spent considerable time down there and been frightfully meticulous. There were even exits leading to villages, some of which were barely more than a name on a territorial map.

Quistis fought down the bile rising in the back of her throat. She felt her knuckles turn white on her staff and forced herself to calm. Anger at their own failure in managing this sordid affair wouldn't fix the blunder, and it would definitely not get them closer to uncovering the flesh sellers that had been plaguing Valen's countryside.

Little wonder they couldn't find any sign of the bastards for so long, or hadn't even gotten news of their comings and goings since those first reports of missing people. There were tens of places to slip in and out of the tunnels, dozens of routes, even more that were still secret.

"Complete failure," she mused, the words bitter as she wandered away from Barlo's track. "Rats wiped out. Nothing to follow up on. We had one lead and we mismanaged it."

Quistis was busy enough being miserable that she didn't notice the burnt skeleton until she tripped over it and went down with a brief cry and a splash.

"I see ye found 'im."

Barlo was trying not to laugh. He was failing.

"Not a word, Barlo." She picked herself up from the muck and tried to shake it off her clothes. The stink would be with her for days. "It's a burnt-out skeleton. How do you know it's a shaman?"

"Larger shoulders than the rest of the rats in here. See? And there's a half-burned wooden staff over there."

He raised his torch to the wall. The light shone on the burnt, greasy outline of a ratman caught in an explosion. Fire had blackened the rest of the wall. He whistled.

"Pyro work, sure as winter's cold. Mean one, too."

Quistis wasn't listening. She had found the shaman's resting nook. Some of it had survived the destruction.

"Pry this open for me, please," she said and showed him a battered old metal chest. "Would it be too much to hope that the rat would've kept some records?"

"They're not often literate. But ye can hope."

Barlo unclasped his spiked mace from its hip harness and brought it down two-handed on the chest's lid. He bashed it again and again, until the lid bent out at the corners, enough for him to slip his fingers between. He ripped it off without even straining.

"All for you, my lady." He presented the mangled trunk for inspection with an overdramatic flourish.

It was filled with papers and coins. Quistis dug through the contents, her sprite hovering near her.

"No names, but there are orders here. And dates. This one either was literate or held on to someone else's accounts. We're taking this with us back to the Fortress."

Finally, something to brighten up the trip. Maybe—

"Quistis! Barlo! Come help."

The call had come from the side tunnel. Both Storm Guards rushed over. Quistis slipped through the hole while Barlo stopped to smash open an entryway more appropriate for his size.

Vial, wearing his full armor, had been propped against a wall, panting and bleeding. His helmet was off, and he was deathly pale. His armor looked to be the only thing still keeping him in one piece.

Rumi leaned against the wall as well, chest heaving with the effort of having carried him. Her short white hair was damp with sweat. It must've been a real effort, seeing how Vial outweighed her thrice over.

Quistis went to work. "What happened?" she asked, hands busy inspecting the wounded soldier.

Barlo trotted over and took up position as a guard, mace in hand, facing the opposite end of the tunnel.

"It's bad down there, Captain Quistis," Rumi said. "Throne, it smells worse down there than here."

"Report."

After downing a healing potion and receiving magical mending, Vial could stand, albeit dizzily. For the moment, at least, he was out of immediate harm's way. Quistis mixed him a tonic from the flasks in her satchel.

"There's nothing sane down there. I can tell you that much," the white-haired scout explained. Then she leaned forward, hands on her knees, and dry heaved. "We barely made it out. I think it used to be a sanctum, but it's dying out. We need to call in a Vitalis to take charge of it. It's full of chimeras, and they're all crazed."

"Are you hurt?" Quistis noted her state.

"No. Just bloody tired, Captain. Vial's bloody heavy to carry."

"What kind of chimeras are we talking?" Quistis knew the creature by theory, but she also knew that a Vitalis could breed any kind of these monstrosities.

"Human, for the most part. I think this is where the missing people ended up. We didn't get far, though." Her breathing steadied, and she pulled herself up. She ran a nervous hand through her hair. "It's huge, Captain. Whoever it belonged to has been active for a long time here. There are a lot of bodies down there."

"Thanks, Cap. And I owe you one, Rumi," Vial said before he drank the concoction Quistis had offered him. Color returned to his cheeks and a shine to his eyes.

"Don't mention it. Don't need it again, please," Rumi replied with a shaky grin.

"How in the bloody throne did ye get taken down, lad?" Barlo asked over his shoulder, grinning. "I saw ye fight daemons. These can't be worse."

"You fight them," Vial grumbled. "If you cut a daemon's head off, it bloody dies. These things keep coming. Had to hack them to bits and even then they still kept trying to bite my ankles off. My sword broke, and we got swarmed."

"You can stand down, Barlo," Rumi said. "There's an elevating platform. We got it moving and we came back up on it. I didn't hear it go back down." She sighed and turned to Quistis. "We need to go back. I caught a whiff of something down there, but I can't be sure without going in deeper. It could be a big problem on our hands."

If Rumi said it was important, then Quistis needed no other explanation. They had learned all they would in that stinking place. The only way to go, it seemed, was down.

"Barlo, hand Vial your spare sword. We're going back."

The vanadal drew his broad-bladed curved weapon and handed it over without a word. Vial needed a two-handed grip for the weight. He tested the edge with a gloved finger and whistled.

"It's tight down there, Barlo. You won't have room to swing that mace."

Barlo raised his chin, the vanadal version of a grin. "I'll manage."

Nonetheless, he uncrossed his lower arms and rested hands on the pommels of his daggers.

"I'll take point. Make sure ye don't give the captain more work, eh?"

Rumi kicked him in the back of the knee and scowled up at him. He only chuckled, unperturbed.

"Just jostling ye, speck. Don't take jesting so hard."

Quistis stepped between the two warriors and pressed her hands to their chests.

"*I require a Blessing of Cassandra*," she chanted in prayer to the Goddess. Her palms flared up with blue lights and left behind an imprint of her fingers on their armor.

"Are you fit to fight, Vial?" she asked as she rotated some of her flasks inside the pouch at her hip.

"Fit and eager to get payback, Cap," Vial confirmed. He had his helmet back on. Deep gashes scored the metal, which told Quistis all she needed to know of the creatures waiting.

"Whistle when you need barriers," she barked. "Rumi, you're the eyes on the back of my head. We do everything smart and neat." The entire unit confirmed.

The platform descended with a sound of grinding metal gears and stone scraping on stone.

"No element of surprise. Whatever's there will know we're coming down," Quistis said as she paced the rim of the platform, keeping a mental check of the depth. The sanctum had been dug deep under the mountain, deep enough that no Egia could ever sense it from the surface. Only blind bad luck could otherwise bring anyone close to it.

Smart. Terrifying, but smart.

"What exactly is this place?" Vial asked. "Never seen anything like it before."

"Vitalis sanctum," Rumi replied from beside Barlo's tall form. She was producing knives from somewhere and fastening them around her belt, within easy reach.

"I got the name. But what is it?"

Quistis answered ahead of Rumi, drawing on memories from her earlier days of training, "Place of power. Channelers sometimes build these as fortresses where they can work unimpeded. Vitalis ones aren't even the weirdest of the lot."

"Throne eternal." Vial whistled. "I'd rather I went back to the daemons at the Twins."

"Wait till ye see a Crepuscular's sanctum." Barlo chuckled. "First one'll strip sleep from ye fer a whole season. If yer lucky."

The air stank at the bottom of the shaft. Its humid, cadaverous stench clung to them as they walked out into the waiting dark.

Seething, writhing masses and lumps of fleshy protuberances covered the tunnel walls. They were everywhere, from floor to ceiling, and moved and extended feelers towards them as they passed by. Their steps squelched, the morass floor sucking them down, trying to climb up their legs.

The smell grew worse as they followed the tunnel. Small eyeball-like lamps on the walls gave off a twitching, blinking white light that followed their progress. Quistis brought her sprite close as one tendril grew teeth and snapped after it. Human faces sometimes formed out of the walls, moving soundless lips at them, gaping mouths that turned inside out when looked upon.

Barlo spat. "It reeks of fear," he grumbled as he stomped on an eyeball growing on a flesh stalk.

Sounds exuded from the walls in a continuous echo of almost-human sighs, whispers in unknown tongues, groans, and humming. The cacophony only got louder as the passage widened into a circular chamber that split apart in various directions. Eye lamps blinked, and the light of the room focused on the group as they entered. There was a momentary pause in the noise, but it resumed as if it had deemed them of no importance.

"Place looks very alive to me, Rumi," Quistis said. Her sprite moved in circles around them to show the flesh of the walls writhing and squirming.

"It's dead. It just hasn't finished dying yet."

Putrefied corpses littered the room. One burst with a wheeze of escaping gas. Whatever it had been was impossible to determine.

Barlo grumbled and hefted his mace.

"Yer a strong lad, Vial, but this ain't yer work," he said as he turned in place to take in the devastation. The piles of rotting corpses rose as tall as he was in places.

"Nah. My pile's over there." He showed some fresh bodies cooling among the rest.

"Ye, feared as much. Captain, yer thoughts?"

The room whimpered as the sprite got closer to the walls. Craters in the flesh growth showed signs of battle. Fire had been applied with crushing fury.

"Big fight went on in here," Quistis said, stating the absolute obvious. Her lunch wanted to come up for a look around.

A wailing creature ripped itself out of a wall and charged at them. Barlo reacted before anyone else, stepping in its path and bringing down the mace, pulping it on the spot.

"See, Vial? If it's mulch, it stops moving."

More howls followed as the tunnels spat out more creatures. Walking rotting corpses rushed them on decomposing limbs, waving weapons of splintered, sharpened bone.

The vanadal warrior whistled as he drew his daggers.

Quistis erected barriers on their flanks, enforced them, and made a bottleneck that led into the two warriors up front. Rumi pressed her back to hers just as Barlo waded into the throng.

He swung his weapon in a wide arc, mowing down anything that got within reach. They fell to him in numbers. Vial guarded his back, his borrowed sword cleaving clean through anything that got close enough.

Quistis's barriers cracked under the pressure of bodies. Barlo whistled again, and she added more invisible walls to his flank.

"Push," he calmly called over his shoulder.

Vial obeyed and moved out of his shadow of slaughter. They advanced, keeping a weapon's length gap between them, and broke the assault.

Quistis studied one creature mindlessly throwing itself at her barrier.

It was impossible to determine what its base species could have been. Someone had grafted parts where they didn't belong, had amputated limbs and reduced them to spears of bone. The head . . . she couldn't look at the head. Its eyes were lidless, terrified, still very much alive. Some intelligence still shone there, but it had clearly been driven into insanity by whatever had been done to the poor thing.

Its suffering ceased when Barlo's mace crushed it down into a pile of mashed organs and bone fragments. He dragged another of the chimeras off his back and slammed it into the barrier by a foot. The leg broke off at the knee, and he beat the wailing creature to death with the stump.

The assault ebbed, the creatures running cowed into the safety of whatever nest had spawned them. The warriors let them run. In due time, they would purge the sanctum clean of all atrocities.

Chimeras, along with grave horrors, skirted the edge of necromancy. Empress Catharina had passed an edict two centuries back, calling for their destruction. Any Vitalis mage found to be making such creatures was to be executed on the spot. By the state of the place, Quistis imagined someone had already enacted justice.

"Got a nasty bite here," Barlo called out and showed one of his naked lower arms.

Quistis rushed to his side and inspected the wound. The creature had bitten straight down to the bone. Some of its teeth were still lodged in the muscles, along with an entire jaw that kept gnawing on the arm. Barlo pulled it off and crushed it in his large hand.

She opened a flask and washed the wound, picking out teeth fashioned like fish hooks from torn muscles. Blood flowed purple for a moment, then lightened in color to the soft pink of the vanadal constitution.

Quistis pressed her hand to the clean wound.

"*I require this one to be mended,*" she chanted. When she took her hand away, only soft scar tissue remained.

"I don't think we're done with our hosts," she said as she replaced the flask in her bag.

"Nah, but we smote fear in them. Vial, ye still in one piece?"

"Safe and hale, brother. I need to get me one of these when we get back," the other warrior said as he shook gore off his borrowed blade. There was a ring of ruined corpses around him, parts of them trying to crawl away. He slammed his armored foot down on some.

Quistis urged them forward into one of the open tunnel mouths. Rumi was quiet at her back.

"Seeing anything?"

"Shattered bits of weave," the Egia replied. "There is that pattern I saw all the way up top and in the tunnel, but it's faint now."

"Keep at it. At least this answers some questions for us. Something like this doesn't just grow overnight."

Oh Goddess . . .

A nightmare room welcomed them. Quistis knew it for what it was the moment she stepped inside, and her stomach lurched into her throat at the very notion of its existence.

A single orb, somewhere high above, still twitched and lit up the ruins. Bodies were embedded in the wall, all of them charred black.

Barlo got closer to one and grunted in disgust.

"Used to be female, if I'm any judge," he said, voice low. He swung his torch around. "All of them. No limbs. Held in cradles. There are tubes going inside the corpses." He spat.

"I can't count them all," Vial added as he moved around with Quistis's sprite. "There's so many." He stopped by one body. Its abdomen was distended and had burst. A mound of flesh had leaked out and putrefied on the floor. All unfortunates in there had been cooked alive.

"This used to be a breeding room," Quistis said, just so the words would be out of her. "Chimera stocks were being bred here. Just buying warm bodies wasn't enough."

The Academy and the empress had stamped out the more abject Vitalis practitioners. She had read of the purge years back. It seemed they had missed one.

"Someone used a devourer in here," Rumi said. "Its weave lingers."

"Can you say which one?"

"I think this was Titan's Punishment," she said quietly. "Yes, that's the one. Not a pattern I recognize on the weave."

"So there was a powerful Metal Mind down here, picking a fight with whichever Vitalis nursed this atrocity. We should thank them if we find them."

Quistis fought back a shiver of revulsion as her sprite went up, showing row upon row of burnt cadavers. The cavern had been packed tight, every nook occupied by at least one cradle. There were easily a couple hundred.

"Or have them executed for murder."

"Mercy killing," Barlo corrected. "The Punishment woulda killed them all in a blink. Good control too. Didn't punch off the mountain's top."

Quistis wanted to argue for the sake of her sanity but decided against it. Would they have done differently? Probably not. Only so much could be done for victims of a Vitalis, and death was kinder than survival.

Some of the other rooms showed similar devastation.

There was a destroyed laboratory, equipment reduced to melted lumps of glass.

Holding cages had been opened up, their contents splattered into gore.

An operation room, with bone tables and instruments, lay intact, gruesome work rotted through, unrecognizable.

They lost count of the corpses they found. The sanctum had thrown a wall of claws and teeth at its invaders and had been beaten back. The creatures that assaulted Vial and Rumi were nothing more than the surviving dregs, doomed to slow decay.

Then they found the stairs. A perfectly even set ran down into a deeper, blacker darkness.

"There," Rumi said. "It all leads down there."

"Can't be worse than the rest," Barlo grumbled as he went down into the inky dark. He barely fit through the narrow tunnel, his head scraping the ceiling.

The stairs led deeper under the mountain. Air, thick with the stench of putrefaction, seemed to congeal around them, as dead as anything else in there. For the first time in hours, Quistis was happy to have the mask on, both for the protection it offered and for hiding her face. Blood ran down her chin from where she had bitten through her lip.

Decades of horror within a stone's throw of Valen. What are we even doing if we've allowed this to happen at all?

She ran into Vial's back as the stairs ended and they emerged into a cavernous room.

A throne of bones and viscera dominated its center—or had at some point. Now it lay toppled over and half-burned.

"They fought in here," Rumi said, looking slightly sick. "There were two of them. They were spectacularly powerful. Someone of Adjunct Leea's caliber, I would say."

She walked around, eyes unfocused as she read only what only she could see in the pitch. Her steel-toed boots clanked on solid stone.

"Another devourer was used. Here." She tapped the naked stone with a heel.

Quistis's sprite showed a triangular patch of floor with no growth on it, clean and smooth.

"Titan's Punishment again?"

Rumi shook her head.

"No, this was a different one. Much more vile." She concentrated for a moment and closed her eyes. "Life eater. Wild." Her brow furrowed, and she looked pained in the light. "Poisonous. No!" Her eyes snapped open, and she reeled back.

Barlo was at her side in a moment, mace hefted, looking for whatever had frightened her. Vial grabbed her shoulder to steady her.

"Captain, this is bad," Rumi said, shaking with every word. She shook her hands as if to get filth off them. "We need to go back to Valen and get the commander. We're in trouble."

"Talk to me first, Rumi," Quistis said as she headed to her side. "What do you see?"

"This was Disintegration." She pointed at the bare rock. "And the rest was fire. There's only one channeler who could have wielded that monstrosity. And she's dead."

Oh no.

"And does this channeler that makes ye piss yer pants have a name?" Barlo grumbled.

Rumi scowled up at him.

"It's Cinder, you blockhead." She spat out the name. "Bloody thrice-damned Cinder was in here, where you stand right now." Shaking off Vial, she moved some steps forward. "A portal was used right here, and someone walked through. If so, Cinder could be in Valen right now, right under our noses."

Barlo's free hands balled into fists and his jaw tightened, all levity gone. "Are ye sure? An awful lot of assumption on that," he said, voice like rumbling thunder.

"It doesn't matter if she's sure," Quistis replied. "If there are two channelers that we don't have tabs on, who can use devourers of that magnitude, then we need to consider a worst-case scenario." She had already opened a portal straight to Valen's illum hearth. This needed acting upon.

"There's a corpse here," Vial called from the opposite end of the room, where the cone of devastation hit the wall.

"There are corpses everywhere," Barlo shot back.

"Aye, but this one moves."

Quistis cursed and headed over. The day held only surprises, and none of them had been pleasant so far.

A woman was entombed in the wall, a complicated lattice of tubes pocketing her flesh and holding her upright. The spell hadn't hit her fully, but it had been enough to char half of her. The other half had bloated with death. But Vial held at sword point something different.

On the floor, cowering before the corpse, was a figure. It approximated a woman. She was skeletal thin, wilted and disheveled. Thin wisps of white hair clung to her scalp, and bones poked out against her skin. She hid her face and tried to shy away from the light, hissing when Vial took a step closer. His sword's killing point was aimed straight at the thing's throat.

"Don't touch that," Rumi called from behind. "That's a flesh doll. Survived her maker and is now dying along with the sanctum. She's bleeding illum."

Quistis looked at the creature and then at the corpse. "I guess this was our Vitalis." She put a hand on the remains, to the flesh doll's hissed horror. The skin was cold and wax soft, yielding to her touch. They wouldn't get anything from that.

But the doll . . .

"Vial, be ready to take that with us."

It growled at her, showing rotted needlelike teeth. It was too weakened to do much more than growl and shrink back against the wall at the feet of its maker.

"*I require this to be preserved,*" Quistis chanted. A shimmering translucent barrier encased the flesh doll and held it in place. Even so wasted, it struggled against the bond, enough that it proved troublesome.

"I can hold it long enough to get to Valen. Pick it up and be ready to move," she ordered. "Barlo, can you make your way back up to the cave on your own?"

"Give me two of yer drafts and I'll be fine," he replied. He looked like he would enjoy cracking some more chimera skulls.

She threw him the flasks.

"Get up there and get that chest of papers. You can handle yourself out of the tunnels after that. Drop it off at Lucian's. Tell him that if I don't see sorties go up for a thousand griffons each, hunting any leads on whoever the rats dealt with, I will have him flogged and salted."

"Aye, ma'am."

"Rumi, you head straight for the gate. I'm giving you special permission for its use. Go to Aztroa Magnor and find Falor. He's visiting the empress. Find him and tell him Tallah Amni is active again, and likely in Valen. Do not let anyone belay you."

Rumi saluted with her right fist to her left shoulder. "Yes, ma'am."

She rushed through the portal without waiting for further instructions.

Quistis waited until Vial had the struggling creature on his shoulder and had passed through the portal. She took another look around the room, raised her mask to spit blood and bile on the memory of that sanctum of horrors, and went through.

CHAPTER FIVE

Vergil Vansce

In the sublevels of the hospital, far beneath the day-to-day bustle, Vergil believed he was dreaming. He lay on a rough bed of interwoven white roots with their thin, hooked thorns digging uncomfortably into his skin. He was dimly aware of a transfusion hooked into his arms, and of some exchange between him and the ancient tree but could make no sense of it. Something inside him was blooming, ripening, changing, though he couldn't think straight enough to understand what. He flickered around the edges of consciousness, a corpse that hadn't been allowed to fade away and rest.

Who were the two women he'd seen by firelight?

Where was he?

Why didn't it all hurt? It had hurt for so long, so deeply, that he felt the absence of pain like an absence of himself.

Women in green bustled about him. He didn't know any of their faces. They came and went like visions of a world he wasn't sure was real.

Pain, his beloved pain, had become a memory of a dream, fading just like him in the sterile white light of the leaves. Whatever his headware had to say had become just a tangle of absurd strings of characters. He couldn't keep up with the constant red-flagged alerts.

Vergil Vansce fell headfirst into a long dream of a time before . . .

"Damn, my shift starts in fifteen minutes. I'm going to park my character here and finish up the mission when I get back."

"What's your assignment today, Vansce?"

There were three men around the campfire, all three wearing mismatching sets of armor pieces from a dozen time periods. The dead littered the ground around them in a grim display of bloodshed.

"Carbon dioxide scrubbers, S14. Routine check."

One of the knights shook his head, making a sound of disgust. His armor rattled dully.

"I don't envy your schedule, man. It stinks down there."

"Don't I know it. Anyway, I'll come back online after. Don't kill the boss without me. I need the levels. I don't want to wait another six days for it to respawn."

The knight nearest the fire waved a salute to the others and then reached over his head. The neural connector disengaged with a barely audible click, and the gray reality of his small cabin reasserted itself.

"Vergil Vansce, please report for duty at: Carbon Dioxide Scrubber, Section 14. Details have been uploaded to your heads-up display. Ten minutes to start of work shift."

Argia's slightly metal-tinged voice echoed from a speaker in the wall as if on cue. Vergil sighed as he dressed in his work overalls, banging his shoulders and elbows as he struggled in the cramped space. The trick was to fold himself instead of the clothes and do up the zip only after walking out.

"Natural born, how lucky I am," he griped for maybe the millionth time as he tried to stretch without banging his head on the low ceiling. A family line that had no truck with genetic tampering had produced him much too tall for the *Gloria Nostra* and then discarded him as soon as he could be put to work. How lucky indeed.

A natural-born male was worth exactly as much as his excrement to the gynocracy that led the *Gloria*.

His cranial implant already fed him the day's assignment as well as directions towards his planned work location. He didn't need any directions, especially as the route Argia suggested was always longer than it needed to be. She said it was safer, as if there was anything to be safe from.

His cabin door slid open with a slight electric whine, and the light inside went off. In a few minutes, the inside would be sweltering hot as all power was cut from it for the duration of the workday. How lucky he was to be of use at such a tender age.

Vergil knew by heart the maze of ducts, walkways, and corridors that made up the lower levels of the *Gloria*. Most of the ship's operation was automated and barely ever required human supervision, so he would very likely be alone for the entire day. Again. The quiet thrum of machinery working as intended accompanied him as he made his way towards the outer ring to the literal belly of the ship.

He paused by one of the rare observation ports, a window in the side of the ship no larger than his head.

Bright blue stretched away from him, the curve of the planet below just barely visible on the edge of the port. His HUD attached a pointer to it. It was designated as Athos III and had been there his entire life. He tried to crane his neck and catch a glimpse of the other two SPRAWL ships that he knew were also in orbit, but they were out of position at that hour. Nonetheless, the sight of the planet improved his disposition. It often did. A storm brewed above the planetary ocean, and the angry swirl of clouds drew his attention for a few moments before an angry red text popped up in his display to hurry him along.

Some of the guys from his alternative-reality experiences had said the *Gloria* would be breaking orbit before the year's end. The terraforming of Athos III had been completed, ahead of its century-long schedule, so all three SPRAWLs were preparing to head back out into deep space once the space port for their youngest sister was completed. He could see the shape of that floating on a lower orbit, ships moving in a slow dance around its massive hulk.

"Not long now," he mused.

The idea of that single observation port filling with blackness made an ugly lump in his throat.

"Argia, would it be possible for me to transfer to a surface colony?" he asked the open air, savoring the sight for a minute more.

No, came the reply as a text in his vision. *All five colonies on Athos III have reached stable population thresholds. No new personnel will be allotted for planetary settlement.*

Pity. Not that he would have ever qualified for settlement duty as a male with no higher qualifications, but it was worth asking.

Despite Argia's laid-out route, he opened an access hatch close by and took the ladder down. It would bypass several levels. Engineers never bothered to lock the hatches properly, not down there, and Argia's complaints could be ignored while he was out of her many-eyed sight.

Very few other workers ever had cause to venture so low, and the state of the shaft showed their neglect. Loose panels on the walls, exposed wiring, air vents that wheezed with accumulated filth. Even the ladder was barely fastened to the wall. Its rattles echoed as he descended.

When he was just a few yards off the lowest deck, the ladder shook. He clung tighter to the metal rungs and produced his flashlight. Something scrambled into a vent when he tried to shine a light on it.

"What was that? Argia, is there someone else on the level with me?"

Negative, came the text reply. *See secondary assignment for the day: Find missing specimen / burn possible nest. Please use approved route.*

"What missing specimen?"

Details available in work file.

With the ladder stable and nothing moving down towards him, he finished his descent.

If that wasn't just fantastic! How lucky he was. The scrubbers were some of his favorite places on the ship precisely because they were quiet, deserted, and generally did not give him any work to do. There was nothing in the air scrubbers for pests to feed on.

Secondary assignment: Specimen retrieval / removal. Specimen appears to be aggressive. Caution is advised.

Vergil reviewed the files uploaded to his headware. Normally he wouldn't have bothered, but normally his ladder wouldn't shake in the dark. Some pictures of the creature were also available. It had broken out of a containment tank in one of the ship's bays and bolted for the air ducts. Covered in carapace, four-legged, about a yard long, and with a wicked-looking tail, it looked like something Vergil would not enjoy finding.

"What a wonderful life I live," he mumbled as he walked the narrow passageways, his motion detector in hand. Lights flickered to life and died away as he made his way deeper into the ship, motion sensors his only company for a long time.

He had to stop at one point when he ran into a group of five women. Three wore the gray uniform of engineers, and the other two were in full-body armor and armed with some nasty-looking rifles. He turned towards a wall, lowered his head, and they passed him by without harassment. By their conversation, they were also looking for the missing specimen.

Seeing the security detail escorting the engineers brought the unfamiliar and uncomfortable feeling of danger. Hairs on the back of his neck rose as he unholstered his own special-issued plasma pistol. It was considered non-lethal for humans but powerful enough for most critters that would infest the ducts. Vergil, as a pest control technician, had only fired it half a dozen times in the three years since he had been assigned to the job, and intensely regretted his lack of practice.

With the motion detector in one hand and the pistol in the other, he walked slowly among the tall machines that produced the very air the whole ship breathed. Most of them were hidden behind thick protective casings that only the maintenance crew could access, so that only left the corridors and general access hatches to check.

Lights failed to turn on down one of the corridors.

"Argia, I am at corridor number seventeen, sub-level three. There's no light," he informed the machine spirit of the *Gloria.*

Motions sensors do not register movement at hatch seventeen, sub-level three, came the instant reply.

Vergil waved his pistol towards the usual placement of the motion sensors. "I'm here and moving around."

Maintenance ticket has been created. A maintenance crew will be there shortly to investigate malfunction.

The motion detector in his hand came alive with a beep.

"Of course there's something right in there." Vergil sighed and clasped the detector to his waist to free a hand for his flashlight. It could be the missing specimen, but it could also be any other pest chewing through the cables. He had given up trying to count the number of times that had happened with critters brought up from the planet. Too many of them had a taste for copper and silver, sometimes even for electricity. If he left it for the maintenance crew, he'd get scolded and punished again.

The motion detector beeped as he walked into the dark corridor, his shadow long ahead of him. There was no sound aside from the constant echoing beeps in the narrow space. He stopped. The beeping stopped. When he moved, it started again. The light from the main scrubber deck turned off after some time, and he was left only with the narrow cone of the flashlight and the sickly green glow of the motion detector.

He spun in place, a creeping fear mounting on the nape of his neck.

Nothing behind him. Nothing to the sides.

Whatever it was, it moved quietly through the wall.

All in all, a good sign. If it was that quiet, doing that much moving around, then it couldn't be the missing specimen. A thing that size would register somehow.

He looked for and found a wall access panel. With a set of screwdrivers, he pried it loose and stuck his head in the crawlspace. Sure enough, the smell of burnt electronics hit him instantly. Somewhere to the side something threw up sparks, and he could hear the whine of a damaged electronic component.

"Argia, I found the damaged area," he said when coming out. "There's a strong smell coming out of wall panel D, in—"

Pain flared under his chin. Something sharp stabbed up through the soft tissue there, went up through the roof of his mouth and punched out through the center of his face. He choked on blood and spasmed in shock. Like a fish on a hook, flailing his arms and kicking his feet, he was lifted into the air.

In his final terrified moments of consciousness, Vergil saw the creature slithering out from among the mess of cables crisscrossing the ceiling.

The specimen had grown. Its long, serrated tail effortlessly brought Vergil level with its head. He gurgled thick, hot blood. The creature's black lower jaw opened up into two pieces, fangs as long as his fingers shimmering in the dark.

Angry red messages crowded for attention in Vergil's dimming field of view. The shine on the silver fangs was infinitely more fascinating and urgent.

The pain lasted for much more than a moment.

The noise made him stir.

Something was wrong with the noise.

He stirred in his sleep and turned over, but that felt wrong too. His cot was too hard and rough, the shape of it unfamiliar somehow.

He mulled it over in the half-awake state he enjoyed just moments before the ship's intercom came alive and Argia woke him.

The ship? Something was wrong about the ship. His eyes opened sharply and then closed instantly, obscenely bright light blinding him. He couldn't hear the ship, the background noise of his life so far. Everything was gone, from the quiet thrum and vibrations of the engines to the air cycling through his cabin and the soft buzz of the lights when they turned on automatically.

It was all gone.

The noise replacing it resolved into a cacophony of voices talking over one another, yelling, and even laughing. He had never heard so many voices all at once, all vying to be heard above the din.

Slowly, carefully, he opened his eyes again. The world around him was tilted at a strange angle. No, no, *he* was at a wrong angle. He was lying in a cobbled alley, on his side. It took him a moment to process the strangeness of that.

There was stone beneath him. It felt real.

He had never seen stone before, not actual stone. His reality had always been metal and plastic imitations. Stone was not as interesting as he had always imagined it to be. It smelled strange as well, but it was the air around that was foul. He pushed himself up and heard clanging. His clothes clanged and were heavier than expected. He almost fell back on his face.

He looked up and squinted against a bright blue sky, dotted here and there with soft white shapes of clouds. For long moments, he couldn't tear his eyes away, caught between fascination and absolute terror of being sucked up into that infinite azure.

Whatever alternative-reality experience this one was, it was genuinely immersive. He couldn't remember another one quite so vivid. It almost seemed real.

It felt real. He couldn't remember logging into it, nor falling asleep.

Weirdest dream . . . I must've been dead tired to drop while playing.

With some uncertainty, he moved his hand to the back of his neck, folding his fist over empty air. Normally that would have disconnected him from his entertainment system. There was nothing to grip.

Pain. He remembered, too clearly, the pain of something biting into him. He put a hand to his face and searched for the wound he knew was supposed to be there.

No scar. No wound. No connection port on the back of his head. There weren't even signs that he had ever had connection ports.

"Argia?" he called out. Even his voice was different.

He waited for a second, and then some more. Argia normally replied instantly to anyone on the *Gloria*. It monitored everything, including the experiences.

"Argia?" he called out again. It unnerved him to not have the machine spirit reply.

Connection unavailable. Please consult Maintenance at the earliest convenience.
The text scrolled on top of his vision.

Switching to Independent Mode. Some functionality may not be available.

Argia and Athos III had been the two real constants of his life. Both . . . gone? That sank in his stomach with the weight of a black hole that threatened to turn him inside out.

He waved his hand, gesturing like in the virtual experiences, to see his menu and character. Nothing happened.

With a different gesture of his hand, he tried again, repeating for every experience he had ever played. Nothing happened.

Even as he tried to not rush over the precipice of panic, Vergil found himself smiling.

He had seen this before, somewhere in some experience once. Hero died and was taken to a strange world where his true destiny was revealed. All rather trite, but . . .

Could he have died? Was he living out some absurd fantasy in the final spasms of his life?

Could it be real?

He would have laughed if not for the people peering at him through the mouth of the alley. A madman gesturing at the air and having a quiet moment of panic in the crook of a dead end?

If he was dreaming, he might as well get the most out of it. If not, well, it was still a step up from being a male on the *Gloria Nostra*. Wondering too much on the whys and hows wasn't going to get him answers.

Okay, let's think for a moment. First things first.

He looked down at himself and his clothes. The clanging he heard was a chain mail vest he wore underneath a green tunic. Lower, he saw that he also wore metal shin and thigh guards clasped over tanned leather trousers. They felt uncomfortable, a size too large maybe, and cumbersome.

Resting against one of the walls were a bright yellow kite shield and a short gladius sword. He recognized the combination as starter equipment befitting paladin inductees from some of the experiences he'd spent his free time on. This looked, down to the pattern on the shield, like something out of *Crusade of the Innocent.* He'd been playing just that morning.

I'm a paladin.

Was he?

The prospect of serving as a warrior of faith destined to protect the weak and vanquish evil made him giggle. He knew that was the motto of the Paladin Corps but had no idea where he'd learned that or what the Paladin Corps even was. Maybe this was an experience after all, and it functioned on the same principles as the others.

"Argia, have I had any data packets downloaded without my consent?"

No reply came. Not even a text.

Could it be real after all?

He grabbed the gear and walked out into the sunlit plaza beyond the mouth of the alley.

And immediately turned on his heels and retreated right back.

A riot of colors assaulted him with dizzying patterns and motions, along with a buzz of activity he could never have imagined in his wildest waking dreams.

Men were everywhere, walking, talking, discussing with other men. And with women! Those gave him a moment of pause, and he instinctively drew back from the sight, dread drenching him in cold sweat. Sixteen standard years of conditioning told him to turn around, face the wall, lower his head, and wait until the women had gone on their way.

But they weren't the imposing, frightening figures from the *Gloria Nostra,* just other people. They didn't look down on the other men on the street but were talking and laughing and interacting with them, as equals. It looked that way, at least.

Vergil kept telling himself that as he plucked the courage to go out through the crowd.

He walked out into an open-air marketplace. Stalls of produce and meats and condiments lined the narrow, cobbled streets. The colors dizzied him.

Aromas of rich condiments coated the air. Fresh and seared meat followed, fish on ice, perfumes, and herbs. He couldn't begin to identify most of them, but they made his head spin with the vast newness of it all.

His stomach growled. A quick check of his pockets revealed that he was penniless.

Price of a loaf of bread: 12 Valen eagles.
The Valen eagle is a subdivision of the Valen griffon.
Exchange rate: 1 griffon = 10 lions = 50 eagles.
Source: Unknown.

Part of him wondered if his headware was making things up. The rest was too fascinated by the sights, sounds, and smells to care.

There needs to be some sort of Guild that employs new arrivals. There's always a Guild in the experiences. He clung to the idea and made a goal out of it.

He stopped a passing man to ask for directions. Except that it wasn't a man, not a human one, at least. The stranger was even taller than he was and had the most strikingly beautiful features Vergil had ever seen. He had a hawkish face with large amber eyes and high cheekbones. His frame was lank and supple, and he moved with such grace that Vergil became conscious of his own stooping gait.

The man smiled encouragingly as Vergil stepped in his path and opened his mouth . . . and immediately forgot everything he wanted to say.

"May I help you, young human?" Even his voice was wonderful, like cool water running over white marble.

In that moment, Vergil panicked. He hadn't considered if his character spoke the local language or if he would just sound like an imbecile. He understood the man, so he tried answering.

"Uh . . . yes, please. I'm sorry for bothering you." The words rolled off his tongue, alien sounding, yet as familiar to him as the back of his hands. Strangely enough, he spoke as if he'd always spoken that strange flowing language. An itch pestered him somewhere in center of his skull but was easy enough to ignore.

"I'm new here and . . . it's overwhelming." He hadn't meant to be so honest, but his fascination for the strange man overrode anything else.

"Ah," his interlocutor said, and then smiled the most dazzling smile Vergil had ever witnessed. It couldn't be real. "Well, I'm an aelir. I imagine my kind are not very common where you come from. Don't worry, I get this kind of reaction quite often when I visit here."

"Where are you from?" Vergil was certain he wanted to ask something else, but he couldn't rightly remember what it was.

"From Nen, across the Divide."

It took a couple more vapid questions to the aelir before he remembered what information he needed.

The Guild Halls were in the Inner Plaza, just opposite the Paladin Corps recruitment office. Vergil couldn't miss it if he kept walking towards the Upper City in the distance.

What Vergil didn't have was money, and credentials from an established workshop or a military branch. He needed money to pay for admission into the Guild, and he needed to be part of an established trade before he would be licensed as an adventurer for hire.

Finding all that out had cost him an entire day of aimless wandering and short panic attacks whenever he had to interact with a female representative. They weren't so bad. He couldn't meet any of their gazes, but they weren't being actively unpleasant to him.

That first night, he slept huddled in the same alley he had woken up in. For the first time in his life, he fell asleep on an empty, grumbling stomach. The more the feeling sank in that this might be reality, the more he avoided looking up at the sky. Even glancing at the star-speckled expanse made him sweat and shiver as if there was a gaping maw up there that waited to swallow him whole.

On the second day, he manufactured a story about coming from a small village somewhere in the middle of nowhere, his dream of being a great protector of the people, his inherited weapon and shield and so on. The Paladin Corps recruiter, a bored man named Louis, didn't believe him much, but a new member from out in the sticks, with his own gear, was a member he didn't need to spend time and money equipping. He said as much.

Vergil received basic training, his induction into the local paladin order, and some basic skills with the sword and shield. To call him an amateur was a kindness. At the end of three weeks of training, he was given the choice between enrolling as a soldier bound for Aztroa Magnor or being licensed for adventuring sorties.

Adventuring seemed like the less-dangerous path, so he decided on that. Maybe it should have rung a warning that, out of all fresh recruits, he'd been the only one to refuse recruitment into the ranks of the empire.

The Corps was kind enough to offer him Anatol's Blessing as a parting gift, a sort of tattoo that was infused with words of power from the god Anatol himself. It promised to heal most scrapes and minor wounds, just what a rookie needed. Just his luck.

Argia was still in his head as a heads-up display, but her functionality was almost nil. Without the *Gloria* and the machine spirit, all that this hobbled version could do was translate text and run some self-diagnostics on his state of being. Her text updates mostly consisted of failed connection errors or random facts about the city. Most of them seemed like fabrications.

Why he even still had it was a mystery that he decided wasn't worth thinking on.

Once he had his induction, the Guild posed very little challenge. They didn't care where he had come from or where he wanted to go as long as he got them results and he could be held accountable for his misdeeds. All adventurers were the same in the eyes of the recruiters and were treated the same up until results came in. The Guild cared and paid only for results. He got his adventurer license with half a day of questions and form filling and was then shown to the rookie-aimed billboards bursting with sortie offers from various merchants, farmers, or other folk of Valen that needed cheap work done quick.

He could scarcely believe it was as easy as that.

Vergil Vansce was officially a rookie paladin adventurer looking for a group to take on his first missions on the path to fame, glory, and wealth. That was what the Guild promotional banners promised.

Why is everything moving so fast? Vergil thought as he stood outside the Guild Halls, staring at the scroll and token that acknowledged his status. *This can't be right. I just got here.* The thought struck him as odd. He had been in Valen for weeks already. He even knew the city somewhat.

He had worked some days as a menial for one of the many construction sites rebuilding what looked like the ruins left by a great fire. He was given bread and wine by the workers and made small talk, got to know some of the markets, and even had the temerity of exploring more of the Lower City and its twisting, winding, narrow streets.

Weeks had passed . . .

Why would he think otherwise?

What's going on?

Vergil stepped outside himself for a moment like a passenger leaning out of his own head. Life rushed around him, forward, sideways, sometimes backward, sometimes skipping between moments. It felt like someone searching for one frame in a video file, and it wasn't him doing it.

What's happening? I . . .

'You're too perceptive for your own good, lad,' a woman's voice answered with impatience. 'Put him back and take it easier, girls. Let's not have echoes, or we'll never be done with him.'

And back he went into this new, wonderful life. The future had looked so bright in those first days, and he was excited for the first time ever to live it.

CHAPTER SIX

Breaking Open

Tallah watched the blizzard with a mug of tea held in her hands. Winter had followed them down from the mountains with dogged determination and had now stationed itself outside her window. Snow built up outside as if determined to swallow the city whole.

Her head was filled with strange images of sail ships floating through emptiness, carrying people to unknown worlds on invisible tides.

There were unknown worlds out there. There were unknown people.

The possibilities. She couldn't keep her thoughts away from the amazing things Sil had gotten from the boy's head.

A chance meeting in a cave, a hostage of ratmen saved to be eaten later like some cheap cut of smoked meat. She'd shown a moment of mercy in the slaughter, stayed her hand for a brief instant, and had been rewarded with finding an Other.

It stank of fore-planned coincidence. She couldn't help but keep mulling on what exactly had stayed her hand. Was it the state of the wretch? How he had strained against his cage to warn her of danger?

Or something else entirely?

She scrunched up her nose and grimaced at her misty reflection in the clouded glass.

"You're quiet," Sil said from her desk. She had Anna's wand on a support in front of her and prodded it with an array of small, sharp utensils. She'd been at it for days.

Tallah pressed her forehead to the ice-rimmed window and closed her eyes.

Her fever ran high, higher even than when she infused. The chill helped keep her mind clear while her thoughts chased one another and jumped fences they shouldn't.

"I'm just thinking."

"Bad kind of thinking? Or good?"

"Neither. Just . . . thinking."

She tried to pull in illum and instantly regretted it. Acid flooded her veins, burning from her heart to behind her eyes. Tears welled up until she released the power.

Fighting Anna had been sobering. Even with Christina aiding her, she had barely survived the clash. Victory coming on a coin toss was barely anything to be happy about.

Anna had grown incredibly powerful while in hermitage, doing her dirty experiments, never known, likely rarely challenged.

Deidra, on the other hand . . .

She let out a groan. Why did it have to be Deidra and not Lucretia? Why was Lucian so blasted useless when she needed the sleaze?

Deidra was a bad idea altogether. She closed her eyes and let out a long, slow breath. Thinking of Deidra inevitably brought up Rhine. It always did, as the two of them had been so bloody close for so bloody long. Her younger sister's dimpled smile and bright hazel eyes loomed up from the folds of time, and Tallah was drawn to the memory like a moth to murderous flame.

She tried to keep Rhine's real face in her mind's eye for a heartbeat longer. Her sister's fire-red hair, so much like hers, falling in waves down her shoulders. Hazel eyes that lit up the darkest, most hopeless odds. Her laugh and her fury that could charm and shatter armies.

Even as Tallah's lips creased up into a thin, trembling smile, the memory crumpled.

The starlight in her sister's eyes darkened to a hollowed-out stare that saw nothing. Her smile withdrew into a thin-lipped gash on a gaunt, alien face.

Who she'd found under the mountain hadn't been her younger sister. That she could never remember Rhine properly but only as that bloody wraith made her stomach fold in on itself in anger. She snapped off the mug's handle without meaning to, nearly spilling tea all over herself.

Deidra was striking out for her own vengeance, of that much she was certain.

And Tallah couldn't afford another hairbreadth close call. Anna had been a frothing-mad, cornered animal, and had been put down like one. For Deidra it would be personal, and it would hurt worse than anything the blood mage had inflicted. This time Rhine's memory and their shared love for her wouldn't be enough to keep them from killing one another.

They should be allies. It would make sense to pool their strength and go for Catharina's throat together. But she knew better than most that it wouldn't be enough. It'd barely be enough to reach the thrice-damned empress. Only through the plan would they have a chance of surviving, and there was no way Deidra would accept it willingly.

She bit on a knuckle and worried at it with her teeth until she felt the metal taste of blood on her lips. It chased away some of the unwanted ghosts of memory. They still scratched at the scabs of wounds that refused to close. An ember of a dead smile. A ragged, shuddering breath. The emaciated, ruined figure shuffling towards the bars.

Tears stung at the corners of her eyes, and she growled in frustration.

'Rest more, you child,' Christina whispered in her ear. 'Illum still comes at your calling. You have avoided the worst consequences of your gambit. Rest and stop torturing yourself over memories and failures.' The honeyed tone and poorly veiled criticism only served to get Tallah's blood boiling. The pity in the mental voice salted her old, festering wounds.

'You need to stop fretting, dear. It cannot be productive. You have come too far on this mission to start questioning yourself on this hour.' And now Bianca decided to weigh in as well. Of course she did.

"Are you all insistent on mothering me!?" Tallah snapped out loud, tone terser than intended. She wiped her eyes with the sleeve of her nightgown.

"I haven't said anything," Sil replied, distracted. "Keep your annoyances with your ghosts to yourself." She leaned back on her stool, stretched, and yawned. "Oh my soul, this thing is infuriating."

Tallah turned away from the blizzard and picked up her mug of tea from the windowsill. It had gone cold. On impulse, she tried to reheat it and failed.

"What are you trying to do?"

Sil had been poking the bone wand for hours, and it showed. Her eyes were red from the chemical fumes she used for her tests, and her face had gone paler than normal.

"Your creepy friend had this thing imbued with all sorts of interesting little effects. But it's made of bone. And I'm certain it's one of her own. Even with its master dead, it's still trying to protect itself. It's the cheekiest little piece of pettiness I've ever seen."

She demonstrated this by pressing the soft tip of a brush on one side of the wand, trying to add ink into the etched grooves. The nail-high runes shifted immediately, folding in on themselves.

"Anna was always secretive, Sil. All blood mages are. She's had a century to make that wand. You won't crack it in a couple tendays."

Sil gave her a level look that spoke of what she thought of that assessment.

"You and your clique weren't as clever as you all thought you were," she said. She bent back over the wand and donned her loupe. She wrote her notes left-handed and kept teasing the weapon with a burin.

'Why is she like this?' Bianca asked and let out a mental sigh that grated on Tallah's nerves.

Everything grated on her nerves since they got back to Valen. Waiting for news about the boy was its own brand of slow torture. What Sil had told her were fragments of a fever dream that she couldn't fit together in any useful way. The boy was *alien* and full of promise but stuck in a husk that may never be salvageable.

Was he even worth getting stuck in Valen over winter? They could still leave for Solstice before the week was done, while the high passes were open. She could manage the journey even with Sil chewing her ears off for not resting.

'You won't make the passes in your condition, even with a caravan,' Christina said, and accompanied the thought with a memory of last year's blizzard that had almost buried them in the forests of Solstice. Sil had nearly lost two toes to frostbite. 'At your age, you should have a much better understanding of your limits, chit.'

Tallah opened her mouth for a cussing reply, thought better of getting goaded into it, and instead moved closer to Sil's desk.

"Why is it so interesting to you?"

A tome waited open on her own desk with her half-finished translation on a separate scroll. She couldn't focus on it no matter how much she forced herself to sit still and work.

"She channeled through this from a distance. Her flesh dolls shouldn't have been able to channel anything on their own. I know that much about blood magic. This should have only worked in her hand, but the dolls were passing it between them. It's how they kept you so easily pinned down." Sil had to create a light sprite and orient it around the wand. Minuscule shadows lengthened as the runes came into relief. She grinned ear to ear, too many teeth showing as she scribbled new notes.

"And how's that going to help us? I can't make duplicates of myself, and I don't use my wand." She took wounded offense at the idea of being *easily* pinned.

"It'll sate my curiosity for one thing. Unlike you, I intend to someday live peacefully somewhere and ply a trade. I don't want to spend my entire life skulking in cold, dark places." Without looking up, she gestured with her burin at the wrapped form of the staff that hung on the wall. "For another, if I can modify the enchantment on that, I wouldn't need to haul it about everywhere we go."

Tallah picked up the cursed horned helmet and juggled it one-handed as she paced the room. She tried not to laugh at the idea of a life after the mission. Sil generally took it poorly if she did.

Anna had been creative in the way she used her dolls, that was true enough. So many of them at once, all channeling as if they were the bitch herself. No wonder it had taken her so long to find the real body and deliver the killing blow.

Anna had had a century to become what she did. What would the empress be? She'd seen the woman in battle, been at her side, witnessed the raw strength she could muster . . . and knew in her bones that she'd never seen Catharina truly unleashed. What a horrific spectacle that must be.

She pushed the thought away. A long way to go still, and at least one old friend's blood to be spilled.

"I need to go see the old man," she mused, restless in the cramped, shadow-strewn room.

A gale groaned outside the window, forcing the snow into a mad dance. Tallah shivered, ten paces away from the glass and with the hearth burning at her back.

"You're still feverish. Angledeer can wait. I bet he's quietly and drunkenly hibernating." Sil did not look away from her work as she spoke. "You should get some sleep."

As if I could get any sleep. Again, the thought only served to annoy her further. It wasn't enough that her power had been maimed, she couldn't even rest properly and recover.

Instead, she said, "I owe him. Without him, we'd still—"

"He'll keep. He's got nothing but time. Go sleep. It'll do you good."

Tallah forced herself to drink the cold, sour tea. She set the empty mug on top of the mantelpiece. Normally it would annoy Sil, but she was too entranced in her work to notice one more mug where it shouldn't be.

"I don't want to dream."

Sil's hand stopped scribbling in the middle of a word. Dark blue eyes rimmed with red turned away from the wand and stared at her with worry.

"What?" Tallah asked, finally settling down at her desk. She threw the helmet across the room into the open storage chest. It clattered as it hit the lid and bounced away.

"Nothing."

Quill scratched on paper again. Ice shards pattered against the window. A log snapped in the fire and threw embers against the iron grate.

"When did you start dreaming again?" Sil asked.

"Before we went into the caves. I don't want to think about it."

"Is it bad?"

"Bad enough."

She dreamed of the mountain. Always the mountain and the cruel, dark cold beneath it, the rattle of chains and the creaking of the rack. She rubbed at her left eye to dull a phantom sting and the feeling of cold metal sliding through flesh.

Now she'd also dreamed of Rhine. The promise of sleep terrified her worse than the empress's torturers ever could.

"Are you hearing the song?"

"No."

'Don't lie to her, you absolute child,' Christina warned. 'She will find out sooner or later and bleat at us for a tenday because of your cowardice.'

Tallah pulled her notes closer. Words danced and swam on the page, teasing her. She squinted and tried to force herself to focus and get her mind back on her work.

The words didn't care. They kept on dancing to the sound of sweet, distant music. Somewhere, beneath the mountain, her gallows sang out to infect her dreams and every waking moment.

CHAPTER SEVEN

Early Return

I'm not going to get any work done tonight," Quistis whined from her desk, a mountain of paper scrolls threatening to collapse on top of her.

Barlo set a mug of coffee on the sole free space of the overladen desk.

"Drink this. Slowly. Elend stuff," the large vanadal said and picked up some of the papers to take to his own desk. "When'd this become our job?"

"If you somehow find out, let me know. I'd really like to know too. I've got reports coming in from all over, and Falor's pushed it all onto me. How's that fair?" She sipped her coffee. Despite all the complaints, she was making a sizeable dent in the workload. A few more hours in the night and she'd probably not think of burning the office down anymore.

"The commander's visiting the empress," Barlo said. "We hold down the fort in his absence. It's only normal."

Quistis glared at him over the edge of her glasses, and he pretended not to notice.

"Kiss-ass," she muttered.

"I heard that. 'Sides, imagine the mood he's gonna be in."

The door to their office nearly snapped off its hinges and slammed against the wall with a sharp, deafening crack. Falor walked in, still dressed in his white imperial regalia, with Rumi following him. She was dressed in an ill-fitting blue imperial uniform that looked to have been sized for someone at least twice her build.

"Lord Commander," Quistis greeted him, holding down the stacks of scrolls against the inrush of air. "It's nice of you to join us, a tenday after the fact." Her glare snapped to Rumi in a way that promised an extensive debriefing.

"My mother is a very demanding woman, Quis," he said without preamble. He had dark rings around his eyes and looked haggard. When he passed by her desk, he picked up the mug of still-steaming coffee and downed it all. "I've finished a season's worth of meetings and negotiations with the militant lords in a tenday. The paperwork will be forthcoming." He gave her a smirk. "I'll have it all on your desk by this time tomorrow. It's coming here in a chest."

He sat heavily in his high-backed office chair and sank in it with a sigh. "It's damned good to be back, all things considered. Has news of Cinder reached the high lord?"

"No," Quistis replied, still working on the papers. The lord commander never minced words if he could help it. She had expected him to want an update on the situation the moment he got back. "Vial and Aidan are pursuing current leads but otherwise we've kept a tight lid on the information. I don't want another imbecilic panic and subsequent witch hunt."

"Which is why we's in here, doing clerical work, instead of out there, ripping the city in two trying to find 'er," Barlo added, flourishing his quill. "Nothing's wrong, all's lovely, there's no insane sorceress running loose in beautiful Valen."

Falor turned to the scout, who was sitting at attention by Barlo's desk. "For my mother's love, change out of that ridiculous outfit, Rumi. I have work I need you to do."

"Am I allowed to burn it?" she asked with a hopeful grin.

"You're not allowed to destroy empire property, but do it in your spare time. Now get going. We're about to get very busy."

She saluted and hurried out of the room.

"Who's on guard duty at the illum hearth?" Falor asked, ticking off concerns.

Quistis plucked a paper out of the pile and read off it. "I have our squads down there, rotating out every six bells. One mage killer is always present. We're not going to have a repeat of that disaster."

"Have there been disturbances?"

"None that we could link. If she's here, she's hiding, and she's doing it well. We assume she's got some new allies that she's likely using as a front." She finished off a stack of scrolls, set it aside, and turned her attention fully to the conversation. "Commander, we don't have a solid lead just yet, aside from Rumi's reading. We only have the two rookies that produced the maps, but they've proved harmless thus far."

"Define *harmless*."

She extracted another scroll from a different pile on her desk and adjusted her glasses as she read off it. "Tianna of Aieni Holding, in Calabran. Daughter to one Fyodor of Aieni Holding and Saveetha of Merchal Holding. Budding pyromancer. Studied for one year at Hoarfrost Academy, then moved her studies across the Divide.

"Silestra Adana, of unknown parentage, as per School of Healing edict. Aelir. Unknown age, of course. Appears to be a house medic of the former and accompanies her as a healer. Duration of association unknown."

Falor wrote down the names and tapped the paper with a finger, thoughtful.

"Aieni Holding leads a significant trade company. I had a meeting with some of their representatives just yesterday. I expected to see Fyodor, but he's apparently become reclusive in his old age. Why's the daughter in Valen?"

Quistis shrugged and ruffled some of her documents. "According to our sources in the Guild . . ." She made a face at that. The sources were all Lucian's, and dealing with him for information was like handling a pig dipped in lard. While you were naked and dipped in the same lard with him. "She's in the midst of some sort of rebellious moment and seeking to build a name for herself as an adventurer. She rarely undertakes any sorties and mostly spends obscene sums on luxurious living. Either gets outlandish results when she goes out, or she wanders off from the task and never turns it in. Makes for an unreliable asset to the Guild."

She sighed and took off her glasses to clean on her dress, more a tic than a need.

"I've had Vial following them around Valen at a distance, but so far it seems they're just . . . boring."

Falor furrowed his brow, and for a moment, Quistis worried about him. She doubted he had slept at all in the last week. His dark eyes seemed even blacker than usual, and he looked pale. He hadn't found time to shave, and the stubble was threatening a full-on beard attempt. It didn't look good on him.

She wished she had more information, but it had been a fruitless search ever since the caves. All that fire they'd felt in the caves dulled by the lack of anything concrete to go on, and the only real connection was stonewalled against their attention. Approaching someone with such ties in the Imperial Court needed a subtle hand.

"Does being quiet and neat sound like Cinder to you?" he asked. "When has she ever kept a low, quiet profile?"

"It's a miracle she's still alive at all considering how badly you trashed her during the illum hearth ruckus. Maybe she's just passing winter here at familiar haunts. Or maybe she's moved on already and we're chasing echoes and ghosts."

Falor steepled his hands over the desk and cracked each finger joint in turn, deep in thought.

"I do wish you'd stop doing that. It's disgusting," Quistis complained.

Falor ignored her.

"For the moment, we will work under the assumption that she is here, or somewhere hereabout. We've got reasonable confirmation that she's still alive and doing something we are not aware of. Either she had a meeting that went poorly with that Vitalis in the caves, or she went there with the express intention of killing whoever owned the sanctum. If she's scheming something, I want to get ahead of it before she ends up down my throat again."

"About that," Quistis said, interrupting the lord commander's line of thought. "We recovered one of the mage's creations. It's completely feral and degrading quick, but we have it with that bastil whose name I can't pronounce. They should be able to have a memory map for us in a few more days. If luck holds, we should get the name of its creator, so I'm personally following up on it."

She'd had to promise the bastil a look into Valen's deep vault as recompense for their help. Falor would likely approve, but that was a matter to discuss later.

Falor nodded. He had started drawing a schematic of known information and unknown factors. Quistis would have to look over the draft and fill in the details later to make it readable to others as a plan to follow.

"We need to get Cinder's allies." Falor circled something on the paper. "She's never been one for idle friendship, so whatever friends she has will be of great value to us if we manage to identify them. Big unknowns there."

He turned to Barlo and raised an eyebrow at the sight of his largest warrior crammed into a chair much too small for him. The vanadal's secondary hands were busy scribbling reports while the mage killer himself looked bored.

"Barlo, see if we can learn anything more about these two rookies. If I'm guessing correctly," he said with a meaningful glance at Quistis, "our source in the Guild is Lucian. Have a chat with him and explain, calmly if you may, just how interested we are in all he knows about them."

"A'ight, Commander. Do I break his fingers if he's being pigheaded as usual?"

"Please don't break his fingers, Barlo. It'll come back as a headache for Quis. Take Rumi with you. She should be convincing enough."

Barlo saluted, extracted himself carefully from the desk and sauntered off after Rumi. He looked relieved to be away from the papers and his quill.

As they remained alone in the room, Falor finally let out a heavy breath and slunk back in his chair.

"Do I look as tired as I feel, Quis?"

"You look ready to kick the bucket, so I guess about halfway there," she replied. "Before you ask, I refuse to give you anything for the fatigue. You're going to go rest, and then we'll tackle this with fresh eyes."

He closed his eyes, leaned his head back, and sighed heavily. Nothing followed for a while except the sound of her quill on paper as she tackled some of the other reports.

"I think I'll do just that," Falor finally said. He rose and walked slowly to the door, stopping by her chair. A warm hand rested on her shoulder.

"Are you joining me?" His voice was soft and his touch even softer.

She pressed her cheek to his fingers and closed her eyes for just a moment, as if she meant to give the offer consideration. In truth, she really wanted to go, but the work needed doing or it'd only pile higher.

"I'd love to, but my lord commander, at about fourth bell of the night, has added a big headache to my workload. So he's going to go rest while I put things into motion. You know, like I always do?" She grinned up at him.

"I don't know what I'd do without you, Quis," Falor said, laughing softly.

She pushed him away. "I imagine you'd overwork yourself to death. Go away. I don't want morning to find me here."

The moment the door closed with a creak and a tortured click, Quistis allowed herself a jaw-popping, eye-watering yawn. She looked forlornly into her empty mug, barely having had a chance to taste the coffee. And the closest place for more of it was all the way down into the city proper, with nobody around to go and fetch it for her.

"Bastard," she whispered, and smiled to herself.

CHAPTER EIGHT

Goboid Hunt

Vergil dreamed of late wither, of when it was still pleasantly warm under the two suns. Neptas was quickly becoming a pinprick of light in the noon sky while Cares grew ever brighter. That the first snow hadn't arrived yet promised a long and angry winter to come.

He learned that in an orientation class. The Guild offered many of those.

The overcast sky above still wanted to drink him whole, but it became easier to ignore day by day. Mostly, he ignored it by being indoors rather than aimlessly walking around the Guild Halls. Handlers refused to offer him any sorties as a new member without at least another rookie taking on the same mission and agreeing to co-opt the pay.

Vergil found himself, as before, terribly alone.

And woefully hungry.

Hunger chased away his fascination for the Guild's splendor, its imposing statues and gilded halls, and for the throngs of people bustling in and around the great courtyard. No amount of wonder or dread could fill the yawning gap in his stomach.

He could go find work as a menial, he knew, but that would put a definite end to his hopes of adventuring. And with winter coming, he expected work of that sort to dry up for someone with as few marketable skills as him.

If he returned to the Paladin Corps, he'd sign on as a soldier and be sent for further training in Aztroa Magnor, then deployed for duty in some faraway outpost where the empire's rule was still contested. If he survived his first three summers, then his overall survival odds were statistically sound, per Argia's calculations.

Well over half of the fresh recruits never survived their first summer unmaimed.

Death by a spear to the throat, or death by starving on the streets of Valen with winter's chill looming ever closer.

With those pleasant prospects in mind, Vergil did what any reasonable, budding adventurer would: He bused tables at the Sizzling Boar for five Valen lions a week, a meal a day, and a dry place to sleep in. On the *Gloria*, he'd worked more for far less.

The Sizzling Boar was a small, out-of-the-way tavern that existed because it needed to. Every large city needed a place like the Sizzling Boar, where those down on their luck, aimless and lost, found cheap beer and even cheaper rooms to contemplate exactly how life had conspired to dump them there.

Vergil worked with the diligence of a man one lost meal away from desperation. In a week's time, he began feeling quite at home, though still hoping an adventuring opportunity would present itself. Then he met Sidora Adana, Merk Armcast, and Davan Steir.

They sat huddled around a small table, hidden away in a barely lit nook, wearing their misery as a cloak and talking in hushed, angry voices. Each of them nursed the cheapest, stalest mug of ale that the Boar served, alongside equal portions of the perpetual stew. Vergil had spooned and served those himself.

The discussion, as he strained to overhear, revolved around finding a fourth member for their group.

They had gone into the wild and got ambushed by the very animals they were supposed to be hunting. Poor coordination coupled with even poorer leadership—if what one of them was whisper-shouting was to be believed—had almost ended their budding careers as dray chow.

In short, they were ripe for approaching. He just needed to figure out an opening.

He found it around the third round of ale.

"You're going to need a tank," Vergil commented offhandedly as he set down the relatively fresh mugs. From the weapons laid by the feet of the table, he was dealing with an archer, some form of infantry warrior, and a healer. No shield. They needed someone who could protect them in case of an emergency.

"Excuse me, a what?" One of them, Davan, it seemed, threw him a black look. He had a nasally voice that made all his words seem unnecessarily belligerent.

"Someone that can take a beating and hold the front line for you. I noticed you haven't got a shield with you."

"I don't hide under a stinking shield."

Okay, so he wasn't one to just accept a stranger throwing in his opinion. His displeasure was boiling over into rage. Vergil assumed he had struck a nerve.

"As you say." He walked away but not quite out of earshot. He dropped off his tray and slunk back around through the midday crowd, just close enough to listen without being obvious. It seemed that a fresh round of hostile reproaches was underway.

"He's not wrong," the aelir woman, Sidora, put in, moving food around on her plate, separating the vegetables from the unidentifiable brown meat. "No offense to you, Davan, but you rushed ahead and left us to fend for ourselves. That was unkind of you."

"My friend, I almost had the seats of my trousers ripped off by the wolves you failed to draw away. We had to climb trees to get out of the way. I soiled myself, ye? We need more people," the other man said between spoonfuls of the stew.

"I still say we don't need another guy with us," Davan insisted, fist on the table. "I can protect us next time."

Sidora and Merk looked at one another.

"All those of the opinion that Davan is full of shit, raise your hand, please." Merk raised his hand, and Sidora laughed, raising hers as well.

"Majority rules. Davan is full of shit. Mate, we need a fourth person. Less money coming in, sure, but less money we spend on getting patched up. It's a win for us however you look at it."

Davan tried to argue his point further, but Merk quickly talked over him.

"Who specializes in getting their arse whooped and enjoys it too?" he asked his companions.

"I do." Vergil pounced on the moment. He had poured himself a mug of ale and, to the chagrin of many other patrons, sat down with the trio. After all, allegiances of opportunity were the main stock in trade for a place like the Sizzling Boar. The innkeeper would understand.

"I'm fresh out of the Paladin Corps, and I need some paying work, as you can see." For good measure, he also placed the metal disc marking him as a licensed adventurer down on the table.

Davan glared at him, but Merk shook his hand eagerly.

"I'm Merk, this is Sidora, and the stupid one is Davan." Vergil already knew all their names but thought it more prudent not to mention. They'd likely not appreciate his eavesdropping.

"I'm Vergil. And I know a few things about squad roles. I can help you."

He turned to Davan and extended his hand to him too.

"One sortie. I'll suggest how we go about it. If we don't get good results, then I won't take my cut of the reward and will be gone from your hair. How about that? You can't lose much just by trying." He smiled at the man, hand still outstretched. Davan shook on it after weighing the proposition for a few moments.

Vergil remembered men like Davan from the experiences, desperate for some measure of control and recognition. He felt that way sometimes too. It also wasn't the first time he had to bribe his way into a social group. His family had hated so dearly that he'd been born male that they'd arranged for the very worst, most isolated job available on the *Gloria Nostra*. He would go weeks without meeting another person outside the virtual space that they couldn't deny him.

He did his best not to look at Sidora. She made him uncomfortable in a way he couldn't understand. The aelir in general had him sweating whenever he drew close to one. It made it difficult to look the woman in the eye when she spoke to him.

"You seem quite down on your luck," Sidora said. She smiled so bright that he felt ashamed of himself for existing next to her. "I don't mean to offend you, Vergil, but you smell. May I buy you a token at the bathhouse?"

"I'm . . . sorry?" he said, taken aback by the disarming brusqueness hiding beneath that smile. "I do bathe, but it's a tiny pail, and my room is small and . . . well . . . I . . ."

Davan laughed loudly, swinging his ale pitcher.

"Don't listen to her, Vergil. Men should smell of hard work and conquest. Leave the baths to the gelded and the womenfolk."

He said *men*, but both he and Merk were barely past seventeen standards by Vergil's estimate, close to his age, if not younger. Sidora was older, in the same way all aelir were older than most anyone else in any room. Vergil had learned about aelir near-immortality, bar accident or sickness, from a Guild orientation class aimed at people coming from the more remote villages of the empire. Many species weren't a common sight outside the larger cities such as Valen or Drack.

Hands were properly shaken, and mugs of ale were knocked back. Vergil settled his dealings with the innkeeper and got paid his week's half griffon in advance. If he wanted to come back, there were always pots that needed scrubbing.

Next came the posting from the Guild. Queries and special missions were posted regularly, with an appraised difficulty rating and recommended number of people for best results. There were missions for agricultural help, pest control, property or lost-person retrieval, and a wide variety of miscellaneous odd jobs. On special billboards there were bounties for various individuals, as well as assassination requests, though these had to be cleared with the Storm Guard before undertaking them.

Vergil already knew what they needed to do. He'd spotted the perfect job days before and had waited for the right people to come along. Luck had been kind.

"This one would be perfect for a party of our size that needs to raise some quick spending money," he said as he took the notice off the wall, showing it to the others.

"Goboid pest control?" Davan sneered at the idea but stared closer at the paper. "Why's the rating so high for that low of a pay?"

"It's out in the sticks," Merk said. "Vergil, that's out of Valen's influence, and the pay is really poor for that sort of work. Land's real dangerous beyond the plains."

"Yes, yes," Vergil conceded. "But listen, there's a bigger picture to this. I've seen this notice hanging here for weeks—"

"Because nobody sane would touch it," Davan interrupted him. "It's pest control for no money."

"No, it's because nobody has the imagination to see this in the right light."

Everyone stared at him, so Vergil kept talking. He had thought about it a lot, so much so that he'd even studied the map hanging in the central pavilion of the Guild Hall.

"Look, this isn't that far out from Valen. At a brisk walk, we can be there in about six days, give or take." He led them to the map and showed the place. "The road ends at this village. A vein of the mountain comes real close to it, so it's a dead-end place. No road, no trade, no brigands or bandits. At worst, some animals on the road."

Merk snorted.

"You say *at worst*, but that's what got us in trouble the last time." He glared at Davan. "Money's still low for that sort of travel."

"Bigger picture, remember?" Vergil grinned, finally coming to his conclusion. "Goboids are always popping up here and there, right? The thing is, they hoard a lot of what they steal."

It had been in one of the orientation classes. The trio hadn't taken any of them.

"All right, so?" Davan moved closer to the map and inspected the route. Vergil could see his mood turning to his aid now that Merk was skeptical.

"They're easy to kill and easy to track for any tracker with some experience. If we follow them back into their lair and slaughter them, we'll probably find a lot of things they kept from raids. They like shiny things and will steal almost anything that's not bolted down. We can sell whatever's valuable. Two days' work, probably, and we'll have a good fund to get better gear and go on better missions. Unless otherwise stated in the notice, any loot we find in a warren is ours to keep. Guild rules."

Merk was pensive and scratched his cheek.

"People go missing in the hills. But the plan has merit." He turned to the other two. "Vote?"

Davan clapped Vergil on the shoulder. "With him," he said.

Sidora shrugged and raised her hand. "Safer than what Davan chose, I think. If we keep to the road, we should be fine up to there."

Decided. Vergil felt a flutter of pride for this as Sidora took the note from him and headed to the reception desk to get details about the location and contact person on site.

"Smart reasoning," Merk commented, rubbing the patchy stubble on his cheek. "I can track them to their lair, Davan can do most of the actual killing, and you can keep me and Sidora safe in the tight space. I hope your instincts are as good as your head."

Davan nodded along.

"I read a lot," Vergil lied. He was barely literate and never once bothered with literature in his life. When he looked at the local letters, he could only understand their meaning once his implant translated the text. He could speak the language like he had been born to it, but his reading and writing were patchy at best.

Sidora soon returned holding a rolled-up map.

"It's way out in the sticks. The map here is generous," she told them, spreading out the updated map received from the Guild. The goboids were raiding some small villages in the hills with irregular hit-and-runs. It was about a week's walking journey to there, but the actual reward specified on the posting had actually been increased due to low turnout of adventurers.

"We shouldn't waste time," the healer went on. "Talk from other adventurers says the weather may get bad soon. We should do the job while it's still fairly warm out, or we may get stuck out there. I don't fancy spending winter tending to chickens and goats."

It took them seven days of hard marching to reach the small village of Nest. Vergil shared a tent with Sidora, as hers was the most spacious, and it wasn't uncommon for adventurers to share cover at night. He was on edge the whole trip. Being under a single tent at night, aware of her nearness as they slept back-to-back, had him sweating to the point of dehydration.

She and the others had formed up some months back, at near the end of thaw, and had done a bit of odd work here and there, so they were used to each other. She was an initiate healer, and as part of her training, she had to do field work. She had met Merk the same day she arrived in Valen from the School of Healing, and Davan soon after.

She was being kind and trying to engage with him.

For his part, Vergil was only too keenly aware of her and unable to offer more to the conversation aside from grunts and short, vague answers.

It came as a relief when they reached their destination, and none too soon. The supplies the other three had bought were gone by day six, and the last day of travel was accompanied by unhappy stomach growls. Even so, they did not stray from the road.

Vergil felt anxious about the whole thing now that he was face-to-face with it. If his insight proved wrong, they'd have a very hungry and sullen trip back to Valen. He may well remain behind to tend to chickens, whatever those were. "A goboid alone is as dangerous to any of us as a ten-summers-old human child armed with a pointy stick. The largest of them will grow to about a yard in height, with a thick greenish-gray skin, pointy ears, and the relative intelligence of a particularly forward-thinking rat. They become a nuisance when there's a lot of them gathered and their thieving becomes bold. Honestly, all of this was in the Guild orientation classes."

"Nobody goes to those," Davan said as the small, scattered village of Nest came into view among the tall trees lining the road. "Why waste your time with classes when you can go out and kill beasts for money? Besides, they don't say things we don't all already know. I've killed plenty of goboids in my village."

"You go to them to make sure you don't go hunting anything really dangerous, like a corallin or a dray." Vergil was making a very determined effort to get his party mates to agree to take the classes once back in Valen.

"Corallins are big kitty cats. They're not that dangerous for three people."

"They hunt in big groups and lay down ambushes. Like goboids. It's not uncommon for large bands of goboids to seriously injure or even kill people they rob."

"I swear by all the gods, you're relentless," Davan said, exasperated.

Merk snickered behind him. "Oh no, you let him have it, Vergil. Maybe he'll finally listen to someone."

"I have had a very hard time finding people to work with," Vergil said. "Do you have any idea how many dishes I had to wash so I could eat? I need all three of you alive and well. I'm not going back to the dishes." He had tried his best to befriend Davan, and it had worked for the most part.

"All right, you preaching bastard. We'll go to the orientations when we get back. Are you bloody happy now?"

Sidora had gone ahead to confer with the village head. When she came back, she showed the way to a secluded homestead and a patch of forest from which most incursions came at night. They set up camp and spread out in search of good watch posts.

The plan, concocted during the trip out, was to let the goboids do their raid and then have Merk track them back to the hidden entrances of their lair. Easy pickings from there.

But raids had become rare in recent weeks. Villagers had started locking away their valuables in strong boxes and then bolted those down against thieving critters. The thieves had become, for most people around Nest, a kind of nuisance they had learned to live with. Their notice asking for help in the big city had gone unanswered for near a whole season, and the local militias had more pressing matters to deal with.

It was uneventful for the first tenday, as no raid happened in Nest.

Sidora brought tea to the men during the watch hours to help them stay awake and did not relent in her efforts to get Vergil to talk to her.

After the trip out, and now around the fire, he found that she wasn't quite as terrifying as the women aboard the *Gloria* and even felt comfortable to have her around as long as he could sit to hide her effect on him.

He also learned that it was offensive to refer to her as a *woman*. That was human talk. She was an aelir'rei and preferred to be spoken of as such. Most humans never learned to make the distinction. Aelir society was complex and strict, and using human terms for them was considered the height of rudeness. Taking revenge for slights was an art form for the aelir, though Sidora assured him that she had no such intentions for him. The right poison took a long time to brew.

Vergil tried to commit the distinction to memory, even if he really couldn't understand it.

They slept in the mornings and in the evenings for a few hours, while in the daylight they helped with odd jobs around the village for food and some money. Vergil found that he was terrified of birds when the first cockerel charged him. Sidora had to calm and coax him down from a tree he had climbed, to the amusement of the others.

"Gods help us if the goboids dress in feathers," Davan ribbed him during their modest dinner in camp that evening.

Vergil blushed and stared down at his cheese and onions. The experiences couldn't compare to the feeling of growing closer to actual people.

Nothing could. The loneliness and isolation squatted down in his memory like great beasts just waiting to snap at him. He'd do anything to keep them away forever.

"What the matter, Vergil?" Sidora asked him. Merk and Davan had sauntered back off to their watches. There was a chill wind coming down from the mountain, a first tender caress of the cold winter to come.

"Nothing," he said, running a palm over his face. "I haven't really been with people before. This is my first time working with someone else. I'm happy, even if I spend my days up in a tree."

Sidora laughed, and it was the most beautiful laugh Vergil could possibly imagine. Her wide eyes reflected the firelight as she leaned towards him, looking mischievous.

"I will tell you a secret, if you promise to keep it," she said and pressed her third and fourth fingers to her lips.

Vergil leaned in, his heart thundering in his chest. She had finally managed to get him to look at her, and he couldn't pull his eyes away.

"I promise."

Sidora smiled and winked at him. "We like you too, Vergil. Even Davan. If this doesn't get us money, we'd still like you to stay with us. Will you?"

He smiled and nodded, not trusting his voice for more.

The raid came that very same night. About twenty small figures crept from the dark of the trees and proceeded to steal whatever they could grab. They made off with cheese and meat, eggs and a few chickens they killed on their roosts. Vergil spotted one of the small creatures as it was making its way across a reaped field and immediately signaled for Merk.

The ranger made his way back to camp late in the morning, red-faced from effort but smiling wide. He had followed the creatures all the way out of the forest and into the skirts of the mountains. They had an entrance cleverly concealed behind some stone pillars, practically invisible until you either fell into it or had the right angle of sight to see it opening up. Merk hadn't gotten the angle and found it the old-fashioned way.

"I was enjoying myself helping around the village," Sidora confessed as she sat with her arms around her knees in front of the fire that evening. "It's so quiet out here compared to the city."

"It's too quiet," Davan protested. "I could hear Merk every time he went for a leak. Pisses like a horse." He got an elbow to the ribs from the ranger.

Sidora laughed quietly. "It reminds me of home, actually," she said, sipping her tea with a faraway look in her eyes. "The quiet rustling of the leaves in wither. Smell of cut grass in the morning. Friendly people that say hello when you walk by. It's just so different from Valen. I had forgotten how this felt."

It got quiet around the fire for a few heartbeats. The wood crackled and snapped, sending up a few embers in the dark night sky.

"So, we go in the morning?" Davan broke the moment, stabbing with his sword at the fire pit.

"At first light. They should be asleep, and we'll have the element of surprise," Vergil confirmed. "Take care of the shadows and nooks as we go in. They're cave animals, so they'll hide and try to surprise us if they get wind we're coming. Plus, they'll probably have a lot of side tunnels to scurry away through. We should kill as many as we can so they don't return any time soon."

The rest nodded.

"What do we do if they have a live chicken in there?" Davan couldn't help himself. The rest laughed, Vergil included.

Finding the warren proved a lot easier than any of them had expected. There were just a few tunnels and intersections, and all were marked clearly by goboid tracks and droppings. They were upon the sleeping group of creatures in less than an hour after entering the tunnels. They slaughtered most of them before the rest woke, and only one managed to escape the killing grounds, running screaming into the deeper tunnels. There was no point in chasing a single goboid down into the dark.

Davan and Vergil took turns at dragging the corpses to the center of the lair to form a large pile. Merk shifted through the assortment of junk collected there, picking out valuables. It turned out to be quite a haul after all. The thieves had collected weapons they never used, coins and jewelry, and even an odd assortment of books with particularly colorful covers.

"Sidora, this would look nice on you," Merk called to the healer, holding up a thin silver chain bracelet that had probably been stolen off some merchant's cart. "Sidora?" he called again when no answer came.

Davan and Vergil both stopped their work and looked towards the section of cave where the healer had last been. She wasn't there.

"Sidora!" all three called out.

Something moved in the mouth of a tunnel, but it wasn't the wayward healer. Three ratmen walked in, furry faces grinning, each taller than the humans. Three more walked in through the opposite tunnel, hissing a low snarl of threat. One of them held Sidora by the hair and dragged her around. Her face was bloodied and her body limp.

Another of the beasts held the crumpled body of their missing goboid.

Davan charged before the others even reached for their weapons. The ratmen, tall and brawny beasts, were armed with swords and clubs. He didn't get the chance to swing his sword before one of the creatures grabbed him by the neck and slammed him headfirst into the wall. He went down in a pile with barely a noise.

Merk was back-to-back with Vergil, and they were surrounded. One of the rats hissed at them and lunged. Vergil managed to deflect the thrust with his shield but realized the feint too late. A steel-encased fist knocked him flat, his vision swimming from the pain.

Merk dropped his crossbow and surrendered. Him, they beat into a ragged ruin.

'Steady there, lad. We've got you.'

Vergil did not recognize the voice. It didn't fit with the rest of his life just then. A woman was speaking, but he couldn't see her. Her voice was a balm to dull the teeth on the terror gripping his heart.

The ratmen were taking them deeper into the caves. They dragged Sidora by her hair, kicking and screaming. Davan tried to fight, twice. They broke his arms for it, twisted them at odd angles with bones pushing out against the skin. It washed out any resistance left in him.

Merk was pushed and dragged along, too shattered to manage more than a couple steps on his own.

Two scores of ratmen infested the large cavern at their destination, gathered in clusters around small fires burning around a central blaze. The smoke slowly filtered out through a gallery of cracks in the ceiling, but the musk of animal filth overpowered any other smell.

"What this?"

Vergil raised his eyes to the gravelly voice and saw a ratman nearly twice as large as the rest, with gray fur and milk-white eyes. It held a gnarled staff. Unlike the rest of the horde, which wore various bits and ends of armor, this one was wearing a black robe adorned with bones. It clattered when the monster hobbled over to look them over.

One of the ratmen let out a long series of hisses and grunts. The old rat struck it over the knees with its staff and snarled.

"You guard. Not hunt. Hunting for smart clan, not dumb pup." It spoke in broken, hissed Imperial, making a mockery of the words.

A flicker of hope ignited in Vergil's chest but quickly went out as the creatures roughly undressed them.

"These two, cage," the shaman said as he inspected Davan and Merk. "Female, spice. Knifey-ear taste better than human."

That only left Vergil. Warm piss ran down his legs as the wizened ratman loomed over him, close enough for Vergil to taste the filth in its fur. The monster sniffed and let out a rasping laugh.

"I wonder if this one can starve. It reeks of Anatol's incense. Up," it ordered the other beasts.

They threw him in a cage fashioned out of gnawed bones. It reeked. Strips of rotten meat hung in tatters off the grisly construction. His stomach turned over and ejected the sparse contents of their last dinner as he was hauled two yards or so above the lick of the cook fire. Only smoke marred his view of the cavern as he slowly rotated in the draft of hot air.

'Steady, lad,' the voice-like-a-balm said. The edges of reality blurred, like colors running down a wet painting. 'Found a cluster. We start here. Move outward.'

Who's talking? Vergil looked around, trying to find whoever it was that talked right in his ear. Again, that feeling of stepping out of his head, of hitching a ride on someone else's life.

The world bucked and bent around him. He'd seen experiences glitching sometimes, images and events shuffling together. This felt very much like that. There was no connection port on the back of his head, no matter how desperately he groped for one. If this wasn't real, he needed it to stop.

It all kept playing forward as he wailed and smashed his fists against the bones.

'Bugger, you're a stubborn blighter. Mistress Aliana, please go to him. He's going to twist something out of place if he keeps at it.'

Vergil screamed until he frothed pink at the mouth.

Sidora wailed when they dragged her out of the cage for the first time. She screamed and cried and pleaded as they held her down and chopped off her fingers.

Vergil was sick with the sight of so much blood spilling at once, stunned into silence.

The shaman forced the healer, clawed fingers clasped around her nose, to drink something out of a dirty bowl. The bleeding stopped, but she still cried for what felt like days.

Her fingers were ground up into paste and mixed in with the gruel boiling over the fire.

Spice, he realized with a rising sense of horror. Just as the monster had said, they would use her for spice.

You appear to be in distress. Mood regulation attempted. Please consult Medical at your earliest convenience.

Vergil looked through two sets of eyes. One pair watched Sidora kicking and clawing with her unmaimed hand when she was taken out again. The other watched him watching her. A sort of strange calm washed over him as he separated from the first and drifted above the pain and the horror of it all, above the shame of what he'd done to them.

"Take him! Take him! Please, no more. Please!" Sidora begged. They stretched out her other hand on the chopping block. "I'll do anything. Please, not—" The hatchet came down, and her voice rose into a keening, rattling wail. More blood. More screams. More curses and hate.

Days passed. Or weeks. Maybe even years. An eternity of hunger and shame in his tight little cage, slowly going insensate to it all. Sidora cursed him every single moment she was awake and not screaming, all the way until they took her tongue. From there on, she merely glared up at him until she had nothing to glare with.

Colors ran together and moments skipped forward. Silences filled small crevices in his life where he was sure there were supposed to be cries, clangs, clatters, curses, pleadings. Ghosts whipped past the Vergil that watched, apparitions in white that manifested for a moment and stole away something of him.

He felt it happening but never knew what went away.

Davan and Merk were made to fight one another, to bite and scratch and try to rip each other's throats out. They were even fed bits off Sidora when the rats drank too much of their brews.

Something changed in them. They lessened, but not how Sidora did. Humanity shed off them with every drop of spilled blood until they were little more than feral, twisted things that snarled against the grates of their cages. Ratmen prodded them into fighting frenzies and treated them like pets. They fed them rotting carcasses nearly stripped of all meat, and some of their fetid potions.

'That never happened, lad. It was a nightmare, nothing more,' said the voice as the watching Vergil cried behind the eyes of his corporeal self. That other him had stopped caring, had quieted down and suffered the gnawing hunger.

SEVERE STARVATION afflicts your body. Death is imminent. Please consult Medical urgently.

Blessing of Anatol has activated. Death is no longer imminent. Please consult Medical at the earliest convenience.

It happened irregularly, and it made him scream.

On the verge of death, of sweet release, that thrice-damned blessing dragged him back. Every single time! If he still had the tears for it, he'd cry when the jolt of healing clawed him from the precipice and forced another hour or another day of watching Sidora and the pure hate in the pits that had been her eyes.

Was it all really happening?

'There we go. Seed of doubt is flourishing. Give him a couple of days before you start growing out new memories.'

The hunger gnawing at his insides was all too real. When the ratmen cut off Sidora's arm and roasted it over the fire, he drooled for a bite of it. He begged with a ragged voice for a sliver of the charred meat. They teased him with it, waving it up at his cage just out of reach of his outstretched fingers.

It wasn't my fault! They weren't supposed to be here! Guilt burned worse than the hunger, worse even than the fire. Nothing they could do to him compared to the simple fact that he'd damned them all.

'It never happened, lad.'

It happened! I was there. I hated her. I hate her. I hate her.

'Steady, lad. She was the first to die.'

Yes, she was.

She died when there was nothing more to cut off her. She died before the stranger got there. She . . .

No! That's not right.

Sidora had died in the goblin warren, head split open by a ratman axe. She died with a spasm and a sigh, painless and quick.

No.

She . . . she . . . was eaten? She wasn't. They killed her first.

When the stranger had come, he was alone in the cavern, the only one left. Merk and Davan had died in the warren. They hadn't changed. They hadn't been sicced on the stranger only to be gutted by lances of white fire.

Sidora had been the first to die, hit from the back by the ratmen. She . . . she hadn't suffered. It had all been quick, painless.

Yes, that made more sense than the horror he'd been imagining. He rose from it as if from an early-morning nightmare. It was already fading into formless mists and rags of memory like all bad dreams are wont to do.

He had mourned them all, for endless days of endless hungry terror. Then he was bored and hungry. Then, just hungry. No rest for him, not when the blessing kept shaking him awake.

In the low firelight of what was probably night, he saw the stranger approaching.

Firelight glinted at the mouth of one tunnel. There had only ever been darkness there before. It grew in brightness by the moment.

Someone walked out of that normally empty tunnel. It wasn't a verman. There were supposed to be guards in that tunnel, but the newcomer walked through as if the notion was ridiculous. Shadows parted as the stranger advanced and Vergil felt an odd excitement swelling in his chest.

Men came to the cavern sometimes, to deal with the ratman shaman. Coin pouches were passed between them, scrolls were locked in a metal box, ratmen were sent out. They would return later carrying bound women. Once they brought three young girls bound together into a bundle. Every time they'd open a secret door to the side of the cave and carry their victims through.

Only the ratmen ever returned.

The stranger wasn't someone Vergil had seen before. This one wore black garments and a shining mask upon their face. Fire and shadows reflected in it.

He wanted to shout a warning. There were scores of vermen in the cavern, laying strewn about, out of sight, armed and armored. No matter how he strained and fought to gather strength, he couldn't do more than lift his desiccated arms in a gesture of warding.

More meat was coming to the fire. The stranger looked like they would take a long while to be eaten. That thought fled his mind as if chased by hounds.

I'm hallucinating things. This can't be real.

There were fireflies flitting around the stranger like motes of dust catching the uneven light.

One ratman sounded the alarm, and the cavern exploded into action. Vermen scrambled to their feet and rushed the intruder with weapons held high and fangs bared. Doom descended on the unwary fool.

Fireflies swarmed away from the figure, flying out like rays of light. Each one hit a different rat, stumbling their rush for a heartbeat.

Some ratmen faltered in their charge, gazed down, and burst apart like overripe fruit hitting the ground. Flesh and entrails erupted as the stranger approached the fire, barely concerned about the carnage.

It was a woman, Vergil saw, with red hair and a tall frame that almost matched the vermen. She had a thin sword at her waist but did not draw it.

Her hands flashed into fire. The first verman to rush her exploded into blood mist as she unleashed a lance of flame on it.

Air boiled and screams evaporated into echoes as balls of fire exploded with blinding flashes. Vergil was tossed inside his cage like the near-corpse he was when the blast wave hit him. He saw, in brief gaps through the smoke, the woman killing the shaman with a gesture. She turned him into a burnt-out skeleton as if he were of no concern to her.

It lasted for a moment. A breath, maybe.

Then his cage crashed to the ground, and the world lurched out of shape.

He hoped he was now dead. For a long time, he saw nothing but the crimson puddle of blood in which he lay. Bits of fur and offal broke the surface. An arm's length away lay half a corpse, burnt nearly black, staring with empty eye sockets at him.

By the time the Goddess came for him, he'd screamed himself mute.

Her touch was warm and soft on his face as she turned his head over to gaze into his eyes. She was a vision of beauty with glacial blue eyes and hair the color of the midday sun. She spoke and pressed her fingers to his forehead, but his mind slipped around the words.

"*I require touching this mind,*" she said. He heard the words, but they meant absolutely nothing. Colors ran behind her.

He begged for death with soundless words. She was a goddess, she should know that in his head there was only guilt and the wish to end this life. Why prolong his suffering?

She was gone in a flash of bloodred, her touch ripped from his skin with a clap of thunder.

Why?! No! Please, no! Kill me. Please—

'None of that, lad. That Adana may be many fine things, but she's no goddess. Let's not keep that silly notion.'

Maybe he was just imagining everything. Maybe he had lost his mind while watching Sidora's long murder.

But Sidora had died first. That didn't make sense.

'By the Goddess's horns, you're stubborn,' the voice snapped at him, suddenly impatient. 'Why are you fighting me, boy? Don't you want to be free of it all?'

The stranger in black loomed over him. There was smudged blood on her mask. She wore a long black coat with gold trimmings, almost like some kind of uniform.

Her mere presence caused him more suffering. She manhandled him and threw him about like a rag doll. Every time she moved him, it reminded him he was still alive. He found new depths of hatred. He couldn't live and couldn't die, and he hated her for not letting the rats or the hunger finish him off.

'Stop struggling, boy. Let it all go. There's a good lad.'

The goddess was back, talking to the stranger. Blood ran down her face, as if she'd hit her head on something.

'She's not a goddess, Vergil.'

They stuffed a helmet over his head. The stranger argued with the other, the not-a-goddess goddess. He could only look at them. His voice refused to obey him and stop its braying laughter.

When had he started laughing?

Why am I laughing?

Why a helmet? Why give him a damned helmet? Couldn't they show mercy and just end his suffering?

Muted echoes penetrated the helm's thick metal. The not-a-goddess hid behind the stranger in black and aimed her staff at him over the other's shoulder. Blue light blinded his vision, and fire flared up in his chest as bones knit painfully back together and his breathing came easier. It made his arms and legs spasm and jerk around like the limbs of a marionette, and then he was still again. Even out of the cage, he was too weak to even crawl.

Physical ailments have been healed. Pain muting has been deactivated.

SEVERE STARVATION afflicts your body. Death is imminent. Please consult Medical urgently.

Something clicked in his head.

The light fizzed out, and he saw the blonde *woman* peering at him over the shoulder of the frightening stranger, looking ready to duck back at any moment. She raised her staff again, and a moment later he felt very wrong.

His voice was no longer his own, the braying laugh taking on a manic, desperate edge. He tried to and found that he actually could move his head around. A thin golden line connected his chest to the goddess's. The line pulsed faintly, its glow dimming and intensifying in rhythm with his thundering heartbeats.

'Mistress Aliana, please attend. This . . . we can't get rid of this. Look, see how tight it's latched on to him?'

'This thing is going to be trouble,' another, rougher voice said. 'I'm going to skin those two.'

Something felt horribly off. Words crowded his field of vision, but they meant nothing to him.

His right arm jerked up of its own accord and pushed him to his side, the effort igniting new fire in his bones. The left arm became rebellious as well and, helping the right, pushed him up to his hands and knees as if he were just learning to move again. His entire body moved and rebelled violently against his wishes of lying still to die. Impossibly, moving in jerks and starts, he came up on his own two feet.

Everything hurt. His feet and legs hurt just from supporting him. Bones ground on bones and sent daggers into his laughing brain. His hands and arms hurt just from pushing him upright. Every breath hurt his chest. He tasted blood from something rupturing somewhere.

Despite it all, he drew in a sharp breath and bellowed out a war cry that made his own blood run cold.

Where had that come from?

Something flowed out of the helmet and into his head. It pushed his consciousness aside as if he were nothing. It laughed and laughed and screamed its way to the surface of his thoughts. It was malice, angry and hateful, barely conscious of itself. Vergil felt the shape of the mind that occupied his, and it made him recoil from its cadaverous touch.

His voice cracked halfway through the war cry, and he gasped for air, choking and coughing viciously. He inhaled sharply, and with alien strength he bellowed again and banged his worthless fists against his naked chest.

Except that he wasn't naked anymore. Translucent plates of armor now covered him from neck to feet, and his fists rang out like the tolling of a bell.

From a cage of bones now into a cage of thought. The cave faded away, and only the malice remained, pitch black and all-consuming.

The spirit of Horvath, the Hammer, has taken over your body. No actions are available at this time.

'What in the Goddess's teats do we do about you?'

CHAPTER NINE

Sweet Cravings

Winter had hammered Valen for five days straight with what was considered one of the most vicious blizzards anyone had ever seen, especially for so early in the season. For its part, the city took it in stride and merely slowed its operation. Otherwise, business as usual.

"I refuse to go out there," Tallah protested as Sil tried to drag her chair away from the table. "It's bloody cold and blowing knives."

"We need winter gear, you mule-headed creature. I refuse to portal out of some cave again and freeze my arse off just because you're too stubborn by half."

The argument had been going on for the better part of the morning. Tallah's fever had broken during the night, and she could finally focus on her work.

Sil had different plans.

"It's a bit cold out. So bloody what?"

Tallah had half a mind to let go of the table and give the annoyance a face full of chair and irate sorceress.

"I like my work clothes just fine," Tallah said. "Go out yourself and leave me alone. I want to work."

"We've been cooped up in here for days. I need fresh air, and you need sunlight. You're paler than cheese."

"There's a blizzard out there, Sil. I'm very certain the only color I'll be turning is blue. I'll throw you out buck naked if you keep insisting."

Sil refused to be deterred.

"Your fetish work gear is a bunch of ribbons holding together out of spite. You need new clothes." The healer had changed tactics from dragging her chair to shaking it. "Let's go already. It's not even that cold out there."

The windows, frozen solid, shook when a howling gale swept through the alleys around the Meadow. Tallah turned to Sil, looked her straight in the eye, and pointed with her hand at the shivering window.

"That doesn't mean anything," the healer protested. "It's a bit nippy. It'll only get colder from now on."

"If you want to go and see your lover, you really don't need me as chaperone. You're a big girl."

Sil paused for a heartbeat then recommenced her attack. *Well, that didn't work as intended.*

"If I wanted to see her, I'd say so. Stop being stubborn for once in your miserable life and let's. Go. Out."

Despite herself, Tallah sighed and gave up.

'Please, Tallah, go with her,' Christina groaned. 'If I still had a head, it would be throbbing after a bell's worth of her braying. Please, just go with her. A bit of air will do you good.'

Sil, to her dubious credit, had a knack for cutting through Christi's patience like an oblivious knife through soft butter.

"Great, now Christina's agreeing with you. All right! We're going. I'm going to push you into the deepest, coldest snowbank I can find."

A knock on the door drew their attention. They shared a look before Sil went to answer.

'Do not sulk. For once she is right. You lack winter gear. The cold will bite until you recover enough of your ability.' Now Bianca pleaded Sil's case.

"Shut up," Tallah groaned, putting her head on the tome she was trying to study. "One of her is enough."

'There is really no need to insult me. I was merely suggesting.'

"I want you insulted."

'Testy and sullen. Fresh air will do you good.'

"Mistress Tianna, there's a runner from High Priestess Aliana here," Sil called from the door. "Could you bring me some coins, please?"

Tallah perked up and bolted for the door. "What's the news?" she asked as she handed Sil two silver lions. Way too much for a runner, but she didn't care.

"Mistress Aliana of the esteemed Sisters of Mercy would like to inform you that the ward you left in her care is now recuperating steadily from his injuries. He can be discharged into your care at your earliest convenience," the boy at the door said crisply. "She would also like to inform you that the agreed-upon rate for her service has been increased twofold to cover the terrible stress put on her priestesses, as well as a tax for, and I beg your forgiveness for quoting this, 'dealing with that pissant.' She thanks you for your understanding and would like to know how soon you will come by."

The boy had caked-on snow up to his knees. He spoke with hands behind his back and, at the end, extended a hand for his tip. Sil paid him and added one coin more than was customary.

"Tell her we'll pick up our friend tomorrow morning at the earliest possible hour. We also agree to her adjusted price. Go now."

He pocketed the coins, nodded curtly to them, and rushed away.

Finally! Tallah's excitement nearly bubbled over into giddiness. She had been sitting on needles ever since Sil had related what she had seen in Vergil's mind. Even the fever hadn't dampened her enthusiasm.

Most of what she had learned from the healer had been completely unintelligible, while other things presented tantalizing possibilities that promised fresh ways for her to expand her power. She had grown restless waiting at the Meadow, and sometimes wished she had never asked.

By the time Sil had made sure nobody had followed the boy and returned to the study, Tallah was already half dressed and giddy.

"We go right now," she declared.

"We go shopping right now," Sil corrected, and got back to preparing for a cold trip out. "Helmet Boy will also need some warm clothes. Unless you plan on dissecting his head there and then. Which I'd really love to see you trying after Aliana spent so long getting him to his feet."

Tallah's eye twitched so violently that she teared up. It still stung at night.

"All right, all right," she conceded, taking a deep breath, "fair point. I hadn't thought that far ahead. But we're still going tonight, not tomorrow."

"We've got plans for tonight. He'll keep, my plans won't. Now that you got your arse off the chair, we should hurry up."

"We have plans? I don't have plans. What plans?"

"The last time we were in town, I made us some reservations at Mistress Fugue's. It's normally booked weeks in advance. I will not miss that reservation," Sil replied, very carefully avoiding eye contact.

It might have been a trick of the light, but had she blushed?

Tallah's mouth hung open for a moment.

"Isn't that a pastry place? In the Agora? Next to the . . . uh . . . that other stupid place you like?"

"It is."

"But we really didn't know when, or if, we would be coming back at all."

"We did not."

"And you still made reservations?"

Sil smiled wistfully. "I was hoping we'd manage somehow. And now we're here. And we're going. Anything else can and will wait."

Tallah rubbed the bridge of her nose underneath her glasses.

"Take Mertle. You owe her. I can get the boy on my own."

"No. You're joining me." The terrified look she gave her cut off any other protestation.

'Why is she like this?' Both Christina and Bianca reacted in unison, beating her to the thought.

Would the boy keep? Of course. Aliana was likely busy purging the memory of him from her priestesses and would be in her foulest mood. Waiting for morning rather than facing her at the end of the workday wouldn't be the worst thing in the world.

"Far be it for me to get between your sweet cravings and a pastry," she said with a weary sigh, defeated in battle against the temptations of sugar-rich confections. She would still roll Sil through the snow, just because—

Another knock interrupted their conversation. Had the runner forgotten something?

"Verti? Is something the matter?" Sil asked when she opened it. Tallah looked over her shoulder, still half dressed. It was unusual for Verti herself to come up from the common room without very good cause.

The elendine was dressed in her usual dark work clothes and pristine white apron. However, even with her reddish complexion, she looked flustered.

"Begging your pardon, Your Graces," she said with an undertone of annoyance, "but there is someone asking after you. They are terribly insistent and threatening to stop asking politely."

"Rare to see you get worked up, Verti. Who's the nuisance?" Sil asked with forced levity.

"Rude is who they are," Tallah said as she stormed off to finish getting dressed. "I'll be right down, Verti, and I'll give them a piece of my mind." Probably one of Tianna's father's people come to pester her again to return to Calabran. They came around every once in a while, and sought her out.

Maybe the daughter could get ol' Fyodor back out into the world from wherever he'd holed up, that was what most of them seemed to hope.

'Ill timing,' Christina whispered in her ear. She ignored her. Christina would see ill timings if Tallah stepped on a particularly sharp rock.

Sil stepped aside and let the elendine enter, both bowing respectfully to the other.

"Again, I must apologize. I make it a rule of the house that my guests cannot be bothered. But it is very difficult to get rid of this person. She claims she is an envoy from the Storm Guard, but she is out of uniform and very pushy.

She gave a name, but I couldn't catch it in the noise of the room." She fidgeted with her apron, anger tightly held back. "I respect the Guard, but the way she's acting makes me suspicious. I had one of the girls keeping her busy while I discussed the matter with Your Ladyships. If it's a bother to you, I'll have Tulip and Pert throw her out."

That prickled Tallah's ears. So, not an envoy from the Aieni Holding but much worse.

'Ill omen,' Christina repeated. 'An invitation now would be too far ahead of schedule.'

'We can't be certain this visit is within our plan, Christi,' Bianca countered. 'The Guard does not recruit people while out of uniform and in informal settings. We need to assess what they seek of us.'

Tallah only half listened to the two ghosts as she perfumed herself and powdered her face. Becoming Tianna took a horrifyingly long time, and she usually just half-arsed it if she could get away with it. Now she needed to become the spitting image of the annoying upstart. She should have left with Sil a bell's strike earlier.

"I'll be right down, Verti," she called out. "Can we have a private booth where we can talk? I would be ever so grateful."

She heard the door closing behind the elendine.

"If I miss our reservation, whoever this is gets strangled," Sil grumbled outside the bathroom. "Should we worry?"

"No flaming idea. We'll see. Let them wait for a while before we deign to show up." Tallah was trying to apply red pigment to her lips. She had to start over twice.

Sil paced in and out of the room. "Is that wise?"

"It's what would be expected of me. My father never met immediately with anyone that came calling unless it was the empress herself. A peasant can wait until we're good and ready." She growled at the image in the mirror. "Help me with this before I end up drawing blood. Rhine used to do it for me. I never got the knack."

Music filled the common room. Crystalline voices rose above the raucous noise of the crowd, clear as spring water. Two elendars, on a small stage off in the corner, swayed as they both sang for the crowd, graceful bodies dressed in their traditional Beril garments, long hair adorned with bells and clinking pearls. Another was further back, fingering an elend string instrument and adding his voice when the chorus demanded it.

Verti had arranged for a booth in one of the less-crowded parts of the great room. She had sent one of her daughters to guide them through the throng of adventurers and regular workers. The rooms of the Meadow were expensive, but the food and drink catered to the size of many money pouches.

Tallah's vision flashed red, and a headache burst behind her eyes at first sight of the woman waiting. She missed a step and stumbled but waved Sil back from helping.

The curtain to the booth was drawn aside, and the visitor watched the elend males performing, a mug of ale seemingly forgotten on the edge of the table.

'That is Rumi Belli, Tallah!' Bianca's panic caught her by surprise. 'Do not even think about infusing yourself. Do not draw in illum. Whatever you do, control your temper.'

Who?

The woman was human, ashen-haired and green-eyed, with a slightly pinched face. Couldn't have been older than thirty summers. Looked almost like a young Empress Catharina to Tallah's eyes.

She rose when she caught sight of them approaching. There was, in that simple motion, the impression of a cat unsheathing its claws. She greeted them with a lopsided grin. Her head only reached up to Tallah's chin, but her eyes locked onto hers with a predator's insistence.

"Good evening, Lady Aieni," she said and stuck out her hand. No curtsy. No sign of subservience. She spared no attention for Sil. "I hate to cause a stir, but this would have all been done so much neater if your host had just cooperated with me."

Tallah looked at the outstretched hand. Calluses and white crisscrossing scars marred the exposed sun-kissed skin.

'Take her hand, Tallah. Just take it. Do not insult her.' Bianca's voice had fallen into small, terrified whispers.

"You offer your hand in greeting, know who I am, yet do not present yourself? I thought the Storm Guards of Valen were trained and educated in Aztroa Magnor, by the best teachers of Court. Perhaps I have been misled?"

She stared the woman down, refusing to take the proffered hand. Not all Storm Guards were actually trained in the empire's capital, and most were barely educated at all, but that was the kind of story that would travel all the way into Calabran.

'Tallah . . .' Bianca whined.

Nothing showed in those green eyes except growing amusement. Heartbeats passed in terse silence. Finally, the other pulled her hand away and inclined her head. She never stopped smiling.

"My apologies, Lady Aieni. I forget my manners when among the rabble. My name is Rumi Belli. I am a special liaison from Aztroa Magnor to the Valen garrison of our force." She looked back to Tallah, and something eased in her expression, but that mischievous glint in her eyes only grew brighter. That, more than Bianca's whimpering, set Tallah's teeth on edge.

"May I ask you to sit with me? I only wish to discuss your recent expedition. It is of some interest to us."

Better, but her manner irked her. Tallah had the distinct and unpleasant sensation of being called into a spider's parlor. Worst yet, she had already walked in only to find the exit blocked by the type of polite request that couldn't be ignored.

She sat down opposite the woman, and Sil waited by her side, hands clasped demurely at her front. Belli still hadn't acknowledged her.

"Do you normally call on adventurers while out of uniform, at their place of residence?"

Rumi wore dark blue trousers and a loose tunic over a long-sleeved undershirt, a simple cut, yet excellently tailored. A cloak of similar color hung on a peg by the booth. She sat sideways on the narrow bench and crossed her legs, face turned to the performers.

It took a moment for her to reply. "As a rule, no."

"Then why are you here, Miss Belli?"

Again, a long pause.

"I enjoy seeing elendars performing. They're so rare and precious." She smiled wistfully before turning her attention to them.

What a crock of nonsense. Elendars were a common sight in Aztroa Magnor. If anything, outside of their own homeland of Beril, the empire's capital had the most of them applying their arts. Not that Tianna would know of such things, all the way in Calabran.

"I want to ask you about the maps you sold to Lucian about a tenday or so ago." She put her hands on the table, one over the other, drumming her fingers on the lacquered wood. Her nails clinked on the polished surface in an uneven rhythm.

Sil stiffened.

"You should know," Rumi went on, "that Lucian's assurances of confidentiality go right out the window when it's us who do the asking. Do not hold it against him. I can be very convincing when we seek to learn something." Her smile turned nasty for a moment, then returned to its earnestness. Her nails still lightly tapped on the wood as if trying to dislodge some particle of invisible dirt. It was starting to annoy Tallah.

"Miss Belli, get to your point, if you please. So far, you are wasting time I would rather spend elsewhere." She swept a hand across the tavern's packed interior. "Pedestrian performances put on for sweaty commoners are not my idea of a pleasant evening."

The taps stopped for a moment and gave Tallah the satisfaction of finding a chink in the Rumi Belli character. She could play the game as well as any Aztroa-trained pissant. She leaned back and offered her own most insincere smile. "I sell what I no longer need. I am happy it was of some use to you, if that is the case, but there is nothing else to add aside from what I already handed to that unpleasant little man at the Guild."

"Did you kill the ratmen?" The question came sharp, like a sting from behind the smile. "That is a great subject for debate in our cell. I thought I'd best hear it from the horse's mouth."

"What ratmen?"

'Do not play games with her, Tallah. She can see through games. She can see through you. Just answer her questions so she leaves. Please.'

'Shush, Bianca.' Christina intervened for the first time, annoyed. 'Tallah knows her business. You are distracting her.'

She'd need to talk to Bianca once the entire farce was finished. Backing away from veiled threats and intimidation ran counter to everything a pyromancer stood for, especially when one had Tianna's high-stationed lineage. Bianca, given her circumstances, only knew how to bow and scrape before those who she considered her betters.

Tallah had met and worked alongside mind-skinners before. This one hid it well, but there was no mistaking the eyes of a torturer, nor the way they searched and prodded and dug for that one gap where they could inject their venom. If she inhaled deep enough, she'd gag on the stench of blood.

She almost felt bad for whatever Lucian had been put through on their behalf.

"The ones you mentioned in your document, where your maps end. You mention wiping out an entire nest of the creatures. Don't misunderstand, it is a laudable feat in itself, but I would like your confirmation."

"I only purged some vermin. The tunnels are lousy with them." She smiled. Rumi smiled. Silence stretched out between them.

"You also mentioned two victims found there, an aelir'rei and a human male. Both dead of their wounds."

Tallah closed her eyes and pretended to find the memory repulsive. "I remember. They were a big reason of why we decided to end our exploration. Terrible sight."

"Where is the man's body, Lady Aieni? We found the aelir, but not the human."

They went searching the caves. Why? She remembered Sil's words from Lucian, of the interest the Guard had in the old shaman, but even so . . .

"I assume it rots where it lays. How would I know?" She shrugged without much conviction. "Perhaps some other creature dragged it off to crush its bones for the marrow."

That sounded like a poor answer even to her ears.

"Mistress?" Sil spoke up for the first time, and four eyes turned to her.

"Something to add, Silestra?"

Sil smiled apologetically and did not meet either of their gazes.

"We did not kill all the ratmen, if you remember," she went on. "We retreated when your first gambit did not . . . well . . . work out. We aimed to save the man in there but failed." She worked very hard at seeming embarrassed for divulging what her mistress had not. "We ran from the shaman and the other beasts aiding it until you collapsed a side tunnel on it. We assumed it dead. There was blood and . . ." Her voice trailed off, her cheeks turning bright red for the indiscretion.

Rumi's interest devoured every word, and she gave Tallah a side-glance.

"Thank you, lady healer. That does put some things in proper light." She turned to Tallah and tapped the side of her nose conspiratorially. "That shaman is very dead, if you'd care to know, but not crushed under a rock. You owe Lucian an apology for deceit."

That was poor bait and did not deserve consideration beyond an offended glare.

Rumi turned back to the two elendars, face slightly pensive, finger tapping on her chin. They played a slow, haunting melody and sang in their old, odd language. She watched for a while, distracted away from the conversation.

Tallah glanced up at Sil, but the healer knew her part too well to look back. She kept the blush on and her eyes staring right down at her boots. Quick thinking had taken the edge off the conversation when she had floundered. The Storm Guard did not police the tunnels, given up as a lost cause for decades. Them going down there themselves had caught her off guard.

"You should not go alone into the tunnels again," Rumi said after a while, voice low. "We've had many reports of people going missing in the Ruffle. Mostly common folk, but there have been some adventurers of repute disappearing. You were in great danger, Lady Aieni, and you had no idea." Mischief glinted in her eyes when she turned back to Tallah. "It would be a shame for a pyromancer as promising as yourself to end up someone's plaything in the dark."

She downed her drink, now likely gone stale, and placed a coin next to the empty mug.

"In due honesty, I came to meet and warn you. Some of my superiors were interested in you for a time, and now I am too. It would be such a shame if something were to happen to you now, Lady Aieni. You are quite the promising pyromancer, if I'm any judge."

"I doubt I will be heading into those horrid places again anytime soon," Tallah said, almost eager to move away from the subject. "Winter is here, and my curiosity is sated. I find cartography boring and exhausting, thus I plan on devoting myself to other pursuits."

Rumi kept bloody smiling. The horrid gash of her wide mouth seemed plastered to her face, and only a chisel and hammer were likely to budge it.

"I haven't delivered my warning yet." She leaned forward, over the table, and spoke in a whisper. "I'm convinced that you realize why asking after certain people can be . . . unwise. Some of my superiors certainly think so. If you insist on knowing more, we can have a private chat, you and I. Though I can't promise the setting would be quite as pedestrian as this one."

She took out a pair of gloves from an inside pocket of her cloak and slid the left one on. It was armored across the knuckles, and blood spatter marred the fur lining. Tallah was certain she had been allowed to see, as clear a warning as any of the evening.

The nerve! Fire ignited in the pit of her stomach and clawed up into her chest, pain and all. She fought to restrain herself from grabbing the woman and slamming her face into the table. Tears welled up in her eyes from the shock of the sudden infusion.

'No, Tallah. She is Egia. She can see the weave. We are almost rid of her.'

That got a grip on her growing rage, enough that she reeled herself in with a sharp breath. Her eye twitched. By Rumi's expression, she had completely misunderstood the effect of her words.

A large man moved through the crowd, parting it as a dray hound would scatter a herd of goats. He towered over most of the people there and was wider of shoulder than the largest of Verti's hired muscles.

Tallah knew him, as did most others in the room. Barlo. The Miscreant. Part of Prince Falor's own inner circle and a bruiser like few others in the empire. Mage killer. He was also dressed as a civilian, but people moved out of his way regardless as he came up to their booth. Sil drew back from him when he filled the entrance.

"We done here, speck?" he asked Rumi. So, he was her insurance in case the conversation turned violent. Tallah was certain he was heavily armed, even if she couldn't spot any weapon on his excessively broad person.

Rumi donned her cloak and fastened it, then stuck out her naked hand to Tallah.

"It's been a pleasure meeting you, Lady Aieni. I do hope I haven't made too poor of a first impression."

This time Tallah did clasp her hand. She still fought to push the fury down. The handshake was firm but just as frigid as the woman's eyes.

Tallah mirrored the other's grin and spoke through nearly clenched teeth, "First impressions can always be mended, Miss Belli. Thank you for your concern, and for your warning." She squeezed the hand tighter. "I take them both to heart."

Rumi had to wrench her fingers away, the grin now strained on her face.

"What was that about?" Sil asked as the two Storm Guards moved out into the cold. She sat on the newly freed space and gestured for a coffee to one of the servers.

Tallah sighed and collapsed back on her cushioned seat. Her hand trembled as she shook off the cold feeling.

"Bianca says that was an Egia, but I doubt she's one of your school's lot. It's a good thing I'm as messed up as I am right now and can't infuse myself properly. She wanted to see if I could have done what we wrote I did."

"But why?"

"Because they found Anna's sanctum and can't be certain if we were involved. We left a bloody good trail to follow in there. Why they care, I couldn't say." She shrugged and gave a long sigh. "Quick thinking on your part. Saved my blunder."

Sil cursed under her breath. "There weren't any queries related to your friend. I checked. I spent all thaw making sure we weren't getting in the Guild's way on this."

Tallah took Sil's coffee as the serving girl put it down.

"I don't know. For now, you get your wish. We're going to be eating sugary confections until we're both sick, and then go frighten some shopkeepers."

"Aren't you in the least worried? That was the closest we've been to the Guard since . . . you know, the whole hearth incident."

'Oh, look, Bianca, Adana is as witless as you in such matters. I hope you are very proud of her.' Christina's mockery got a smile out of Tallah. Bianca sulked in silence in the back of her mind, emanating a feeling of intense relief now that the mind-skinner was gone.

Christina's insult was dulled by the reality of the fact. Sil and Bianca were both of common stock originally and hadn't been brought up to recognize the usual games and veiled threats of the gentry. Tallah had grown up among false smiles and sharpened tongues.

Tianna, had she survived the storm, would have inherited a veritable armada of trade ships and enough money to buy half of Valen wholesale. Without Prince Falor himself calling for her head, she was untouchable.

She imitated Rumi Belli's infuriating smile and spoke with the same sticky-sweet affectation that the mind-skinner used.

"Why would I be worried, Miss Silestra? I'm an innocent pyromancer that has been warned away from danger, out of pure, sweet kindness. Why would that disrupt my life in the least?"

She knocked back the coffee and grimaced at the sweetness. Verti's girls knew Sil's sweet tooth and prepared her drinks accordingly. This had been more sugar than coffee.

"What did you think about for that blush? That was a work of art."

"For me to know, and for you to mind your own business."

CHAPTER TEN

If I Were You

I'm sorry. I don't remember you."

Tallah had half expected some inane, screamed battle cry out of the boy and was surprised by Vergil's actual calm, measured voice. Even if it was still weak, it held a certain resonance that she found pleasing.

He was barefoot and wore only a pair of green trousers embroidered with the same white leaf pattern that was common in the hospital. He had filled out somewhat, though he remained pale and gangly, his cheeks drawn in and hollow. He had brown eyes and a mess of shaggy, mousy gray hair that had grown down over his eyes. All in all, a stark contrast to the half-dead wretch she'd spared in the caves, with promise left over.

Sil inspected him a lot more carefully, relentless and impervious to his obvious discomfort. She looked at his sunken cheeks, the different shades of color in his hair, how his arms shook, and more. She'd been peppering both him and Aliana with questions about his recovery for the better part of a bell's strike. After how much she'd chewed her ears off back in the caves, now she was mothering the sod.

"We're going to need to work on you," she finally said. "I am very impressed with your work, Aliana. He's unrecognizable." She stopped behind the boy, squinted, and smiled. "I see you got rid of that tattoo he had. Good."

Aliana gave Tallah a look of pure, obnoxious triumph.

"You could stand to learn some of her manners. It would do you a world of good if you showed proper gratitude to those of us putting up with you."

Tallah rolled her eyes and waved away the notion. Aliana would see gratitude from her on the same day she saw the back of her own head. Maybe even the day after that.

"They brought you in, Vergil." Aliana was at her most motherly now, still playing the concerned caregiver. They all sat in her office. Vergil tired easily, so two other priestesses had helped him come up from the care rooms.

"I—I think I know that. I remember two women in the cave, but it's all hazy. I can't remember much . . ."

He teared up and sniffled as a shadow passed across his face. They waited for him to calm down.

His voice cracked when he tried to speak again. "Is it normal that I feel numb?" he asked without looking at any of them in particular. "I think I should be feeling . . . I don't know. Different. Sad? But there's nothing. Are you sure my friends haven't revived at the Guild's chapel?"

He kept his gaze downcast, only rarely stealing glances at them. Tallah couldn't help but notice how he kept squeezing his hands together.

"Isadora is not the most reliable Goddess," Tallah said. "And it's probably for the best that your friends have passed on. Revivals aren't . . . safe." Of course the Guild had promised him what they usually did, that it was possible for fallen adventurers to be revived by the patron Goddess if their valor and morals were high. Isadora favored the aelir on Nen and couldn't give a rat's arse for humans.

She turned to Aliana. "You did great work. I wasn't expecting him to be coherent." The compliment was given begrudgingly, but it was honest.

"It's why you brought him to me. I don't do less than *great work*." She had her hand protectively on Vergil's arm. The message was clear: Pay up or he's not going anywhere.

Sil produced a small ornate box out of her satchel. It was just a hand's width across, gold trimmings on ebony with a mirror shine. When she opened the lid, the room flooded with emerald light. It drowned out all other colors and shaded all shadowy nooks in deep black. A sliver of irregular green crystal lay at the bottom of the box, nestled in its padded interior.

"I should've known you wouldn't pay in anything I can actually use." Aliana shielded her eyes from the glow and reached out for the box. "What is it?"

Tallah grinned. "That is one of the few slivers left of Salmek's illum hearth after it detonated. It's dead, so you needn't worry about hearth's flame or any other ill effect. We had it appraised in Drack at almost a hundred thousand Valen griffons. It should cover him, me, my debts, and your discretion all at once. I'm pretty sure it also covers whatever fancy drinks I ever nicked off you."

"Insanely valuable for a piece of glowing crystal. Have you gone daft?"

Tallah savored the look of surprise on Aliana's creased face. She so rarely got to see the old beast gaping.

"Perfectly sane, thank you so very much." She tapped the crystal lightly. "You can make a shard pair out of this. Either get your Goddess to break it in two for you or find a resonant for it. Regardless, I think it's worth giving you a gift that the empire would burn a city for."

Aliana reached over for the box and closed its lid smoothly.

"Where do you even go to get something like this?"

Tallah raised a finger to her lips and winked at the priestess.

"You got paid, and our debts got squared several times over. I'm not telling you more until I owe you more."

"If you ever shush me again, Tallah, I'll see you banned from this place for the rest of your unnatural days." Aliana peeked under the lid of the box again like a curious child; it turned her dark eyes bright green.

Her threat was genuine but not one she hadn't made before. If Tallah had a griffon for every time the two of them butted heads, she'd have paid that and kept the shard.

"You'll get over it, I'm sure. We'll be moving on come thaw, and it may be a while until we circle back again. The heart grows fonder in absence, or something of the sort."

Aliana looked over to Sil, who confirmed this with a silent nod.

"You take care of yourself, Adana, since you insist on letting this lunatic lead you astray."

"I'll miss you too, Aliana." Tallah smiled and wanted to rise from her chair. "Get us a couple of girls to help dress the boy and we'll be on our way."

"Sit your arse back down, girl. We're not done yet." It was Aliana's turn to point the sorceress down with a self-satisfied dramatic gesture. "My girls had their memories of Vergil purged last night, as per our standing agreement. I will do the same for myself once you're gone, be assured of that."

"We don't need confirmation, Aliana," Sil said. "Your word is good enough. It has always been."

Even Tallah nodded.

"Don't be stupid. Of course you trust me. Mine's the only word worth anything in this city." She shook her head and looked over to the boy. "No, this concerns Vergil. We had trouble purging his trauma. Something fought us every step of the way. If we picked clean a cluster of memory, it got restored before we finished working on the next. I admit we got creative with blocks rather than use the more stable wipes."

"Trauma?" Vergil tried to interrupt but was pointedly ignored.

"There's metal in the boy's head. And it's a living sort. Whatever we tried to do, it undid. I've never seen anything like it, metal that thinks. It's built like a kind of mesh in his head and gave one of my girls an ugly shock when she tried to reach into it. She's still being cared for."

"I told you not to mess with whatever you found out of place," Tallah said.

Aliana shook her head. "It wasn't the magical block, sorceress. We found that, and the girls kept clear of it. That's a completely different nastiness, alien to him. It *watched* us. What I speak of is part of him."

"Are you talking about my network implant?" Vergil asked.

All six eyes turned on him.

"Your what?" Sil reacted first, her interest suddenly piqued.

Tallah could see her eyes brighten.

The idea of a living entity in the boy's head, something artificial, perhaps, was now squarely in Sil's area of interest. She had talked about a very vague idea of something like that from his memories, but it was so basic that it meant nothing to either of them.

Vergil pressed a bony finger to his temple, tracing a line to the back of his head. "I have a microchip implanted here. It's a . . . uh, call it a thing that does complex thinking for me."

Tallah shushed him. This was exactly what she wanted out of him, but this wasn't the place. Rather, she worried about other things from what Aliana said.

"Should we worry about the work you did on him? How likely is he to go loopy again?"

The priestess shrugged. "Can't say. We've built blocks and reroutes for stressful stimuli, but I can't be completely sure of that kind of work. You know too well how fickle these fixes are and how memories bleed. I can't say what could trigger him, but I do advise you keep him on a tight, short leash. The less you stress the boy, the better."

She drummed her fingers on the lid of the ebony box.

"I would worry about that helmet," she mused. "I'm not convinced that enchantment is without risk. I would rid myself of the thing if I were you."

With her warnings delivered, she called two other women in and had Vergil changed and discharged from her care. Mother Aliana had been dismissed in favor of the efficient priestess. She'd been paid, and Vergil ceased to exist for her. Outside her door, those seeking her aid were legion.

Vergil had no idea what had just happened, or, for that matter, what was happening still. The two women picking him up seemed to regard him as a particularly interesting piece of decor they were taking home.

He would have wanted to ask more about his friends, about what was to happen to him, or why they had even paid for his recovery. He couldn't have heard right how much they paid for him. It was ludicrous that they'd hand over more money than most adventurers saw in a lifetime.

He got jostled about, undressed, redressed in new clothes, and sent out in the freezing cold.

It was all happening to someone else, and he was just along to watch the show.

Nothing to do but meekly follow along, head tucked between his shoulders in the thick fur lining of his new cloak. There was nowhere else to go, nothing else to do but—

The cold shocked him back into a semblance of reality, and the falling snow stopped him dead down the steps of the hospital. He knew snow existed somewhere. It had featured in some of his experiences, but it was a distant concept that he had never connected to.

Valen was a very different place through the lens of snowfall. Flakes danced in the air and scattered with the wind. They died on his skin and melted into sharp chills that got him shivering.

It finally, somehow slotted into place the fact that he was very far from home, and he wasn't going back. Home was a distant dream now faded in the gray light, and he was lost in the static of the blizzard. His head felt light and full of steel wool.

His new companions noticed they were walking alone and stopped to look back. Vergil tried to catch up, but the wild patterns of falling snow kept snatching up his attention.

"If I understood you correctly," the scary one said to the other, "his life before was in a large metal box floating in nothing."

"He's never seen weather at all," the aelir'rei confirmed.

"Helmet Boy," the scary one called to him, seeming to lose patience. "It won't stop for the next few days at least. You can watch it all you want when we get somewhere warm. Come on while the storm only looms."

That snapped him back to himself, and he hurried after them, catching up with huffing, steaming breath.

"Your name is Tallah. And you are Adana. Is that right?" he asked.

It didn't seem right to think of them only in terms of how much they unnerved him. They had, after all, rescued him. The scary woman's eyes widened, and she looked around suddenly, as if worried someone would overhear.

"I'm Sil, actually," the tall aelir'rei said. "Adana is my Hepius calling. And she's Tianna. If you'd like to keep your head, I suggest you don't mention the other name again."

The threat had been made with such ease and honesty that his cheeks burned. A chill wiggled underneath his clothes and made him shiver.

"Um . . . I—" He floundered for words. "Miss Sil, I—"

How can I tell her about her sister dying?

It had been on his mind ever since Miss Aliana mentioned the name Adana. He couldn't find his words as cold tears ran down his cheeks.

"I think I . . . knew your sister, Miss Sil. I'm sorry. The ratmen. They, uh . . ."

Sil shrugged, and Vergil's mouth dropped open.

"I don't have a sister. Adana is a calling, not a family. Whoever you knew, they weren't related to me more than any other sister of the trade. If I cried for each of us meeting a horrible end, I'd never stop grieving."

"But—"

"Close your mouth or you'll get a sore throat," she said and reached to tighten his cloak around his shoulders.

"This is all very touching, but it's bloody cold. Start walking or I leave you both here." Tianna had already started walking away, towards the slope that led into the Lower City.

"I'll take him back on a carriage," Sil said, putting her arm under his.

Vergil shied away from her like her touch was poisonous, but she would have none of it. She held on tight to his arm and led him towards one of the stations, its outline visible only by how packed down the snow was by countless feet. Tianna followed, a look of intense unhappiness on her face.

"I'm coming along too," she said, and stood by to wait for the carriage.

"Oh, this should be good. You've finally decided to join us in the modern world?" Sil mocked her friend.

They were completely alone under the falling snow. Vergil had enjoyed the early mornings of Valen while he'd been alone. It was a wonderful time when the city was almost quiet, with the day shift not yet awake, and the night one still at work.

Now the city frightened him. Loneliness waited for him, now that Sidora, Davan, and Merk were gone. Their absence left a hole in him that he had no idea how to deal with.

"I could be at the Meadow in less time than it takes you to freeze out here," Tianna argued, unhappy for some reason. "Bianca would be all too happy to get me away from your stupid grin."

"But Tianna can't do force manipulation," Sil said in a low, sweet voice. "Even a promising pyromancer can't fly. One of our watching friends catching a glimpse of you flying around would be quite an unfortunate turn for us." Her evil grin widened. "So, you're stuck walking or catching a ride with us."

Tianna scowled.

"What's wrong with catching a transit carriage? They're free," Vergil asked. He'd ridden in them before while exploring the city. They reminded him of the monorail trams that ran across some portions of the *Gloria*.

"Tianna gets sick on them. Violently."

"Oh. I'm sorry. We can walk."

"No. Me and Tianna can walk. You'd likely expire on the stairs, given your condition. She's going to be a big girl and suffer for a bell strike."

It was a horribly uncomfortable, cramped ride for both Tianna and Vergil. The carriages were heated, after a fashion, but were also overcrowded, as no one relished the idea of waiting for the next one in the freezing cold. A thick, cloying smell of animal hide and perspiration clogged the air in the tightly packed space.

Tianna looked like she was trying very hard to keep her breakfast down.

Vergil felt sick with himself. Having the aelir'rei pressed against him in the crowd, her arm around his waist to steady him, was like a red-hot band of metal coiled around his naked body. It brought up a memory of Sidora, of the tent and . . .

"Breathe slower," Sil whispered. "Deep breath. Slow."

Had she noticed? He tried to pull away, but there was nowhere to go. She pulled him closer to herself.

"Panic is manageable. You are safe. Close your eyes if you need to, but if you don't slow your breathing, you are going to faint. We will not be gentle if we need to carry you."

She said everything in a calm, quiet monotone, for his ears only. Vergil squeezed his eyes shut and forced himself to slow down.

"Good, like that," she said encouragingly.

It wasn't working. All the bodies pressing into him forced his mind back to the cave, back into the cage. He trembled violently in spite of the healer's quiet coaching.

Someone pressed into him. His stomach dropped. The carriage had stopped on the elevator platform that took it into the Lower City.

"Open your eyes," that someone whispered right in front of him.

He obeyed without thinking and found himself staring down into Tianna's midnight blue eyes. They were almost forehead to forehead and closer than he felt comfortable. Her stare ran him through and chased away the firelight from his imagination. Her pressure overwhelmed any semblance of thought in his head, leaving him an insect pinned to the wall.

"Stay on your own feet. I am not carrying you," she said, pushing the words out through gritted teeth. Her voice was as sharp as razor wire, the threat almost palpable.

He managed a weak nod as she kept her eyes on his. Sil's tight hold relaxed as she chuckled gently.

Vergil had heard about the Meadow. Everyone knew about the place, but very few adventurers ever reached the kind of wealth and status to afford a room there, let alone an apartment sized for an entire extended royal family. Four rooms, two of which were bedrooms with richly sculpted king-sized beds dressed in soft furs and silk sheets, were connected by a smaller, central hub into which the main door opened.

The largest room it connected to was a sitting room with a fireplace dominating one wall. Along the walls there were bookcases and wardrobes, all with crystal glass doors. Two long tables were piled high and orderly with books, scrolls, quills, and a glass apparatus.

He was led slack-jawed through the corridor and helped by Sil out of the heavy coat he'd been gifted. There was even a cart of food waiting in the central hall, the aromas making his mouth water and his stomach rumble. Both Sil and Tianna ignored it.

Tianna took him by the arm and dragged him past the food and into the study. For someone as dainty as she seemed, the girl was immensely stronger than him.

Sil disappeared into one of the bedrooms.

"Stay there," Tianna instructed, pointing to a spot in the middle of the room.

She walked to one of the tables piled highest with scrolls and thick, ancient-looking tomes. She undid the clasps of her thick dress, letting it slide down her body to reveal a tight, body-hugging white blouse and leggings underneath. Vergil's face and ears burned, and he became acutely interested in the toes of his boots. If Tianna cared at all, she didn't show it.

"Hold this."

Vergil found himself cupping with both hands a dark gold chalice studded with dull gems around its circumference. It was just slightly larger than a pitcher of ale at the Boar.

"What's this for?" he asked, turning the thing in his hands.

Sil returned after some time. She looked Tianna over and sighed when she noticed the dress strewn about the floor and the sorceress strutting about in her underclothes.

"Really, clean up after yourself. There's a hamper for wet clothes, you know."

Tianna waved her away impatiently and thrust a staff tipped with a blue jewel into her arms.

"Spare me the lecture. I want to see his doppel."

There was a quick exchange of glares between the two, until finally, Sil sighed, shook her head despondently, and took the staff.

Holding its blue gem against her chest, she concentrated for a moment and then pointed the crystal at him. A shining, gossamer-thin golden thread appeared between her chest and his, like the first strand of a spiderweb connecting two pillars. He felt weird for a moment, but it was an oddly familiar experience.

The chalice in his hands began filling, from the bottom up, with a black oil-like liquid. It had a multicolored sheen on top that reflected lamplight as a distorted rainbow. It overflowed the chalice and covered his hands, thick as tar and cold as ice. He tried to drop the goblet but found his fingers refusing to unclench.

He looked in panic to the two women who stood abreast a few steps away from him, watching as the tar formed into a long shadow of him, a pool in the center of the room. As liquid flowed, strength sapped out of him. The liquid shadow coalesced and rose high, turning into a naked copy of him.

"What the hell?" he stammered.

Drawing breath was an effort of will. So was speaking. Only his eyes still obeyed as they should, and he hated what he saw. The black body turned towards him with a predatory grace. It looked like a mirror image, if the mirror had been warped by heat. Its posture was slightly hunched, with the impression of a coiled spring ready to snap, while its face had a savage ferocity that scared him down to the marrow of his bones. Featureless voids occupied the spaces where its mouth and eyes should have been.

"What the hell is this?" His voice almost cracked, sounding high and shrill even to his own ears. The thing in front of him mimicked his outburst but added outrageous body language.

"We call it a doppelgänger, an avatar of the state of your soul right now," Tianna answered.

Sil called the creature over with a gesture of her hand.

"How is that my soul? Why does it look like that? Why are you taking it out?" His voice was still shrill. He had started breathing shallow and fast, pain flaring up in his chest.

"A *representation* of your soul, not your actual soul," Sil answered calmly. "That bit is a lot harder to take out without killing you."

The doppelgänger mimicked every word Vergil said, and it flayed its arms about in a simulated panic.

"Stop that and calm down. Don't be a child. We're not hurting you." Tianna's words cracked like a whip.

Sil walked around the cowed, twitching creature, her face twisted into an unpleasant expression. "You have been starved for a long time," she said and scrunched up her nose. "Hunger is a powerful transformational state for a person, of any species. While you've been in that state, you have been tempted by your captors and have broken under that temptation, in some way I'd rather not know about."

She waved a hand at the doppel. "This is the transformation your inner self was undergoing when we found you. Had Aliana and her priestesses not cared for you, this is what you would have eventually become. This, or dead."

"Teach later. Pay attention now," Tianna intervened. "Come and look at this."

She pointed at the thing's chest, above where its heart would be. Under the shiny, oily surface mimicking skin, a deep red cancerous growth pulsed steadily. Sil walked around to it. Red tendrils extended like veins, pulsing in a steady rhythm.

"It looks like an infection," Sil said. She sketched and wrote in a leather-bound booklet. "Does it feel familiar?"

"I've never seen anything like it. I assume it's divine by the way it's built, but I have no idea which one of the maggots could have made it. Seems too subtle to be Ort or Isadora. Definitely not Anatol."

Tianna prodded the heart—at least, that's what it looked like to Vergil—with a gloved finger. A spark of electricity danced on her finger as she did.

Vergil screamed, and the growth on his copy pulsed in agitation, more tendrils growing out of it and stabbing at its host.

"Hostile little bugger," the sorceress noted while Vergil calmed down, breathing hard.

"You prodded it." Sil shrugged. "I'd be hostile too if you electrocuted me."

"Please don't do that again. It hurt." Vergil felt faint. He wasn't sure he would still be standing if he weren't quite literally rooted to the spot.

"I don't have equipment here to excise it without killing him, I think." The sorceress looked up at Sil, who shook her head. "It's latched on tight and reacts this hard, even on the doppel. I need it separated to study it properly. I could just capture it whole . . ."

"You can't kill him. Aside from the fact that it would be daft to do it now, after we dragged him here and paid a small fortune for him, you'd announce yourself to the entire Guard. They're jittery enough already." Sil gave her a long look with a raised eyebrow. "Remember the chaos you caused when you took Bianca in Aztroa? With an Egia sniffing about, you'd just as well go up to the lord commander and kick him in the shin."

Tianna cursed and walked away.

"Sorry." Sil shrugged and, with a gesture of her hand, released Vergil from whatever curse was holding him.

The copy shivered in the air as if struck by a heat haze and then puffed into dark smoke. The sorceress cracked open a window.

Vergil collapsed to the floor, the goblet rolling away from him. His teeth chattered. He wasn't so much cold as intensely terrified of his two saviors, of how casually they had discussed possibly executing him, of the disappointment in the sorceress's voice and the pain they had so casually inflicted on him. He couldn't parse which horrified him more.

"I need to have him along until we get back to Solstice." Tianna poured herself a glass of some yellow liquor from a carafe, looking out the window morosely. "I have things in my sanctum that will help me study it without killing him."

"I'm not babysitting," Sil was quick to reply, hanging up and covering her staff. She sat at one of the worktables, lighting a brazier.

"No, we'll put the helmet back on him, and we'll take turns in keeping the effect going. At least we'll have a front line like that—if the ghost plays nice."

Vergil tried to stammer something, but neither woman paid him any attention. Whatever they had done to him, he could barely move, his body turned leaden. He couldn't take his eyes off them, though, afraid one of them would hurt him again.

Sil was studying a bi-horned helmet on her desk. It had a penis drawn on one side in bright red paint.

"I really wish I hadn't used such good pigment for this. Now it'll draw attention," she mumbled, scratching at the paint. It stubbornly refused to flake off.

"Least of my worries." Tianna set her empty glass on her table and walked towards the door, stepping over Vergil's splayed form. "I'll have a long bath, and then we'll see how we plan our next moves. He's all yours, healer."

She talked to herself. Vergil couldn't catch the words, but she was having a conversation on her way out of the room.

It took some time before Sil remembered he was still there. She scribbled in her notebook and nibbled on the end of her pencil, completely oblivious to him struggling to crawl away.

Where to, exactly? He had no idea. But he'd seen this sort of people before, on the *Gloria,* in every core crew member who looked at him like he was less than human.

The helmet clattered at his feet, bounced twice, and stopped against his leg.

"The weakness will wear off on its own. Don't force yourself." Sil was looking at him from her table, her chin resting in her palm. "Congratulations, Vergil. You now own a cursed artifact. Don't poke an eye out with it, all right?"

He stared at the ugly thing resting against his trouser leg. It was little more than a gray metal dome with two horns fastened on top of it. A T-shaped visor had been roughly cut in one side of it, just enough for whoever used the helmet to see out of.

Malice radiated off it. For some reason he couldn't explain, he wanted to pick up the ridiculous thing and settle it on his lap.

"Who are you two?" Terror strangled the words into a squeaking mess. At least he had gathered enough of himself to look up at the healer.

Her lips quirked into a mirthless little smile, and he felt like a child ready to wet himself.

"Two very unpleasant and dangerous people. And you are an excessively unlucky one," she responded candidly.

A pregnant pause stretched out between them. She moved away from the table, and he managed to get himself up in a sitting position. Breathing came easier, and he was already feeling tingles in his hands and feet, sensation returning slowly and painfully.

To his surprise, Sil came and sat next to him, an arm's length away. She sighed heavily.

"In the interest of honesty, I need to confess that I have touched your mind, Vergil. You were in no state to consent, so I apologize now for the invasion." She shrugged, not waiting for an answer from him. "We weren't intent on saving you. I was dead set against it, actually." She had no remorse to show over this. Her voice said as much. "What I saw in your head, about the . . . what was it called? The *Gloria*? Yes, that. It interested Tallah a great deal. It's why you're here now and why we paid for your treatment. This is not a blessing in disguise."

Vergil didn't know how to respond to any of this, and it didn't look as if Sil expected him to have an opinion. She went on.

"I think I have an idea of what you must be thinking now. We frighten you. This is not what you may have hoped for when waking here. You expected adventure. And maybe some glory? Instead, there was blood and death, and you fell into the care of two bastards."

She sidled closer and inclined her head towards him. She kept her eyes staring forward as she talked, her voice lowered to little more than a whisper.

"I'm impressed you're taking it as well as you are. Understand, however, that there are no heroes here. There is no righteous cause to follow, no glory to earn, no dragon to slay." She stopped and thought for a moment, her smile turning just a fraction. "Well, there are dragons. But slaying one is a faer tale at best."

"What do you want to do with me?" Vergil asked. He darted a look after Tianna, fear of her returning clawing inside him. "Is she going to kill me?"

Sil shook her head. "I doubt it. She likes to talk big but doesn't kill on a whim. You are interesting to us. When that interest runs out, we'll cut you loose if we're certain you won't be an issue. Will you be an issue, Vergil?"

Her eyes now bore into his, and she smiled so like Sidora that it twisted the words out of him. "No. I swear on my life that I won't be."

"You have no idea what you're saying. It's adorable. If I were you, I'd weigh my words more before spilling them out." She shrugged, pushed herself to her feet, and offered him a hand. "Stand. You should be able to by now."

He gingerly took her help and rose to his feet, his other hand holding the helmet tight. The soles of his feet stung as if he stepped on pins, but he stood unassisted and shuffled about.

"Go and eat something. Don't be shy about it, but pace yourself. Sap healed you, but it did not nourish you. Eat slowly or you'll cramp up, and you're in no fit state for any of my medicine to help."

As he turned towards the cart of food, she went on, her voice quiet enough that he strained to hear.

"I will remember what you just swore to me. Tallah's fire is much kinder than what my talents can do. You'll remember that, I hope."

She dismissed him with a gesture, not expecting an answer from him as she sat at her desk and wrote in a thick leather-bound book.

He ate as instructed, small nibbles of food such as he'd never tasted before, making a determined effort not to gorge himself. For some reason, he had no taste for meat. The smell of it, when he uncovered the pot, made him gag. Instead, he filled a plate with vegetables, cheese, bread, and an odd assortment of spreads, and sat in a chair in the common room, creeping about to not disturb the aelir healer.

"You don't need to carry that around, you know."

He jumped at the words and choked. He hadn't noticed her move from the desk.

Sil offered him a pitcher of water. "Easy, boy, I don't bite. Put that down."

It took him a moment, once he forced down the lump in his throat, to realize that he was holding the horned helmet on his lap. Reluctantly, he set it beside his chair.

She held a notebook in one hand and her gnawed-on pencil in the other. "Eat. I'll ask some questions. Answer as you can."

"What about?" he asked, cringing back. Their curiosity, he feared, was a mercurial, terrible thing. It had saved his life, true, but who knew how long that goodwill would last.

"Relax. Let's talk for a bit about that place in your head. The *Gloria Nostra*, yes? Tell me about that thing thinking for you."

CHAPTER ELEVEN

Head Names the Price

They followed.

Small slips, here and there. A glance away too quick. A stumble over someone in the crowd. A rattle of armor when she took to deserted narrow side streets or through snow-covered construction sites.

They follow, but I'm being led to believe that they're incompetent. Cheeky bastards.

There was someone she couldn't see who was doing the actual following. She was certain of it when she passed through the Guild's large ornate gates. The ones drawing her attention were far observers, too distant to listen in on conversations, pointless for anything more than annoying her.

As she headed to the postings, shouldering through the wet throng of snow-laden bodies, she looked behind as if reacting to a noise from the crowd. Nobody followed, not even the minders from earlier.

Am I being paranoid? She'd been cooped up inside with Tallah for too long. It was about time she started imagining things.

"You're a pleasant surprise, Miss Silestra."

She startled and turned around with a yelp. Lucian was by her side, offering a smile that managed to be both apologizing and ingratiating. The man must have walked out of a wall.

"My apologies if I startled you."

There was just the barest outline of a fading yellow bruise over his right cheek. Hair-thin lines of scars showed on his lips, almost invisible on his pale, parchment skin.

"Good morning, Master Lucian. You did. I hadn't seen you approaching."

His smile broadened. If he held any grudge for whatever the Guard had done to him, he didn't yet show it.

"Given the crowd we face, one must learn to move unseen. What can I thank for the pleasure of your presence here today?"

Sil started forward again, and Lucian fell in step by her side, hands clasped at his back, almost slithering through the push and shove.

"I wish to have a look at recent postings."

"Is winter boring the mistress?"

Sil smirked and offered a small shrug. "It is. And we'd like to take more active roles with the Guild come thaw. A bit of travel, if you understand."

"Ah, the days of chafing. I remember them well." He drew ahead by a step and opened a path for her. "I'm not surprised the mistress would like a change of pace. It's been a remarkably quiet few years here in Valen."

"Quite."

Quiet wasn't how she thought of the time since she and Tallah had begun their work. They'd arrived and set Tianna up in Valen just a mere season after the fire and had been working restlessly since then. Five years, two hunts. First Bianca, for whom they'd had to steal into Aztroa Magnor, a plan that ate up two years of their lives. Then Anna, a frustrating series of false leads and dead ends that had grown more and more aggravating by the day.

It hadn't been quite so quiet.

Another of Empress Catharina's wars would have helped them move about more easily, but the allegiances with Valen, Calabran, and Ria held strong.

The Maggot War droned on in the heavens, so the empire wore its cloak of peace.

"Any particular interests?"

Sil pulled herself out of her own head and stared ahead at bursting billboards. Guild officials were setting new ones up, fighting against the crowd of adventurers to pin new notices up. The clamor had Lucian yelling to be heard over the din.

"As you can see, it's a very lively time for us here. Very exciting. You couldn't have come at a better time."

With the boy taking up so much of their time for the past few days—infuriatingly so—she had forgotten the date. This outing was more so she wouldn't strangle the frustrating wretch.

"Ah," she muttered to herself. Then, to Lucian, she said, "New postings came through the gate today?"

"Precisely. Isn't that why you're here?"

No, not really. She and Tallah wanted to start looking for new information on Deidra Aratol and her movement. Guild postings, out of date as they would be over winter, were a good place to start. She had completely forgotten about the mid-season delivery from Aztroa. No wonder the place teemed with people.

Well . . . bugger.

"Excuse me, Master," she said as she pushed forward, drawing a scroll out of her satchel.

For better or worse, if there was someone keeping an eye on her, this wouldn't tell them anything of worth. Just another adventurer come for the fresh missions. Most of them had come hoping for paying work come thaw. The actual commissions wouldn't get handed out for at least a few more weeks, but it was worth being among the first to apply.

Someone pushed her, and she shoved back, fighting her way to the front of the lines. One look at her wooden staff sent most adventurers to the side, shoving a clear path for her.

It didn't pay to upset a healer, not when you might be working with them one day, especially an aelir. Their memory for slights ran decades long.

Lucian followed quietly in her wake, hands tucked inside his vest pockets, as she scribbled down notes. Most of them were nonsense that Tallah would throw out. Others were of interest.

"The mistress seeks to work you hard again, I see."

Old Forge. It came up time and time again. Unrest. Bandits. Monsters sighted. Even a dread chimera, which was sure to bring in experienced adventurers. Forces were being amassed there.

"Every time I believe myself getting a handle on her, you show up and ruin my delusions," Lucian said as she copied down the details of some request that promised bugger all of interest. "I can't see her doing work as plebeian as what you're perusing now."

"She'll likely not even deign to read the details. But my instructions are to bring back whatever gets us traveling. We've seen quite enough of Valen's countryside."

Lucian seemed thoughtful as he watched one of his assistants put up another series of queries.

"I imagine her father's minders are bothering her again. We've had an influx of requests about Her Ladyship. Mind you, these were from before the snows came, so likely out of date."

Sil grinned and leaned into the broker, elbowing him slightly.

"Free information, Lucian? Coming from you, I might get very confusing ideas."

He scratched at the thin stubble on his cheek and twisted his face into an amused grimace. "I dislike highly insistent parties, Miss Silestra. Call it a professional courtesy extended towards your mistress." He smiled, gray eyes twinkling bright in the sprite light. "And, if I can be honest, I'm very much looking forward to the oddities you two might bring back. Your last delivery led to some interesting conversations."

She couldn't help but raise an eyebrow and stare at him. His eyebrows in turn rose as he kept smiling, mirth turning to polite inquisitiveness.

"I'll . . . I'll be sure to let Mistress Tianna know of your interest." She stumbled over the words and hastily turned back to her notes.

"Please do that," he said and turned his eyes back to the new postings. "You might be interested in that one, right up top, by my assistant. Yes, that one."

Glaring down at her from the page was a sharp-featured, deeply lined face painted in color. Ashen-colored hair braided into a narrow strip hanging over one shoulder, eyes the color of summer plums staring from behind round spectacles, high cheekbones, a crooked nose, and thin, cruel lips. Deidra Aratol, wanted dead or alive. Dangerous in the extreme. The list of crimes levied against her filled a scroll as tall as Tallah.

Ice stabbed into Sil's spine, and she felt color draining from her face. She had to gather herself before slowly turning to—

"Miss Silestra," Lucian's voice whispered in her ear, "I counsel caution. Spending one more thaw with us might not be so terrible. Until certain embers cool."

"What do you m—" She turned sharper than she meant towards the voice.

Lucian was gone from her side. He had melted into the flagstones or something to the effect, for she hadn't even felt the crowd shifting to allow him passage. A look back showed nothing but more bodies crowding the entrances, and one of her minders getting an unceremonious elbow to the ribs.

Sighing and worrying at her lower lip, she turned her gaze back to the portrait. Empress Catharina had deemed Deidra a big enough nuisance to formally call for her head.

"Head names the price," she read. Others had noticed, and many whistled in appreciation. Low grumbles made the connection just as quick as she did.

The last head to name a price up on a billboard had been Tallah's.

Sil nearly stumbled over the boy's cot in the hallway. She'd forgotten seeing Verti's men hauling it up the stairs just as she was leaving, at Tallah's behest.

Vergil lay on it, huddled tight against the wall, his sheets a sweat-stained, crumpled mess. He whimpered softly and kicked out a leg like a dog having a bad dream.

Three or four drops of burn-leaf extract a bell's strike after his evening meal would help ease his rest. She'd get some more the next time she went into the Agora. Tallah was taking it with her tea and had nearly depleted their entire stock.

"I can't leave you alone for even a spell, can I?" she asked as she walked in.

Tallah was at her desk, head on the smooth black wood, both hands pressing on her temples. She let out a whimper as the door creaked open.

"You've been trying to channel, haven't you? Do you never learn?"

Red splotches of burst capillaries rimmed the sorceress's eyes when she finally looked up. There was a smudged streak of dried blood on her upper lip, a clot in her nose, and the accompanying stain on her arm. She groaned rather than answer Sil's question.

"Did Verti ask anything about Vergil?"

No answer, just an endless stare to somewhere far beyond the walls. The corner of an eye twitched spasmodically.

"You're an imbecile."

"We've also told her. She refuses to listen." Christina's pitiless tone rose hoarsely from Tallah's throat.

"Give me something," the idiot in question followed up.

Sil set her satchel down at her desk and emptied out the scrolls and odd assortment of engraving supplies she'd picked up at the stores outside the Guild's compound. She'd taken some measure of pleasure from keeping her Guard minders out in the falling snow, stamping and shuffling their feet through the freezing cold. They hadn't even tried to hide.

"Misery suits you. I think I'll leave you like that."

"Sil!"

But she had already lit a brazier and adjusted its flame.

"Yes, yes, I'll have something ready in a bit. Don't wet yourself."

Two measured thimbles of her potion base got poured into a tube and set above the fire. She softly hummed the melody she'd known her entire life, measuring the time for the currant's preparation. She dropped various other ingredients into the tube, following the words to her mother's rhyme.

"Eye of toad, and tongue of worm," she cooed over the bubbling currant as she added in a pinch of dried bloodberry. "With a thumb of goose and an ear of corn."

Nonsense that coaxed a smile out of her. She stirred three times with a thin metal rod, then took the tube off its fire with pliers, opened a window, and plunged it into the snowbank outside. The rhyme counted out the cooling time.

With another pinch of beaster's salt sprinkled in, she handed it to Tallah.

"One gulp. Straight down."

"What's in this?" the sorceress asked after obeying, face twisting into a painful-looking grimace of disgust.

"This and that. You'll feel better in a bit. It'd be best if you slept on it for a couple bells."

Of course, Tallah wasn't listening. She adjusted her spectacles, stumbled to her feet, and moved over to the waiting scrolls.

"Right, then," she breathed out, a sigh of relief in her voice as the lines of pain on her face eased out. "What do we have here?" She read the first scroll on hand, crumpled the paper, and threw it into the hearth. "You were followed?"

"Guard cronies. And Lucian, for some reason. I wrote down everything in sight so he'd get bored and bugger off."

"Did he?"

"Eventually. Strangest thing, though." She shoved the bounty scroll under Tallah's nose. "Either he's got a weird read on me, or he thought something of our previous talk, but he directed me to this—and then warned me away."

Tallah read and scrunched up her nose.

"Head names the price? Deidra must've really pissed in Catharina's coffee."

"We'll have competition."

A shrug, a different crumpled scroll, another crackle in the fire.

"There's a map in the chest. Bring it, please." She moved the pile to her desk and dove into the work. Pointless drivel was crossed out with a charcoal pencil. An array of random words was circled and then copied to a clean sheet of rough paper. "Is this exactly as it said on the billboard?"

"Of course."

"Fancy that."

Sil took away some of Tallah's overcrowding tomes and cleared up a space large enough to unroll the map. An inkwell and a snuffed-out candle held it in place.

"Anything interesting?"

"Lots. Also lots of nothing. Need to sieve out the chaff."

She brewed tea over her burner while Tallah worked, then steamed a pouch of kinnettle petals above the kettle. While the tea infused her own blend of herbs, she checked in on Vergil and set the pouch on his pillow, by his head. A few breaths and his fits subsided. Finally still, he looked every bit the child that he actually was.

"What's all that?"

A string of words crowded together on the fresh scroll in gibberish arrangement. Old Forge was circled on the map, and thin lines connected the smaller settlements around it, going nearly to the very edge of Vas, to Amaranth.

"Code. Now would've been the best time to get ahead of her. By thaw, most of this will be cold trails and trampled routes, but at least we know where we're starting from."

Tallah reached out and plucked the steaming mug from Sil's hands. She sipped, grimaced, looked incredulously into the cup. A slight gnashing sound came from her as she struggled to chew the half-melted sugar slush.

"This one's yours. Stop taking my drinks."

They swapped mugs while Tallah wrote down some more seemingly random words plucked from the Guild's listing.

"Right. Anyway, look at this."

She traced the path from Old Forge, down the river Calis, into Amaranth.

"The last time I dismantled Deidra's faction twelve summers ago, she had been operating out of Neant. She's moved on to the mainland now, striking out from Amaranth and seeding discord up along the river, into Old Forge." She drank, adjusted her glasses, and traced the string of words. "These are all Claw postings. They're scheming big."

"Through the Guild?"

"Through the Guild, yes. They code the message for embedded agents and distribute it to the most likely affected areas. That you found these here means that there's a chance unrest will bloom nearby. They think Deidra's coming to Valen."

"What happens if some hardheaded adventurer decides they want to take on the mission?"

Tallah grinned. "How do you think we've been recruiting our best Claws over the years? When someone outside the Guard turns in the request, they'll find themselves joined by someone very insistent on partaking of the mission, even without a cut. Generally, it'll be hard to refuse, as they'll often be Iluna or a sheathed Claw."

"Huh. Never knew."

"Very few people outside the Claws know this. I had to burn it out of Caragill when you were recovering, back when I tied up loose ends."

"Ah."

She sipped her tea and looked closer at the map. She'd been to Old Forge once, when she had been a girl, and found it a quiet, rather droll place compared to her native, dark-walled, raucous Drack. Granted, that had been two lifetimes ago, but she remembered liking the place. It would be a nice change of pace compared to Valen and Aztroa.

"What's our move forward?"

Tallah's shoulders slumped, and she sighed over her tea. "I'll get better first." She spat the words out indignantly, loath to give her and Christina the satisfaction. "And then we wait for thaw. You'll book us—"

She looked back towards Vergil's cot and frowned. "You'll book all three of us as a party heading into Old Forge. Peacekeeping, bandit hunting, monster suppression. Nothing political. I'll tell you which is which."

"And from there we try and pick up the trail?"

"That's the wide of it. We'll keep an eye on the postings until then. There should be another set coming in a couple tendays or so. With any luck, I should be able to predict where the empire thinks Deidra's heading."

"You're putting a lot of stock in these."

"It's a start. The first time I went after her at Catharina's orders, it took me four years before I caught up, and I had my own Claws. I don't expect it'll be any faster now."

Sil sighed and chewed her tea. "Solstice first?"

"Definitely. I want Anna's strength. Deidra was easily Christina's equal at Hoarfrost." She grimaced as if struck, then resumed. "Even if her pride still won't admit it. And the witch has the gall to call me a child."

"That still leaves the Storm Guard dogging us. I can bet that Rumi character is either a Claw or she has some of her own. They've been following me all day."

Tallah waved an impatient hand and rolled her eyes. "Lay low. Stay quiet. I doubt they have anything on us worth a lick of salt."

"Then why—"

"Because they can't be sure we weren't involved in killing Anna's sanctum. It doesn't take a terribly sharp Claw to see that some very powerful people had a violent disagreement in there. If it were me asking questions, you'd already wish you'd have let the chimeras eat you." She looked up at her and cracked a nasty, evil little smile. "If it were me, I'd have picked you up long before coming in for a chat like that upstart brat. Tianna's brick-walled, but you'd be fair game."

Yes, next time she'd let her suffer. That, or spike her currant with a diuretic. She still had some corallin's tooth stems somewhere.

"Charming."

She drifted away from the sorceress and watched the gathering dark outside. Bells sounded in the distance, but she didn't count them. Ancient instincts warned her of a danger she couldn't see, and it turned her skin to gooseflesh. She'd been careful. Anyone making a report on her would only note on how dull she was and what a waste of time trailing her had been.

It wouldn't be enough to shake loose the invisible pinch of the Storm

Guard. She couldn't say how she knew that, but she did, and the thought refused to be ignored.

"Why isn't your old friend already in chains?" she asked without turning her gaze away from the people moving in the streets.

"Deidra's a Crepuscular."

Ah. That explained absolutely nothing. A dagger stare at Tallah's back provided no elaboration. Not like it mattered. Tallah would find this woman even if she was hidden under Catharina's own throne. Now that she was animate about the hunt, there would be nothing stopping her until she got exactly what she wanted. There were two more soul gems resting at the bottom of the chest, ready to be filled.

What do I want?

She knew what she wanted. She longed for it. It gnawed at her peace.

Add another corpse to your pile, Silestra. Do it. You know that's the only way it'll end. You can't help it.

Sugar turned to ash on her tongue, and she set the mug down. Stupid to want and stupid that she was tempted to go back out into the cold and make her way to the Agora, into that narrow alley and through that rickety door past the anvil . . .

"Festival's coming up." She needed to fill the silence with something before her feet took the decision away from her. "You expect any of them to show?"

Tallah shrugged without turning.

"Isadora or Cassandra. Maybe. Depends which one's got the figurative black eye. Ort definitely won't come down. Anatol, like any good pet, won't leave his master fighting alone." She took a piece of blotting paper and carefully removed a smudge from her writing. "It'll be a hot day under Cares when the Dryad deigns to show. She hates winter."

"I doubt my Goddess will show up," Sil said. It was absurd to even consider. Blessed Panacea had only shown up once for the Festival of Awakening, slapped Ort's incarnate avatar, and then vanished without a word to the gathered people. It had started a war.

That had been so long before Sil's time that it reeked of myth rather than reality.

"I haven't been to the festival since I was a girl," she mused to nobody in particular. She remembered it vaguely, an outline of a memory rather than anything clear. It started up a headache, like most of her remembrances did, when she tried vainly to focus on it in her mind's eye.

She had learned to give up before it became overbearing. She did so now and refocused on the moment and her selfish, niggling wants. Out of the fire and into the pan . . .

"Take the boy when you go. It probably won't make him any stupider," Tallah said with a hint of malice in her voice.

That's unkind, Sil thought but immediately stifled a chuckle of her own. After a tenday with Vergil, she was no better.

"Actually, really do take him if you decide to go," Tallah said after staring out through the door for a few heartbeats. "Doubt he's ever seen something like it. May do his misery some good."

CHAPTER TWELVE

Waste of Breath

Stop! What are you doing?"

Vergil tried to squirm out of the sorceress's grip, but she had his arm painfully twisted around and had forced him face down on a table. Her strength was truly monstrous in comparison to her stature.

"This would be painless if you were more cooperative," she commented, a slight edge of annoyance in her voice.

Sil paid them no attention from where she worked, so no help would be forthcoming from there. She was watching a flask come to a boil above some kind of burner. A caramel-covered pastry lay half eaten on a plate next to her.

"I've already told you I'm cooperating. You don't need to put that on me." Vergil groaned in pain, his voice muffled by a stack of papers pressed against his face. "Stop already. Please."

He felt a pinprick at the back of his head, followed by a sharp, stinging pain that mellowed into a slight pinching pressure. The grip on his arm slackened and went away.

"See?" Tallah said, pushing him away from her table. "That wasn't so bad. All that fuss for nothing."

Vergil salt bolt upright and immediately palmed at the back of his head. The thing she'd put on his neck bit his fingers with a jolt of electricity.

You have equipped a magical item: SILESTRA ADANA'S BINDING STUD.

You have been electrocuted and your right hand is now afflicted by PARTIAL PARALYSIS.

He ignored the messages.

She had put a smooth, perfectly round crystal stud on the back of his head. It dug into his skin with needlelike clamps and caused a blinding headache.

The crystal's twin was on a silver armband on Tallah's wrist. Sil had called that a special limiter and warned the sorceress about abusing it. Shattering that one would trigger its twin.

"Why?" he asked, blinking back tears. He tried to massage feeling back into his right hand. "I haven't done anything to you."

Tallah—for that's how Sil always addressed her in spite of the initial warning—returned to the work of translating some large tome covered in symbols that kept shifting in Vergil's eyes. It was what she did most days, cooped up in the room with her books and her translations. He had tried to peek once, but she shooed him away.

"It's a leash," Sil explained absentmindedly while Vergil tried to get a glimpse of it in a mirror. "I wouldn't touch it again if I were you. I've built it so that it gives a nasty shock to whoever tries to remove it. If you get further than, hmm, about half a mile from Tallah, it will detonate and take your head off." She looked back at him over the rim of her boiling flask. "It'll hurt like you wouldn't want to imagine. Be a good boy and keep close. All right?"

"But why?" he asked again, a slight whine in his voice. "Where would I go? I've got nowhere to be. My only friends are dead. I'm penniless and, as you said, considered dead. I either stay with you or I freeze to death out in the streets."

Sil shrugged. "All the same. Go watch the snow or something. We're working."

She dismissed him from the room with a wave of her hand, like always, as if he were a bothersome child.

Both she and Tallah had interrogated him relentlessly for the better part of the tenday, going so far as to wake him from his fitful bouts of sleep whenever they felt they needed clarification on some point or another.

She would call him back when she'd need him again, though in the last two days, that had become increasingly rare.

Whatever information he could provide from his world had been sparse, which depressed him in probably equal measure to them.

How did the weapon he used for his job work? Was it some kind of crossbow? Where did the bolts go?

He pressed the trigger and it fired. He didn't know anything about its inner workings except that it needed some kind of a battery. Or was it called a clip? He received one of those every fifteen work cycles when he turned in the old one.

What was a battery?

It stored electricity.

How?

He had no idea. How had he never even considered that?

How did the *Gloria Nostra* travel between stars? What was it made of? How did it fly?

May as well have been magic as far as he knew. He knew of the ship's purpose, of course. But for his entire life, the *Gloria* had been in orbit above Athos III. They didn't fly, just . . . floated there. It was something to do with something called orbital mechanics, or something like that.

What was that?

He had no idea. Argia knew.

Could Argia explain, then?

Technical database unavailable.

How was the *Gloria Nostra* society structured? How had the structure come to be?

He had gaped at those two particular questions. He had never been part of society on the *Gloria*, just a drudge in the outer ring. As far as he knew, the ship was run by women, and there were just a few other men, all of them scattered in menial jobs.

Why was it structured that way?

"I was a pest removal technician. I killed bugs. In the sewage systems and in the walls. I barely know how to read," he told them, incredulous. "I was one rung higher on the social ladder than the critters I was killing."

How did he travel to other worlds with his mind?

His interface chip did that for him.

How?

He didn't know.

What, precisely, was a *chip*?

He didn't know exactly. Some kind of computer.

What was a *computer*?

A thinking machine.

How did a machine think, exactly?

He didn't know.

Really, how had he not considered any of these things?

They were just there . . .

And so on. Questioning him had frustrated Tallah, and then it had frustrated Sil. He was the first Other they had ever encountered, and he was, by their estimation, a complete waste of breath.

"Others like you pop up from time to time," Sil had explained to him in one of their sessions. "They claim to be from other worlds, brought here by forces unknown. None, as far as I know, have lasted long here. Disease, assassination, loss of faculties, you name it. You did well to keep your mouth shut about your origins."

And then the questions started again, on and on, of an increasingly obscure nature.

Was he shocked when awakening on Edana? How was he coping with the extreme social discrepancy between his ship and Valen? Why did the sky make him anxious? Could he describe the feeling? These were mostly Sil's questions, and she had a habit of niggling at everything he said until she was either pleased or too frustrated with him to keep going.

"If I understand everything you've said, and it has been a challenge to make heads or tails of it, then you're lucky that you have that thing in your head," she had said after a particularly long questioning. "Is it normal for all of your people?"

He had to think on that. Argia provided the answer.

"It's mandatory for technicians and core crew. For others, it's optional."

She jotted that down.

"Your so-called *implant* is acting as a buffer and interpreter as far as I can figure. Some of its function seems to be to sedate or regulate your mood, which I expect exists for medical purposes. It's fascinating, really. I hate that I don't have another case to compare you to."

Of course, she tested out her theories by having him under the effect of various artifacts and magic effects. Argia, limited as she was, offered up almost precise estimations and interpretations of the effects he was experiencing. That was useful. It turned him into a cheap, hapless appraisal expert.

An unexpected boon that earned Vergil his first kind word from Tallah had come after he'd read the name of the helmet. Argia had attached a marker to it for easy identification. Horvath the Hammer's Cursed Helm, it said, and that had really gotten Tallah excited.

Horvath had been a dwarven hero that had, in her words, led a desperate defense of the Lang Fortress wearing nothing but a loincloth and his helmet against a host of invaders, likely some form of daemons. They had burrowed in from underneath Lang in the dead of night and caught the entire garrison with their literal pants down. Horvath died in that defense, of course, and the entire fortress had been burned to the ground.

Apparently, the helmet contained some sort of echo of him. It had Tallah cooing over it for days afterwards.

"I don't know how safe it is for you to use this. Aliana certainly thinks it's bad for you," Tallah had said when they tested if he could use it on his own. "It was created in a very different way than we do enchantments now, so we don't exactly know how potent this possession is. It's clearly cursed, as we understand the concept, but it's got some good uses. Sil could probably take it apart eventually, but we'd lose the artifact, and I think it's more useful as is. We'll keep studying it and see if we can find a way around its more damaging aspects."

Vergil didn't even try to worry about the risk. He understood that the helmet made him into a fierce warrior if powered by one of them. Not being responsible for his actions was more comforting than he would have liked to admit.

All in all, Vergil had mostly enjoyed the ten days since he had been taken in by the two channelers. He'd learned much and had been . . . safe? Aside from the early fright they'd given him, they'd mostly been kind. Sil had taken a keen interest in getting him into some sort of healthy shape. She kept mixing bitter tonics for him and mandated daily exercise.

Which he was to do now.

Having been dismissed for the day, Vergil slunk away from the room, still massaging his numb hand. Pins and needles were starting up, and he found that he could flex the fingers after a few minutes. After the first day of interrogations, they had a servant's bed prepared for him in the central hallway as well as a washbasin, a table, and a wardrobe to store his clothes. All in all, these were the best accommodations he had enjoyed in his entire life. How lucky he was.

Will they throw me out when I'm no longer interesting for them? Will I be alone here? Again?

He still massaged his hand as he sat down heavily on his bed. The room spun for a moment. Horvath's helmet clattered to the floor from where he had set it on his pillow. He picked up and set it back on the bed at some unknown whisper inside him that demanded it.

And it also told him he'd never be quite alone again. Maybe Sil had cracked a window open because he felt the cold at the base of his spine with a shuddering jolt.

"Vergil," Sil's voice called him back a moment later.

He had aimed to spend the rest of the day trying to read one of the many martial books that Tallah had given him. His literacy was steadily improving, and she seemed genuinely pleased whenever he showed an interest in learning.

He groaned as he had to get up again, head still light.

"Yes, Miss?" he answered from the doorway.

"Sil is just fine. I don't need you to always *Miss* me about everything," she replied and beckoned him back in. "Get dressed. We'll head out to buy you some proper clothes and armor. The Corps must have given you at least some basic plate training. Right?"

"Yes, Mis— Y-yes, Sil," he answered. A lifetime of instincts had a small disagreement with his new orders.

He avoided looking at Tallah. Her displeasure could ignite entirely without warning. She didn't look to be much older than him, but when her gaze turned his way, it was always with the same terrible intent of pinning him to the wall, blasting out his soul, and then sieving it for any scrap of knowledge or secrets he might have hidden away.

The sorceress looked up sharply from her tome. He flinched.

"We need to see the old man," she said, turning to Sil. "What time is it?"

Sil gazed out the window at a mostly clear dark blue sky tinged with a soft hue of purple. There had been a few hours' gap in the snowfall on that day, and the light out was suggesting afternoon. It also suggested a fanged chill that lurked at the edge of night.

"Still early, I guess. Second bell of the evening? Does it matter?"

"Excellent. We shop for Helmet Boy here and then we go see Ludwig."

Sil groaned and put her head on the table.

"Why must you ruin this for me?" she whined, to Vergil's puzzlement.

They acted so different with one another than they did with him.

"I had no idea that buying him armor meant so much to you," Tallah replied, eyebrow raised in as much confusion as he felt. "By all means, go and have him try on armor. I'm not stopping you."

"I want something sweet, Tallah. I'm sick to death of Verti's pastry chef. Everything's caramel with that girl, no fruit, no butter, no nothing. Caramel this. Caramel that. My teeth hurt from so much bloody caramel."

The sorceress walked past Vergil, snorting. Her laugh echoed out of the shared bathroom.

She laughs like a horse. He banished the traitorous thought, lest she somehow hear it.

Sil apparently remembered Vergil was still there and blushed slightly. "Ludwig is an old teacher of hers," she said. Her deflection had no subtlety whatsoever. "He drones on and on, when he's not being insufferable."

"You were using me as an excuse to go out? For sweets? Why?"

"Because I'm a fickle woman, and I do fickle things," she replied crisply. Even smiled slightly.

Tallah poked her head out of the bathroom and called to them across the hallway.

"I want something sweet—and savory too, maybe. I'll shop with Helmet Boy; you find me something that fits my cravings." The door slammed shut.

"I stand corrected. We're both fickle women. I could kiss her sometimes." She looked at him and frowned. "Close your mouth, Vergil. You look like an imbecile."

Vergil did just as instructed.

"I don't understand you two," he said in a small voice.

"You'll get used to it."

Tallah made a spectacle out of the shopping trip into the Agora. May as well, if the Guard were set on watching them.

Dressed in a richly embroidered winter dress, with a deep black fur over-coat ripped off some poor Nen-bred corallin, she left the hotel hanging on to Vergil's arm as if they were out on a grand date. Sil followed just two steps back, dressed modestly, as befit the live-in personal healer to the gaudy sorceress.

She needed to drag Vergil. There was something wrong with his legs, considering how he kept staggering and freezing in place.

"Walk straight, boy," she ordered. "Sil, why's he stumbling all the time?"

A soft wind blowing in from the mountains brought with it the smell of charcoal and burnt stone, of alchemical setters and freshly mixed paints. The sounds of construction echoed in the chill evening. Snow and cold would not deter the Enginarium from pushing forward with the work that had been commissioned to them by both the empire and Valen's council. So much of the city's burnt husk was being torn down and built anew that Tallah wondered how much of it she'd even recognize once the work was done.

'I can only mourn what we have done here,' Christina sighed in her ear. That unmistakable smell of smoke always brought to both of them the echoes of screams.

Tallah gritted her teeth and pushed the ghost's guilt back. She sank into Tianna's persona and allowed herself to be what her father had once wished she were.

It wasn't even third bell of the evening when they approached the Agora's large plaza, the crowds already thick and still swelling. Lanterns had been lit on high poles. They illuminated rich snow-laden stalls, all selling knickknacks and supplies for the upcoming festival. Music slithered above the din, sweet and soft, festive. Some string band played drunkenly under a tent, ignorant of the cold.

After the third jab to the ribs, Vergil did as instructed and straightened up. Tallah barely had to twist his arm to get him to walk properly as she took to the role of gaudy imbecile excited by a new toy.

She laughed and cuddled up to him, talking much too loudly about small things. The weather was so beautiful this time of year here in Valen. So many people. She wished they'd be done already with the ungodly noise. Oh, that armorsmith looks glorious. Let's check that place out.

Tallah could almost *hear* Sil behind them, trying to melt into the flag-stones out of embarrassment.

"Oh, Vergil, dear, look at all this . . . tosh," she said loudly, as they walked into the first armor shop. "Pity, the outside façade promised so much more."

"Uh, ma'am, what might we interest you in?" The vendor, an aelir, hurried over to their side just as Tallah turned to leave. "I can assure you we can satisfy even the most eccentric needs."

Tallah turned and feigned an interested smile.

"Oh, do tell. My father always spoke highly of Valen's artisans." She pursed her lips as she took another critical look around. "Then again, he is very old."

"A-Are you looking for yourself, ma'am, or—"

"Goodness, no," she interrupted and beamed a smile at Vergil. He blushed furiously. "My dear Vergil needs the best armor for when we decide to go on another dangerous Guild mission. We can't accept just any ol' piece of rust-eaten farmer's iron."

To her credit, the aelir took everything in stride, though her smile started fraying at the edges.

"Of course, ma'am. Uh, sir, please step on the podium, and we'll have you fitted in just a moment." An aide had come from a back room, measuring tape in hand.

Tallah latched on to Vergil's arm and drew close to him, making sure that the coin pouch at her hip jingled obviously.

"I just don't believe it's worth wasting our time here. Do you have anything actually good aside from this tosh up front?"

"If— Uh, if it's your pleasure, ma'am, please have a closer look—"

Tallah turned around and dragged Vergil out past a red-faced Sil, who had become extremely interested in the carpet's patterns. She left the seller talking, her voice petering out along with the jingle of the doorbell.

"I think I'll drop dead if I feel any more secondhand embarrassment for whoever's caught in your path," Sil said after she made her apologies to the flabbergasted vendor. "Is all of this necessary?"

Tallah cackled. "There's four more to go," she said, infinitely pleased with herself. "Which one do I humiliate next?"

"I'm going to go find me some alchemical compounds. You can do this whole thing on your own. Meet me after."

People gathered around them, pushing them closer together. The evening crowd had grown dense. The press of bodies was nearly overwhelming as they tried to go their separate ways.

"Our friends are back and watching us," Sil whispered by her ear. "On your right, edge of the plaza, between the bakeries."

"Watching, not following. I know. Saw him."

"We are watching him back," Christina said. Her voice manifested as an undertone to Tallah's.

The crowd carried Sil away, and Tallah was left alone with Vergil.

She was almost certain he whimpered when the healer disappeared from sight. One of her best glares got him straightening up better than a hot poker up his arse.

They perused the wares of no less than four other smiths in the Grand Agora, with her doing all the talking. She demeaned every single armor piece that the store clerks dutifully presented to them and had them storming out of each establishment. Let whoever watched try to find some semblance of coherence from that.

The Grand Agora radiated out from a central plaza in an almost organized set of small streets and alleys, with shops packed tightly together and bright sprite-lit signs vying for the shoppers' attention. In fairer weather, the central plaza contained stalls selling fresh produce, meats on ice, or condiments, but in winter, the city's council converted it into an open-air skating rink. Just like the alleys around, it was packed with people.

"This looks like a place that may sell some high-quality armor, dear," Tallah chirped as she and Vergil stopped in front of Merg's. She'd been carefully maneuvering through the crowd so that they should have disappeared from their watcher's sight at least two stores back. Still, it was worth keeping up appearances. Just in case.

Despite her loud announcement, the shop wasn't much to behold. It occupied a small, misshapen building just beyond the mouth of one side alley, away from the center of the Agora, and had a small anvil and hammer statue outside. In white paint and deformed handwriting, the name Merg's was plastered above the door, almost as an afterthought.

"Seriously?" Vergil asked in a small voice.

Tallah dragged him inside.

Merg's storefront was a workshop rather than a store, with blacksmith tools strewn about and only a small selection of armor and weapons on display. There were no prices shown on any piece of armor, the light inside was poor, and the chilled room smelled of armor oil and various other chemicals that left a tang on the air. There wasn't even a little bell above the door to announce a patron walking in.

"Mertle," Tallah called out, as there was no one to greet them up front.

No one replied.

"Mertle!"

Still no answer.

She motioned for Vergil to get up on the raised platform by the sole grime-encrusted window when a rustle stirred in the back room. A crash followed, and then the sound of many metal pieces tumbling loudly to the floor.

"By my pledge to the Frozen Hands," a gruff voice swore in the back. "I'll be right out. Mertle, one of these days, all of these are going to come down on your head. Clean them up, please."

Thuds, crashing, more metal tumbling. The whole building shook for a moment.

After a few moments of silence, the door to the back room swung open, and a giant walked out. He had to bend to get through the doorway, and the top of his head brushed against the ceiling when he straightened.

Vergil openly gaped at the sight. Tummy had that effect on people meeting him for the first time. His raven-black beard and hair were both unkempt and slightly smoking. He wore a charcoal-stained brown apron and black tanned trousers, with nothing else. A thick jaw and a small, crooked nose that had been smashed once too often completed his savage look.

"What can I help you with?" His voice boomed in the small room as he offered them a poorly practiced crooked grin. Vergil still gaped like a cretin.

"Your best armor. And your best leather worker, please," Tallah replied.

He looked down at her and squinted, seeming to just now notice his clients weren't as big as he. A massive bricklike hand dug into one of the many pockets of his apron, and he produced a pair of almost comically small round spectacles with a leather strap. He fastened them over his head and took a better look at them. A bellowing laugh erupted from his chest.

"Mertle!" He turned around and knocked loudly on the door, prompting more clanking metal beyond. "Get out here. Our kooky friend is back."

"I'm busy. Which kooky friend?" a shrill female voice shouted back.

"The one with the leather fetish."

"Which one?"

"Come out and see." The big man turned back to them and spoke in a lower, pleasant voice. "She'll be with you in a bit."

"Actually, I have business with you too, Tummy," Tallah said, beckoning him forward.

"Oh?" Tummy's brow creased, and he walked across the room, his great big steps dislodging dust from the ceiling. "Are you finally getting some proper protection on that skinny arse of yours?"

Tallah laughed. "No. I'm still very much a leather fetishist. But you can help me by dressing up the boy here." She pointed with her thumb at Vergil. "Sit up straight, boy." The command was like a whip, both in tone and effect.

"Twitchy little thing," Tummy commented, rounding on the boy. He offered him his outstretched meaty hand. "Name's Tummy Toh'Uhm. And who might you be?"

Vergil looked uncertainly towards Tallah. She nodded at him encouragingly.

"Vergil Vansce. Pleased to meet you, Mister Toh'Uhm." He mangled the throaty pronunciation, but the large man just laughed.

"Just Tummy to my friends. If you're her friend, then you're mine as well. What armor do you need?"

"I have no idea. Today's been weird," Vergil answered candidly, looking again to her for help.

"Make him something sturdy that he can grow into," Tallah said. "I need it to be strong, magically resistant plate, preferably, and easy to adjust. He's still filling out after some bad times. No frills, and nothing to attract attention."

Tummy scratched his large chest, thinking. "What about weapons? You need any?"

Tallah tapped her lips with her index finger and turned to Vergil. "Do you have any axe training?"

"No, none," he replied. "I can learn, though."

It was as satisfactory an answer as she could expect. He would likely be useless with any weapon, but the ghost in the helmet was a dwarf, and axes were a preference for his species. Tummy produced a small writing pad on which he took notes with a sharpened piece of charcoal.

"You told me once that you had some friends here from old Lang. I need hand axes, four of them, modeled after what the dwarves used to wield. Also, a short sword. Something like a gladius, not like the ones you made for me." She thought for a while more while he finished scribbling down her order. "And you can make him one of those stupid big claymores, and a war hammer. Weight them up for yourself."

Tummy raised an eyebrow over his round spectacles and then looked at Vergil more closely. The boy shrugged. He looked like a dressed bag of bones held up straight by force of will.

"Pull the other one. It's got bells on," Tummy said.

Vergil looked similarly confused.

"I have high hopes for him." She brushed off both of their stares.

"Fine by me. Hold this, Vergil."

He handed his notepad to the boy and began patting his pockets until he produced a worn measuring tape.

"You tight for money?" he asked and retrieved his notepad. He began sketching with a deftness that seemed almost unnatural for his large build.

"How soon can you have it ready?" she replied.

"How soon you need it?"

"Soon. I need to train him before thaw."

"Couple of days. Got other work, but it'll keep," he rumbled, scratching his cheek with the charcoal tip.

Tallah smiled. "Then you know I'm good for the money. I'll be settling my debt."

He chuckled at that. If she could settle her entire debt to him and Mertle, she could as well be buying half of Valen. She knew it well enough, and he was kind enough not to say it to her face.

Since Mertle hadn't made an appearance while they were talking, Tallah left Tummy to measure and question Vergil for the gear. She made her way to the backroom door and gently pushed it open. Nothing clattered to the floor, so she opened it fully and stepped into the workshop proper. The heat was stifling inside, with a forge fire burning bright in the back. Tummy was melting some lump of metal in a crucible.

Diagrams covered the walls, and tools hung on supports, neatly stacked and labeled, very different from the front image. Tallah stepped carefully past the pile of metal odds and ends that had dropped off an overloaded shelf. It wasn't the only one.

This place keeps getting more and more cluttered. At some point, I won't be able to even find them in here.

The elendine worked bent over an overcrowded table. Her attire mirrored Tummy's, revealing her tattooed bare back. She was carefully inscribing the inside of a leather doublet with runes that burned with a soft light before sinking into the material. Each intricate rune was no larger than a fingernail, and she worked with slow, deft strokes of her quill.

"And here I thought you'd be jumping for joy to see me," Tallah said as she walked up to her.

Mertle startled at the interruption and misspelled the rune she had been painstakingly working on. The doublet immediately turned gray and collapsed into a pile of ash that spilled off the table.

"Aw, poop," she said, with an almost-sad sigh, quill in one hand and inkwell in the other.

"I hope that wasn't too valuable," Tallah said.

"No, no, it was just three days of work. I'll start over." Mertle spun around with a jolt, dark eyes widening in surprise. "Tallah!" She threw her arms around the sorceress. Her entire inkwell spilled on the floor. "Oh poop, not again." She pulled away and ran for a mop before the ink could start eating its way through the smooth stone.

She was short, her head barely up to Tianna's chest. She wore her red hair long and tied in an intricate braid down her bare back. Two jagged, curving bone horns protruded from her brow and arched back over her head.

"Considering your trade, how in blazes are you still such a klutz? That stuff can't be cheap." Tallah had stepped aside while Mertle took care of her corrosive ink spill.

"Don't sneak up on me like that, Tallah," she admonished while she mopped up the sizzling ink, running twice to a bucket of water to clean the well-used mop. The ink boiled the water. "You could set us both on fire. Or explode. Or . . . I don't know. Something bad." Words tumbled out of her as she cleaned the floor to a mirror shine. "Don't sneak up on me, all right? I've missed you. When did you get back? Where's Sil? Is she still mad at me? I hope she's not still mad; I didn't mean to laugh at her about the whole, you know, incident."

Tallah held her hands out and gestured for the elendine to slow down. "Easy, Mertle. Breathe. Sil's doing some shopping of her own. She's assured me she's not still mad at you."

Sil would, in fact, become livid if Tallah so much as breathed a word about the incident. Christina had made it a personal mission to insert comments about that moment of carelessness with the helmet at every possible opportunity.

"Are you sure?" Mertle's slanted, deep black eyes stared a hole through Tallah's.

"Fairly sure, yes," Tallah lied with a smile. "We've missed you too, Mertle. How about a cup of coffee? I think Tummy and my friend are going to be a while up front."

"You have a friend?! Who?"

"I'll introduce you later."

The elendine set down her mop in its bucket against the wall and rummaged through a cupboard for two clean cups. She set them down on her workbench and brought a kettle of hot water off a small stove. From another cupboard—the chaos of her arrangements never ceased to amaze and intrigue—she brought out a tin of dehydrated coffee. Three teaspoons for herself, one for Tallah's mug. Elend blended their coffee strong enough that it wasn't quite safe for human consumption. Or for any other species, save vanadals. It outright killed the aelir. Tallah suspected that was the original intent for the drink.

"I assume your hunt went well if you're back?" Mertle asked while sipping from her cup. She burned her tongue but didn't admit to it. It showed on her face. She had propped up some boxes as chairs for them while they caught up.

Tallah sighed and nodded. It wasn't a subject she was ready or willing to breach, and Mertle, for all her air-hotheadedness, understood.

"I need you to make me some new gear. My old one got cut to ribbons. I think most of its enchantments got destroyed."

Mertle wrinkled her nose at that.

"You never asked me to design them to be cut-proof," she said with a pout. "It's why I made you the carapace."

"That carapace was all I had hoped it would be. Make me a new one like that. Old one got stabbed too many times."

The glare she got back could have stripped paint from the wall.

"What did you do, Tallah? Is Sil all right?"

She chuckled and sipped her deathtrap coffee. "Sil's fine. She handles herself better than an Iluna when we're out and about. We have a bodyguard now. He's the friend up front with Tummy."

Without slackening the glare, Mertle thought for a time. "I've had some success with my current batch of runes. I can add something experimental to your usual. I've actually been testing many of the new combinations I got from the tomes you translated for me."

She blew on her coffee before taking another sip.

"Your translations still need work, if you don't mind me saying. I set Tummy's hand on fire with a rune word that was supposed to make an object heat resistant. *Heat resistant* and *highly flammable* are not the same thing, you know."

'I told you so, child. She should have made a pair for you.' Christina forced an image of a smug grin into Tallah's imagination. 'Next time, remember which of us is the more accomplished scholar.'

"Have you had any success with exotics?" Tallah asked, hiding her grimace behind her coffee mug. She pointedly ignored the psychic jab.

"Dragon scales, you mean? Got a few. Bought them off an adventurer. Tummy's infusing some silver chain weave with their essence right now. I was saving it for you. I think it's exactly enough for a pair of gloves."

Mertle's glaring gave way to squeaking excitement, and she almost dashed away to bring the red-hot weave. Tallah grabbed her by the hem of her apron before she bounced away.

"I'll trust that it's excellent, then," she said calmly. "How much heat will I be able to output with that?"

"Oh, I don't think you need to worry about heat any more, not for your hands. They should be able to resist anything short of actual dragon fire." She stopped talking and stared at Tallah for a moment, frowning. "Can you reach as high as dragon fire now?"

"Ha! I wish. Still far from that."

"Good. The convection will be an issue since neither my breathing masks nor my tunics are yet that good. But if you push heat away from you, you'll be good to go as hot as you want."

Tallah made a mental note of that. Her fireballs and heat lances would improve if she could increase the temperature without fear of the backwash, which would have her rely less on more aggressive and illum-inefficient weaves. The bonus was that Sil would worry less about her illum expenditures and stop chewing her face off every time she needed to exert herself.

"And you're in luck. I have some really good gold-tongue hide for a *new* carapace." Mertle twisted the word, displeased that her work had gone to tatters again.

She had her old sketch pad out, leafing through the ripped and falling pages until she found a tightly annotated sketch of Tallah herself.

"When do you need everything?"

"Soon as you can, like always. But don't feel pressured. I'm waiting for a caravan to come through the snow from Drack so I can head to Solstice. But you know that won't happen until we're on the lip of thaw," Tallah answered, putting down her empty cup. She refused a second.

"Aww, you're leaving again? You owe me dinner," Mertle whined at her as she made her annotations on the drawing with the new requests. "I'm not giving you a single piece of gear until you take me out to dinner." Her eyes twinkled.

"Sil owes you dinner. How about I tell her to be a big girl and come take you out?" Tallah asked, a bit of mischief in her voice. "She's had time enough to grow a backbone since we've come back."

'Maybe it's what she needs to stop niggling us.' Christina scoffed.

Mertle blushed all the way to the top of her ears, turning her already tan complexion almost black. She tried to stammer out an answer, but Tallah understood every unsaid word.

"Tomorrow, then, about this time. You know what she likes."

"Can she be herself? Please?" Mertle almost whispered, still mostly black with embarrassment. "It feels wrong to hold hands with an aelir."

"I'll ask her nicely. For you."

"Do you know that you look about two missed meals away from starved? Does Tallah know?"

Vergil didn't know what to make of the questions, and more than that, he didn't know how much he should say to Tummy. He had his arms outstretched as the smith measured him every which way imaginable.

"I . . . don't know how to answer that," Vergil replied candidly. "I have no idea what this is even about."

The smith furrowed his brow and looked at him critically. That he had used Tallah's real name did not escape Vergil's attention.

"Figures. Come here."

Tummy showed him to a stool and then produced a bottle and a couple of glasses from behind his dusty counter. What he poured out was nearly black and had the consistency of syrup. He stopped, looked at Vergil more closely as he perched on the stool, and then emptied half of one glass into the other.

"We drink now. You tell me who you are and what you're trained to do, and I decide what to make for you."

Vergil took the half-empty glass and darted a look to the back room. "I don't think she'd like that."

Tummy poked him in the chest with one meaty finger. "Not her shop. I ask and you answer, or she can take your business elsewhere." He held out the glass and clinked it against Vergil's. "First, drink."

He did. It was sweet and thick, but the kick was like a punch to the back of the head. Vergil's eyes watered, and he struggled not to cough it out. It didn't so much go down as spread into him, like molten iron exploding in the pit of his stomach. Even Argia's text appeared garbled in his vision.

"Not all at once would have been best, but your face is fun to watch." Tummy drank in dainty sips, his smile broadening. "Now we talk man to man. And I don't want to hear anything about the mean lady in the back."

Vergil wiped his eyes on the sleeve of his tunic and struggled to find his mangled voice.

"What is this?" he rasped out, still feeling the drink clawing up his insides.

"Summer wasp venom. Good for the nerves. Good for digestion. Loosens tongues."

"Sil said I'm not supposed to drink anything but water and her tonics."

Tummy shrugged and looked around. "I don't see her in here."

Vergil grinned. It may have been the drink, but he found himself intensely liking Tummy.

"You're not afraid of them," he said and immediately blushed. "They both scare the living daylights out of me."

That was definitely too much information to give. He stared incredulously into the dregs of venom in his glass.

"Is this truth serum?"

"Close as. Doesn't last long."

"Tallah's going to be upset."

"I'll bring out the privy rag for her to write complaints on." He swirled his drink in the glass and matched Vergil's grin. His demeanor was infectious. "So, she hasn't trained you at all. Two mistakes in one go."

Before Vergil could rally his response, he went on, counting off his fingers.

"One, you drank with someone you don't know well enough to accept a drink from." He downed his glass in one swig. "Could've been poison. Could've been actual summer wasp milk in here, and you'd be screaming for days when the eggs you swallowed hatched." He shrugged, seeming none too impressed by Vergil's gasp of horror.

He raised two fingers. "And you confirmed her name to me." Now the levity was gone from his voice, replaced by a hard, harsh note of disapproval. "That one's real bad."

"But you . . ."

"Not your fault," Tummy said, refilling his glass. "But it tells me you're green and not of our class of people."

Vergil slumped back. He could see a lecture on the horizon, either from Tallah or Sil, that would make him feel even more the child. Tummy swirled his drink now, watching him.

"Who starved you?" he finally asked.

"Ratmen," Vergil answered miserably. "My party got wiped out in the caves." He gestured vaguely to the air without looking up from the tarry surface of the drink. "Somewhere out in the sticks. Tallah and Sil found me half mad. I got better, and they kept me around."

They had only told him not to speak about being an Other. The rest, he figured, was nothing to keep secret even if it shamed him.

"I got my friends killed." He finished the glass and held it out for a second shot. Tummy obliged. "I don't know why I'm here or what good it'll be to get me armored up. Tallah uses an enchantment on me, and I fight without a thought of my own in my head."

He drank slower. The drink didn't kick as hard anymore now that the initial shock wore off. It left behind the heat in his guts.

"It's eating you alive," Tummy surmised after allowing him some time for his silence.

"I guess it is."

All of it. Davan and Merk, cut down. Sidora, brains splattered on the walls. Being helpless. Surviving. Being useless.

Things missing in him . . .

"What's your training?"

"Paladin Corps. Basic." He wiped his nose on his sleeve, then his eyes again, the short moment of kinship earlier having melted away into misery. "Just sword and a bit of shield."

"Who?"

"Master of arms, Harlem."

Tummy nodded, drink set aside, and pulled his goggles up to his forehead. His eyes seemed beady now without the thick spectacles, as he regarded Vergil thoughtfully.

"Harlem's good but only really trains those that sign on as soldiers. Did you?"

Vergil shook his head and chuckled slightly. "Adventuring seemed safer."

"More fool you. Adventurer is another word for mercenary. It only adds worse pay and much worse odds."

Tummy moved to the back of the room and opened the door. He beckoned someone to him and, a few moments later, Tallah appeared in the doorway.

"Is he giving you lip?" she asked and gave Vergil a black glare.

"I'm not making you a single piece for him," Tummy said without any preamble, face stony.

Vergil shrank into himself. Should've kept his mouth shut. Now he'd failed what had certainly been a test. Small wonder both women considered him a waste of breath.

"What?" Tallah's glare snapped to Tummy, unimpressed that he towered over her. "Why?"

"For the look on your face most of all." The smith crossed his arms and gave Vergil a side-glance.

And a wink?

"Send him round every other day, 'bout eve time. I'll beat some proper sense into him. I'm not wasting good gear on a green leaf that can't use it right."

Tallah's eyebrows nearly climbed off her face. "You want to train him? You barely agreed to train me. I pestered you for weeks."

"You're loud. He ain't. Deal or no?"

She looked to Vergil. He was sure his face matched hers in amazement.

"Deal, of course. Saves me the trouble," she said, voice softer than Vergil had ever heard from her. "Why?"

"I'm not wasting good work on an untrained boy you found somewhere," the smith said as he picked up a sword from a rack on the wall. "Hold this, Vergil."

Vergil accepted the weapon. He nearly toppled forward when Tummy released it to his grip.

"That's a crock of nonsense," Tallah insisted.

"I'll charge you two griffons per training bell if you keep pestering me."

"That's robbery."

"Five, then."

That shut her up. Vergil still struggled to lift the sword upright and hold it steady.

"Tell Silestra I want him eating properly from here on out. Proper food. Meat—"

"I can't eat meat," Vergil hurried to say and then blushed. "I'm sorry."

"Proper food to build muscle. I'm sure she's doing all right by him, but remind her that tonics do not stand in for actual food." He poked Tallah in the sternum. "Same goes for you."

"You can't know . . ." She blushed and did not meet his glare.

"I can and do. Eat. Or I'll have you back here, with him, before I let Mertle make anything for you."

He also selected a scabbard and showed Vergil how to fasten it at his hip.

"Put that down before you poke an eye out. Wear the sword when you go out. Get used to it and learn not to stumble over it. I'll see you here tomorrow."

CHAPTER THIRTEEN

Debt to Pay

Tallah and Vergil found Sil next to a brightly lit cart at the edge of the skating rink. It served a kind of waffle twisted into a cone, filled with a thick white custard and topped with various jams, all of it steaming hot in the crisp cold.

Even the air around the cart smelled sticky and sweet. Tallah's teeth hurt as they got closer.

"You're having dinner with Mertle tomorrow," she said by way of greeting. "You've sulked long enough."

"Am I now? After how she laughed at me, do you think I want to see her?" Sil pretended to pay extra attention to the man serving the confectionery treat. Her ears and cheeks turning red were just due to the biting cold. "Why's Vergil grinning like an imbecile?"

"She really thinks you're upset with her." Tallah walked up next to her and jabbed an elbow in her ribs and got back a very satisfying flinch. "Two more of what she's having." She glared at Sil. "Don't do that to her. She thinks she's hurt your feelings."

Sil carefully bit into her confection and still managed to get jam down her chin. "What time do I need to show up?"

"Third bell. No knife ears. I'll help you sneak out of the Meadow."

Tallah took the two cones the vendor offered and absentmindedly handed one to Vergil. He accepted sheepishly, shaking out of the stupor he'd been in since Tummy had patted him on the back before they left the shop.

"Thank you. Why?" he asked.

'Is he broken? Or simply dumb?' Bianca wondered.

'Frightened stiff, more like,' Christina said.

'Of us?'

'Tallah, be nicer to him. He's impressed Tummy. You couldn't.'

"Because it's yummy," Tallah replied, talking slowly. She ignored her companion ghosts. There was a lull in the melody singing out to her, so they got chatty.

Sil snickered. "If you won't have it, I have room for seconds."

"Why are you being nice to me?" he tried again, walking quickly behind them as they made their way through the jostle of bodies.

Skating was a popular pastime in wintertime Valen, and the crowd swelled and surged towards the rink. Evening rolled in with the conspicuous calm of a planning storm.

"You'd prefer I be mean to you?" Tallah asked the boy. "Fine, then. Give me back the cone."

Vergil almost complied. He had the confection held out before catching on. "You're making fun of me."

"I am."

"Why do you act like this? One moment you threaten that my head will explode. The next . . . pastries? New armor and weapons? Someone to train me? Why?" He waved the confection around, almost spilling jam on himself.

Tallah caught his arm and steadied him before he made a mess of the thing. Sil couldn't contain herself and laughed openly, even as she struggled not to slip on the black ice. There was salt underfoot, but it hadn't made it any less treacherous.

"Oh my, Tianna, you're confusing the boy," Sil said, wiping her eyes with a glove, still chuckling.

"Am I? Oh dear. How mean of me." Tallah cupped Vergil's cheek with a palm and talked softly, pouting just so. "I'm sorry, darling. I promise I won't do it anymore."

Vergil drew back so abruptly that she half expected his skin to leave his bones. She was enjoying the routine a bit too much, though.

"For now, we're in Valen and it's safe. When we head off, I won't be able to care for you at every turn," Tallah explained in Tianna's singsong voice, leading their small group towards the Enginarium Quarter. "Thus, I got you armor and weapons from someone that does actual good work here. Second, it's getting late, and we'll likely go without dinner tonight. So I got you the same snack we're having. It would be rude otherwise." She finished eating and licked her fingers. "I can't understand what part confuses you."

"You are not a servant, Vergil, or a slave," Sil put in. "We paid a small fortune to get you back on your feet, but we don't expect anything in return from you. We leashed you because we have concerns about our own safety, not because we want you to serve us. And it's certainly not our goal to mistreat you."

"I can't get what I want out of you yet, and I can't kill you for it. May as well be civil." She locked her elbow onto his and almost dragged him forward, with Sil trailing behind.

"That's what worries me. You're civil because you can't kill me. How is that normal?"

It began snowing again while they ascended the stairs up onto the elevated Enginarium grounds, heading for the Alchemists Quarter. A pungent stench of chemical compounds and volatile oils struck them as they emerged out of the stairwell. Even with the sparse snowfall, the air was oily and thick with gagging wisps of smoke, not helped in the least by the sector's reliance on old-fashioned gas lamps for artificial light. A greenish fog covered the dense, mis-shapen architecture of the place, with monstrous heads of masonry gargoyles peeking out through the airborne soup.

Something exploded in the distance as they made their way through the small, cramped alleyways, down and up flights of stairs that made no sense to anyone not already familiar with the place. Distant cheers erupted as the echoes of the detonation died out.

Someone cursed loudly nearby, muted echoes bouncing around the alleys.

"How can you eat in this?" Sil had taken note of Vergil taking small bites out of his now-stone-cold pastry. "You are the slowest eater I've ever seen. Watching you gnaw at that thing in this stink is turning my stomach."

"What do you mean?" He finally finished and even licked his fingers for any traces of runaway jam.

"Did you lose your sense of smell in the caves?"

Vergil sniffed at the air and made a sound with his mouth as if he were tasting it. He shrugged at her, unimpressed.

"It's not that bad. Oily, maybe, but I used to work and eat in worse on the *Gloria*. This is actually pretty pleasant by my reckoning."

They passed narrow slits of light scratching the gloom. Workshops had their gates open and inviting with the sound of industry within. Apprentices and novices were being sent out into the night laden with materials on unknowable errands.

Despite the sparse foot traffic and the poor light, there was energy in the air, laced into the fumes, crackling with potential. The Quarter offered a strange kind of privacy made up of tight streets, cacophonous echoes, and hurrying ghosts.

If Tallah learned that someone, somewhere in there, was melting down diamonds, she wouldn't have been surprised. The feel of the night made any-thing seem possible.

Tianna was no longer useful in there, and Vergil's fidgeting started getting on her nerves. She released him from her arm with a shove and pulled two steps ahead, guiding their progress.

"Do you think we're still being followed?" Sil asked as they stopped by an overlooking balcony that gazed into the maze of buildings some distance further down. Warm forge lights shone through the murky wet fog, waxing and waning as the miasmas traveled.

The entire place sloped down towards Valen's wall, built to dump its excesses outside the city.

"Someone following us in this soup would be nipping at our arses to keep up."

Sil was unconvinced. She looked over her shoulder and fretted, restless like a spooked corallin.

"They were very keen on us in the Agora. That Egia could follow us easily enough."

Christina took over Tallah's voice and spoke with infuriating disdain. "She was not in the Agora. We are watching for her. You are safe, hen. Leave the worrying to your betters."

Tallah reeled in and muzzled her willful ghost. Banging and clanking, curses in at least three different languages, and the sounds of detonating apparatuses made up the voice of the Quarter. Their discussion was drowned in the background noise.

Truth of the matter was, in spite of Christina's boasts, that it would be harder to catch any whiff of someone trailing them. A mugger wouldn't be much of an issue, but it'd leave a mess behind. Someone tracking them with no intention of revealing themselves?

Hairs on the back of her neck prickled, but that was just Sil's whining getting on her nerves too.

"Safe from what?" Vergil asked, echoing Sil's worry as if it mattered to him. It was too long and too tedious of a story to get into for his curiosity's sake.

Tallah walked on ahead. "I think we're coming up on the church. Or we should be."

Ahead, two flights of stairs down, they reached an open square. The blind light of the lamps illuminated the hazy outline of the Church of Old Hope, its crooked sharp roof and bent bell tower peeking out through the murk. Handling highly explosive compounds mixed well with faith in a higher protective power. Hymns to Cassandra could be heard echoing from within. Far as Tallah knew, Cassandra had never acknowledged the Old Hope as a cult dedicated to herself.

They headed behind the building to find a flight of narrow steps going down at a steep angle.

"Was that belfry always this bent out of shape?" Sil asked Tallah, looking up at the sloping outline of the building.

"I think that was me." She couldn't help but feel smug. "They chased me over this way last time, and I collapsed it on top of a couple of them. Nothing gets rebuilt straight around here."

"Who's *they?*" Vergil asked.

"The Storm Bellends," Tallah answered, almost dismissively.

"What's a *storm bellend*?" Vergil couldn't take a cue to shut up if it hit him over the head. Tallah considered actually hitting him.

"The Storm Guard, Vergil. Tallah's just being affectionate," Sil replied in her stead.

"*The* Storm Guard? From the Fortress?!"

"What are you, an echo?" Tallah asked, annoyed. "Yes, those guys. We don't get along."

Vergil stopped dead in his tracks, hands on the side rails.

"But . . . they're the law of the empire."

"Yes, yes, quite so."

"You're a villain?" He even managed to sound incredulous.

"Be honest, Vergil. Does that even surprise you?" She turned around and gave him an encouraging smile, complete with a mischievous tilt of the head and doe-eyed stare. He flinched.

Sil groaned.

"Don't scare him, Tallah. He's spooked enough of you. We're not villains, Vergil." She gave it a little more honest consideration. "All right, she is, but not how you'd imagine."

That reassured him even less. He had the look as if ready to bolt back up the stairs and into the night. It was rather endearing.

"But the Storm Guard are keepers of the peace. At the Corps, they were extremely proud that they had members serving, even right here in Valen."

"Yes, yes, they're all very valiant and honorable and whatever else makes you feel good and tingly," Tallah said, with as much venom as she could be bothered to show. "Don't be simple."

"Can we please move on from the subject?" Sil glanced over her shoulder again. "I feel like we're inviting attention."

"You encouraged him. You deal with it."

Something somewhere exploded. It lit up the hazy darkness for a fragment of a moment, and the boom shook the ground. Tallah waited for the echoes to dampen before continuing to descend to her destination.

Behind, Sil tried to reassure the boy.

"We used to be in the Storm Guard, Vergil. There are a lot of things the Guard does that aren't noble, or honorable, or even moral."

Tallah felt Vergil's gaze on the back of her neck as he and the healer hurried to catch up.

"But she's so young," he said in what he thought was a conspiratorial whisper. "You're an aelir, but I didn't think the Guard took in people as young as her."

Tallah burst out laughing, followed immediately by Sil.

"I love him," the healer said. "He's like a puppy, all innocent, wide-eyed, and dumb as a brick. He makes me want to feed him treats."

"I wonder if we were also that dumb at his age?" Tallah asked, elbowing Sil in the side.

"You're not that much older than me," Vergil protested. "They kept going on about the Guard when I was in basic training, like it was the highest calling we could aspire to. I thought they were all grizzled veterans and wise scholars."

Sil blew into her hands for warmth as they finally reached the bottom, and Tallah checked their bearings again. They went down another tight, sinewy alley, no different from the many others they'd followed. If the two following her noticed they had gone in circles at least twice, they didn't mention it.

"We're much older than you, Vergil," Sil continued. "And we're not good people, if I'm perfectly honest, but neither are those in the Storm Guard. The difference between us is that we've stopped pretending."

Tallah spied their destination in the gloom and backtracked them some dozen paces. So easy to miss the hovel in this accursed place. One more mis-shapen box among many, torn down and rebuilt so many times over Valen's lifetime that its origin was lost to the folds of time. The two-storied, sharp-roofed home looked as if it had just barely survived a hurricane's fury and was held up by leaning against its equally humped and broken neighbors. Maybe it had collapsed in on itself a bit since her last visit?

A single gargoyle peered down at them from the eaves—Ludwig's obses-sion with an architecture style dead for more than a century—with a beaked face frozen in mid-roar, ready to vomit water onto the cobbles below.

At least there was a light shining on the upper-level window, flickering candlelight casting thin rays into the fog. The trip wouldn't be a complete waste of time.

"Burn my eyes, would have walked right past it again."

Sil grabbed Vergil's arm and halted him, backtracking to Tallah.

"How did you end up with the Storm Guard as your enemy? What did you two do? Did you betray them because you didn't agree with their methods? Are you renegades?"

Now he was gushing, bordering endearing and imbecilic in his new-found enthusiasm. Any more excitement in his day and he was likely to wet himself.

"She's in their bad books, not me. I doubt anyone in the Guard even remembers me," Sil replied and shushed him afterwards. "Maybe I'll tell you about it some other time."

Tallah knocked loudly on the small door and got back a loud groan from the entire building. She knocked again, louder. The old bastard would see them or she'd kick his door down. Finally, something shuffled within, and the light at the upstairs window moved away. The latches were pulled back with glacial slowness after what felt like an age of waiting.

Ludwig's gnarled hand emerged first, holding a tray with three barely burning candles. His decrepit, sharply angled, dried-leather face followed, hooked nose underlit by candlelight. He grimaced upon seeing who his late-night caller was. A ridiculous, floppy nightcap hung haphazardly across his ear.

'I will never get used to seeing him like this,' Christina groaned. 'I used to think him distinguished, not . . . this.'

'Teacher's pet,' Bianca chided.

"This is a very strange hour for visits," Ludwig said, voice still carrying the sonority of his teaching days.

"I know you burn both ends of the candle," Tallah replied. "When have you ever not liked visitors in the night?"

"Always." Ludwig swung his light around and took them in, stopping on Vergil. "Who's he?"

He lifted the candles higher for a better look, but Tallah shoved him aside. The blasted feeling of someone watching out in the gloom, as irrational as Sil's worries were, frayed her patience worse than seeing the ancient bastard usually did.

"I'm not here to be kept out in the cold, old man." She and Sil walked in, while Vergil remained outside, barred by the old man's scrutiny.

Ludwig turned around and slammed the door in Vergil's face.

"Do we leave him outside?" Sil asked. "He's too dumb to catch a cold, but still."

Tallah opened the door as the old man shuffled away. She grabbed the boy by the lapel of his shirt and dragged him in, slamming him face-first into the header with a dull thud.

"Why?" he groaned once he shook her off and shuffled inside.

"Next time, if I tell you to move, you move," she snapped at him while Sil took a look at his nose. Bent, red, and slightly bleeding. Not broken. She could have pulled harder.

"But you didn't."

Whiner.

Ludwig blew out his candles. He clapped his hands, and three large light sprites appeared to properly illuminate the room. He wore a patched and battered old nightgown draped over his long, thin frame. With a sigh, he sat tiredly onto a dusty armchair that creaked under his familiar weight.

His books, old and new, littered the room, stacked in haphazard towers that threatened collapse at the slightest disturbance. Workbenches were overladen with apparatuses and experiments half completed, all strewn about in drunken chaos.

What the room lacked were chairs.

"It annoys me more than I like admitting that I can't figure out how you can make three of these," Sil said, poking at one of the sprites moving lazily through the air. "Why do you even need candles if you can make sprites? Or just buy a sprite-lamp. They're cheaper than candles nowadays."

She and Tallah had relinquished their wet fur coats, hanging them on an ill-used set of hangers on the wall. Vergil followed their lead, though he kept shooting looks for the old man's approval.

"I dislike reading by cold sprite light," he said in a tone of voice that didn't betray any of the constant annoyance etched on the features of his face. "Candles are kinder on my soul. I could teach you, if you'd like."

"I'll have to refuse. I'm certain I don't need to hear another life story for the five heartbeats of actual learning that it would lead to."

He produced an ancient corncob pipe from somewhere and lit it with a small crackle of fire from his fingertips. Ludwig reclined back in his chair and looked to his visitors with a raised eyebrow.

"Suit yourself, Miss Silestra. While it gladdens me greatly to see the both of you safe and hale, I assume you haven't come to bother me just for a friendly chat."

"Could it ever be just a friendly chat, you old fart? No, I came because I owe you my ear." Tallah tried to find somewhere to sit. A stack of books sufficed. She refused to be made to stand for him. "I would cut it off and send it by runner if I could. I'm here. Feel free to bore me."

Ludwig gave her a gap-toothed grin. "It was her, wasn't it? Who the rhyme spoke of? It was Anna."

"It was. Your contribution was less than useful, but it did get me on the right path. I'll listen to your plea, nothing more."

"How is Anna these days?"

"Dead, cold, and rotted. Good riddance."

"Did you really seek her out just to put your old grudges to rest? I thought you above such childishness."

She fought back a smile. Yes, she had settled an old score. But it hadn't been about it at all. She and Anna would probably butt heads again on that particular issue come thaw.

"Wish that I could just grow old and waste away like you, but alas, I've other interests. On the road to the empress's forgiveness, settling grudges is just a happy occurrence."

He nodded almost sagely and smiled above a plume of pipe smoke. Yes, that tickled the perpetual empress-botherer just fine.

"It pains me somewhat to learn of her death. I hope you were swift in your execution."

"Too swift. I've rid us of a monster that should have suffered." Tallah bristled. "It would be best if I never learn you had any dealings with her."

The old git chuckled at that. "I haven't seen her since you lot were still at Hoarfrost. I told you as much."

Ludwig had told her. Appealing to him had been a last-ditch effort before moving on to the next name on her list, and he'd provided a cryptic children's rhyme from a village out in the Ruffle.

Tallah and Sil had spent weeks up in the high hills looking for that village. A near-nameless place, hidden in a deep gorge, lived in by some hundred people collecting healing herbs for Valen's apothecaries. Children recited the rhyme in their games, as if to ward off evil by turning it into something mundane and ridiculous.

She comes, she comes, the blood queen comes,
Your sight she'll break; your heart she'll take,
She comes, she comes, the blood queen comes,
Your mind she'll snare; your soul she'll scare,
She comes! She comes! Here the blood queen comes!

Pity more than nothing to go on, but it served. A creature dwelt in the deep tunnels under the Valen-Drack mountains, the elders of the village had said when inquired. It carried children off into the night, bled them, turned them into monsters and wights. Some of the lost had returned once twisted and broken, made into near-mindless monsters that had needed to be put down. Pleas to the Guild had gone unanswered.

Of course they had. Too close to the mountains, too little pay. No sane adventurer would go near that place for the kind of money those unfortunates could muster.

Tallah could recognize the work of a Vitalis mage even when twisted into local folklore. Anna's lot were a decaying, dying breed, but always tightly knit. If she could find this "blood queen" of the rhyme, she'd either find her wayward old friend or someone who knew whether she was alive or dead.

In the end, she had found her prey, hidden away and grown frightfully powerful in hermitage. Killing her had not been easy, not even with Christina lending her strength. The less said about the aftereffects of the battle, the better.

She gave Ludwig a long glare. *If this helps me, I will come back, and you can lay out your request, old man.* Those had been her exact words to him. Ever since her raid on Valen's deep vault, he'd been adamant about getting her to help him on some matter he never fully disclosed and, in return, she wasn't interested in it.

Now he had her captive attention. May as well get it over with.

"This had better be a good use of my time, old man. My gratitude only got me to the door."

Ludwig blew out a ring of smoke and settled back in his chair. "I'm certain it will be, if you're inclined enough to listen and think on the matter before you dismiss it, as you're wont to do. I believe it could profit us both greatly, and even spare you your bloody quest."

Acid rose in her throat as she readied an answer about what she was wont or not to do, and where he could shove his tone, but Sil cut between them.

"Behave, Tallah. You haven't dragged us out through this place's stinks just so you two can get into another shouting match. Let him speak, and maybe it won't take all night."

"Thank you, Miss Silestra. You are very kind."

"I'm minding the hours, not your sentiment." Sil gave him a thin smile. "Just tell us what it's all about so we can leave."

That dampened Ludwig's spirits.

"So you can leave . . ." He sighed. "Why even come if you can't entertain the idea of helping me?"

"Because I owe you. I've said it before, I'll say it again: Start talking, old man. Let's see if your need is worth considering further."

For some reason, she had thought she'd be more inclined to patience this time, more willing to indulge his bloody way of talking around what he meant to say. She had made the promise and was behooved to it, but she would rather have fought Anna all over again.

The back of her neck and her palms itched with the silent touch of unseen eyes waiting somewhere in the gloom outside.

"Well, the both of you are pitiless to an old man," Ludwig finally said after chewing on his pipe for a long time. He brought his sprites closer, as if to give himself a theatrical spotlight, sipped his foul tea, and sighed. "You make it so hard to address a subject, like walking on eggshells for fear of dismissing your hard-earned attention."

Tallah failed to stifle a jaw-cracking yawn. She waved him to go on.

"Like with all great issues, we must first look at the root of things. If you do not understand the context of my plight, you will not see why it is of such importance to me."

Christina and Bianca failed to stifle a mental groan.

It took just one moment, one look at the old man steepling his hands and leaning back in his chair with half-closed eyes, and they were all back in Hoarfrost, suffering another interminable lecture that added nothing more to their lives aside from a single nugget or two of new knowledge. Even the smell of dust and old waxed paper was the same in his home as it had been in his cramped office a century back. Even the stench of that foul thing he regarded as "tea" was the same.

I can't do this.

Tallah got up and wandered away to peruse the shelves. She took his candle tray and got the wicks burning again with some difficulty. Sil gave her a suffering glare.

"This happened before my tenure at Hoarfrost by a good few decades. Five, I think, or maybe even seven. Time becomes harder to manage and keep straight the more it flows you by. I was a different man then." He ignored her departure and kept talking. "I don't say this to justify my actions. I don't expect you would take kindly to something as blatant as that. I merely wish to offer you a complete account of what happened back then that derailed my life."

Tallah dragged a leather-bound book off a too-high shelf, and the remaining stack collapsed in an avalanche of dust and loose pages. He hadn't touched those old tomes in years, maybe decades. Paper flaked away even under her gentle touch.

Old, obsessed bastard . . .

"This was sometime on the tail end of the first Unification War led by Empress Catharina, blessed may she be always. Injury in battle robbed me of a chance to serve the empire further than the conquests of Drack and Ria, so I turned to other pursuits where my experience would be of value. I became, like many retired soldiers in those days, an explorer of the Old World, of the ruins on which we were building a bastion for our species."

Tallah threw a glance at the other two captives. Vergil actually listened with rapt attention, eyes fixed on the old man. Sil picked through Ludwig's alchemical implements strewn across a devastated workbench that hadn't seen proper use in years.

She couldn't help but chuckle. Soldier turned explorer was a pretty way of saying soldier turned tomb robber.

'Let him have this, Tallah. There is no gain to be had from calling the truth from him,' Bianca whispered, as if she were still a student in class passing on a message.

"Queen Catharina the First, soon to be empress, supported and blessed my endeavors. Aztroa funded my work. Valen offered me the men I needed. Those were my halcyon days, Tallah, when I built something that truly mattered." He fell into a long silence, smiling wistfully.

"Isn't the empire . . . ancient?" Vergil asked. "I mean, it's called the Eternal Enlightened Empire. How old are you?"

Sil was right to call him a puppy. If Vergil had a tail, it would be wagging in excitement.

"My boy," Ludwig replied in the tone of the patient professor, "I don't rightly know anymore. I've lived through at least two hundred summers, if not more."

"His memory's not as good as it used to be," Tallah said with mischievous delight. "I'm surprised he still recalls his own name going by the crap he's trying to feed us."

"Tallah . . ."

She sighed and waved Sil's exasperation away. "I'll be nice. I promise. Go on, old man." She gestured with the opened book towards Vergil. "This one is dying to know more of your illustrious life as a sanctioned tomb robber."

"I am not and have never been a tomb robber, you blighted ash eater," Ludwig shot back, nearly pushing himself out of the chair. "I brought back knowledge lost to the ages, knowledge too valuable to even express in words. I helped start the Adventurers Guild in those days. Show a morsel of respect."

"You helped found an enclave of thieves with sanction from a conquering queen hungry for power. What you brought her were new paths through which to march her armies so she could catch her enemies unaware. Best to call a duck a duck." She turned her attention to Vergil. "Believe maybe a word in three if it comes from him. There's not much left or preserved of his discoveries, not after being trampled to dust by armies coming and going."

She squinted at another book and tried to drag it off its shelf. By candlelight and without her glasses, she could barely make out what was written on its spine. Could have been a cookbook and it still would have been preferable to the old man's sweetened accounts.

"Regardless," Ludwig said at length, "I don't intend to defend myself. Just listen, please."

"Agreed. Please go on, Master Angledeer, before morning creeps up on us." Sil sent a sprite to Tallah's aid, and a glare to warn off further interruptions.

"My travels ultimately led me to the gateway of a civilization so ancient that barely any legend of them still survives. But their power, in those rare myths that have survived decay, was believed beyond comprehension. They had unlocked the stars, ladies. Can you even imagine that? Finding a way into their inner sanctums, into the heart of their sealed city, would have changed the face of Edana. Not even the aelir have a claim on history as old as this.

"This wasn't a path to march through. This was pure knowledge, pure history that wanted, no, that needed to be uncovered. Empress Catharina gladly gave me all I asked for in this pursuit. Men, warriors and thinkers, weapons, money, resources. This was to be my life's greatest achievement, my claim on the immortal soul of the empire."

"And yet, here you are. Vergil, come here and hold this for me. It's filthy and I like this dress."

"And yet, here I am, yes," Ludwig echoed her words as Vergil reluctantly shuffled over to her. The old man smoked more pensively, the fire seeming to leave him. "I did find the city. I found the door to it. I found that it was open, but there was no safe passage through. Death lurked beyond it, death unseen and unheard. Something beyond resisted us . . . and we succumbed. The cost in lives was . . ."

He pressed a gnarled hand to his eyes and looked away, into the shadowed nooks of his home.

"Riveting. If you want to try again, I'm not interested." Tallah handed the heavy tome to Vergil and moved him around so the sprite's light would serve better. "I don't care to become another casualty of your ambitions."

"I didn't fail. That's the core of it. In the end, I succeeded." He drew in a deep breath and held it for some time. When he spoke, it was low enough that Tallah had to strain to hear him. "I needed a cipher to go through. I sought audience with the empress herself, and was granted it. I prostrated myself to her and made a plea. I needed a cipher breaker, someone that could see what both was and wasn't there. I needed an Egia."

Sil let out a slow laugh.

"And you didn't ask for one of the moons too? Egia were even rarer back then than they are now."

"I was young, foolish, and too confident in my abilities. The empress nearly had me thrown to the dogs. But in her wisdom, she thought on my request for a long time. I had the determination and my past successes. I knew she would see the value in my efforts, so I waited, right there, on my knees, for two whole days.

"I was thrown out after the Court got tired of tripping over me. Days later, an aide sought me out and brought me to the first gate. It activated, and through it stepped . . . Erisa." He whispered the name, like trying to shift a heavy stone off his heart. "She was barely fifteen summers, still flowering, a dark-eyed girl that regarded me with curiosity and eager wanderlust. I was told she had been born to the School of Healing and had never seen anything but its walls and gardens. She held the empress's hand but was not afraid.

"'I entrust her to you, Angledeer, as she was entrusted to me by the school. If any harm should come to her, I will have you flogged within a hair's breadth of your life,' she told me. I barely heard the threat. My mind was filled with the triumphant song of destiny made manifest at long last.

"And I was a fool."

"So . . . what happened?" Vergil asked as Ludwig lapsed into silence.

Tallah, despite herself, was intrigued.

'He was onto something if the empress actually granted him an Egia,' Christina mused. 'If this is going where it appears to be, then I think Professor Angledeer might have made a grave mistake.'

"Of course, I wasn't entrusted alone with her safety. The empress chose minders from her veterans to accompany us on the journey, some of the first of the newly established Storm Guard. Her enemies were rallying then, on the Summer of Bastra's Humbling. We set out on our journey into the Crags while she marched down into the south, on a beautiful early-summer day.

"Erisa was everything I had hoped she would be and so much more. Where I'd lost over forty people on my previous attempt, I now only lost five to carelessness and mischance. She guided us through the danger, fast and true, straight into the embrace of history. Beyond the passage, our prize awaited."

Vergil trembled with excitement like a child listening to bedtime stories of faer folk and dragon kings. That, despite her shriveling patience, got a smile out of Tallah. The coming ending to the remembrance, like for all good faer stories, would be tragic. For his sake, she held her tongue.

Ludwig sighed, reached for his cup, and took another sip of tea.

"It all went wrong once we reached the city. Creatures such as I have never encountered before assailed us the moment we emerged out of the passage, before we could bask in the glory of our success. Our first clash was vicious and bloody, but we endured and pushed back the tide.

"After that, we began to die one by one. They hunted us down, grabbed us in the night, from our sleep, from making our water. Our strength lessened by the passing hour."

"Wh-What was killing you? What were they?" Vergil asked with a shaking voice.

"I hesitate to call them spiders, but that is as close as I can describe those nightmarish apparitions. Something as mundane as that, grown by some cursed means to the size of a man, even larger, with razor claws and envenomed fangs. We were powerless against their tide.

"The evil in there—for there is no other word that serves for it—jealously guarded its secrets. We barely made it beyond the threshold, and we had lost half of our strength. Half, Tallah. Good men and women of valor that had laid down their lives for our mission. Their dying cries haunt me still."

Tallah yawned. Ludwig kept going.

"Whatever controlled the creatures sent an envoy on our third day there. We were weary and tired, bloodied and desperate. Bone-white monsters came up to us, and without words, I knew what they wanted." He sighed deeply, sipped his tea, and held the cup in both hands on his lap. "They wanted the girl. They wanted Erisa. I do not know why or what for."

His sprites dimmed out until only Sil's was left. The long shadow of a bookshelf settled over him as he finished his tale, face lit by the embers of his pipe.

"I accepted. To my eternal shame, I accepted. What choice did I have? I gave them the girl, and they, in turn, showed us safe passage out. It was easy for them. We lost people that couldn't keep up the pace.

"Fifty and five people left Aztroa with me. Eight got back."

"I don't expect the empress enjoyed the news you brought back," Sil said from where she sat on the edge of the work desk.

Ludwig chuckled grimly.

"She had me flogged, then imprisoned in the darkest, smallest cell she could find in Aztroa. After weeks of agony and filth, she had me flogged again, then thrown out of the city with nothing but the bloodied rags on my back. I was promised the headsman's axe if I ever set foot again within a league of the capital. I've never dared check if the edict still stands."

Tallah waited for Ludwig to go on, but the old man lapsed into silence. A small crackle of fire showed him lighting up his pipe anew, but he said nothing more.

"Put this back on the shelf. It's more religious garbage from the Dominion." She slammed closed the tome she had been reading and brought Vergil out of his fascinated stupor. He blinked at her and then turned back to Ludwig.

"What happened next?" he asked, maybe still hoping for a happy ending. There couldn't be one.

"Next, lad, was a long life of regret," the old man said as he let out a heavy breath.

"Which doesn't tell me what you bloody want," Tallah snapped at him as she physically pushed Vergil to do as she bid. "The girl's dead. The empress's angry. All of it seems like a done deal to me."

"I want your help to get back into that city and find the girl."

Very few things in her long life had left Tallah at a complete loss for words. Rhine giving birth. The empress betraying her faith. Maybe a few other scattered moments.

The sheer stupidity of Ludwig's request was now added to that short list.

"Have you gone daft?" she finally managed. "Why would you want to go back there? What for?"

"The girl haunts my dreams, Tallah. I see her every time I close my eyes. I haven't had a night's full sleep since we escaped that damned place. You are my final chance at setting right the wrong I enacted so long ago."

"Master Angledeer, there is no possible way in which the girl could still be alive," Sil said, echoing Tallah's thoughts perfectly. "Going back there is a fool's errand at best."

"Yes, it's an old man's folly," Ludwig agreed. "It could have meant something once, when it would have mattered, but now it is only an old man's folly. I know that, Miss Silestra. You would think me mad, but I know the girl, or something of her, still endures. I have proof of it."

"What proof?"

"I'd much rather not say. If you must take something on faith, then take that."

He summoned his light sprite back and moved it around the room as if looking for something. "It is also a matter of redemption in the eyes of the empire."

Tallah laughed, at both the absurdity of taking anything on faith and at his dreams of redemption.

"The empire doesn't even know who you are. It doesn't care."

"It doesn't matter."

"The empress will still have your head on a spike the moment you step into Aztroa, carrying the bones of the girl or not. I doubt she still cares about you, but that only means she's never rescinded her edict."

"It doesn't matter. I will have completed my duty and can happily die once that is achieved."

Sentimentality and zeal always made for the worst combinations in people.

No, this isn't about either of those, Tallah thought as she studied Ludwig's serene expression.

'You doubt him,' Christina said, pensive. 'There is more to the story than he tells.'

There always is. I expect he wants his bloody place in history back.

Out loud, she said, "I don't see my benefit in any of this." She gestured to the room in general. "Your theatrics were all very fine, I assure you, but I don't see why all of this is something I would care about."

He gave her a patient look, like an expectant teacher on the verge of disappointment.

"I would think it obvious. You're on this bloody penitent mission for whatever you did to wrong the Storm Guard and the empress's faith. Bring her this bounty, Tallah, and she will forgive you, regardless of sin."

There. She almost laughed. He truly believed the lie she'd fed him seasons back, about her motives and her discharge from the Storm Guard. And he tried to use it for his gain. Which was . . . what?

She played along for a while longer as she dusted herself off. If nothing else, he had at least managed to rouse her curiosity.

"I don't see the value in tracking down a corpse. Even if there's anything left to find, you'd never know it. One bone's as white as another," she said. "We both know it's foolish. I'm not so desperate yet that I'd turn to faer stories for my deliverance."

Ludwig blew out a plume of blue-gray smoke and grinned with mischief.

"I never expected you to agree to this for the sake of naked bones and sentiment," he said. "This could be worth your while if you'll allow me a few moments more of your attention, now that I finally have it."

"By all means, beg away."

"This is not about begging. I do not plan to beg. I have that much dignity left."

He got up slowly and walked over to an overburdened worktable. One wayward spark could turn his home into a crater, considering the overabundance of magical tomes and old, brittle paper.

He dislodged a single large tome from a scattered heap and blew off the patina of neglect from its covers.

"This place is a sty," Sil said as she covered her face in the crook of her elbow. More books fell, and the dust rose thick as the chemical mist outside.

"I still recall what drove you, back when you would still call me *professor*. I expect it has changed little in the decades since."

He gestured Vergil to him, unwilling to bring himself over to where Tallah had perched in her exploration. At a nod from her, the boy obeyed and brought the book.

"This, I believe, might change your mind."

'He means to bait you,' Christina said, echoing her own thoughts. 'He is old, not foolish. I doubt he ever expected your better nature to jump to his aid.'

When Vergil presented her with the metal-dressed tome, she heard its call immediately. It was barely as thick as her thumb but so richly dressed in illum that she could actually sense it. If she had her mask, it would likely show a tapestry of woven power so dense that it would be blinding.

"Marvelous," she whispered as she ran her fingers down the smooth, time-worn protection plate on the cover. "I don't recognize this lettering." She caressed the words imprinted on the shell and could hardly resist the temptation of peeking inside. But opening a tome so thick with illum without proper precautions could be catastrophic.

"Neither do I," Ludwig said as he sat back down and lit his pipe again. "Neither does anyone. You hold the sole artifact I managed to hold on to from that cursed expedition. To my knowledge, nobody in Aztroa Magnor has managed to decipher any of the others."

He leaned forward as he smoked, letting the pause speak for his intentions.

Sil sighed heavily. "You're offering her power." She clicked her tongue in annoyance. "You're a malevolent old fart, did you know?"

Tallah looked over to them to see Sil glaring at a very self-satisfied Ludwig. The glare snapped to her.

"We are not going in the middle of winter to some dusty old ruin in the middle of nowhere!"

"I never said we were going at all, winter or summer," Tallah protested.

"It's on your face," Vergil said sheepishly by her side. "We can all see it."

"Oh, spare me," Sil snapped at her. "When have you ever ignored a chance like this? The woe story was an excuse to have you sitting still for two moments, but this horrible old bastard knew exactly where to pinch to make you giddy."

'That is a particularly disgusting mental image. Thank you for that, Adana,' both Christina and Bianca complained. Tallah shrugged off their indignation.

She held the book out and waggled it at Ludwig. "You could have shown me this at any time, and I would have been tempted. Why not lead with it? Why bore me first?"

Ludwig reclined in his chair and puffed out more blue smoke. "I am not a fool. You being in my debt is the only reason you'll even listen to the next part."

She raised an eyebrow at that. Sil had crossed her arms at her chest and seemed particularly displeased about the whole discussion.

"Had you known about the book, I fully expect you would have gone into that city of your own volition for more and cared very little about my wishes on the matter. But you see"—he gestured with the tip of his pipe—"I want to come along. I need to come along when you go. My business with that place is not concluded."

"You will aim us in the right direction, and that will be the end of your involvement," Tallah countered. "If I go, it will be in my own time, on my own terms. You don't have a say in that."

Ludwig shrugged, unmoved.

"I am coming. I don't care when. You owe me at least this." He talked with such certainty that it made her blood boil.

"I could just extract the path from you, old man," she said, meaning every word. "Do not test my patience."

The git stared at her levelly. "Do your worst. I am either coming, or you shall never get there alive." He tapped his temple with two fingers. "I am the only person living that knows the way. I've made certain of that. The empress never had the time or inclination to risk another incursion. After my colossal mishap, she lost the trust of the School of Healing, and that rift has never mended since. And the one artifact that could be used instead of an Egia belonged to Valen, not the empire, and is now in your possession." His eyes shone with the fire of purpose. "I need to go, Tallah. I need forgiveness and to be freed of my ghosts and my failure. You will take me there because you have no other choice."

So bloody pleased with himself. He fashioned that he'd made his case and won her compliance. As if she were a child to be placated into behaving by being offered sweet meats.

Tallah smiled her best grin and threw aside the tome.

"Well, get buggered, then. Enjoy your dreams of the corpse girl. Come on, Sil, we're done."

Ludwig's jaw dropped, and he sputtered, pipe almost falling from his lips. He'd had it all planned so well. Tempt her, offer a trinket, make promises of power and knowledge, even redemption to seal the deal. But she had listened to the story and weighed its allure against her needs.

What was there really to gain?

Weeks out in the cold. A delay to plans half a decade in the making. More strain on her when she was far from well and recovered. Come thaw, she'd need to head towards the Inner Sea, and from there, down the swelling Bistry River towards Old Forge. Deidra had been sighted there last. Ludwig's errand would happen now or never . . . and she saw no profit in it.

"You owe me." His face grew hard and pale, a bloodless mask draped over old, gaunt bones. "I gave Anna to you. I offer you power like you can scarcely believe. The secrets there—"

"Secrets are worth less than nothing to me. Legends grow fatter in the telling. I promised I'd listen. I did. My debt is complete." She kicked aside the pile of books on which she'd sat and walked to him. "Do you think me a child, *Professor*? Do you think you can waggle vague promises at me, and I'll lap it up, eager to bound off into the dark because you said there would be sweets there?"

She pitied the old fool. She pitied the way he lived and the way he regretted that he lived. Alone, forgotten, abused by his memories. He surrounded himself with dust and the detritus of countless wasted years, and just waited to die.

Well, she refused any part in his drama.

"I—I can give you . . ." He faltered for words. Wide eyes searched around the room, desperate for something else to back up his pleas.

"What can you give me, *Professor*? Even for Anna, all you gave us was a rhyme you heard in some village. We followed that trail on our own."

And now it was all getting rather pathetic. She gestured for Vergil to bring them their cloaks.

The boy was looking at the discarded book, head tilted sideways, muttering. He leaned over and picked up the tome, staring at the cover's odd letters.

"The letters are really weirdly drawn, but it says *Understanding the Correlation Between Illum Conversion and Intrinsic Personality Biases*. It says it's volume three of five."

Ludwig looked as if he'd been smacked over the head with the metalbound book.

"Fancy that," she said nastily, "I don't even need to go there for a cipher. Can you give me Deidra? Or Lucretia? Or the exact day Ort returns from the Maggot War?"

Of course he couldn't. His jaw snapped closed, and he gazed up at her with honest loathing. At last, a spark of honesty from him.

"You won't forgive yourself even if you do go back there, Master Angledeer," Sil said as she donned her thick cloak. "Learn to leave the past in the past and move on. Going back to the place of your failure will not atone you, not even to your own conscience."

He turned sharply to her, hands balled into white-knuckled fists. His eyes were feverishly bright. "She is alive, Miss Silestra." Old fists struck the armrests of his chair. "Alive! I know that with every fiber of my being. Take the book and leave me be. Just remember, Tallah, that I know you're in Valen. I—"

He stopped and seemed to think better of the threat he almost voiced. Tallah loomed over him and gave him time to consider his words.

"No. That is unfair. I apologize." He deflated and passed a hand over his eyes. "You are right. You only ever promised to listen, and did so. I was a fool to think you'd accept such an undertaking, especially on my terms."

"At least there's still a shred of wisdom in you, *Professor*."

Sil glared at her. Christina too. Tallah relented in her mockery.

"If I learn of anything in my travels that may aid you, I will pass it on. You at least have my promise on that."

Vergil brought the book and their cloaks. For better or worse, the evening hadn't been entirely without merit, even if her relationship with her old teacher would never mend. Him threatening her was not going to be forgotten.

Ludwig did not rise to see them off. Sprite light faded when they opened the door and the night's fog and chill rushed in. They left him brooding in his chair, clad in darkness and accusing silence.

"For a heartbeat, I thought you'd accept," Sil said as they made their way back out of the labyrinth.

"For a couple, so did I. But it's a bad time for flights of fancy, especially when they're not mine."

Again, the prickling sensation on the back of her neck, like someone tugging on hairs. She turned and startled Vergil right behind her.

"What?" he asked, brandishing the book like a shield against her attention.

Behind and over his shoulder, the night stretched on, now old and gloomy, threatening a storm. They'd stopped between the narrow cones of two streetlights, down a final flight of steps before the Agora, utterly alone. A faint noise of cheering and laughter came from their destination, but behind them, all had grown still and quiet. Shifts would be changing soon.

"It's nothing," Tallah said after listening for a time. Sil tugged on her cloak, eager to be down in the city proper, away from the heavy chemical stench.

"Dealing with the old man was more tiring than I thought. I'm imagining things." She hooked her arm around Vergil's elbow and dragged him forward. "Let's go try this skating thing people here are so crazy about, my dear. It's bound to be such lovely fun."

"At this hour?" Vergil whimpered.

Sil chuckled.

"My dear, Valen never sleeps."

And the back of her neck still prickled.

CHAPTER FOURTEEN

Learn to Attack

Quistis kneeled over Falor and inspected the wound.

His breathing wheezed through the gash in his side. True sight granted by the Goddess showed two . . . no, three shattered ribs, and his right lung quickly deflating. He tried to smile and say something but choked on blood.

For all the power the commander wielded, he was impulsive and poorly practiced with most mundane weapons aside from his great warhammer, something Barlo was determined to beat, smash, and impale out of him.

She dug through her satchel and handed him two mixtures to drink. One to offset his blood loss, the other to strengthen him before the actual healing. It took some effort for him to down them.

With a palm on his mangled chest, she requested the Goddess's aid. "*I require this one to be mended.*"

That put her at half of her daily allotment. She'd stop the training session after the next wound. By how things were going, she wouldn't be out in the cold for much longer.

It was a credit to Barlo's skill that he had managed to inflict such ugly wounds without outright killing the lord commander. Three crushed ribs and a collapsed lung just on the tail of a full-body impalement, a near severance of the commander's right arm at the shoulder, and a crushed eye socket . . .

She sighed as Falor stumbled back to his feet, rolled his shoulders, and sauntered away to pick up his weapon. He spat a glob of blood, coughed, and spat another into the fresh snow.

Barlo, stripped down to the waist and barefooted, paced the outer rim of the sparring ground. Steam rose off him in thin wisps, curling around the edges of his bone-plate carapace. Vanadal carapace never stopped growing, and Barlo didn't file his smooth like tradition dictated, allowing it to grow into a spiky, jagged mess that gave him the look of a long-ago savage.

He held his swords loose at his side and waited for his willing victim to come back into range.

She caught his eyes and the question there, then replied with a nod. Yes, Falor could continue training. For as mercilessly as Barlo beat him, he would never go a single step beyond her mandates. She could stop their session with a single gesture, but that would injure the commander's pride much worse than the Miscreant's blades ever could, especially if Quistis could still heal him.

Some soldiers were gathered on the other side of the arena, watching in silence the lessons administered. Each of them had been in there with Barlo before, and all knew intimately the edge of his blades. None cheered or commented on the exchange of blows.

Snow fell in thicker swathes now as both men took up position and raised their guard. Barlo's weapons of choice for the day were his ugly curved blades, one in each dominant hand, while Falor faced him with a wide-bladed halberd. Quistis washed her hands in snow and scurried back into the cover of the pavilion overlooking the sparring grounds to watch another bout of the massacre.

Falor's warhammer, a particularly nasty piece of star ore, rested next to her chair like a squatting great hound waiting for its master's return. It was decidedly too heavy for her to move away, so she moved her chair instead. Something about the weapon always got her teeth itching, and being alone with it only made it worse. When the master got hurt, the hound growled, and she felt its resonance in the pit of her stomach.

Any moment now, Quistis thought as she looked into the still-darkening sky. By her reckoning, it would be past the third bell of morning, but the darkness hadn't abated. A storm brewed above, gathering malice to unleash onto Valen.

Weapons clashed with dull rings of metal on metal. Falor came out swinging, trying to force the point of Barlo's weapon away from him and thrust for the throat. He had the conviction for the swing but sadly not the strength. As large and well-muscled as he was, Barlo was simply much larger and much stronger. He barely flinched when attacked so brazenly, allowing the point of the halberd to pass by his face, and moved in to deliver a vicious punch rather than outright kill with his sword. He'd already demonstrated that technique earlier.

Falor had to dodge back or get his head punched off.

"You miserable bastard," he groaned as Barlo kicked his halberd back to him. "I'll bloody you today, or so help me . . ."

His threat was met with a raised chin. Barlo exposed his throat, said nothing, charged with a scissor slash of both swords. It got the commander backtracking, desperately trying to push back the rampaging bull with a slash of his axe head. Barlo's large sword pushed down the haft of his halberd, and the other swung for his neck.

Quistis barely followed the next exchange.

Falor pushed forward and ducked under the slash. His halberd's hook passed behind Barlo's calf, and he tried to reverse the motion to rip out his opponent's ankle. The Miscreant took it in stride and moved forward with the motion of the weapon, hook scraping against the armored heel of his boot. He smashed into Falor, forehead to nose bridge, bone-armored torso against blood-soaked tunic.

Another loss for the commander. Quistis got ready to go back out and heal him.

Something crackled in the air, and Barlo jumped back.

"Oh no."

The warhammer burst out through the chest-high ring wall in an explosion of pulverized stone fragments, straight into Falor's hand. She turned away and shielded her face against the kicked-up dust.

"Temper, temper, Commander," Barlo said. He still held his chin up. "We're not training against sparkles today."

Falor's nose was broken, and blood ran down his face, but his eyes shone with crackling power.

"Let's see how you keep your temper, Barlo, if I knock you around until the bells toll." The words came out slurred through cracked teeth and lips. Their intent was clear enough. Lightning arced down the hammer's long shaft and discharged into the bloodied mud.

Quistis rushed to intervene, but a gesture from Barlo stopped her behind the ruin of the wall. He would ride out the storm.

The thick-skinned bastard never lowered his head.

Lightning sheathed Falor as he swung the hammer with practiced ease and infused strength. He swung at the ground and coils of electricity rushed Barlo.

"This be a bad time, Cap'?"

Quistis almost jumped out of her skin. She hadn't heard the man walk in, hadn't seen him get close. The only entrance to the sparring ground was directly opposite her vantage point.

Aidan had always made Quistis's skin crawl. The man wasn't much to behold, and even less to remember by. He was of average height and average build and had a face that a mother's love could think of as homely. He wore loose clothes, grays on blacks, and looked like nothing more than an overworked bureaucrat of the Fortress. Dark skin, dark eyes, raven black hair, not a smile in sight.

He was Rumi's shadow, her assigned Claw. If Rumi hid what she really was, Aidan wore it on his sleeve with a semblance of pride.

"I wasn't expecting a report this morning." Quistis composed herself and turned back to the sparring. Barlo held his own, but Falor's bursts of power kept him on the backslide and off balance. The commander, even when angered, held himself in check and made sure his outburst didn't spill out of the fighting arena. Nonetheless, she'd need to intervene before he put the warrior beyond her help and into the Sisters' care.

"Aye, but me thinks you'd get prop'ly wobbly if I'd waited," Aidan replied with mischievous delight. "You's not gonna like this."

"I'm listening. And speak properly, please. I haven't had enough coffee for you to speak Rian at me."

He chuckled, swallowed, and made the effort. "I followed the two doves you was interested in. Well, they's three now. Third's a boy toy. Lives with 'em. I's lookin' at 'im, but gonna take time."

"Mm-hm."

Barlo dodged a serpent of blue-white energy and switched to the attack. This time, Falor forced back the swing of the swords with his hammer. He spun around, carried by the momentum of the heavy weapon, and smashed Barlo in the chest with bone-cracking fury. Lightning flashed on impact and sent the vanadal sprawling through the mud.

It wasn't enough. The Miscreant rolled with the blast and was back on his feet before Falor closed the distance. His lips cracked into a full-fanged grin, but he still didn't lower his head as he met the commander's next swing.

"So, did we learn what other pastries they like?" she asked, eyes fixated on the duel. After the first couple of weeks of looking into the sorceress and her healer and getting absolutely nothing of worth, she had put them out of mind. She could read only so many reports of where they took their desserts before it got rather yawn-inducing.

Rumi was less inclined to leave them be. Either as prospective recruits, or for other reasons Quistis didn't want to think about, she had taken a curious interest that refused to abate.

"Aye. Waffles with custard, in the Agora," Aidan said with dry amusement.

She glared at him. The spy grinned, too pleased with himself for her liking.

"They met with someone last night, someone you'd care to know about. Ludwig Angledeer, by Lady Cassandra's Old Hope Church."

"Why do I care about him?"

She'd heard the name somewhere, but it wasn't on her list of troublemakers and potential problems. Maybe some sort of scholar? She remembered a book by one Angledeer, but what it was about wouldn't spring to mind.

"Cinder's teacher. Last one alive."

That pried her interest away from the exchange of blows. He went on in the usual dry monotone he used every time he reported something to her.

"Hard to get close to 'em. Very hard. They's got eyes in the backs of they heads. I couldn't hear the talk, couldn't be that close, but kept up with 'em and followed through the Alchemists' soup. I know who he's about because Lady Belli drew up a list of the sorceress's old acquaintances. Just in case."

He glanced over her shoulder and moved two steps aside.

"Another thing, Cap'. That flame-breath and her crony? They be acting peculiar like when away from eyes. Very careful in public, very prop'ly posh. But not so much when they thinks it's private. Other body talk, not lady and servant. Me nose don't likes it."

That was too much coincidence to ignore. She'd accepted the explanation for young Tianna's interest in the troublemakers of Hoarfrost. There was never a shortage of young, misguided people interested to know more about the most powerful students the Academy had ever trained up to Falor. Some even sought to imitate them.

But meeting with someone that was an actual, living connection? There's interest, and then there's troublesome obsession that always seemed to land in her lap.

"I want them marked and—"

Barlo crashed into the pavilion, flew through the space Aidan had occupied, and hit the back wall with a stone-cracking thump. He landed in a heap, lay still for a few moments, and then hauled himself to his feet with some difficulty. His chest carapace was shattered, and he had to lean against the wall to steady himself, but still made the effort of raising his chin.

"Bloody bastard—" Quistis turned to Falor as he leaned on the ruin of the separating wall. "You got me again," he said through gritted teeth.

The commander had dropped his hammer and held his stomach with both hands. Soft, pink entrails poked through the net of his fingers.

"Need a touch of help, Quis." His knees gave out and he fell into the mud, groaning in agony.

Quistis spared a glare for Barlo before vaulting over with her medical supplies.

"If I could heal you so that it kept hurting for a fortnight or more, I would." Another ugly wound that would scar, and it wasn't even necessary. She dug her fingers into his opened abdomen, feeling for the damage. He clung to consciousness and tried to smile at her anger, stoically failing to not wince as she checked him over.

Without a healer on hand, in actual battle, that wound would be a festering nightmare. She knew it. He knew it.

She let her silence scream invective at him.

"I didn't cut him deep," Barlo rumbled above, looking down over the shattered rim of the wall. He peeled off shattered bits of carapace, purple with viscera, and tried to round off the edges with a bloodied dagger. In a few days' time, his armor would be regrown even stronger than before, and the edges would be gray scars on white bone. "If someone goes fer yer belly, commander, don't step into the swing when that someone's got a second blade ready. Killing them won't be worth much if ye ain't fit t' fight the next bastard."

"Shut up. I bloodied you." Words gurgled up bloody from the commander's throat.

"And I killed ye. Hope it was worth the captain's ire."

Quistis groaned her displeasure, packed Falor's guts back in, and healed him. She would treat him later with salves to reduce the scarring, and purgers to clear up any rot that may have gotten into the cuts. As far as she was concerned, this morning's sparring was finished, and she dared one of them to contradict her.

"Aidan," she called out, "please fetch Rumi and Vial. Barlo, get cleaned up and join us." She handed him an accelerant to hasten his natural recovery. "You too, Commander."

"What'd I miss?" Falor wheezed out when she helped him up. There wasn't much left of his clothes but tattered, bloody rags.

"News on our Cinder situation."

"She's surfaced?"

"No. But a cold trail started stinking." She washed the blood off her hands with snow as she walked away from the sparring ring, giving a wide berth to the discarded hammer. "May be nothing. Still, I don't want to chance it."

Storm winds picked up, and the shingles above rattled like dead men's fingers, welcoming the coming tempest.

CHAPTER FIFTEEN

Learn to Defend

"Come on, just put your hand in this," Tallah told Vergil as sweetly as she could manage to twist her voice. She even tried giving the boy an encouraging smile. Something must have shown on her face because he refused the lure.

"I really don't want to touch it." He moved further away from her, keeping Sil's high-backed chair between them.

"I could simply throw it at you. I guarantee I wouldn't miss." She had to chase him at her slowest pace lest she lose the thread of concentration. It allowed the boy too much freedom to dodge her.

She held her hands out, and thin strands of black lightning arched between her fingers. They ate light with every pulsation, erratically dimming the room as she stalked him. It took a lot of concentration at that stage of testing to keep the effect going. Even if she wanted to, she couldn't actually hurl it at him. She and Christina could barely manifest and keep it coherent, and Vergil had unwittingly called her bluff.

Her chest burned when channeling. Pain lingered even when she didn't channel. It took a real effort of will to force illum into this new form, and the blasted boy refused to help her test it.

"But electricity could fry the chip in my head." He excused himself again, moving in circles around her work desk. "You wouldn't set your own research on fire, would you?" He sounded a lot less sure when she vaulted onto her books and files, scattering them.

"I know you're lying, bucket-head," she said. Her control slipped, and the lightning licked back at her, unruly and wild. She cut her illum flow and started again, forcing herself through the white flashes of misery. "Blast you. Sil had me electrocuting you exactly five times so far, and your thing is still chirping away."

There was a sound from Sil's room, and the large black door opened with a slight creak. A nearly nude, bleary-eyed Mertle walked out, stumbling over Vergil's small bed in the main hall. She stopped in the doorway to the study room and stared at the cat-and-mouse game.

Vergil hadn't noticed her walk up. His attention was solely on keeping at least out of Tallah's arm reach.

"I really don't want to touch that," he said, backing away. Nimble little critter when he wanted to be. Tummy's teaching must have been sticking somewhere, for the boy was getting cheeky with her.

"It won't hurt," Tallah replied, smiling as he backed into Mertle.

"I'm sorry, but I—I—I really don't believe that."

". . .'s privy?" Mertle asked, two steps behind him, in a quiet, sleepy voice.

"What?"

He turned for a moment, surprised, and Tallah pounced on his moment of distraction, getting both hands around his throat for direct skin contact. Nothing happened for a heartbeat, and then he collapsed, frothing at the mouth, body convulsing violently. He did not make a single sound.

Huh. That was unexpected at least.

The elendine looked at him, then at her, and frowned. "Why?" she asked, eyes squinting.

"Door opposite this one, Mertle," Tallah said as she walked around the convulsing body. "Vergil's helping me test some things. He'll be fine. Probably."

She crouched next to the boy and inspected his fluttering eyelids. The spasms came and went, and he curled up into a tight ball on the floor to gibber away in a language Tallah couldn't understand. That was also unexpected. He seemed to be cursing at her.

Mertle shrugged and swayed softly from side to side, a large grin plastered on her sleepy face. "Sil's not upset with me. Yay."

"That's nice. I did tell you so."

"Thank you." She hugged Tallah's back and then walked away to the bathroom. After a while, she walked back to Sil's room and closed the large door behind herself.

It took some time for Vergil to regain the use of his limbs, and then a few heartbeats more before his gibbering stopped. Tallah poked him in the cheek with a quill.

"What's your head-thing say?" she asked, excited, notepad prepared.

"That you're a horrible person," Vergil muttered and tried to pick himself off the floor. He could move, but coordinating seemed particularly challenging. He managed to get up on his knees and hands but crashed back on his face in a tangle of limbs and cusses.

"I quote." He groaned. "'Your body is afflicted by alcohol poisoning. You are now confused and dazed. Motor skills, vision, speech, reason, and sexual drive may be impaired and respond erratically. Do not operate heavy machinery. Seek medical aid.'"

"Sexual drive? What?" Tallah barely contained her laughter as she wrote down Vergil's interpretation of what had happened to him. Basically what she expected and hoped for, with some flourishes.

"It thinks I've drunk myself stupid, and it's exactly how I assume it feels." He kept trying to get up. "I wouldn't know."

He failed again and dropped down on his face. Tallah made no effort to help.

"Did it endanger your life in any way? Does it say anything about organ damage or anything similar?"

"Nothing like that, no. It doesn't even hurt." Something sparked in his eyes as he finally managed to get some semblance of coordination back. He got up in a sitting position and tried to pull away in a panic.

"What?" she asked, more and more excited by the results.

Vergil looked horrified. "I'm seeing three of you."

That earned him a smack over the head and another face-plant on the floor. He half chuckled, half groaned, sound muffled by the thick carpet.

"I think I'll put down impaired judgement," Tallah said and left him to manage on his own.

She headed to the study and closed the heavy oak door as Mertle's soft giggles could be heard two rooms over, and a bit more than that. Sil got self-conscious about those things, and it'd make her more comfortable if she found the door closed when they inevitably came out for food. Sometime in the tenday, maybe.

Vergil had managed to find his feet, and he wobbled his way into a chair in front of the fireplace. If nothing more, he made for the perfect test subject. It helped to have someone who could somewhat accurately describe what he was experiencing instead of simply whining.

"You can create magic?" he asked as he sat down heavily, head held in his hands with his elbows propped on his knees. "Isn't magic all in dusty tomes and . . ." He gestured to where his helmet lay on the mantelpiece above the fireplace.

"New channeling effects are easy to produce. You need a bit of imagination and a great deal of understanding of yourself and the natural world." She finished her notes and began copying them more neatly in her grimoire.

"Repeating this by instinct is the hard part. Takes practice." She gave him a level glare. "And a willing, cooperating subject."

It was Anna's mastery over her flesh dolls that had sparked the need for this particular variation of Christina's stunning bolt. To kill a doll with fire took a lot more illum than it did for Anna to make new ones and keep up her assault, especially in her overfed sanctum. A way to disrupt the connection between maker and creation would simplify the problem in the future. It could also make things easier to manage when she needed a quick exit and did not wish to leave a trail of bodies behind.

With nothing of any real worth gained from the boy, she had all winter to either sulk or work. And working kept her mind off other things. Rhine's wraith threatened intrusion even now, and she was determined to avoid it.

She shook herself out of her reverie. Vergil was talking to her.

"Come again?" she asked. He looked expectant of her, as if he'd asked a question she hadn't caught.

"Could I also learn magic?"

"No."

"Why not?"

Tallah raised an eyebrow and then pointed to his horned helmet. "You can't generate the helmet's effect at all. That means you're impervious to illum, a blank. Without illum conductivity, which occurs naturally in most people, you can't channel illum into effects. You can do it or you can't."

Vergil deflated. "So it's not just chanting out words and making things happen? I thought that's how it worked." He gestured weakly with his hands.

Tallah raised her index finger, and a flame flickered to life a few inches above its tip.

"Channeling, or magic, if you'd like, is all about transforming illum into an observable effect." The flame on her fingertip changed color from a playful red to bright blue, its contour sharpening. "The more illum you channel into an effect, the stronger it becomes, up to a threshold."

The air began to sizzle, and she put out the fire. She looked at her blistered finger and then stuck it in her mouth, reminded that she shouldn't do demonstrations without her gloves on. She pointed with her free hand to a crystal vial on Sil's desk and gestured for Vergil to bring it over.

He uncorked the healing potion and offered it without a word. Instead of drinking it, Tallah stuck her finger in and swirled the liquid around.

"No point wasting a perfectly good mixture for a burnt finger," she said.

"Sil always chants something when she does magic," Vergil said, curiosity giving his voice a near-childlike wonder.

"She's a healer," Tallah replied and wanted to leave it at that. The boy looked at her so expectantly and leaned in so close that she begrudgingly went on. "Healing channeling is different from whatever we're taught at Hoarfrost Academy. It's a whole different school of thought, and the bastards refuse to share anything with the rest of us. They can get the same results regardless of how much illum they channel. The normal laws somehow don't apply to them. Selfish buggers."

She went back to work on her grimoire, meticulously writing in her observations and diagrams. Some things would need to be adjusted later down the line, what with her current abilities being diminished, but the core fundamentals of the new effect were sound. Once she worked out how to apply it without direct contact, she'd have a new weapon to add to her repertoire.

There was plenty of time for experimentation until thaw and still a few days until the Descent, when she'd have to quiet down and wait out the misery. Even with the certainty that Ort wouldn't descend on this occasion, the worry that he might gnawed at her. Maybe she'd get on a cheese cart and take that woman in the hills up on her hospitality promise. Maybe if the cart could take her all the way over to Nen. Or to one of the moons . . .

Vergil hobbled away from the desk and went to where he'd set down the sword and scabbard. She'd told him to take them off for her test, and now he did what Tummy had instructed him to.

Good boy. A black eye was starting to darken on his face, one that was certainly not of her making, and he moved with careful steps. She'd watched him catch more than a couple of the smith's love taps to the ribs.

"Not that way, boy, you'll get your wrists broken. No, not that way either. Don't lock up your elbows again or I'll break 'em myself."

Tummy had been as relentless as she knew he'd be.

"By my oaths, are you trying to fall on your sword already?"

It had been an entertaining afternoon for Tallah. She'd half expected the boy to sulk after getting back, but he had the sword out and was going through some of the stances that Tummy had taught him. There was a kind of grim determination on his face that got jotted down in the mental schematic she kept of the boy.

When Tummy had given her a first taste of his teaching methods, she had ended up throwing a full-blown, explosive temper tantrum at him and got slapped back to her senses so hard that she sulked for days. It took Sil hauling her back there by the ear.

"When we go outside Valen," she found herself saying as she watched him, "Sil and I will be rather different than how you've seen us so far. There's very little room for sentiment out in the wild, and we don't take kindly to distractions or delays. I will defend you, but I won't baby you."

For as determined and enthusiastic Vergil had proven with Tummy, he was still scared of her. Any hesitation on his part could prove dangerous at the wrong time.

Time she fixed that. He had been compliant with their wishes, and they'd not been kind to him in return.

"I expect that you learn well what Tummy teaches you. I won't tolerate you endangering Sil when we're out there."

'Now that's a peculiar reaction,' Christina noted with interest.

Yes, it was.

Vergil had stopped dead with his sword's point lowered to the floor. Tears welled up in his eyes, and he tried to wipe them away. It made it worse.

"Hardly a reason to bawl." She groaned. "What's the matter with you?"

She had never had much patience for crying children, not even with Rhine's own ill-fated son. If Vergil was going to start doing that out of the blue, she'd rather he was somewhere where she wouldn't see or hear him.

And Sil was occupied . . .

"Stop that," she demanded, temper rising. "You were fine until a moment ago. What's gotten into you?"

He sniffled and tried vainly to get back to his exercises. She wanted him less scared of her, not more.

"I'm sorry. I'll stop. Just . . . Sorry."

He did not stop. Tears blinded him as he tried to swing the sword like Tummy had shown him. He managed to shear off a candle's top. Wax scattered in fat droplets. The more he tried to compose himself, the worse it got.

Tallah caught his wrist when even she could see that he'd end up hurting himself if he kept it up.

"Stop this. Are you scared of going outside the walls?"

Tears turned into wracking sobs. The uneven light of the fireplace masked him in devastating misery.

"I—I got them all killed," Vergil hiccuped. He was fighting in vain to keep his voice from cracking. "I t-told them I'd protect them. I only got them killed."

She raised an eyebrow. What was he on about?

'His friends from the cave,' Christina provided. 'The ones you incinerated. He thinks they died because of him.'

'They were beyond help,' Bianca put in. 'The girl was screaming on the fire, and the other two were wargged. Killing them quick was a kindness.'

Tallah felt that wasn't what the boy needed to learn just then.

"You couldn't have done much in your state. Anyone taking the Guild's coin faces the risk it brings." She tried to sound kind but only managed to be dismissive. It reflected on his face. "I don't expect you to protect anyone, least of all myself or Sil. We're quite capable on our own, I assure you. As far as I'm concerned, I'll only need you to wear the helmet."

That made it worse. How?

"For pity's sake, stop that." She slapped him and wrenched his sword away. "I don't have the patience for th—"

"I've been such a fool. Tummy's wasting his time on me." He gritted his teeth so hard that Tallah heard them gnashing together. Left without his weapon, he balled his fists and repeatedly slammed them down on his thighs. "I thought I was clever. I thought I had something figured out. I was so fucking stupid."

His sudden burst of whatever this was brought her up short. First time she'd ever seen genuine anger from the lad. Impotent rage did not suit him well.

"Pardon?"

"I hate feeling like this." Vergil stared down at his hands as if willing them to still. "I don't know how to deal with this guilt."

"It really wasn't your fault."

Vergil rounded on her, and a wild, desperate boy stared through his eyes. She took a step back and nearly ignited a fireball at the ferocity in that grimace.

"I don't feel anything about their death. Not a thing. I killed them, and I don't feel it ripping me apart. What's wrong with me?!"

Ah. This was Aliana's work through and through, just one in a number of insurances the priestess would have built in him. Most people would be happy to be unburdened of their guilt and failings, but Vergil seemed made of something much different. Despite herself, Tallah was impressed.

A day with Tummy had taught him exactly how little he knew. And he'd made it into a grievance with himself. It would keep cascading if she allowed it to.

'Fascinating,' Christina whispered. 'Let's see what he does.'

"What's done is done. No amount of prostration is going to change what's happened." Tallah lifted his sword and poked him in the shoulder with the tip. "What I'm curious to know is what you'll do next. I've already killed the rats. There's no revenge left for you."

'You're being a cow. He's going to start crying again.' Bianca radiated disapproval. Not of the boy, but of Tallah pushing him.

Vergil measured out his words, still regarding her with that impressive intensity. A child, yes, but one who could be nourished to grow into . . . Well, who could say into what, exactly? An itch in the back of her mind suggested she bring out the chalice again, but she ignored it.

Much more interesting to see the changes filtering through him.

When he spoke, the tremors were gone from his voice. He breathed in deep, exhaled, met her gaze. "I'll live. No other choice but to live, seems to me. I'll do my best to pay back the ways in which you've been kind to me." He shrugged despondently and pressed both hands to his eyes. "I don't know about the rest. Wait it out?"

'I hardly recall us being kind to him.' Christina snickered. 'Do you reckon Tummy's hit him too hard? Or is he plotting revenge?'

"Can you help me learn more? I can't pay back what you spent on me, but I can make myself useful. I want to be useful."

Tallah chuckled. Vergil's swing on his mood was something to behold. Desperate one moment, rallied the next. Tummy had seen it before her and made the call. "And what makes you so certain that I'm able to train you, bucket-head?"

Anger made way to a kind of wounded dignity.

"I'm not stupid. You were Storm Guard. You fought against them and came out on top. I'd need to be brain-dead not to figure out you're not just a snotty rich girl." Streaks of tears dried on his cheeks into white lines. He held out his hand, and she passed him the sword back. "I don't know what you can do, but I expect it's powerful. But if you or Sil get hurt wherever we go, I'll become a liability if I can't use the helmet. Going to Tummy every other day doesn't seem like nearly enough. Can you help me?"

Another annotation got made to the boy's schematic. It was the first request he'd made of her directly. And one that was attainable.

'He's got a bit of a spark in him,' Christina observed. 'I like how he got up on his own.'

'He works things out,' Bianca followed up. 'He is a simpleton, right enough, but maybe not a useless one. We should consider if we can't make better use of him.'

"Go bring me a sword from the trunk in the hallway. Let me see your basics first," Tallah said as she stretched. The ghosts kept chattering on in her head. Some exercise would shut them up and shake the stiffness out of her. Tummy was right. She had been neglecting herself.

She considered getting dressed in something more than just smallclothes but decided it wasn't worth the trip to her room. She wouldn't allow him to even nick her.

Not the best place for a bit of sparring. Even if she could move the heavy desks without spilling all of her papers and Sil's alchemical compounds, it'd still be too narrow a space for two people swinging blades. Right, that wasn't thought through.

"Bianca?"

Furniture lifted and moved aside gently without so much as a tremor.

Bianca's power coursed through her, and it burned. She gritted her teeth against its tide. Slowly getting better; achingly, terrifyingly slowly getting better. Never again.

"This one?"

She turned to Vergil as he brought her a thin, ebony-black scabbard. She pulled out the sword and inspected the blade. Not really a sword at all but a long knife that fit her build better than the broader blade Tummy had gifted the boy.

"I probably should have these honed," she muttered as she took a few experimental slashes against the air. Even dulled from months of heavy use, the blade sang in her hand, eager for blood. Of the three she owned, this one was definitely her favorite.

Her good gloves were ruined from the Anna clash, so she opened a small rend and rummaged about for a spare. She put on only the right-hand one and flexed her fingers. A small flame danced over and around them as she limbered up.

"You're left-handed?" Vergil asked, eyeing her sword.

"No."

"But . . ."

"When you see someone like me with a weapon, worry about the empty hand." Flame erupted over her glove, encasing it in white-hot brilliance. Maybe not so much power for a bit of exercise, but regulating her output proved difficult after weeks of meekly waiting to heal. Her limiters warmed up as she adjusted.

'Use my ability,' Bianca said in her ear. 'Less chance of stupidity ensuing. And you need the practice.'

She swept the sword about, and Vergil took a step back, giving her the room she needed to warm up. Jerkily, she started a sword dance. Well-practiced stances came easily to her even if she felt her muscles protesting.

He followed in mirror movement next to her. Tummy had shown him the dance, but once would not have been enough for the exercise to stick. May as well work on it together.

"Learn the dance like you learn to breathe your fire," Tummy had taught her. "Do it daily, like your meditations and your breathing exercises. It needs to be a part of you." Her cheeks flushed thinking of how easily Tummy had seen her lapse of discipline.

She slowed her movement so Vergil could observe her better.

Watching him watching her was interesting. He didn't so much copy as adapt. With each repeat of the dance, he made minute adjustments to his pose until he reached the correct one. There was a method to his learning, and that showed her that he had the patience for it.

"A spar, then?" She pointed the tip of her sword at his feet and invited him to a duel. "I'll hurt you. If you cry, I'll throw you out on your ear."

It wasn't an empty threat.

Vergil readied himself in an amateurish defense stance.

A familiar flame lit in the pit of her stomach, and she breathed out an exhalation of heat. She drew in more illum and infused herself to near-full capacity. The dance had loosened her up, and that pleasant warmth smothered some of the pain of channeling. Bianca's strength overlaid hers, and she felt more like herself than she had in weeks.

"How do I fight someone left-handed?" Vergil asked.

"Stick them with the pointy end. Try to not get stuck back."

'Cow.' Bianca snickered.

They circled each other, step by careful step. There were too many openings in his defense, and he watched the wrong things.

With a swift move of her right hand, she reached out a kinetic lash, yanked him straight to her across the width of the room, and hit him square in the cheekbone with the pommel of her sword. He dropped on his arse.

"In battle, I would've had my sword through your throat. Diagonal cut so a healer would have little chance to get to you before you bled out."

That looming bruise Tummy had gifted him would turn black now.

He blinked away the hit, rose, and picked the sword back up. "How do I defend?"

Tallah's impression of him grew another measure. "Expect it. React. Stick them with the pointy bit."

He gave her a level glare and immediately attacked. A quaint thrust that seemed to wholly rely on her being unprepared for it. Silly.

Well, play silly games . . .

She parried his sword too easily and readied to smack him down. The back of his empty fist came for her face even as he stumbled from the parry. Were he slightly better trained and better with his timing, the blow would have caught her neatly across the eyes.

A quick step back and a lean away had his stumble sending him to his knees. A kinetic push blasted him straight into the wall with a crash. *That should put the wind out of the cheeky bugger.*

"Second death in as many heartbeats. Isadora would enjoy a full feast on your expense today. Don't use gambits. They'll get you killed." She was aware of the irony even as Christina got ready to call her out on it.

Vergil groaned and picked himself back up. "Why are you so strong?" he asked breathlessly, voice hoarse and cracked.

Tallah shrugged. "I'm enchanted. Why are you weak?" she asked back, without a hint of a smile.

"I've been sick," he replied and grinned at her.

Back in his stance, his eyes flickered between hers, her sword, and her open hand.

The next bell was an education. She spared him no pain. She cut, blasted, and burned him mercilessly. Without Sil's treatment, his face and nose would probably swell up something fierce by morning. He bled all over the carpet, and the clothes on him wouldn't be fit for use as dustrags.

Tallah's bare feet squelched on the blood cooling on the carpet. The iron stink of it filled the room enough that she had to crack open a window. As far as she remembered, Tummy had not been as kind to her as she had been to the boy. Vergil got to catch his breath between executions. She hadn't been allowed that.

The memory brought a smile to her face while Vergil lay on the floor, panting and bleeding.

"And there's your final death, by bleeding out," she said, standing over him and wiping the tip of her sword on the tatters of his shirt. "Pick one death and I'll teach you how to avoid it." She picked up the already uncorked vial and handed it to him. "Drink this. It'll stop the bleeding."

The light-amber liquid sloshed in the crystal vial, and Vergil downed it greedily. He winced as the cuts healed. He'd be plastered with angry red scars for some time to come, but that didn't seem to faze him. He was back on his feet immediately, though swaying. She picked through Sil's supplies and handed him something to offset the blood loss and dizzy spell.

"Thank you," he said as she helped him stay upright. "For the lesson, I mean." Both the carpet and his clothes were beyond salvation, but he looked happy for the first time in weeks.

Tallah nodded curtly. "Rest up, eat, and we'll start again," she instructed him and set her sheathed sword against her worktable. "Change and run down to the kitchens and order us something for lunch." She looked out the window and thought better of it. "Or whatever time of day it is. Get something sugar-rich for those two." She thumbed in the general area of the bedrooms.

She avoided imagining how Sil could have ignored the noise of the last bell's strike.

Mertle had never stayed anywhere quite as regal as the Meadow. Her own little cot back at home could fit in Sil's bedroom three times over, and there would still be room for her worktable. It was all a bit too much.

"What are they doing out there?" she asked as another thud and crash came from the common room.

"If I know Tallah, she's either experimenting on Vergil or teaching him something. Either way, my latest batch of potions is at their disposal."

"She was doing something to him earlier, but I didn't think she'd try to kill him."

"He'll live. Don't worry about them."

Sil had her head nestled in the crook of Mertle's shoulder and her arms wrapped around her chest. Their legs were intertwined underneath the heavy quilt.

"That feels good," Mertle said as Sil tightened her embrace and kissed her neck softly.

"It should," the healer replied sleepily, cuddling closer.

They had used every pillow available in the apartment. Sil had even taken Tallah's, since the sorceress never used them. They had constructed a nest of comfort, and Mertle lay in its center, idly caressing her lover's back. These moments came all too rarely and far too distant from one another, so she was set on enjoying the time they had together. For as long as winter could last, it would still be too short.

"You know what I've never understood?" Sil asked in that dreamlike state that only late afternoon allowed for.

Clear winter's light had drizzled away into before-dark gloom. Candlelight caught in Sil's golden mane. Mertle sieved it through her fingers like the finest sand.

"What?" she asked.

"What color is your skin?" Sil asked and kissed her neck. "It's not red. And it's not brown. What do I call this in-between? I don't want to think of it as rust."

Mertle grinned as fire spread through her veins from each of Sil's caresses.

"It's the color of dark honey," she replied. "I have skin the color of dark honey and bloodred hair. That's how you should always think of me, like a poem."

"I'd expect that to offend."

"Polite elend get offended by too many things," Mertle replied with a mischievous smile. "I'm not a polite elendine. And that's how I want you to think of me. Only you. Nothing of me is to be shared."

She shifted around and slid down on the pillow until her face was level with Sil's. They kissed softly, almost timidly, and her hands slipped underneath the quilt.

A loud thud resounded through the wall and prompted wisps of dust to dislodge from cracks in the walls.

"Is she killing Vergil? Do you need to go out there?" Mertle asked with just a slight pout at the interruption.

Sil didn't respond and instead kissed her again, harder, much longer. She always ended up taking control if Mertle let her. She bit the healer's lower lip and pushed her away with her forehead. A strand of golden hair caught in her horn.

"I want to talk a bit," the elendine whispered, feeling uncharacteristically shy.

"You say that, but your hands are giving me a completely different message," Sil said with a sigh of pleasure.

"Well, yes, they've got minds of their own. See? I can't tell them what to do. They just do things, and I'm along for the ride. Pay attention to me, not to them."

Sil's legs tensed around her own.

"Mmm, right."

Mertle pressed her forehead against her lover's shoulder, hiding away her awkwardness.

"Can't you stay? After winter passes? I miss you when you're gone. And then I need to coax you to me when you come back. Just . . . stay? This time?"

"I miss you too when we're gone. And you know I can't. When the roads clear and the snow melts, we need to head into Solstice. Without the gates, it's a long trip."

She could feel Sil's strong heartbeat thundering against her forehead. Whatever was in Solstice, in Tallah's hometown, it was important. She understood that and was resigned to it but still had to ask her question.

"Why?"

There was a moment of hesitation, a lie built up. Sil never spoke of Tallah's ends, of her great, dark mission, but Mertle knew that was what kept her going away. Solstice held the key, for it was where they always went after their hunts.

They never spoke of it, not really. Always cryptic, never honest.

"So we can keep on living. So I can keep coming back to you."

That made her smile. It was a silly lie coming from a silly place of worry. Mertle could go with them, if allowed, and she wouldn't be a burden on whatever the mission was. Tummy would handle the shop without her just fine.

"I'm not getting younger, you know," she said, almost too quiet.

"None of us are getting any younger. I'll stay longer next time. I promise."

Mertle raised her head and met Sil's eyes. "Liar," she whispered, and kissed her again.

CHAPTER SIXTEEN

Dead Things Need No Lies

Where are we going?"

Quistis heard Vial's hushed question to Barlo. Sound carried well in the narrow stone corridors. It made for an unnerving trip.

They made a long procession through the innards of the fortress. Falor and Quistis had the lead, Rumi and Aidan made up the center, and Barlo brought up the rear with Vial. It was a long descent from the high tower of their office to the depths under the hearth's ever-burning flame.

Falor's mood was foul.

The high lord of Valen had sat in on their meeting, called in by Falor himself. He disliked the pinch-faced man, but the empress's orders were to obey and respect Valen's will in all matters that concerned the city. That unfortunately meant obeying High Lord Diogron, an unpleasant, portly man who spoke in a high-pitched, nasal voice. He was plagued by a bad habit of fidgeting incessantly. It made him annoying thrice over.

Falor had called Diogron in and had to wait three full days on his pleasure. With the festival less than a tenday away, the fat bastard showing up was nothing short of a miracle.

The meeting did not go well.

"Commander Falor, if there is reason to suspect these two nobodies might be dangerous, why are you not apprehending them?"

"With all due respect, my lord, there is no real reason for us to arrest two adventurers for simply walking about. They haven't done anything to upset the peace," Falor replied. "Also, the sorceress is heir to a powerful trading company from Calabran. It wouldn't be wise—"

"A pox on wisdom." Diogron harrumphed and angrily paced the room, throwing indiscriminate glares at anyone meeting his eye. "I was here, Commander, when Cinder nearly burned this city to the ground. I was sick for weeks after you chased her off. I lost a daughter to her evil. That incident cannot be allowed to repeat."

"There is no need for alarm—"

"Either you arrest them or I will have my men do it. Am I understood?"

High Lord Diogron's normally red face threatened to turn purple. He waggled a finger at Falor as if brandishing a sword and threatening to stab him with it. The lord commander put a calming hand over the high lord's and spoke as levelly as he could manage.

"We have taken steps to ensure nothing like the incident can ever happen again, Lord Diogron. You have my word that everything is under control. If—and I stress this—if these two women are somehow connected to Cinder, we will find out, and we will take measures. For now, it's best that we observe." He gestured to Aidan and Vial, who skulked by the door and passed a lit cigarette between them. "These men are making certain we know their every move through your city. Our eyes have been on them since winter set in."

Diogron pulled his hand away and huffed. He wore purple robes richly embroidered and hung with gemstones, the official dress for Valen's opulent ruling council. Gems clinked angrily as he paced the room.

"Why are you fretting, man? If they are connected, let us force her to come out of hiding and protect her allies. We both know she will. It is that witch's single saving grace."

Falor smiled and looked to Quistis for help.

"Lord, you know as well as we do that it wouldn't be wise to force a confrontation with someone of her potential," she said, as placatingly as she could manage. "It needs to be well planned and perfectly executed. If they aren't connected and it turns into a fiasco for us, then it will only send the sorceress deeper to ground."

Again, Diogron wasn't impressed. Moreover, now he rallied on her, crystal-blue eyes pinning her with hateful intensity. Quistis was reminded of just how much the people of Valen lost on that day, six winters prior, and how much they still hated the memory of Cinder. Her own presence and the entire Storm Guard contingent was an appeasement act from the empress towards an ally who had been deeply wronged by one of her agents gone rogue. That, and the empire's coffers financing more than half of the rebuilding effort.

Lord Diogron walked up to her, almost snarling. He leaned over her work desk and spoke close enough that she could smell the flowery waft of his breath. True enough, Hearth's Flame still afflicted many around the city. It had taken the lives of three potent channelers to stabilize the illum hearth and avoid Salmek's fate altogether, but ill effects still lingered.

Diogron was rotting from within. Spittle flew when he talked.

"The lord commander bested her once. I am certain he can do it again, for good this time. She either comes out and dies the worthless death she is destined for, or she goes away. Either outcome suits me perfectly well."

"With all due respect, my lord," Falor said, trying to pry the man's gaze away from her, "Cinder is not one to be taken lightly. I wish to avoid, if at all possible, another confrontation with her without my veteran mage killers at my side. They are occupied somewhere else currently."

"But you are vastly more powerful than she is, man. You are Catharina's own blood! Why all this hand wringing and secrecy? Let us get it all over with and finally close this shameful chapter in the empire's illustrious history."

Now he was appealing to Falor's pride. The man wasn't stupid, but right then he spoke from the heart, not the head. News of Cinder's survival and return had caused a stir around the council's round table, and none were more unnerved than the high lord himself.

Even he was aware, in spite of his outburst, of just how destructive a battle between Falor and Cinder would be if she were allowed to clash fairly with him. After the incident at the hearth, she had cut a bloody path through half of Valen in her escape. Six years later, the damage she'd caused was still not completely accounted for, much less repaired.

"Cinder goes straight for the throat, as you well know. It is my interest, as protector of this fairest of cities, to avoid unnecessary loss of life." He held up a hand to stave off more protests from Diogron. "I do have a plan in place and two more puzzling pieces that I need to fit together. Once that is done, I will inform you of my further actions. I insist on your patience and on your support for what follows."

More yelling and veiled threats followed. It ate up a good chunk of their morning, but Falor finally managed to get his point across. And after a private conference she had not been allowed to attend, Falor had walked out of the council's chambers with a grim smile on his lips.

Which begged the question . . .

"Where *are* we going?" she echoed Vial's question as they descended further and further into the bowels of Valen.

"To check the vault, of course," he said. "And I need all of you to find what I'm looking for."

"And that is?"

"I have no idea."

Well, that's maddeningly unhelpful.

An edge to his voice and a weight to his every step. Sparks of electricity danced in the air around him and discharged into the metal railings of the stairwells they were descending. She pulled her hand away. Vial let out a curse behind her.

"Do you think there's something missing that we don't know of?"

"It's just a feeling, Quis. It's been in the back of my mind since Rumi found me in Aztroa. Aidan got me thinking."

"But nothing else was missing from the inventory aside from the mask. We checked. I personally double-checked."

"When you're absolutely certain, it's still best to check one more time. Rumi will investigate some things for my curiosity's sake. We need to keep in mind that Cinder knew the vault well before she turned traitor. She'd likely been planning her theft for years in advance. If she expected to survive her raid, then we should reconsider her motives and plans."

Something occurred to Quistis as they descended deeper, one set of stairs following another, ever screwing down into the bedrock.

"Have you informed Her Majesty about this?"

That got a dark chuckle out of Falor. "Like I could keep it from her after rushing my diplomatic mission. She would be very grateful if I were to arrange a meeting with the crazed pyromancer if I manage to find her. Apparently there are some things my mother would like to ask her."

"Like why she deserted and murdered her entire cell in the process?"

"I expect so, yes. It won't be a pleasant, peaceful conversation, I believe."

"And are we going to oblige?" Quistis expected she already knew the answer, but it was a long trip down to the vault, and the stairwells had a whispering draft that unnerved her. Her people whispering behind her was only adding to the uneasiness.

"My mother has a knack for setting impossible tasks for me to achieve." He chuckled grimly. "I expect Cinder will want to properly settle her score with me. She's never left a humiliation unanswered. I really can't see how I'd manage to subdue her without killing her." He let out a long, despondent sigh. "I still need to try, though."

Cinder and Empress Catharina together in a room sounded like a perfect formula for a calamity. Thankfully, Falor hadn't inherited his mother's volatile nature. His efforts to minimize damage those six winters prior had likely been the only edge that allowed Cinder's escape. They had thought her dead, fallen in the Alchemists Quarter's all-consuming fire as it nearly devoured Valen whole.

The smell of charred wood on every breeze blowing down from the mountains was a constant reminder.

Quistis thought on the likelihood of Cinder answering any of Falor's questions. The Daughter and Mother moons had a better chance of moving backward in the night sky.

"Taking her alive seems unlikely, but what if we do manage? What do we do with her then?"

It took some time for the lord commander to answer. They walked in companionable silence, listening to Aidan's mutterings to Vial about the superiority of Rian tobacco compared to the more exotic varieties brought in from the Dominion. Sprite lamps guided their path, flaring to life when they approached, dimming back to near nothing after they passed. The Enginarium were getting more and more creative with each passing season.

Quistis sneezed, and the echoes took a long time to settle. She caught sight of one of the many guards hidden through side passages and in secret compartments, checking in on the noise with crossbow in hand. He saluted and melted back into the dark.

"I'm going to have her blanked," Falor said just as the silence started fraying at the edges. He spoke only for her ears, voice low enough that it wouldn't carry to those behind. "If there's anything left of her mind, I'll hand her over to my mother. Seems fitting."

There was no wind in the maze of tunnels and corridors. In spite of it, Quistis shivered.

"I know you disapprove," Falor said without turning to meet her gaze.

Images of bloody needles jutted through Quistis's imagination. She had seen the procedure performed on several occasions. It gave her nightmares. She squeezed her eyes shut, as if to ward off the mental image and the memory of the survivors' empty stares.

Blanking took away a person's . . . person and ability to channel. So simple a procedure, but so grotesque in its effects. She couldn't help but imagine the needle, long as her forearm, and the way a mind-skinner would insert it through the corner of the victim's eye . . .

She fought the impulse to look back at Rumi.

"It would be kinder to kill her," she said finally, aware of how her outrage seeped into her words and gave them a bleeding edge of revulsion. "I will not be made an accomplice to that barbarity."

"I wouldn't ask it of you. If we manage to take her alive, I'll take full responsibility. She's come back from the dead once. I won't allow it a second time."

"So kill her."

"Were it so easy, Quis. What if she yields? What if I best her? I would need to kill someone that has surrendered herself to me. What would that make me?" He fell silent again. Echoes of their footfalls slithered in and out of the enveloping dark, dogging their advance.

Falor's aura of power dimmed, and the static in the air died away. Quistis no longer felt her hair standing on end next to him. It didn't help her be less angry with his decision.

"There's trouble in the south," he said, as if groping for some justification. "My mage killers are stalled in Old Forge. One of Cinder's old friends, one Deidra Aratol. She's gaining support there, rallying people to a cause of rebellion, spreading lies. Mother wants an example made of Cinder, her old protégé."

Old Forge was an old story by now. She'd read some of the reports. Empress Catharina branded as humanity's grand traitor, the jailer that served powers bent on the eternal subjugation of every man, woman, and child born on Vas. Not a grand unifier but a bloodthirsty monster, a daemon under human guise. And so on, page upon page of hogwash.

"So kill her," Quistis repeated, having decided on not giving any wiggle room to the issue. "Morality over duty, Falor."

He laughed darkly at that. "Wish that I could always have the luxury of choice, Quis. If she dies in combat, it will be no stain on my honor. If she yields and I execute her, I will be a murderer. If I simply take her in and do nothing, I will be tempting another disaster on our doorstep." He sighed again. "I will, of course, do my best. It's all I can do in this."

The vault loomed ahead. It had taken the better part of the day to descend into the deepest reaches of the city, deeper than the hearth and its everlasting flame, deeper even than the holding cells of the underground prison.

They had replaced the old vault door after Cinder had demonstrated that a sufficiently powerful and determined channeler could simply bypass the locking mechanisms by melting through them.

Falor had personally tested the new one after the Enginarium people finished installing it. Twice. Nothing short of a full illum hearth discharge was likely to penetrate the vault now.

Rows upon rows of mechanical locks barred their passage. The lord commander plunged his arm into one of the mechanisms and channeled power inside. The lock tightened around his arm as it recognized him. Only he, Empress Catharina, and the high lord had access to the room beyond. Anyone else would find themselves short an arm and likely a head if the mechanism felt threatened.

How it could feel anything, Quistis couldn't guess, but that's how the Enginarium described it.

It took long minutes for all the locks to disengage. The door, a whole wall section, swung on its great hinges, fully three yards thick, with a low, angry groan of tortured metal and ceramics.

Then came a strange feeling of fabric shifting, of a veil pulled aside to reveal terrors lurking in the deep dark. It hung in the air and spread out from the growing gap. Quistis watched ghostly echoes of herself and of the others screaming soundlessly, running through the rock, coming undone. Things slithered out, half seen and half imagined, and evaporated once beyond the threshold.

Quistis felt her stomach twist into knots, imagining having to contain all of these horrors again. It had been havoc all the way up into the city when Cinder had stolen in and ripped apart wards that needed a small army of inscribers to reset.

Vial gasped and Barlo spat. Opening the vault was never pleasant. Most of what they saw were hallucinations. Some were true visions of realities beyond reality, of the unknowable things lurking in the seas of illum that made up the realm of gods and their ilk. All of them knew that a stray stare in there could drive one into the clutches of madness.

Sprite light flickered to life as they passed the threshold. The cavernous room beyond was filled with glass cases, each containing a different magical artifact, locked away from the world at large. They numbered in the hundreds, every one a different object imbued with dangerous magical effects, each unique. A miasma of illum dregs hung thick around the cases, and eyes peered through slits that shimmered and hazed.

"I hope you didn't have anything else planned for your day, Quis," Falor said as he led them to the lectern containing the large catalogue tome. Aidan and Vial whistled in unison at the wealth on display. Power crackled in the air with the unnerving buzz of millions of insects.

"I wanted to have a long, hot bath later." Quistis sighed. "I guess today's not my day."

Falor smiled and turned to the others.

"One of these, at least, I suspect is a fake. Barlo, you're with me; Vial and Aidan with Quistis. We each bring an artifact to Rumi, and she checks if what's in the catalogue matches what's in hand. Do not pick up anything we don't specifically tell you to, how we tell you to. Some of these can turn you inside out, and that is just the kindest way to die in here."

She wasn't supposed to meet with the bastil for two more days.

After the vault, Quistis couldn't wait any longer.

"The staff's a fake," Rumi had said when Barlo brought her the silver object adorned with a sapphire gem for a head. "It's perfectly made, but the effect is not consistent with what's written here. It repeats it, but only superficially."

Bugger.

Of everything she hoped against, finding that out was the worst outcome possible. Iliaya's Staff had been secured in Valen's vault for a very simple and terrifying reason: It could, in the hands of a competent wielder, radically change a person's physical look to a level of detail so precise that it was impossible to determine the forgery by most means. It could even hide from an Egia's sight, which was why the staff had been secured away.

Iliaya's reign of terror had lasted for nigh a century before the empress put an end to her at the dawn of the empire and took her weapon away to safeguard.

If Cinder so chose, she could . . . Well, she could do anything she set her mind to. The only grace, Falor had read off the catalogue, was that the staff's power waned in mere bells if the wielder parted with it. It was also too gaudy of an artifact not to attract attention.

Small mercy, that.

"You're in a mood, Captain."

Barlo walked with her through the storm, quietly sheltering her in the shadow of his great cloak.

She grumbled at him, too lost in thought, the wind too cold and wild for talking. They were headed down from the Fortress and across the Agora, to climb into the Enginarium's Quarter. Despite her dark mood, she did not cherish the thought of what she needed to do next.

Falor should be doing this, not me. But Falor had remained behind in the vault to finish the inspection. Iliaya's Staff was just one of too many obscenely dangerous items in there. They already knew Cinder had taken the Ikosmenia Mask, which mimicked an Egia's true sight, but maybe there were even more planted fakes. To have found even one meant all others were suspect now. It would take days to re-catalogue them all.

Empress Catharina would have kittens when she learned of this development.

Quistis and Barlo made their slow, steady way to the Enginarium's compounds deep within the Quarter, beyond the Alchemists' mazes and their stinks. Carriages ran poorly in that weather, so they walked there through the billowing blizzard, snow weighing them down and impeding their progress through some of the narrower side streets.

By the time the black gates of the Enginarium Prime compound loomed through the near-blinding snowfall, the cold had wormed its way through her boots and the three pairs of socks she wore as padding. She felt it nibbling at her toes with tiny, insistent fangs as Barlo pushed open the snowed-up gates. A guard ran to his aid from within.

She knew the compound well enough to get past the gates and into the main building unattended. The storm obstructed all sight of it except for the sprite lamps that briefly pried open the darkness. Pity. The Prime building was a beautiful piece of architecture that she enjoyed seeing at night, even if only to admire in passing.

A man dressed in the simple black uniform of the enginaris—Caius, she remembered his name—took her staff and cloak, along with her boots and gloves, to dry in front of a hearth. Barlo just sat down in front of the fireplace, fully dressed, and huffed.

Her face tingled when she took off her scarf and breathed out a frozen breath. She accepted a warm towel gratefully.

"Strange hour for a visit, ma'am. We expected you the day after tomorrow."

"What time is it?"

Caius inspected a device on his wrist and tapped it with a finger, making it light up.

"Well, ma'am, the eighth bell of evening would have sounded a short while ago. Aside from production, we were locked up for the day."

"My apologies, Caius, but events have taken a turn. I trust my coming earlier is not a great inconvenience?"

"No, ma'am. I sent someone to rouse them the moment the guards signaled your coming. Their preparations were done just this evening, and they went to rest for the night." He poured her a cup of coffee from a metal pitcher. "Sugar?"

"I don't touch it. Thank you."

Barlo took the entire bowl of sugar cubes and ate them while his clothes dried. He refused the coffee.

She sat in an uncomfortable armchair and allowed the coffee to warm her while she waited. It fought off the drowsiness she felt after getting out of the cold. The thought of trekking back to the Citadel through that late-night blizzard only served to depress her further.

The room was sparse in furnishing, everything kept utilitarian and monochrome and frightfully unimaginative. Schematics of various clockwork—they abhorred that term, but it was what she'd been taught as a girl—crowded the walls, a mystifying forest of white lines on special blue paper. She had tried in the past to study what was drawn there but found she had no mind for understanding the complexity of the designs.

Another enginaris poked their head through the door at the opposite end of the room. "They are ready for you, Captain."

"Do you need me along?" Barlo asked.

"No. Our host gets fidgety if we crowd them. Enjoy your sugar while I'm gone."

He saluted with the half-empty bowl and popped another cube in his mouth.

Quistis followed behind the enginaris. Sprite lamps lined the walls as they ascended into the compound's upper levels. Most morgues were built underground, but the bastil preferred being closer to the sky. The Enginarium were happy to indulge this particularity as long as it kept their guest happy.

They were waiting for her in a room that had three sides open to the night. Glass shook when she closed the door as the storm whistled outside.

Aarhyansh sat cross-legged in the center of the floor. She knew their name, but pronouncing it . . .

"Good evening, Captain." They saved her the embarrassment of the attempt, speaking in the bastil growling monotone. "Had we known you'd be gracing us with your visit, we would have forestalled our rest. We apologize for delaying you."

"Not at all," Quistis replied. She knelt on the floor, opposite them. "We received your runner this morning. Unfortunately, we had some developments over the day, and this matter became urgent for us."

The bastil smoked their customary meerschaum pipe. Smoke floated lazily through the low-lit room, mimicking the way their fur floated upward; it smelled of spices, sweet and prickly, with none of the harshness of tobacco.

They exhaled a thick plume, blue-white in the light, and then smiled. Quistis dearly wished they hadn't picked up that human custom. A smile from Aarhyansh put her in mind of a dray wolf, except that a wolf's muzzle had fewer, shorter fangs than the bastil displayed.

"Your request was quite a puzzle for us. We cannot be entirely certain that you will get what you need from the made-thing." They shook their head slowly. Small, beady bells adorning their fur rang out a soft, sad melody. "Whatever was done to the maker of this thing, it was frightfully violent. You may get your answers, or you may only get their anger. We cannot make a promise, Captain Quistis."

"I'll take my chances. A name is all I need. If I can get at least that, it'll have been worth the trouble." She fidgeted on her knees. "I'm not familiar with how this works."

Aarhyansh removed the pipe and spent a handful of heartbeats in silence, carefully cleaning it. Quistis watched how they scraped out with a claw the mix of burnt herbs and carefully deposited the ashes into a pouch they wore tied on their belt. Cleaning their pipe was something that couldn't be rushed or ignored, so she sat quietly and waited. It was considered polite not to interrupt.

"We shall guide the melding of your conscious mind with the echo that was imprinted on the made-thing, and we will protect you from invasion. Even with its maker dead, an imprint of them remains behind and can be reached," Aarhyansh spoke as they carefully oiled the parts of their pipe. Names engraved in small runes showed up in the light, covering the entire outside of the pipe's bowl. "Calling on the echo releases it from its bond. How useful it might be depends largely on how strong the maker's self was in life."

It always struck Quistis as odd how gracefully the bastil moved. In one fluid motion, they were on their feet, despite their low, stocky build, and stretched out a four-fingered, clawed hand to help her up.

Aarhyansh led her into an adjoining room. A solid door opened with a hiss and a rush of freezing cold air.

"We apologize for the chill, but we have taken the doll apart in our exploration of its creation. Even in winter, something like it will rot away."

Living things took a long time to rot away in winter, but illum-born creatures weren't as resilient on their own.

"Even with blessed Cares watching from above, it was a stroke of luck that you found the flesh doll when you did. A day, maybe two more, and it would have broken apart."

Greenish-yellow jars lined shelves all around the darkened storeroom. The low light following them through the door showed Quistis the offal contents of the jars. It smelled like a butcher's abattoir. She regretted the coffee.

"We do not believe you will get a second chance, Captain. It has taken great efforts, both of the Enginarium and of ourselves, to keep the remains from wasting away."

A gas bubble floated slowly to the top of one of the jars and popped on the surface.

"And one more thing, Captain." The bastil put their hands together and looked at her with what passed for worry in their milk-white eyes. "We cannot protect you from what this other presence chooses to show you. It will not be allowed to reach into you, but once you establish contact, you will need to break it off on your own. We can do very little to aid you beyond facilitating your meeting and shielding your deep self."

"Well, no time like the moment," Quistis said and steeled herself for whatever was to come.

She blinked and was face-to-face with the ghostly white outline of a woman. It had appeared so suddenly that she flinched back in surprise. The bastil said nothing. They were letting out a slow murmur at her side, an oddly strained sound that seeped into her bones.

"Hello?"

"Hello," the figure replied, its voice dead and distant. It looked around, wary and skittish, then at its hands as if it had never seen them before. "Where am I?"

"Can you tell me your name?"

The figure turned its gaze to her as if just now realizing there was someone there. It raised a hand towards her. Quistis mimicked the gesture. She tried not to, but a will stronger than her forced the movement.

Anger struck her when the tips of their fingers touched, like flies buzzing inside her head. Pain followed. Confusion. Fear . . .

'Who are you?' a shrill voice asked in her mind. It screamed its questions at her. 'Where am I? What have you done to me?'

Quistis stood her ground against the assault of unhinged emotion. She would not be cowed by the echo of a monster. The room grew dark as she was drawn inward.

"I am Quistis Iluna, captain to the Valen Storm Guard cell. And you are dead, whoever you are."

Outrage.

'Do not dare threaten me!'

Jumbles of images poured into her. Scalpels and sutures, silent screams and crying eyes, more than a lifetime of inflicted suffering. It wanted her frightened.

It would eat shit before that happened.

"I do not threaten you." Her own anger rose to the fore, and she bit through her lip, drawing the rich coppery taste of blood. It woke her up in the maelstrom. "You have been killed. I am offering fact."

Flashes of images assaulted the bastion of her mind, a torrent of fury and sizzling hatred. A battle raged and she was part of it. Chunks were ripped out of her and regrown painfully. Her blood boiled in her veins, and she tried to rip herself in two to escape her own melting skin.

She would have screamed but the air burned in her and shredded the ruins of her lungs.

'The whore killed me?!'

Outrage blanketed the pain, muzzled every other sensation. A life's work, burned away to ash. Ambition, crushed. The answers she sought, for which she'd given herself over to the endless work, lost forever.

Fury rose, the foam cresting a bulging wave of despair.

"I don't know who you mean," Quistis pushed out through pained breaths.

She fought back tears as another memory rose, of flames licking at her naked body and flesh melting off bones.

These are all final moments, she realized with a jolt. The echo relived them with horrifying intensity.

'The whore killed me!'

"Who is she? Who are you?" Quistis asked again, allowing herself to submerge under the other's pain. She needed to gain control of the exchange lest the other consume her. A mantra of centering leapt into her mind to prop her up and steel her resolve.

I am one of the many, and I am one of the few. I am—

'Healer, bear witness to her crime.' The presence reached out. 'I demand vengeance for this ignoble death.'

You don't deserve it, monster. I've seen your work. But she couldn't match wills with this other. The echoing conscience was overwhelming and ravenous, so vicious that Quistis feared she might be crushed under its attention. There was an effort made for memories to be coherent.

With titanic force of will, the other built a vision for her.

She saw through countless eyes three people approaching. Her consciousness settled behind the eyes of a doll as it watched the intruders walk into the mistress's throne room.

One was a woman wearing black and gold, a mockery of the Storm Guard uniform. She wore her fire-red hair tied up in a ponytail and had a silver mask covering her face. Quistis recognized it from the catalogue in the vault. Bloodless white lips smiled an obnoxious grin.

The one following her was a blonde woman, tall and slim, wearing silvery-white garments. '*Beautiful work*,' the observing minds whispered.

What did that mean?

And last was a boy, skeletal and malnourished, wearing nothing but a horned helmet. No, he had armor covering him, but it was translucent, like glass. An enchantment, maybe? She could hear his heart, beating like a terrified rabbit's.

"I did wonder who had gotten lost in my home," the echoing voice said, "scaring my children and trampling my work."

That voice commanded her adoration and loyalty. Honey sweet and chocolate rich, it filled her chest with love. Who dared upset the mistress? They would die a thousand deaths for the insult.

Quistis's mind lurched as she watched from too many perspectives at once. She felt every twitch of every muscle of every creature in the room. There were hundreds, packed together tight, all watching the visitors with rapt, hungry attention.

She tasted the magic weave around the visitors, her senses heightened beyond anything human. Both women were dressed in illum, overflowing with it, shaped by it.

In a flash, she was next to them, circling them, drinking in the scent of their power. She saw herself as the doll, opposite herself. There were two, sharing a mind, and she stretched to fit both and know what they learned.

The second one, the healer, had caught their attention. Her borrowed eyes saw beneath the veneer of beauty, into the core of the woman. She couldn't count the scars under her fake skin.

I'm seeing through Iliaya's enchantment. Sure enough, the healer had the staff in hand, looking exactly as the planted fake. Her hearts pounded in excitement at seeing through the deceit, at seeing the horrors the staff's enchantment hid away. Quistis's real heart gave a sharp pang of sympathy for her sister.

"What have you done to yourself, girl?" the mistress asked, malice tinging her words.

"I am not here to reminisce with you, Anna," the red-haired woman said.

"Such a pity. I couldn't imagine what other business the whore of the Academy would have with me and mine."

Anna, and more importantly, Tallah. Quistis had the names. It was enough.

But Anna's echo was not done with her. This wasn't what she needed known. A vice squeezed tighter around Quistis's mind, urging her to watch on.

Anna's questions were light and her tone playful, but Quistis knew the anger boiling beneath, the way the mistress hated the other sorceress. It was just curiosity that kept her children back, the urge to understand why Tallah had assaulted her sanctum. Why, after a century since they'd last seen each other, their first contact was such gross misconduct, unbefitting two women of their high birth.

How powerful was she? Quistis found herself wondering at the strength of the two sorceresses as they stared each other down. Anna's echo had a will of razor-wire ferocity, and she would ultimately fall. She tried to break away from whatever it was trying to show her, but the echo refused her efforts.

'Save your effort, healer. I will release you when I'm done with you. I understand what you did to see this, but I will not be made a simple tool to serve your ends. Bear witness so you may seek vengeance on my behalf. You will have no choice in the matter.'

Witness to what? She already knew the blood mage would die in the inevitable clash.

Tallah undid the topmost button of her coat and reached into an inner pocket nestled against her heart. She produced a black crystal, which she held out for Anna's attention. It was the size of a pigeon egg and black as pitch, swallowing up light like a hole in reality.

Quistis's real breath choked at the sight of that atrocity. So did Anna's, reverberations of horror and disgust melding with her own.

"I claim you, Anna Theala, born of mother Viostra Theala and father Logovich Eilan," Tallah whispered to the crystal. It melted away from her hand and puffed to black smoke. She shook her hand off it. "Does that answer your question?"

A doll pretending to be the mistress was on her feet, trembling. "Have you taken leave of your senses?" Her voice cracked like glass under the pressure of her anger.

"I'm as clearheaded as you've ever known me."

Quistis found herself appreciating Cinder's voice. She saw the storied sorceress for the first time in the flesh, as it were, and the only thing she could think about was how pleasant and calm her voice was. The full horror of what the pyromancer had just unleashed refused to find purchase in her mind.

Soul theft . . .

Revulsion wracked her even as she thought the words. The One Sin. The only real sin in the acceptance of gods and mortals alike. The one unforgivable oath-breaking that could not be allowed to exist. Cinder had performed it so casually . . . so practiced.

Music sang to her, a haunting melody that bypassed all senses to lodge itself into the mind, clawing its way into her very being. She couldn't see where it came from, but she felt it like a draw on her essence, insistent with purpose. Hooks dug into her soul and yanked hard on her life.

Anna produced a bone-white wand and aimed it at Tallah.

"Let's get this farce over with."

The other woman cracked her knuckles and stood defiant against the many that came to the mistress's beckoning. She showed the silver wand at her belt but refused to reach for it.

Anna unleashed her children, and Quistis was part of the assault. She felt her sisters dying, felt herself becoming less and less, until she was the last.

The mistress dragged her out of the melee and sank her under corpses, furiously pouring herself inside until the doll felt like bursting apart. Death breathed on the back of her neck, but the mistress kept her down and hidden, paralyzed for the gambit.

'You can't oppose soul theft, girl,' Anna's echo whispered. They were now in the ruins of the aftermath. Her children lay dead and shattered. More were coming from the farthest reaches of her sanctum, but they could not arrive in time to save her life. Quistis's perspective shifted, and she realized she was seeing from the real Anna's eyes. She waited for death even if she refused to admit she had been spent and defeated.

Cinder approached on unsteady feet, stumbling from her wounds. She held a sword that dripped blood.

'I took the gamble. That's the only way to survive soul theft, the gamble that the black gem accepts the death of the one who invoked it and turns its hunger on them. I failed to give it that.'

Ghostly music howled in her. It was no longer a melody but mad laughter, crying and cursing, agony, ecstasy, fear. It was all being dragged out of her and swallowed by the gaping pit of black.

Cinder had her mask off as she leaned into her, silver eyes staring into the ruin she had wrought. She breathed with a gurgling wheeze.

"I'm sorry," she whispered. "For what it's worth, I'm sorry."

And Quistis felt the heat of the blade as it cut her throat.

She was thrown from the memory, stumbling back violently out of the cold storage. Barlo's powerful hands caught and steadied her as she fought to calm her breathing. Tears ran down her face, and her nose and lip bled. She was screaming herself hoarse.

He spun her around. There was concern in his lined face. He said something to Aarhyansh, but she couldn't make out the words. Music still thrummed in her head, and she felt herself being sucked out through the pores of her skin, emptied out from the marrow of her bones to the thoughts in her mind, poured into a prison of pitch black.

Quistis bent over double and was violently sick all over Barlo's boots.

CHAPTER SEVENTEEN

A Change of Plans

She was shown the point of the needle. Something that small could somehow occupy her entire world in that moment as the blasted mind-skinner prepared. He showed her each instrument that was to follow, now that they were done with the more *mundane* preparations.

"Beatings and starvation will only get you so far, you know. Especially for someone with your grip on yourself. It's best we now start in earnest."

The bastard liked talking about each of his little tools. She knew them all, except the needle. Now she couldn't tear her gaze away from it.

They had her strung up tight for the procedure, all risk seemingly accounted for by long, horrible experience. Was this what Rhine had gone through as well? Had she lain on the same rack, feel herself drawn to her breaking point, and then . . . this?

Had she delivered her sister to this monstrous little man?

Anger lent her embers of strength. Tallah screamed and heaved one more time against her bonds to no effect, the iron shackles cutting painfully into her wrists. It earned her a baton across the stomach and the white-hot pain that followed. She hadn't anything left in her to bring up but black bile and blood. For a moment, the music swelled triumphantly as her grasp on consciousness ebbed.

"This will hurt," the bastard said. "But the pain will pass before you know it. It's for the best, really. You can let go of your anger now."

Oh, she bloody well did not want to let go of anything. She wanted the horrid little creature roasted alive from within. She wanted him cursing her name in all tongues of Edana. If she could free herself for but a moment, she would tear out his heart with her teeth and cook it in front of his eyes. Her hand flashed into fire for a moment, the last dregs of her illum igniting in the incandescent rage that seethed in her bones. It earned her another beating.

"Stop, you oaf. She'll pass out. It's no good if she doesn't see it happening. I have a schedule to keep to."

Ice-cold water splashed across her.

Tallah came awake with a jolt of dread, drenched in cold sweat. Her glasses clattered to the floor along with the inkwell and several scroll sheathes. Muscles cramped up and protested as she tried to shake off the nightmare, phantom echoes of pain lancing up through her joints.

Under the mountain. She had been under the blasted mountain again. It rose in her memories, darker and sharper than she knew it to be, to dominate her nights. Screams chased her among the peaks, chased down by the empress's headsmen and the great beasts that guarded the passes.

A sharp, needling pain wormed through her left eye as she tried to fully come awake from that place's grasp.

Was that what had woken her?

She had fallen asleep at her desk, head slumped over her grimoire, quill leaving a dark blotch of ink where she'd poked the paper.

Blast. It was expensive paper too, hard to get outside of Aztroa or Calabran.

'Something happened,' Christina whispered. 'Something's wrong.'

"I know," she replied, voice low, throat scratchy with thirst. No, it wasn't the nightmare that woke her. She was certain of that at least. The horrors of the mountain rarely pushed her back into reality anymore. Christina and Bianca kept the worst of it at bay when she managed to rest.

At the edges of her consciousness, music hummed distantly. Bianca—it was her turn tonight—shielded her as best she could, but it was still slipping by. It hadn't woken her. Something else did.

Vergil was asleep in the armchair by what remained of the fire, exhausted from the day's training, folded in on himself on the narrow cushion. His sword lay by the hearth, unsheathed, reflecting ember light. He'd sat down to rest for a moment and passed out. She'd covered him with a blanket, but it had slipped off. The boy tossed and turned regardless of where he slept. She didn't envy him his dreams.

Windows rattled, and a chill came down the chimney over the still-smoldering ashes of the fire, ruffling her papers as she tried to clean up the spilled ink. Something rattled ever so slightly over the background noises of the night and the music in her head.

'Something is very wrong,' Christina said again.

"I know, Christi. I felt it."

What had she felt?

She looked over the dimly lit room. Her candles had gone out, melted into puddles now cool to the touch. A red twilight of emberlight shifted shadows around as she paced the breadth of the room, trying to shake loose the cobwebs in her head.

Something kept rattling, and it wasn't the windows. It came from her heavy chest, the one they kept locked. It got louder when she approached.

A wave of nausea hit her when she lifted the lid. Darkness seethed inside, roiling like stormy waters in the confined space. Her mask poked out from the blackness as if floating on top of whatever was happening in there.

The world snapped into sharp focus when she donned it. A storm churned in the room, curdling illum into mercury-like beads of power only the mask could see. They were being drawn into the chest.

Anna. Something of Anna had avoided capture, and the soul trap was unhappy about it. Tallah knew the phenomenon all too well.

"*I told you,*" a bead of illum whispered as it sped by her into the gaping maw of the waiting gem. "*I will have the day.*" Another whisper. Tallah spun on her heels, but Anna wasn't there, even as she kept talking in her ear. "*Now they know, whore. Your sin is laid bare. They will come for you.*"

The beads laughed and mocked her as the silent storm ceased with the suddenness of a snapping rat trap. Like a sigh, the gem drew into itself, sated, contained once more by its box.

Tallah stood by the chest for a long time, cursing under her breath, questions crowding for attention in her head.

Who *they* were was not a mystery to ponder. If the Storm Guard had found the rat cave, they had found Anna's sanctum and whatever else was still down there. Anna's fragment, or echo, or whatever it had been, hadn't just arrived in Valen of its volition. It would be summer at least before the soul gem would've wound itself into enough of a frenzy to reach out for whatever it had missed.

Had they talked to Anna? Could they?

She looked at the horned helmet, hung on a peg above the fireplace. There were ways to communicate with lingering echoes. There were even ways to trap them. It didn't matter where Anna had squirreled away some of her essence, or even how it had gotten loose enough for the trap to sense it.

All that mattered was that something hadn't gone to plan.

"I should have burned it all," she said to nobody in particular. Her nails dug into her palms, and her skin felt too tight over her bones. She raised a fist to her mouth and bit into a knuckle. "I should have burned it all to ashes and left nothing to be found."

'This is your gambit biting back. Regrets are tardy, my girl. We need to take measures and protect ourselves.'

Vergil stirred. First he grumbled about stiffness, then came fully awake with a whimper of pain. Empty vials littered the room. He'd drunk too many again against her instruction when she wanted to end the earlier training, and would pay the price in side effects. A splitting headache would be the least of his worries.

He was the least of her worries.

"Get dressed, Vergil."

"W-What?" He pressed fists into his eyes as if trying to batter away whatever was trying to claw out of his head. "I am dressed. Aren't I?"

"Get dressed to go out."

Vergil groaned and looked around the room with sleep-heavy eyes. He stumbled when trying to get his feet under him and almost landed in the ashes. "It's the middle of the night. Where are we going?"

She paced, still chewing on her fingers.

'You are panicking. We need a clear head now. Wake the hen.'

"I am not panicking."

"I didn't say you were," Vergil replied, looking even more lost and confused than his usual self. "What's going on?"

"I wasn't talking to you. Can you find your way back to Ludwig's from memory?"

'You are panicking, my dear. Christina is correct. We need you to have a clear head before we set upon a course of action.'

"I can get there, yeah," Vergil finally answered after looking bewildered for a minute. "I have a—"

"I don't care, Vergil," she cut him off. "Get dressed. Take the sword with. I'll explain when you're ready."

'What are you doing?' Christina asked after the boy stumbled his way into his makeshift room.

"Preparing a contingency."

'With the professor? He will be useless to us if we run afoul of the Storm Guard.'

"He's got a way out of Valen. Passes out to Bastra and Garet are closed, and it's suicide to try to get into the Ruffle in this weather. The old git's got some way out or he wouldn't have been so insistent for my help."

She was being ridiculous. She knew that.

But the music in her head had changed its tune. Her companion siren call never really went away, even with the two ghosts shielding her, but now it was downright jubilant, celebratory. Instinct poked her in the small of the back with cold fingers that spelled danger. She remembered it sounded just like this, just before the needle—

"Good morning, Vergil." Mertle's voice came from the hallway, entirely too cheerful for the hour. "Good morning, Tallah." She stuck her head through the open doorway. "I need to go and fire up the forge. Tummy's going to have my hide otherwise." She'd been spending all her evenings with Sil, sneaking in and out at odd hours, always somehow managing to pass under Verti's gaze unnoticed.

Tallah stopped herself before waving the elendine away. "Can you hurry up our gear? We may need to leave in a hurry."

Mertle's expression fell. She looked towards Sil's room and back at Tallah. "Why? S-Sil said—"

Tallah rummaged through the chest, moving boxes around. "It doesn't matter what Sil said. We may be in trouble. If you and Tummy can't get it done before we leave, just ship everything to Solstice when the passes clear. I'll get there eventually." She pulled out the leaden box in which Sil had stowed the gem. It buzzed in her hands.

"I'll see what I can do." Mertle's voice had the slight edge that she rarely used to show her annoyance. A bit of her old self talking over the new. "You'll owe me big this time."

"I already owe you big."

"Big*er*. We can deliver two days from now. And you'd better have an explanation ready for me because I had plans and arrangements for winter. *With* Sil." The edge of annoyance bled into cold anger that sent another chill through Tallah's back.

She just stood in the ember glow and stared at the box in her hands until the outside door slammed. Mertle would get her explanation. It was time for one.

But first she needed to get rid of evidence, for all the good that would do her peace of mind.

She couldn't even be mad at Anna, much as she wanted to. Had their roles been reversed, she would have done anything and everything in her power to get revenge. In many ways, she was doing exactly that.

She reached out a hand and focused her illum. Not much pain anymore, just a slight refusal that she had to force aside. Exercising with Vergil had helped her push through the fugue she had settled into, and her strength was returning steadily. Anger still bloomed at her mistake and her weakness, and she used it to stoke the fire inside and infuse herself with its power.

'Far from ideal, but better,' Christina encouraged her. 'You are almost completely renewed.'

Reality warped around her fingers and—finally!—a proper rend manifested, not the paltry slits that she had to force open. Pins of light pricked a dark gash in reality, and she had her storage bubble back. She thrust the box inside and allowed the rend to close.

Vergil watched her from the doorway, dressed for a blizzard.

Sil was behind him, dressed in a nightgown, murder on her face. "What do you mean we're leaving?"

"Are you sure you're not just—"

"I'm *not just* anything," Tallah snapped at her. "Anna talked to someone. We need to treat it as a worst case."

Sil sighed and rubbed her temples.

"She could have been lying."

"She wasn't."

"You don't know that."

"I do."

She glared at the sorceress. Stubborn creature.

There was a gentle knock at the door. Sil had asked Vergil to send up one of Verti's girls when he passed through the common room towards his errand, fool thing that that was.

She changed into the aelir form and went to answer.

It turned out to be Verti herself, up early and about her duties.

"Good morrow, Your Ladyships. What may I get for you?"

Elendine cheerfulness didn't quite match Sil's state of mind. It was too early for it. Worse yet, Mertle had left while she was still asleep, so her mood was as dark as the weather.

"Coffee, Verti, please. Lots of sugar. And some bread and butter and—"

"Jam," Tallah called from the other room.

"And jam, please. Bitter, if you have it." Sil gestured an apology for the inhuman hour. It was likely still a few bells to the crack of dawn.

Verti smiled and nodded back. "There is fresh bread baking if you wouldn't mind the wait. Otherwise, I can have one of the girls make some flat buns."

"We don't mind, Verti. Thank you."

It was too bloody early in the morning to argue with Tallah on an empty stomach. Her paranoia flaring up wasn't the issue, but her solution for it was plainly mad.

"You said you didn't want to go on that absurd waste of time for the old man." She picked the argument right back up when the elendine went away. "You haven't even touched his bribe since we spoke with him. You're being unreasonable. For pity's sake, stop gnawing on yourself."

Tallah paced like a caged animal. Heat wafted from her, sputtering like candlelight in a draft. The fool had forced herself to infuse and was still at it.

"You'll burst a blood vessel if you keep going like that," Sil said as she barred the sorceress's path with her staff. "Stop pacing and start thinking for a bloody moment."

They exchanged glares.

"What would you propose, then? There's a mind-skinner in Valen, and she's already suspicious of me."

"You don't know that Anna talked to the Storm Guard or that she even talked at all. She might have just wanted to rattle your nerves as a last effort at revenge. And she managed that expertly, I might add."

"We can't afford that assumption, Sil. You know that. I know that. Drop it."

"I'll bet you that Christina agrees with me."

That quieted Tallah. She looked as if she wanted to say something on the subject but bit back on the words. Sil grinned.

"You just kept her from answering. We could just change disguises and start over."

"It takes weeks for a new change to take hold. I may not have days, let alone weeks." Tallah looked over their assembled living space, five years' worth of work in building Tianna and Silestra. "We're too entrenched in these roles."

The staff did have those limitations. For any change to be convincing, it needed to take root, to become a second skin, not just an illusion over the old. That took practice, conviction, and a lot of failure. It wasn't a subtle or stable process. Someone like Rumi Belli could see through the weave in those days. Tallah's mask certainly managed if they weren't fully committed to the role. All it would take was one chance meeting.

And chance was not proving kind.

"We could always move over to Mertle's and . . ." The words withered in her mouth as realization hit before Tallah could answer with more than a scathing glare. "We'd risk their safety. You're right."

The sorceress pushed away the staff and started pacing again.

"I know I'm being absurd, but I don't feel safe. Sil, I can't explain it."

"But if we do this, then we're throwing away all the work we've put into getting this far. We won't be able to use Tianna of Aieni Holding anymore."

"Better than risking a battle I can't win right now. I'd rather burn this whole plan than be captured again."

"Christina, please back me on this. We must be able to come up with a better solution," Sil asked the ghost. Tallah normally listened to that one's counsel if she refused to listen to hers, on the rare occasion the ghost agreed with her on something.

"'We agree with Tallah. Plans must be changed if there is the least risk of them failing. But we do not agree with giving in to Professor Angledeer.'" Tallah looked as if she had to vomit out the words. "And neither she nor Bianca has a bloody solution to give me," she finished. "Either figure one out or make your peace with mine. Either way, we're leaving."

Sil sighed and dropped into a chair, hand on her face.

If I were honest, I'd admit I want to run off. It was too easy to get comfortable with Mertle, too easy to start really wanting what she only said she did, too easy to forget she was always being watched. *But being honest and being stupid are two very different things.*

Verti returned carrying a tray of food, and one of her daughters brought a large pitcher of freshly brewed coffee. Its aroma filled the room when they entered.

"Verti," Sil said as she cleared a table for the tray, "have any of the caravan masters been preparing to leave lately?"

The matron thought for a moment and looked to her daughter.

"Master Vulniu closed his credit line two days ago," the girl said briskly. "He's waiting out the storm and preparing to leave for Bastra after the Descent."

"In this weather?"

"He's been taking many meetings with adventurers to help him manage the high passes. I believe he intends to force his way through. I couldn't tell you why."

Sil looked to Tallah, who was still chewing on her finger while looking out the window at the swirling night. She got a slight nod in return.

"When he breaks his fast, would you please inform him we'd like to hire his services?"

The young elendine bowed respectfully.

"Of course, Your Ladyship. Should I ask him up, or will you be coming down?"

"We'll be down to discuss. Thank you, Miria."

After the two left, Sil found that she had less of an appetite than she had thought. She nibbled some bread and drank sweetened coffee but nothing more. Tallah ate jam out of the jar, then the buttered bread. For all her griping and doomsaying, she ate as if preparing for battle.

They were quiet for a long time.

"Was it wise to send Vergil out? Alone, I mean?"

"We'll see."

"He could go to the Fortress and turn you in of his own will." Verti had been kind enough to not mind the devastation she witnessed in the room. "You haven't exactly been kind to him."

Tallah gave her a thin-lipped smile. "The Fortress is exactly far enough from here for your trinket to do its job. If he loses his head, he wasn't worth keeping around."

Sil choked on her coffee. "That's dark. Even for you, that's horrible to consider."

Tallah shrugged. "He'll be back."

"And you know that for certain, do you?"

This was answered by the sound of a teaspoon banging the inside of the jar, trying to get at whatever was left on the bottom. No words.

"How come you've been doing this with him?" She gestured vaguely at the devastated room. She'd been curious since the first day, but Tallah hadn't brought it up, so she hadn't asked.

"He asked to be trained. I obliged."

Sil dropped a fistful of sugar cubes into her empty cup, then poured more coffee over them.

"I'm amazed you bothered, is all. You spend days training him, and then you send him out alone into the storm. How does that make any sense in your head?"

Tallah poured herself a cup of hot coffee and tried to down it all in one go, probably to push down the lump of buttered bread she had just inhaled.

"The boy wants to be useful, and he's scared out of his wits of being discarded." She looked out over the rim of the cup. "I was swayed. Alone, he's invisible. I gave him a mission."

Vergil trudged forward, forcing one foot in front of the other. Trenches had been cut through the snow by much earlier risers than he, but it was still hard work moving forward. Before leaving, Sil had given him something that kept him warm and strengthened him. Two more flasks of it were tucked safely away in an inside pocket of his cloak, next to the letter. The effect of the first was already waning, and he wasn't even halfway to Master Ludwig's home.

When he left, Tallah and Sil were quietly arguing. By the healer's expression, he had expected a bloody row between the two, but it ended up as just a simmering, hissed discussion.

If anything, Sil seemed relieved. Under the anger there was relief that she couldn't feign away.

Whenever I think I get some kind of lock on one of them, it all slides sideways.

Wet cold wormed its way into the toes of his right foot where his boot had sprung a leak. His leg cramped as he forced himself to push forward through the thigh-high snow, walking in a near crouch, bundled in on himself.

Argia guided his progress.

At the next junction, take left-hand passage.
Time to destination: Unknown.
Distance to destination: Unknown.
Oh, just grand. How lucky he was.
"Won't my head pop off if I get too far away from you, Tallah?"
It had been a legitimate concern for him, but the sorceress waved him away. The little thing on the back of his neck felt warm, true, but it didn't hurt. Sil had promised it would if he were too far, and he saw no reason to doubt that.

And why send him, anyway? Why didn't Tallah go herself? She'd probably not struggle going up the bloody damn stairs. So many bloody stairs, even as far as the markets!

Too much pride. Or she's planning something else that I don't need to know about. Yeah, maybe that.
Maybe.
The Agora lay deserted for once. Trenches had been cut by the occasional traveler, but they were few and quickly filling up, most of them leading into the taverns.

Light spilled out of the Ripe Gooseberry, a workers' den, and next door's Godly Pitcher, a popular adventurer watering hole. Without the howling wind, there would be laughter and music filling their little nook of the square, even at that early hour. With the winds, they were just two blobs of ghostly light, flickering through the dense snowfall. He really, really wanted to go inside and wait out the storm.

Ahead loomed the long, steep climb.

Vergil stared up at the winding path stretching into the green-lit dark above. When they first came that way, it hadn't looked quite so terrifying. He stood and gathered his courage, snow banks ever rising around his freezing feet.

With a thick huffed-out breath, he attacked the first flight.

On the third set, he drank another of Sil's mixtures, resolved not to touch the last until he was on his way back. Hammer blow after hammer blow struck his temples from the inside as if his chip were trying to claw out of his head and drag his brain out to air it.

By the end of the climb, fighting against the ice, the blinding snow, the cutting wind, and the bloody wet sock, he was ready to take the express way down over the lip of the wall.

Tallah's frenzied stare when she'd told him what he had to do kept him going. He'd never seen her or Sil rattled before. He took a measure of pride from being given the mission, from being trusted enough to go alone into the blizzard.

They trusted him. Or he was expendable—

Vergil walked head first into what felt like a stone wall. He stumbled back, tripped, and fell onto and into a blood-chilling cushion of powdery snow.

A strong hand reached down into his hole and grabbed him by the cloak. It lifted him as if he weighed nothing at all.

"Mighty sorry for that, speck," a booming voice said over the whistles and moans of wind rushing through the narrow alleys of the Alchemists Quarter. "I didn't see ye."

A vibrantly bright sprite of light hung above the stranger. Vergil had to crane his neck to look up into the face of the man talking. Shining yellow eyes, a flat, crooked nose, and a wide mouth set in a wider jaw met his gaze. A tusk protruded out through the left corner of the mouth, longer and thicker than his thumb.

"I—I'm sorry," he stammered out, terrified by the apparition in the storm. "I wasn't minding my way."

"Are you hurt?" another, gentler voice asked him, by the giant's side.

He swung his gaze around and met the black eyes of a woman protected from the snowfall by the man's great cloak. She had a broken lip, bright red blood frozen into tiny crystals upon it.

"No, no," Vergil said, almost relieved to see another human. "I was just startled, that's all."

The woman looked over his shoulder.

"Are you walking the storm alone?" she asked him, something like concern showing on her face. "You shouldn't be alone in this weather." Her eyes looked him over in a way that reminded him of how Sil had inspected him back at Mistress Aliana's. This one's gaze was harder, more piercing. Her scrutiny made him uncomfortable.

Something like a flash of recognition shone in her eyes.

"I have an important errand to run. I'm sorry for bumping into you, but I'll be on my way now."

"Where to?"

Vergil stared at the large arm that barred his way forward. The giant had moved faster than he could blink. Four armored fingers pressed firmly against his chest. If they made a fist, it would be the size of his head.

"Lady asked ye a question, speck," the giant said. The undertone of his voice suggested that he'd better answer.

"Where are you going, young man?" the lady asked again, pinning him with her black gaze. She held a gnarled healer's staff in one hand, and the other was hidden under her tight cloak.

Vergil stared at her for a moment, trying to match the face to anyone he knew. She wore a shawl under her hood, with only a stray lock of chestnut hair showing. Dark eyes, sharp nose, narrow lips . . .

Sil kept coming to mind, as if this woman were an older, sterner, and darker version of the healer. He wanted to be honest with her, but something in the back of his skull warned of danger.

"I'm going to see a friend. He's sick." He pulled aside his cloak and showed her the metal flask in his pocket. "I'm bringing him some medicine."

The woman's eyes darted from his face to the flask and back up. She smiled finally, and dug into the depths of her own cloak to produce a similar flask to the ones he carried.

"Take this, then," she said as she tried to hand him the flask. "It will stave off hypothermia and keep your blood hot. Try to find shelter soon. You don't look hale enough yourself to be out in this."

Vergil hesitated, and she waggled the flask at him.

"Take it," the giant said, lowering his arm. "The captain's a healer."

Captain?

Vergil took the flask and stared at it. Engraved on the metal surface was an armored fist wreathed in lightning, the Storm Guard's seal. His mouth opened and closed, words failing.

"Is anything the matter?" the captain woman asked. Was she a captain in the Storm Guard? Was he in trouble? Did they know about Tallah?

He felt his face grow hot and red as he tried to stow the flask in his inner pocket. Instead, he dropped it in the snow, bent to pick it up, dropped it again.

The man chuckled. "I think ye scare the boy, Cap." He shrugged off snow that gathered in great piles upon his shoulders. Vergil could hear the unmistakable clanging of armor and weapons under the great cloak.

"Shush, Barlo. Let me help you. What's your name?" She bent and picked up the medicine.

"Uh . . . Vergil, ma'am," he stammered an answer. Should he tell her about Tallah?

No!

He squashed the traitorous thought before it even took root, aghast at the notion. Tallah had saved him. Tallah had trusted him with a mission.

"Well, Vergil," the woman said as she stowed the flask in his pocket, right next to the sealed letter, "my name's Quistis." She adjusted and tightened his cloak, even as the wind kept trying to billow it out. "We're here to help. You don't need to be afraid of us." Her lip bled when she smiled. She had dark lines on her face, as if she'd cried . . . blood? It might have just been a trick of the trembling sprite light.

"Yes, ma'am," he muttered. "I—I'm not afraid, ma'am."

She smiled at him. "Good. Take care, Vergil. See that your friend gets well."

Barlo came forward and held out his cloak over her. It was heavy. Wind barely rustled it.

"Thank you," Vergil said as Quistis waved goodbye. He waited in place until the sprite light disappeared into the bowels of the blizzard. And he waited a few minutes more, a frozen statue slowly buried, just to be certain they were gone.

Please rotate 180 degrees and continue down the path until the next junction. Then take the left-hand path.

Time to destination: Unknown.

Distance to destination: Unknown.

"Shut up."

At least the storm had whipped up the Quarter enough that its signature stink and fog had been blown out of the city for the night. He assumed the stink was gone, at least. His nose had frozen shut even before he'd reached the Agora, and he feared it might snap off if he tried to remedy the situation.

"Why do they need so many bloody stairs?" he gasped in effort as his interface led him up and down the many narrow corridors and passageways. He hadn't paid attention when Tallah had led the way, but at least his headware had. After going up and down what felt like the same stairs a dozen bloody times, he became reasonably convinced that his headware lied with impunity and he was lost.

Your destination is on the right. Accuracy of placement estimated within five yards.

It was definitely lying. There was nothing there but darkness and snow. He should have passed a church first. Had he? Maybe. It was hard to be certain of anything in that weather, at that hour. There wasn't even a hint of light in the sky above, and the green haze of the lamps was sparse and narrowed down to arrowheads.

There wasn't a hint of light anywhere around.

He turned right and walked forward, hands outstretched. Finally, he felt something solid. Wall. Not a door. He walked another step, groping, and his hand slipped into the space between buildings. Then he walked back until he felt the wooden frame of an entrance.

"Well, I'm sorry if this isn't the right place."

He banged on the door.

Nothing happened.

He banged again, harder.

No answer.

Again. Much harder.

"Someone is going to open this door, or I will put my shoulder to it," he grumbled as his fist hammered on the wood. "I am not going back without delivering this bloody letter."

The door swung inside, and Vergil found himself a palm's breath away from a fireball as big as his head. It hovered above a gnarled old hand. If he could still feel anything above the neckline, the heat of it probably should have stung.

"Why shouldn't I burn your face off?" a voice asked from beyond the firelight. Its threat felt very genuine. "Do you know the time, boy?"

"Too early for threats, Master Ludwig," Vergil replied, numb with cold and fatigue, raising a hand to ward off the light. "I was sent."

There was a long pause. Mercifully, the fireball moved aside, and a hard face peered out from the darkness beyond. Yes, it was Ludwig, wearing the same ridiculous nightcap and the same expression, like trying to piss fire.

"Please put the flame out. It's been a hard slog here. Either kill me or welcome me in. I'm fine with either."

There was a moment's hesitation. Blue-red blobs swam in front of Vergil's eyes. Even when Ludwig extinguished the fireball, he was still blind for a few moments.

"Step inside," the old man said, sidling away from the narrow door.

Vergil walked forward and banged his head on the frame again.

CHAPTER EIGHTEEN

Dead and Frozen Somewhere

s this some sick joke? Is she having a lark?"

Ludwig had been drinking. What exactly, Vergil couldn't say, but it stank. His home reeked with the sour tang of bad alcohol and stale food. If the place had been a sty when they last visited, now it was a disaster area of scattered books, scrolls, and alchemy implements, made all the worse by the stray light of haphazardly lain candles and the one flickering sprite. Vergil had been down in the trash compactor of the *Gloria*, and the resemblance was uncanny.

The old man read the letter again, leaning against a wall for support, mumbling the words to himself. Vergil warmed his hands by a candle's flame.

How is he not frozen stiff? It's as cold in here as out there.

"Does she mean to taunt me? Is that why she sent you and did not come herself?" He slurred the words and swayed while waving the piece of paper around. "Has she no shame left for an old teacher?"

"I don't know," Vergil replied earnestly. "She seemed genuine."

"What's happened? What changed her mind?"

"I don't know."

Ludwig stared at him and swayed on the spot, looking sick in the vain light. If his story was true, then he was well over three centuries old and Vergil thought he looked the part at that early hour. Or was it late? Time felt oddly syrupy in the storm outside.

Shutters rattled as the blizzard breathed on Valen again.

"Well, tell that sow I'm not interested in catering to her capricious whims." He fluttered the paper, seemed ready to rip it in two, then started reading it again, mumbling all the while. Now he paced among the stacks of ruined books, the single trembling sprite following him around.

"Why would she do this to me? What's her gain? I have done nothing but aid her at every turn when all others discarded her. I know what it is to fall from Her Majesty's grace." He lapsed into slurred whispers.

Vergil didn't have the slightest inkling of what Ludwig was on about, nor what reply was expected of him. Tallah's instructions were to come back with an answer from Ludwig, regardless of what it was. That looked to take a while, as the old man twisted the paper in his gloved hands again, hesitating.

He was rather certain that Tallah had not been serious when she instructed him to drag Ludwig to her by the legs if he couldn't get a clear answer out of the old git.

Ludwig seemed to rally his wits and stomped over to Vergil, shaking his finger at him.

"She came to me. Do you know that? She sought me out in my home. When the empress had cast her out, she looked to me for aid. And I aided her. I aided her gladly, for she was ever my student." He was now too close, and Vergil flinched back. Alcohol stink wafted off the old man like a vaporous mantle. "I always offered my advice and my aid to her. I kept her secret. And she treats me like trash."

"I don't know what happened, Master Ludwig. She wrote the letter in a hurry and sent me out with it."

"She was cast out by the empress for crimes so great that even she's ashamed of them. There is a price on her head. Did you know that? There is a very high price on her head, but they think she's dead, burned away to ashes." A ghastly grin split his lips, and spittle flew as he wound himself up. "I could turn her in and earn my way back into Aztroa. Has she ever considered this?"

Vergil didn't quite like where this line of thinking was going, not after his earlier run-in with the Guard. His hand grasped the pommel of the borrowed sword. Cutting the old man down wouldn't take any effort at all. No one would even know.

'No one would care.'

He flinched at the thought and spun on his heels. Someone had whispered the idea to him, right in his ear. He had felt the draft of breath on his skin. Nothing behind but the shifting candlelight shadows, flickering in tune with the flame's sputters.

Ludwig read the crumpled paper again.

"Can I . . ." He hiccuped the words, and his shoulders drooped as if the weight of years settled over him. "Can I trust this, lad? Or will she just take what she needs of me again and go back on her promises?"

It took effort to wrench his attention back to the old man. He was imagining things for lack of enough sleep. Pain bulged in his head, a throbbing, stabbing hurt that refused to let up. Tallah had warned him it would happen.

"I haven't known her that long, Master Ludwig, but she doesn't strike me as someone who'd lie to her friends." It surprised him that he believed that. In her own way, the sorceress had shown him . . . well, not kindness, no, but perhaps something close enough to count?

He wandered away from the old man's watery gaze, taking a candle with him. A forgotten cup of tea lay half drunk on the side of a worktable, lost amid the strewn-about instruments. Whatever he'd been working on lay smashed up in a clump of metal and glass, discarded. Empty bottles clattered to the floor as Vergil stumbled over a stack of books.

More experiments lay scattered and unfinished. Yes, the old man had been working on something since they'd last seen him, quite feverishly by the looks of the detritus. A tinge of desperation hung silently draped over the room.

"What were you trying to make?" he asked as he studied some parchment filled with annotations and designs. Glasses? Sil used similar equipment when she tweaked and polished Tallah's spectacles.

Ludwig sighed and sank into the old armchair, earlier mania passed into dullness, his drunken mood swinging him into thoughtful contemplation.

"I never laid all my hopes at Tallah's feet. She's far too wild for that, far too unpredictable." He produced a cup from somewhere and drank deeply. Vergil hoped it was tea. "Her refusal, blunt as it was, hasn't deterred me. I still aim to find my way into the ancient city with or without her help."

He tried to rise from the chair but nearly toppled forward. Instead, he settled back with the same expression he had worn when making his pleas, feigning dignity.

"Tallah owns—or rather, she has stolen an artifact that grants her an Egia's truest sight. It is called the Ikosmenia Mask, and it is of immeasurable worth. She would not part with it for any price. I am attempting to replicate its abilities. I know the principle at work. It was taught to me by bastil Shadow Priests during my travels on Nen. I've been trying for a long, long time, and I shan't give up."

"None of that means anything to me," Vergil said. "I don't know most of those things, and it's too early in the day to learn them."

Ludwig looked at him curiously. He scratched at the patchy stubble on his face.

"Why did you lie about what was written on the book's cover? What was your gain?"

It took a moment to recall what the old man was talking about.

"That? I didn't lie, and I had nothing to gain."

"Then how did you know how to read the words?"

"I can't say. Tallah swore me to secrecy." That was a lie. Tallah had taken it at face value that his chip could simply translate text as well as it helped him understand and speak Imperial, but she'd said nothing about keeping it a secret.

Ludwig chuckled. "She would. Lad, there's paper in the drawer there. Fetch it for me. And the charcoal on the table. Yes, that one."

He wrote on his knee, the letters uneven and sloping down the page. His hand steadied as he went, as if shedding off reluctance and gaining purpose. Heat wafted off him, as it sometimes did off Tallah when she was working.

"I am a desperate fool. She's right on that account. I'll believe again that she needs my aid and will aid me in return." He signed the letter with a flurry and handed it over. "Help me up. My head's swimming in murky waters."

Vergil did, and then helped Ludwig up the stairs to the second level of his home. It was similarly devastated and reeked of old, unwashed clothes and unchanged linen. Under that stench there was the same tang of alcohol and the sweet aroma of tea.

"Take this to her." The old man handed him a closed box about the size of his palm, held shut by a rusted lock. He had taken it out of an old, battered-looking chest that creaked when opened. "I lost the key to it years ago, but I'm certain she'll manage to open it."

Vergil stowed everything in his cloak's inner pockets, secured against the howling wind. When he turned to leave, Ludwig clasped him by the arm. His old hand was much stronger than it had any right to be.

"I trust her words because you do, boy. Had she come herself, I would have thrown her out. Make of that what you will." He seemed to pull back into himself for a moment, and his grip slackened. "You listened." Before fully releasing Vergil to the blizzard, he reached into his shirt and pulled out a small time-worn pendant he wore tied to a silver chain on his neck, some kind of gemstone encased in a mesh of silver thread.

Even in the poor light, Vergil could see it pulsing gently, like a steady heartbeat. It seemed to drag to the side, as if pointing a certain way, counter to the wind rushing in.

"The girl is alive, lad. If you've a heart in your breast, impress on Tallah that I may not survive another disappointment. Not after this."

* * *

I'm lost.

It wasn't a comfortable thought and an even worse realization. Some of the narrower paths he'd followed coming in had snowed up as the storm churned and swirled above, seemingly gaining strength as morning approached. Going through the narrow choked gaps proved foolhardy.

He could try—and didn't relish the thought of—returning to Master Ludwig to wait out the weather. Admitting defeat was better than freezing to death.

Tallah's words were absurd. *Go there, come back, don't faff about.* Bloody damn easy for her to decree, inhuman as she bloody was.

Valen had trapped him in the Alchemists Quarter and kept him trudging in circles. When a path proved blocked, he backtracked, then tried to go around. The whole thing repeated a few too many times, and with so little light, his headware had lost track of his turns and couldn't offer anything beyond vague solutions for guidance.

Staring at an intersection of narrow alleys, the tracks behind him filling back up, he wasn't certain he could find Ludwig's hovel again.

I should wait for dawn. But where? Knock on a random door?

But there were no lit lights, no opened gates, no inviting doors. There was life, yes, by the muffled sound of work getting done, but heavy shutters had been drawn to keep winter and stray fools out.

It was getting harder to think. It was getting hard to breathe. An iron fist made up of night and cold squeezed him as he still tried to move forward. He'd already drunk Sil's concoction, and it did absolutely shit all to help.

And the thing on the back of his head stung. It broke through the chill and kept him on edge, always aware of the heat behind his ears. Was he straying too far from the Meadow? Would it really kill him as horribly as Sil promised?

Of course it would. Tallah wouldn't have lied just to keep him scared. Her wonderful personality managed that job expertly.

"Where am I?" he groaned as he started down another alley and immediately hit a dead end in a narrow slit between buildings. Snow rose up to his hips, and it was soaking through his trousers and into his boots.

He sighed, turned back, took the left path instead of the right, and fell. He stepped onto empty space and went arse over tip down a steep frozen incline of stairs.

This is how I die, he thought as he groped for a rail too far out of reach. He hit the twist in the drop and the flat of the first landing with a bone-crunching thud. Air went out of him in a painful gasp as he scrambled to grab hold of the thin, invisible balustrade, momentum trying to skid him forward and out into the black.

It took a ridiculously long time to haul himself up. Something inside his chest felt tender. He'd fallen quite a distance and was saved by the turn in the stairs, where they'd been built to hug the wall. He would have met thaw dead, frozen and buried somewhere in the Agora below, shattered like porcelain if not for the wrought-iron rail.

There were all sorts of smaller ways to travel between the layers of Valen aside from the lifts. Some were safer than others. Most were closed off in winter for good reason but not sealed off against idiots stumbling through.

"How lucky I am." Pushing the words out hurt. Drawing in the next gasping, frigid breath stabbed into his chest.

Below, the night brightened, and stray wisps of light punctured the dark. He wasn't sure he was seeing spots or if it was the Agora, but going down seemed like a better idea than up. All he needed to do was make sure he didn't slip.

He slipped.

A few yards still off solid ground, his gloved hand caught a patch of ice glass on the balustrade, lost its grip, and he fell again. This time there was enough snow at the bottom to cushion the drop. Barely enough.

Vergil considered lying where he fell. It was soft. He could sleep in the crater he'd made, and everything would be all right come morning. Or thaw. Whichever.

Why even bother getting back? Snow was comfier than the gibbet had been, and he'd been perfectly content to wait to die in the cave. He was starting to feel wonderfully numb and cozy, even warm, in the encasing embrace of the storm.

Seek shelter immediately!

Danger!

Hypothermia onset: Imminent danger to limb and life!

Bold red letters scrolled over the gathering dark on the edges of his vision. They made no sense.

Tallah could hang. His *mission* could hang too. She didn't care if he came back or—

Someone grabbed and hauled him up by the scruff of the neck. A swift, vicious kick in the arse shot him moving forward again, stumbling through the snow. He spun around, but there was nobody there, only the gash he'd cut through the banks.

He was pushed again, towards the light, as if an invisible hand had lost patience with him.

Move, ye dryshite milksop sprig. Yer legs still work.

Danger!

Hypothermia onset: Imminent danger to limb and life!

Sil's tonic bubbled in his stomach and filled him with renewed strength. What was he thinking?! No, he wasn't going to die on a walk from one part of the city to the other. The idea of it was mental. If Tallah heard, she'd laugh her arse off.

Though . . . had Argia just insulted him? He tried to scroll back, but the text garbled up. It kept repeating the danger warning over and over again, the letters rearranging and disappearing.

"What the hell's going on?" he gasped out, feeling like he was losing bits of his mind.

Nothing in his life had been quite as wonderful as the sight of the Agora in the predawn gloom, lit sparsely by sprite lights. Stalls were closed and buried under thick white blankets, barely even resembling their function. But he knew where he was. He had woken up on the first day exactly two alleyways from where he stood just then.

"The Pitcher's just ahead." Ahead, unfortunately, meant all the way across the Great Plaza. Vergil doubted the dregs of strength he was drawing on.

But to the right of him, just a short jaunt away, was Merg's. It occurred to him that Mertle had gone into the night just a short time before he did, and less dressed for it too. He liked her a lot, from the little she'd talked to him when coming and going together with Sil.

Sil, who to his absolute surprise, was human. It made her a lot easier to approach and talk to. The aelir persona made him sweat and stutter and stumble over words that should have been easy.

He pushed on Merg's door, and it swung inwards easily, unlocked, helped by the eager wind.

"Mertle . . ." His voice came out in a ragged, croaking whisper.

Closing the door was almost too difficult to manage. The gale put up a fight. With a creak, and taking everything he had left, he managed to push back the heavy wooden door.

Vergil blinked and immediately regretted it. Bright, intensely hot light blinded him. He blinked again and squinted against the sun flare. For a moment, he feared he was still at Ludwig's door, fainting at the sight of the fireball.

He tried to move.

Something heavy weighed him down. Heat swaddled him. For a split moment, he panicked, remembering the cage and the cook fire and . . .

No!

This wasn't that cage. This wasn't the cave. He'd survived them. He'd been rescued. His heart threatened to burst out of him as he tried to work his arms free of whatever bonded him.

The room resolved in his blurry vision. Straight ahead, there was the coal-burning heart of a forge. Sweltering heat came out through a grate by the side. To his right, there were tools arranged on neat racks on a wall, together with blades of all shapes and sizes. Some looked to have been well used.

"Gave me the scare of my life, Vergil," a voice said from his left. He swung his gaze around and was startled to look into Mertle's face leaning in too close for his own comfort.

"What happened?" he whispered. She brought a cup of water to his lips, and he drank greedily, only now aware of how thirsty he was.

Mertle disappeared from his side and came back a moment later with a refilled cup. He drank it too.

"What happened?" he asked again, stronger now. Blankets were heaped on top of him as he lay on a narrow cot. The smell of dry hay and weapon grease hit a moment later. He'd never smelled anything more wonderful in his life.

"Our door slammed is what happened. We heard it all the way back here," Mertle said as she pried some of the blankets off him, making it easier to breathe. "When we rushed out, we found it wide open and you collapsed against the wall. Looks like it hit you in the face."

It had?

Vergil worked his arm out from the blankets and pressed a hand to his cheek. He recoiled. His entire right side was tender and throbbing with a sharp, cutting pain.

He'd slipped when trying to close the blasted thing. It had swung back at him, and here he was.

"No wonder Tallah wants armor for you," Tummy said from behind. His approach was marked by the room trembling with his heavy steps. "You lost a scrape with our door. I'm honestly ashamed of training you." The smith stopped in front of him and grinned, fists on his hips. "Feeling better, twig?"

"Yeah. Thank you. I didn't know where else to go."

"Glad to hear it. Happy to be of service. Now then . . ."

Tummy grabbed him by the front of his shirt and hauled him up one-handed, neatly extracting him from the blankets. His feet dangled above the floor.

"Mind explaining that to us?" he asked and inclined his head towards Mertle.

She held out a flask. It was the one the Storm Guard woman had given him, shining in the light. Mertle caressed the emblazoned mark on the smooth surface.

"Why do you have this, Vergil?" she asked with the same sweetness she had always afforded him, but the smile on her lips did not reach all the way up to her eyes. The way she looked at him unnerved him even worse than the sorceress.

Looking from her to Tummy, it dawned on him that he'd gravely misunderstood who these two were. If they had truck with Tallah, then there was more to them than he'd been led to believe. The smith held a short sword as wide as his thick arm. Its blade caught the forge light with a malicious glint.

He told them of his morning as fast as his mind could recall and arrange events. He told them of the two he'd met in the storm, of Ludwig and his answer for Tallah, of wandering and falling. When he got as far as the door, in all detail, Tummy finally decided to set him back on the cot.

Mertle regarded him thoughtfully, spinning the flask in her slender hands. Tummy waited by her side, sword still at the ready, an unreadable expression on his face. After some time, she looked up and gave him the tiniest nod.

"Guess something's really spooked Tallah if she's got you running errands in this weather," she said when Tummy turned around and went to his work. Her smile was back and genuine now. There was real concern in her voice.

Tension bled out of the room, and Vergil, as she headed to a bucket and emptied the flask in it. She threw the empty container to Tummy, who tossed it into his crucible.

"I think you shouldn't tell Tallah about your little run-in," Mertle said as she searched for something in the cupboards. "If she's got thistles in her trousers, then this is going to make her insufferable. You don't want Tallah getting jumpier than her normal."

"If I were involved with the Storm Guard, wouldn't it have been stupid to threaten me?" Vergil immediately regretted his words. Out of anything he could have said to fill the silence, he chose to voice the stupidest question he thought of.

But it struck him as so odd. If he were in league with the peacekeepers, who'd threaten him so out of hand?!

Mertle laughed softly. Tummy laughed a lot harder.

"Twiggy, you came in from the storm at an ungodly hour. It wouldn't be much trouble putting you back out in it with your head screwed on backward." He slammed the hammer on his anvil with earth-shaking force, as if to give credence to the words. "Thaw's still a long way away."

"Point taken," Vergil said, swallowing a lump.

"Sil said you have a good head on your shoulders," Mertle said as she handed him a glass of a clear liquid that smelled pungent. It came from a dusty, unlabeled bottle that she dug out from behind the forge. "She also mentioned you're sometimes dumber than one of Tummy's hammers. I think you're sweet for worrying about me when you had bigger things on your mind."

He felt his cheeks burn and looked away from her smile.

She wore leather trousers and a battered apron, like the first day he'd walked into their shop. Her back and shoulders were bare, and he could see the dense cluster of tattoos crowding her skin.

One of them bore more than an uncanny resemblance to Sil. There were other faces, smaller, with names and dates written. The text was too small for him to read at a glance.

Without thinking, and to stop himself from staring, he threw back the drink. He only caught a glimpse of Mertle's horrified expression before the world rotated ninety degrees sideways and all went black.

"I'm going to go look for him," Sil said, impatiently walking across the room.

Tallah refused to budge on the issue. "You're not going anywhere until we have the caravan employed."

"I feel he should have been back by now."

"He's waiting out the storm at Ludwig's. He had enough time to get there before it worsened."

Sil wanted to say something more, but Tallah held up a hand. "What is it with you and the sudden bout of concern for the waste of skin?"

"I have a conscience," Sil said, much more accusingly than she intended.

"I have two of those and they don't kick up this much of a fuss. Vergil's fine."

Sil was bloody sure he wasn't. The boy was held together by big dreams and sinew. Sending him out was beyond cruel, so much so that it bordered on imbecilic. "He could be freezing to death somewhere."

"So could you if you go after him. Sit still and wait quietly. He'll be along after it quiets down out there."

Tallah was back to pacing the room like a caged corallin, arguing in terse whispers with Christina and Bianca. They, too, resented the idea of going with Ludwig anywhere, especially as it all hinged on the sorceress's one bad premonition. Granted, those were usually right, as she had an obscenely accurate sense for danger, but this felt excessive even for her.

"You're fretting your tits off, but you're telling me to be calm?"

There was no spoken answer, just a glare. She turned back to the window, watching for some change in the weather, or at least some sign of the boy stumbling back. Vergil was still in her care and still recovering. Simply discarding him didn't sit well in her stomach.

Verti's girl was due back any minute. Miria had already informed them that the caravan master was taking his morning meal and would be available for a meeting soon after. Vulniu asked few questions and answered none about his cargo and passengers. Traveling with him would be . . . fine.

A knock at the door.

It repeated, insistent.

Why is she trying to break down the door?

She opened it and found herself face-to-face with a runner. Miria was nowhere to be seen.

"Yes?" she asked, more than a little confused. They weren't expecting any word from Aliana.

Confusion turned to surprise, then outrage as the figure walked in, right past her as if she weren't there. He was caked in snow and wrapped in a thick cloak with a head covering that hid most of his face. His footsteps thumped the floor when he walked, chunks of ice breaking off his thick boots to leave a melting trail.

"Excuse me?" Sil said.

He walked right into the sitting room and headed for the hearth. He clinked and clanked as he walked, as if he were armed and armored beneath the layers of padding.

Tallah watched him walk by, gaze swiveling like an owl's to follow his movement. "Welcome back," she said.

Vergil? Sil was having a hard time making up her mind whether to laugh, hug him, or push him into the fire for worrying her.

Vergil raised his hands to the heat of the hearth and slowly defrosted. The first thing he did after was turn to Tallah, raise his right hand, and show her his middle finger.

She chuckled. "I don't know what that means, but I assume it's rude."

"It's . . . b-bloody c-cold . . . out there," he said in a hoarse whisper. His teeth chattered.

"I expect that it is. How's Ludwig?"

"D-Drunk off his arse and m-miserable."

Sil helped him peel off the mask he wore. He smiled at her, sheepish almost, red-faced under the hood. Now that he no longer resembled some strange snowman, she saw that he wore completely different clothes than the ones he'd gone out in.

"Mertle says hi," Vergil said as he unclasped his cloak and set it up to dry by the hearth. "I swung by on my way back."

"She fitted you out well, I see."

Tummy had been busy while Mertle spent her time with Sil. Vergil wore a cuirass breastplate over a thickly padded gambeson. It all seemed very sturdy and functional, as expected of the smith. Subdued greenish grays were the main colors, with only a thick scarf adding a splash of sky blue.

"Tummy calls these *highwayman clothes*," Vergil said, noticing her curiosity. "Said I'm too scrawny for proper plate but that this should suffice for now. Also said Tallah's off her tits if she thinks I'll ever fill up enough for the kind of gear she wanted to waste money on."

Sil laughed, and Tallah flushed to the tips of her ears.

"A fool and her money get easily parted, he also said. There's more to proper defense than how thick the metal you lug around is."

"Yes, yes, I get the idea. I trust he knows his business better than I."

"Oh, this is the very short version. He went on for almost a bell's length. I remember more of it."

Tallah gave a tight-lipped smile and sucked her teeth before changing subjects. "I'm sure. What did Ludwig say?"

"Would you like me to repeat word for word? My headware saved a transcript."

Sil turned his head side to side and inspected his ears. Then she checked his fingers. And finally, his toes. As intact as the moment he went out, even if much pinker in the face and smelling faintly of booze. Mertle must have given him one of her nightmarish distilled concoctions. It explained his sudden bout of backbone.

Released from her attention, Vergil sank into the chair and stretched out his legs. "There's a letter in the inner pocket of my cloak and a locked box. He said you'd manage to open it."

For someone who had spent half the day out in the storm, Vergil looked none the worse for it. It galled her to admit that Tallah might have been right in her own thick-headed way.

The sorceress unfurled the folded paper, stared at it, and went to fetch her glasses.

"How drunk was he?" She squinted at the letter. She turned it upside down. Then tilted it. "Sil, you try. We can't make heads or tails of this."

"Three of you in there, and you need me to read an old man's writing? For shame!" She stomped over.

All right, this is bad.

Words stumbled one over the other and nearly fell off the page. There were no two lines the same height, or even with similar spelling. It trumped even her own horrible penmanship.

"Err, right. How drunk was he, again?"

"Very," Vergil replied and shrugged apologetically. "What do you mean by *three of you in there?*"

"She's got imaginary friends. They're all rude." By his expression, he believed her.

She was just about to correct her explanation when Tallah piped up, annoyance getting the best of her patience.

"The letter, Sil, can you bloody read it?"

"Ah. There's some colorful language on top, and then it basically tells you to use the item in the box and get to him when you're good to go. He'll have his affairs in order in a day and be ready to head out."

Tallah neatly blew the top of the box off with a flame burst. It flew off with a sharp crack, and azure light flooded the room.

"Oh, that old bastard," Tallah breathed out as she picked up the shard inside. Light flowed out between her fingers. "Makes you think, Sil, of what other secrets the old fool's been keeping from us."

"Is that like the thing you gave Mistress Aliana?" Vergil asked. He was keenly fascinated by the glow.

"Yes, but ten times more valuable. This is a live shard, Vergil. It's got an anchor tied to it."

"I don't know what that is."

Tallah laughed. "It's a sliver of an illum hearth." Light pulsed between her fingers, changing through shades of blue. She stowed it back in its box and went to find the mangled lid. "This has a twin somewhere. They're always drawn to one another, meant to come together no matter what. We can portal directly to it without the city's own hearth altering our destination. To the empress, one of these is worth as much as a city."

Sil passed Vergil buttered bread and a cup of hot coffee. He looked like he could use both.

"Which begs the question, why doesn't he just buy her favor back with that?"

"I'll bet you a jar of wild honey that he hasn't come across this by happenstance. Bet you a second one that this is how he's made sure nobody else knows the way to his secret city."

"Lovely. And we're trusting him with our safety. For all you know, that could portal you straight into the deepest dungeon in Aztroa Magnor."

Tallah regarded her with an amused expression. "And you thought I was horrible. If he were to give us up, he'd have done it years ago. No, I think this is safe."

A grimace twisted her smirk into something altogether quite nasty, but it was only a flicker on her face.

"Christina doesn't agree, I take it?"

"And, like you, she hasn't come up with anything better. Like it or not, we're committing."

And, to give finality to her words, there came the soft, respectful knock on the door that announced Miria.

Lovely.

CHAPTER NINETEEN

A Bad Plan's Still a Plan

Vergil slept the sleep of the terminally exhausted, falling off while Sil and Tallah argued on how best to handle the immediate future. By the time he woke and uncurled off his cot, in late afternoon of what felt like a different year altogether, the apartment had become an eerily quiet place.

The earlier headache still dogged him, grown into a mute presence holding his head in a vice-like grip of throbbing pain. A niggling sensation of something trying to scratch its way out of his brain got him to his feet.

Attempted connection: Pending.

Attempted connection: Failed. Error: 432342 [Handshake could not be established.]

Please seek Engineering support via open public channel #2001.

Argia was at it again, trying to reestablish connection to a ship that was a reality away. It'd quiet down after some time.

He stumbled into the common room in time to see Tallah slice open a dark slit in the air. It hovered a palm's breadth above the floor. She widened it with a gesture into something about the size of a door.

"Good. You're awake. Carry these in there," she instructed, as if there wasn't a big rip in the air itself. "Don't gawk. Hop to it."

He stuck his hand in, and it didn't come out the other side. The cold, inside bit.

"It's a hole," he said, too stupid for the time being to articulate anything more profound.

"It's a rend. You've seen them before." She pointed to a pack of clothes on the floor. "Go on, take them in."

It was his first time seeing one as big as this. He'd mostly seen Sil stowing stuff in her little black portals or taking out vials and supplies for her alchemy.

"What's in there?"

"Nothing."

"Why is it whispering?"

Tallah stared at him, then at the rend. She came next to him and placed the back of her hand to his forehead.

"Just daft with an overactive imagination, not feverish," she proclaimed. "The rend's not whispering. There's nothing in there to do anything of the sort."

Vergil heard it quite clearly. Well, not clearly, more like a stream of static that never resolved into a language he could understand, but the impression of words was there.

He really shouldn't accept strange drinks anymore . . .

"Where does it lead to?"

"Nowhere."

He tried to mimic one of the impatient glares Sil always threw around. "Go into the dark portal, Vergil. There's nothing in there, Vergil. It doesn't go anywhere, Vergil. Do the two of you ever hear yourselves?"

Tallah frowned, midway into stowing some books inside her chest. In a minute, Vergil regretted his outburst, as she launched into an explanation of what a rend was in her usual cryptic way that assumed he was either much smarter than he really was or a complete imbecile. Reality grew thin around people like her and Sil because of how they drew illum to them. A skilled enough channeler like herself could rearrange—and here she'd lost him completely—that thin reality into a gap outside of reality that only they could access and use it to store things inside. Clear enough?

Mental. Absolutely mental.

It shut him up.

The two had been busy while he slept, and it made him feel vaguely ashamed for it, and a little uneasy in seeing the room left so bare. Tianna and Sil's lives fit neatly into the large chest that now dominated one wall of the room. What was still out were some clothes, Tallah's trio of swords, and a bunch of labeled jars, the contents of which were either vile or alien to him.

All of it depressing.

He picked up the neatly stacked clothes, drew in and held a breath, and stepped through the rend.

It was like dipping into ice-cold water. The chill knocked the air out of him. He'd expected a kind of midnight darkness but was met by gray twilight.

The walls of the room outside became ghostly and indistinct. He could see Tallah moving about, passing through the empty space he occupied, like two images overlaying.

There were shelves that hadn't been in the Meadow room. Some of them had knickknacks heaped upon them, but most were covered by books and Sil's alchemy supplies. There was a small chest on another with a very large lock set upon it.

The air was thin and smelled faintly of a chemical spill.

The whispers were louder on this side of the portal, buzzing almost, skipping like a bad communication port on the *Gloria*. How could Tallah not hear it? That or she was pulling his leg.

Attempted connection: Pending.

Connection: Successful.

"There you are! Stay put!"

He whirled in place. He'd heard a woman's voice clear as crystal. It had been just there, right beside him. But only Tallah's ghostly figure passed through, crossing the room outside the rend, unconcerned.

Connection: Dropped.

Attempted connection: Pending.

"There *is* something in there." Vergil's voice cracked when he rushed out. Whether from the cold or the shock, he wasn't sure. "I'm not making it up. I swear."

Tallah gave him a suffering glare, walked past him, and disappeared into the rend. She was back out a few moments later.

"Vergil, there's nothing in there. Blast you, I thought you'd finally grown a backbone last night. If you're scared of the dark, just say so."

"I was drunk. And I'm not scared of the dark."

"And it's left you dumb? Get out of my way."

She picked up the sheathed swords and carried them in. Her agitation left him shuffling his feet uncertainly, too red with embarrassment to even look at her as she walked circles around the nearly empty room, checking for things she might have missed. The portal just floated there, its edges rippling slightly as if from an unfelt breeze.

Maybe he had imagined it? The connection log was there, but it had lasted less than a second. Maybe a bug with Argia? Maybe it was finally starting to malfunction?

The unmentionable jars he took in himself. No more connections. No more voices in the dark space. Just the feeling of being watched by something that was constantly on the back of his head, but maybe that was just how Argia reacted to the absurd notion of a rend.

"Where's Sil?" he asked to distract himself from the idea that his headware might be going loopy.

"Talking to Vulniu. Man's merciless. He's charging me two arms and a whole arse for passage on his caravan."

"We're leaving with him?"

"No. But he's charging me too much to take my chest. Said he knows what channelers do with their luggage and how he expects it'll weigh three times what it should." She scoffed. "It weighs five times what it should, but that's beside the point. It's a matter of principle."

She gestured to the large ornate thing that now roosted alone by the wall.

"You can't put it in your . . . uh, in your rend?"

"It's too heavy and carrying too many things imbued with illum. It'd distort the space and make it available for implings and their ilk. Blighters steal everything they can carry and chew on what they can't." She gave him a grin. "Ask Sil about them. I bet she'd love to tell you a story or two about ruined unmentionables. And rightly blame me."

Vergil placed a hand on the chest's polished ebony lid and took another look around the now-empty room. The sight of it stirred something inside him he couldn't quite understand. In the few weeks since he'd met Tallah and Sil, that apartment on the third level of the Meadow had become home, or something as close to it as he'd ever known.

Tallah was doing another sweep of the rooms, checking nooks and corners, climbing on furniture and checking above dressers.

"Can you please tell me what's going on? Why are we in such a hurry to leave?"

She shrugged, not turning to him. "Sil says I've gone mad. She's probably right. But my instinct tells me things have taken a turn that's going to be bad for me. I've enough scars to know when to listen to instinct."

He hadn't expected an answer, much less an honest one. He would've preferred something clearer.

"But, if you're not certain, isn't Tianna suddenly disappearing going to just make things worse?"

"I don't care. I'm burning this plan and scattering the ashes. I'll try again later, in some other way."

"Try what? What was the plan? I'm not bright enough for riddles."

She waved his question away, then gave him a strange look. "What do I do about you?" she asked, voice low, as if suddenly realizing he was there.

Vergil recoiled. "Not kill me, I hope."

"Don't be daft. Why would you— Never mind. I'll cut you loose when we get somewhere safe again. I won't have the luxury of wasting time on deciphering whatever you are."

No. No, he refused the very notion of being left on his own again.

"May I make a suggestion?"

Tallah narrowed her eyes and gave him a long look, as if deciding whether it was worth her time. He went on before she answered.

"If I've pieced things together right, you're worried that Tianna was compromised as a cover. I don't know how or why, but I heard you and Sil talking about some things, and I think you had a long-term plan involving the Storm Guard. You're not just hiding here. You're plotting."

Vergil was supposed to be asleep when some of those conversations happened. By Tallah's deepening frown, she realized this and did not like the implication.

He swallowed and went on, "So I think that you're now willing to drop everything because of something that's happened last night that got you panicking. You're not just hiding; you're really trying to infiltrate the Fortress?" It was a guess.

"Go on," she said, dry amusement coating the words.

"So . . . uh . . . why don't you ask someone else to be Tianna for a time? And reveal yourself as alive, to distinguish the two? Maybe . . . Sil?" he quickly added. "I mean, you know, Tianna is pretty reclusive. Aside from about four people, I haven't seen you interacting with almost anyone in Valen. It wouldn't take much to just show the disguise around and convince people."

Tallah was quiet for a time and then laughed slowly. "Had we not been vain and stupid years ago, that would work. But we both have two disguises already. A third wouldn't stick for weeks, maybe a whole season."

"Me?"

"You'd need to be utterly convinced you are who you look to be. From one sex to the other is . . . complicated for most people."

"Ah." Vergil sat on the lid of the chest, deflated. "Would Mertle be able to do it?"

"With help and time, sure. Though I'm not going to ask her." She sat next to him, stretched out her legs, and crossed them at the ankles. "I'm curious how much else you've been piecing together." There was, again, the same amusement in her voice but with an edge that Vergil wasn't certain how to interpret.

He decided to take his chances. "Ludwig was very vocal about some things. It wasn't hard to connect everything with what I've been seeing."

"Mm-hm, go on."

"You don't want to ask Mertle to do this . . . because she's hiding as well?" He curdled the end of the sentence into a question without meaning to, but the idea had just occurred to him. It made a kind of sense that Tallah would surround herself with similar rogues. That glint in Mertle's eyes, the way she had weighed his words and his life, her will to deal with someone like Tallah. It made sense.

"And where would you have gotten that kind of idea, bucket-head?"

He'd hit a nerve. It was in her voice and all over her face and in the thousand-league stare that avoided glancing at him.

She can't lie to save her life, he realized with some satisfaction.

He told her the full story about the meeting with the captain woman of the Storm Guard. She listened quietly to the entire thing, but a crack showed in her mask. An eye twitched. And he could swear she was getting hot, like a boiling kettle close to bursting under the building pressure.

"I think you're underestimating what Mertle's willing to do for you and Sil," he said in closing, shifting uncomfortably as she kept quiet and got hotter.

A glance over showed her chewing on the knuckle of her finger.

"I could have cut you loose if you hadn't told me all that," she finally said, voice low. "You knowing about me can't be helped. You figuring Mertle out . . . Silly girl, couldn't just play her chosen part."

"You and Sil, for all your threats and secrets, you don't really hold back around me. Sometimes I think you forget I'm here."

Tallah pushed herself to her feet and straightened. Her hands flashed fire for a moment, then sputtered out.

Vergil clasped his hands together and swallowed down the lump of fear in his throat.

"I don't want to be cut loose. I want to help you." Conviction came easily. He believed every word. "I stand by what I said. I don't care that you're hunted."

"Sil said you have some ideas of the sort. The Storm Guard have some particularly nasty things in store for me, and some even nastier ones for those fool enough to follow me." She turned a hard, pitiless look on him. "If I'm to be taken, I will burn you alive even if it's with my last breath. With what you know, I should probably kill you now. But I'll never get Sil to shut up about it if I do."

She would kill him if the choice came to that. He understood this much.

He wasn't afraid to die, not really. The thought of letting Tallah down, or Sil, or Tummy . . .

"You won't be taken." Vergil grinned. "You don't seem like the type to let it happen."

"Fancy that," Tallah said with a voice and expression not wholly her own, "the stupid boy has become a frightfully stupid man, all in the span of one storm and a nap. Color me impressed. His suggestion does have merit if Mergara goes back to bad habits."

Tallah clamped down, bit her lip, and let out a long sigh of annoyance.

"Vergil, meet Christi, the original architect of our entire mess."

"Sil wasn't pulling my leg?"

"Christi's a grafted soul, not an imaginary friend. Sil was being an arse."

"How—"

But she was already moving away, distracted. Her long stare was back. Vergil waited as she paced the room in tight, slow circles. It didn't take long for her inner council to reach a conclusion.

"Get dressed," she snapped. "You're a runner again."

He was on his feet before her first words were even out.

"Where am I going?" He was almost giddy with excitement. His head pounded still. But Tallah was going to give him another mission all of his own.

"Aliana. And then to Mertle. You're to present the plan to them, and—I insist on this—do not try to convince them to do anything. You tell them that I will be making a move and I need to substitute Tianna for a time. For that, I need their help. Whatever they decide, you get right back here once you're done."

"Why Mistress Aliana? What plan?"

"Mertle's an elend. Like you, she can't channel illum, can't use the staff. If Aliana's willing, she's going to do it for her after Sil and I go to ground for a time. She's protected enough by her station that she won't draw suspicion, and even if she does, she doesn't need to care."

Vergil bounced on the balls of his feet as he pulled on his armor and its padding. Tallah helped him draw up the face covering. Her hands were warm, and a light had lit up behind Tianna's midnight blue eyes. Whatever hesitation she had felt before, it was gone now.

She explained what she wanted of Mertle and how to reach Aliana unquestioned. He repeated back every word until she was satisfied.

"When are we starting?" he asked.

"Now. If anything's to happen, it won't take them long to marshal against me. The sooner we get everyone on board, the better."

He ran out into the hallway and into the descending night. It wasn't as bad a storm as the one the day prior, but the wind still cut to the bone. Purpose kept him warm, and the fire he saw in Tallah's eyes lent him strength to wade through the crowd and the snow.

The white-leafed tree shone above Valen's higher quarters, still catching the last wisps of daylight in its silver leaves. A gap in the clouds above, punched through by the hearth's venting, allowed stray evening sunlight to filter through.

Fire hung in the sky, and Vergil pushed and shoved his way towards it.

* * *

'I do not support this course of action, Tallah. This is an even worse plan than your previous,' Bianca whined.

"You've been outvoted."

'How can you, Christina? How do you justify trusting our fate to some elend whelp?'

The ghost was starting to get on Tallah's nerves. She had made her protests, loudly so, and had been outvoted for the final decision. Now, it would be kind of her to bloody shut up about it.

"It makes sense for us. If we salvage Tianna, we won't have wasted five full years."

'And what exactly do you plan to do? You are not fit to face the princeling. If he joins the fray, we will not survive. We will have wasted ourselves on a mindless gambit. Again, I might add.'

"I don't need to win. I only need him to see me. I'm going to rely on you two for the element of surprise."

'You had surprise on your side the last time. It did not work out, as I recall the reports. You survived the fire by the skin of your teeth.'

'Enough, Bianca,' Christina finally said. 'We all know the risk. We can but hope we're enough. Worst case, we have Professor Ludwig's shard.'

'But we don't know where it leads to. This is pure folly.'

"It is what it is, Bianca. We'll manage. I can handle Falor."

'You can't win.'

"I don't need to. Just bloody his nose and run. It'll be good to see how we measure up to him now."

Christina let out an annoyed mental sigh. 'If Anna lied to us, I will give her such a flaying when we bring her into our communion.'

'And what will that achieve? We can't feel pain.' Bianca's high tone was slipping in her impatience. Now she sounded more like her old, provincial self rather than the mock Aztroa courtier.

'It'll make me feel better about this entire sorry business.'

'You two are children. I swear. Worse than. You are petty children.'

Tallah let out a slow breath, trying to calm a cringing thing inside herself. She looked at the empty room and at the empty fireplace and at her empty desk, and felt the familiar, anxious twinge in her heart.

The mountain loomed in her mind's eye, a dark, jagged specter of razor-edged peaks, bottomless gorges, and winds that howled and moaned through crevices and across gaping maws of stone.

Aztroa's Crown wore its own crown of merciless storms with all the grace of a bloodthirsty tyrant and twice the cruelty. Tallah had overcome it once. Against the murderous cold, the mad, laughing wind, and the breakneck drops, she and Sil had endured and walked away from the horrors in the heart of the Crown.

Could she do it again, if she failed here? Probably not.

'Best not to fail, then,' Christina said, intruding on her private thoughts. 'Stop lolling about. We've cast our die. Let's get you fit to face a walking calamity.'

She pushed herself up from the chest's lid and went to Sil's emptied desk. Ten half bands of new metal waited for her, five fresh limiters. Two on each arm, one on her neck. Two by two, they clasped together and then tightened on their own. Cold metal on hot skin. Her furnace fire inside focused sharply as if squeezed by invisible bonds.

She produced a flame on the tip of one finger and ran it across her hands, moving it over and under her fingers, careful not to burn skin again. Her control felt almost perfect.

'She does fine work,' Christina mused. 'For all her faults, she's quite adept at producing these trinkets. Only five do the work of the ten that someone of your capacity would need. Six, if we count the one with the trinket.'

Tallah increased the illum flow. It moved through her with clarity of purpose, like cold liquid fire in her veins. Pain accompanied it, but it was now more a memory rather than the sharp stabs from the first days after her burnout. The more power she used, the more memory threatened to push into reality, but she'd manage.

'Someone's coming,' Bianca said. 'The door. Elend.'

Vergil couldn't have been gone more than half a bell strike. That left Verti or one of her girls. But it wasn't time for supper yet. Sil wasn't even back from her haggling.

"Good evening, Your Ladyship." It was Verti herself. She was red-faced with anger. Pert, one of her big bruisers, stood a half step behind her. He was holding his hat in his hands and nodded respectfully to her.

Verti wrung her hands in her apron and spoke as if chased. "I so apologize for disturbing you, Lady Aieni. But I believe you need to know this. You have been threatened."

Well, that's something to spring on a woman.

"Slow down, Verti. Who threatened me?" Tallah asked, feeling quite sanguine about the news. It made sense that the night would come with more surprises now that she'd committed to a plan of action.

"I . . . I don't know, Lady Aieni. The common room's full to bursting. I was helping the girls when someone grabbed my arm in the crowd. They . . . she? I think it was a woman's voice. It happened so quickly. She said, and pardon me for repeating, 'They're coming for Tianna of Aieni Holding. Third bell of the night. Tell her or this place goes up in flames.'" She cursed in elend and wouldn't meet Tallah's eye. "I have already sent for the constabulary. I will not have my guests threatened in my own home."

Tallah laughed. She looked at the large bruiser, a retired adventurer that Verti kept very well paid to keep trouble away from the Meadow, and she couldn't help herself. The elendine looked ready to sink through the floor in embarrassment.

She wiped her eyes and tried to compose an answer. "I apologize," she said, still feeling the laughter bubbling inside. "Don't mind such things, Verti. A threat on my person is absolutely ridiculous. Nobody would dare."

Oh, the Guard would dare, she had no qualms about that. They'd likely come in force, with no thought spared for the fallout to come, to take out a soul thief.

"Don't look so glum," she went on, taking the elendine's hand in her own and patting it. "I'm certain it's nothing to worry yourself over."

"But—"

"None of that. I assume you brought your guard to ensure my protection?"

"Yes, ma'am," said bouncer replied in a thick, grizzly voice. "At your pleasure, ma'am."

She dismissed him with a shooing motion of her hand.

"Run along. You'd best see to the common room. I believe this was nothing more than some rabble-rouser trying to get you rattled, my dear."

"But—"

She smiled, and the elendine flushed bright crimson all the way up to the edges of her horns, uncertainty washing over her face in waves.

"I appreciate your care. I really do. But this is a hoax. I have no enemies, here in Valen least of all. And my father's business partners are perfectly happy to have me as far from Calabran as possible." She gave another reassuring squeeze to Verti's hand before letting go. "Thank you so much for your concern, but it's really misplaced. And know that I'll be out tonight. I plan on seeing the Descent. If there's any trouble, I invite it to my flame."

Helped along by another encouraging smile, Verti relented, bowed, turned, and left. Pert followed in her wake. Tallah waited until they were safely down the stairs before she slammed the door and let out a slow, satisfied sigh.

'It's a trap,' Christina said.

'It must be,' Bianca agreed.

"I don't care."

Small gasps of laughter slipped out as she returned to the empty room. Without really meaning to, she opened up a rend and retrieved a package from inside.

'What are you doing?' both ghosts asked at once.

Clarity of purpose. She'd missed it. Since Anna's death, stuck in Valen, watching winter's snow churn outside her windows, she'd fallen into a sort of fugue. Cocooned by peace, lulled to sleep by the idleness of a season unchallenged, she'd started enjoying herself. She hadn't been so still for so long for decades. If not for the blasted boy, she would have dragged Sil out into the passes from the first day of winter's coming.

She undid the clasps of Tianna's horrid dress and let it slip off her, like a snake's shed skin, and walked to where Sil's staff hung on its peg, a thin sheet covering it. She touched it, closed her eyes, and let its enchantment unravel.

'My, my, aren't you being dramatic?' Christina couldn't hide her amusement. 'Is that how you're going to play this?'

She caught her reflection in a wall's mirror and smiled.

'Ugh. Don't do that,' Bianca whined. 'You look positively ghastly. Get Aliana to heal that horrid scar.'

Tallah approached the mirror and laughed softly. Gray streaked the red of her hair. She liked the look, though not so much the implication. Her eyes had shed what little shade of blue they once held. They stared back at her, silver and speckled with burst capillaries.

The scar . . . oh, her scar. It showed faintly pink-gray in the candlelight and cracked the mirror on a jagged diagonal.

She remembered the spearhead that had carved her face in two. The blinding flash of pain. The overwhelming iron taste of blood.

And she remembered the spear wielder howling when she fused his armor to his flesh. A boy, really, who hadn't known better and died performing a duty he wasn't fit for. She hadn't thought of him in years.

'Positively ghastly,' Bianca repeated. 'Look away before I lose my innards.'

Mertle would not have her gear ready just yet. That was fine. She still had her old uniform.

And it fit her. In the white and blue of the Storm Guard, she felt like a mockery of herself. It would at least remind the Guard that she had written the book on dealing with out-of-control channelers, and if they wanted to play things cute against her, they'd be walking away bloody. If at all.

'Bianca, you'll be our time keeper for this one,' Christina said in the tone of one laying out a complex plan. 'I'll be shield for tonight unless needed. I need you to be aware of our movement and the time it takes.'

'What for?'

"So we don't happen to kill Vergil."

Tallah pulled on her old gloves and flexed her fingers. Not as good as those Mertle made, but these could handle her heat well enough.

'We'll assume the boy's speed and path from here to the Sisters' and then to the smithy. To be on the safe side, we'll restrict our perimeter to three-quarters of what it would normally be.'

'Those are assumptions piled atop assumptions, Christi,' Bianca said, somewhat reproachfully. 'I will not be held responsible if the boy's head explodes.'

"I will keep a mirror on hand and stare into it every bell strike from now until eternity if that happens," Tallah warned, and relished the feeling of absolute revulsion that washed off Bianca.

'I'd go mad.'

"Good. Christi and I could use the company."

She tied her hair back into a loose ponytail and fitted her silver mask. The world snapped into focus and was bathed in the rich spectrum of illum, undisturbed save for herself.

"I'll swing us by the Agora to grab supplies. Then we'll head to the Fortress." She wrote a note as she spoke, outlining the plan for Sil in their private shorthand. "Bianca, I'll use you for mobility. Christi, if we clash with Falor, I'll need your help. Best we don't play every card right away."

'With a bit of luck, he'll be here while you're carving up the Fortress,' Christina said.

Over the whistling blizzard, she could hear, faintly, the bells of the spires. She counted eight of them. Evening was at an end. Three bell strikes to the moment the warning had mentioned.

Cold mist and fat flakes of snow tumbled into the room when she opened the window that looked down into the narrow streets and alleys. Nothing stirred in the illum flow. Not the raging torrents that accompanied a sorceress, nor the smoother vortexes of healers. She stuck her head out and took in a more thorough look, searching for the minute tremors that announced an Egia.

Nothing. People moved in the streets, huddled under heavy coats and bundled tight in furs, but nothing that spelled immediate danger. Valen celebrated. Three bell strikes to midnight, and people trickled out of their homes to form long columns that shuffled towards the Fortress for the Descent and the festivities to follow. In that direction, illum roiled and churned, a sign of channelers converging to be blessed by whichever deity deigned to show up.

Careful movement would keep her hidden from Rumi Belli's sight long enough for her to reach her targets. From the Meadow to the Agora, and then to the Fortress via the Guild.

'They know you have the mask,' Christina reminded her. 'I would be careful in how I assembled my forces if I planned an ambush.'

'I have a suggestion,' Bianca said, pensive now that they were in motion. 'I will tell you on the way. We may yet limit our risk to something less suicidal.'

Bianca surrendered her power to her use. As always, it was confusing and unwieldy, but it served well enough. Tallah reached out with an illum tether, anchored it to a distant rooftop, and yanked herself off into the night.

Snow crunched softly under her boots when she landed on the slanted roof, her diminished weight too low to dislodge the thick frozen carpet. She turned back to the Meadow and saw Sil's print in the illum moving through the staircase, her power's ripples diluted by distance.

A gust pushed her forward, and she had to enforce her anchor lest she be blown off. Frozen snow stung her exposed cheek, and her ears hurt with the cold, but it all felt so good in the moment. The healer was calm, reflected in how she showed to the mask's sight.

"Good that we left when we did," she mused as she crouched in the snow and swept her gaze over the packed streets. Anyone looking up would only be blinded by the snowfall and the strengthening wind.

'I doubt she would have agreed readily to any of this,' Christina answered.

Tallah jumped off the roof and launched herself towards the Agora. Bianca's power thrummed in her back, and her grip on it was becoming firmer by the moment. She swung herself sideways, gained momentum, and sailed over rooftops in a high-cresting arc. Winds buffeted her flight, but new anchors kept her moving where she meant to, riding storm winds and sheets of sleet and ice.

'We will pay for our supplies this time,' Christina said, a hint of reproach in her voice. 'I will not be made accomplice to theft again. You can afford both the time and the griffons.'

'We may be truly dead in three strikes, Christi. Is this the time for fancies?'

Her conscience let out the imitation of an annoyed sniff. *'It is always the time for being morally upright.'*

"I am going to skin her alive." Sil ripped the piece of very expensive paper into the smallest shreds she could manage. "I'm going to make a whip out of her epidermis. And I am going to flay Vergil bloody with it."

Little shreds of paper got torn into even smaller shreds. She used her nails.

This wasn't how things got done. She didn't get to do as she pleased. That wasn't their understanding. That wasn't how they—

Except that Tallah did do as she pleased, whenever she pleased. She may as well have been angry at the storm. Or at Vergil, for being hapless and eager.

But this was about Mertle! She had been terribly careful not to involve

Mertle in any of their comings and goings. Mertle had other things to worry herself over, not the machinations of one unhinged pyromancer and her two thralls.

A thrall? Is that how I see myself?

Anger brought out the stupid in her. But she wanted to be angry. Maybe Mertle would refuse after all. Or Aliana would. She had little real love for Tallah, and even less reason for it. There was no reason for her to agree to anything so crass and risky.

"Can you believe that fat-headed prim cunt?"

No . . .

Someone was talking very loudly out in the corridor, getting closer.

"Verti, this simply isn't proper. She called me out, in this ugly weather, on Descent Night, just because she thinks I measured her wrong. That is insulting. I barely convinced Tummy not to come here himself. He almost stripped the boy naked and marched him straight out of the shop."

Sil sagged in her chair and closed her eyes, counting down to the inevitable.

Sure enough, here was the knock. And here she was, walking as if to the gallows to answer. She really shouldn't . . .

Mertle stared daggers from under a thick, snow-heavy cloak. Verti bowed next to her, smiling apologetically. Vergil brought up the rear.

She bowed back to Verti and signed her sincere apology then stepped aside. Mertle swept in with a sniff of annoyance, mumbling her displeasure.

"I will try and not let them get too loud," Sil said as Vergil sidled past her. "I apologize so much for imposing on your patience today, Verti."

"Just as long as the mistress doesn't set anything on fire again. Replacing scorched wall is a hassle I wouldn't want to deal with in winter, Your Ladyship."

Sil gave her a tight-lipped, apologetic smile.

"I promise she won't."

"Much obliged. I remain your servant. As does Pert, if the lady changes her mind."

She turned and headed back to her work. Walls and windows groaned in the narrow hallway, the winds outside smashing against the city's inner wall. Above the building's noise, Sil could hear the first bell of the night chiming in the distance.

When she closed the door and turned around, Mertle stepped in and hugged her with such ferocity that Sil feared a rib might crack. She was cold and sodden with melting snow, and she smelled of the storm and said nothing. They held each other for a long time.

"I don't want you to do this," Sil whispered. "Please say you won't do it."

Her lover still said nothing. Only her embrace tightened harder.

"Mertle, this is too much of a risk. You don't know what they'll do to you if the plan fails."

"Tallah told me," she replied, forehead pressed against her collar bone, voice cold. "I know what's at risk. You—" She swallowed, and her fingers gripped at Sil's dress. "You should have told me."

She had been careful. She had been so incredibly, endlessly careful of how she and Mertle went about together, of how they spent their short moments alone, of what others saw. For years, she had never lapsed in her paranoia. And now Tallah wasted all her effort on a gambit.

"I didn't want you to risk—"

Mertle drew back from her with whiplash suddenness. Her finger jabbed Sil in the rib, hard as a crossbow bolt, twice with the intent of one. Opalescent-black eyes tore through her prepared opposition with the intensity of a bolt of lightning.

"What I risk is mine to risk as I please. You don't decide on my behalf." She jabbed her again, then grabbed and pulled her into the most passionate, confusing kiss Sil had ever received in her life. Whatever dregs of resistance she painstakingly rallied crumbled into the pit of Mertle's determination. "I want to help you. Danger be scattered to the winds."

"But— I— You . . ."

Mertle undressed and handed her cloak to Vergil. He had waited very patiently in the doorway to the study, not saying anything up until then.

"Where's Tallah?" he asked after a polite little cough.

"Gone ahead. She's ready to attack the Fortress."

Panic etched itself on Vergil's face. He looked from her to the door, to the empty room, and back.

"Tonight? We . . . we need to go and help her." His mouth worked without sound for some heartbeats. "H-How are we going to . . . uh . . ."

"How are three of us going to take on the Storm Guard at the bloody seat of their power? I sincerely have no idea."

Mertle strode past Vergil into the room as if she hadn't heard the exchange.

"What's her plan?" she asked, much too calmly.

"Attack the Storm Guard before they attack us. Make herself seen. Have you become Tianna. Make yourself seen at the same time. It's mental."

"Good. Doable. How long?"

Sil gaped as she followed her into the room.

"It's not doable, Mertle. We barely have a bell strike left. There's no time. Turning you will take a long time. You need to get out. Me and Vergil, we'll figure something out."

"I've seen you do it in a heartbeat." She warmed her hands by the fire.

Her voice had a strange sureness to it and a slight edge that Sil hadn't heard before.

"Yes, but I'm used to the changes. It took us months the first time around."

"Less time to twaddle, then. Turn me."

"You don't understand. There are limits. You won't be able to hold the shape. It takes days . . ."

Mertle was undressing by the fire, eyes closed and slightly swaying. Her posture changed as she shifted her feet and straightened her back. She lifted her chin slightly, in the same way Tallah wore Tianna.

Vergil turned around and walked out of the room. "I'll bring some of the dresses Tallah left behind," he said.

Sil's heartbeat thundered. Why wouldn't Mertle listen? Time wasn't on their side. It would all end in blood. They would fail to fool anyone coming, and then the empire would remember her and Tummy and . . . and . . . Her fingers closed into painful fists.

Another one for the pile. What's another one, Silestra?

"Stop gawking and turn me." Mertle's voice had taken on the impatient edge of Tianna's condescension. She stood, hands on hips, a slight blush to her cheeks, and looked down at her. It was a marvel, considering the height difference. "With one mask or another, I only need to survive the night."

With roles reversed, it was Sil's turn to embrace her lover. "Thank you," she whispered, face nestled in Mertle's loose hair.

"Yes, well, I'm not getting younger. You and Tallah need to finish whatever it is you're doing before I bite the edge. I don't have the stomach to watch you two lose five years' worth of your thrice-cursed secret work."

Sil took up her staff from its support. "I need you to visualize Tianna. The closer you can, the better the result. It won't be stable, and it will be very disorientating at first. You may be even sick to your stomach. The enchantment needs you to accept yourself as another."

Mertle nodded and set her jaw. "No time like now."

In a flash, Tianna was back in the room, slightly gaunt and maybe a couple fingers shorter. Mertle didn't have Tallah's natural height, nor her wider shoulders, so mass was an issue. Iliaya's Staff could only do so much to compensate for the difference.

"This feels weird," Mertle said. She patted the top of her forehead gingerly, fingertips running the contour of where her horns should have been. "My head feels too light." She swayed but waved Sil away when she stepped in to hold her. "My hands are so pale. Why does she wear her fingernails so long?" She ran a finger along the inside of her palm and scratched at the skin. "No calluses. Never noticed."

Tallah's first time as Tianna had lasted for all of five heartbeats before she twisted back into her own shape and puked in a bucket. Mertle was shuffling about the room, swaying as she tried to get to grips with her new body and its balance. But she was stable. Sil couldn't see a single ripple or mismatched patch of color across the smooth skin, nor any asymmetric bones trying to poke out where they shouldn't.

Mertle straightened up and shut tight her eyes. Her jaw clenched. She groaned and held up a finger.

"Best get a bucket, please."

Vergil cracked open the door and thrust his arm inside, holding out some of Tallah's dresses. "I'll get one," he said without looking in.

"No," Mertle gasped out. "You go and get Verti. I need to talk to her." She was turning slightly green around the gills. "The room should stop spinning before you're back."

"Right away." The door to the study closed with a click. They heard the outer one open and shut.

Sil brought the bucket.

"How are you feeling?" she asked. Mertle leaned against a wall and panted, as if the mere effort of standing up was too much to handle. A ripple passed across her face, shades of her skin intermingling and twisting together before smoothing back out into Tianna's paleness.

"I'll be fine if I don't see a mirror. Help me dress." She dry heaved and shuddered but kept her feet under her.

"Mertle . . ."

"Help me dress. Tell me everything that's happened since you came back from your hunt. Occupy my mind."

Sil told her of the maps sold to Lucian, of the Guard's interest in them, of the figures in the crowd watching them ever since. Mertle shrugged into Tallah's dress with some difficulty. It hung loose on her near-skeletal frame. She listened and asked questions of Tianna's reactions and peeves, of how Tallah played her cover when surrounded by unknowns.

"Big fortune, big head. About right," Mertle said as Sil applied some of Tianna's makeup to hide the gauntness. "That's not far removed from Tallah herself. Should be enough."

When she looked up, her eyes were of mismatched colors. Not something one would notice in poor light, but Sil still redid the enchantment.

"I'm impressed at how well you're handling this. I was a wreck the first time around. I think I cried my eyes out every time I saw my reflection."

"No mirrors," Mertle grunted. "I think it'd undo me. Otherwise, it's just a disguise. It's not my first."

Verti would be a test. Vergil led her in, past Sil's apologies for taking up more of her time on such a night. Tianna sat in one of the large armchairs, legs crossed, a pensive look on her face. Sil closed the door behind the elendine and leaned against it, barring the way out. If anything went wrong, she had a potent sleeping tonic ready. She'd hate herself to lay hands on Verti after all she'd done for them over the years. If worse came to pass, it couldn't be helped.

"Good evening, Your Ladyship. I see you're preparing to leave," the host said as she looked about the now-empty room. "You might have warned me earlier. Will you be returning come thaw? I can keep the apartment ready for you."

"I think I shall be a while in returning. I can't impose the burden on you, Verti. Thank you."

She's holding herself well. A bit stuffier than Tallah talks but close enough.

"I would like to ask for a favor, if you might indulge me."

Verti looked back to Sil and raised an eyebrow. *Is the mistress well?* it seemed to ask. She shrugged apologetically.

"Of course, Your Ladyship, if it is within my means."

Sil gestured for Mertle to relax. Tianna talked much more familiarly with Verti. She had been a guest there for years.

"I believe you know Mertle Mergara?" Mertle asked with a sour smile.

"I do, yes. Her family and mine are quite close, back in Beril." She looked about the room. "I thought she was here. I don't remember seeing her leave."

"Oh, she stormed out some time ago. I believe I might have said something that she took offense to."

Vergil gave a polite cough and interrupted, "She came down with me, Miss. She left when I came to find you."

"I see. You would like Miria to discuss her prices, I assume?"

Mertle's lips quirked as she suppressed a grin. Sil couldn't and had to cough in a fist. Miria was, to some, the bane and secret terror of the entire Agora. That elendine had been born with a forked tongue and a slivered eye. Merchants dreaded her worse than the city's taxation officers. She left them poorer by quite the margin and grateful for her patronage, and it took bells for the charm to wear off.

Mertle, on the other hand, had a reputation for a ruthless no-negotiation policy. Her prices were eye-watering at the best of times, and ruinous if she were ever annoyed.

On any other day, Sil would have brought treats to watch that conversation unfold.

"Exactly. To my great annoyance, she refuses to see reason. Both myself and Silestra here have tried to get her to back down on some expenses, but she simply refuses to be swayed." She gave Verti a doe-eyed look and a sweet, begging smile. "I would be ever so grateful, Verti, if Miria lent me her aid."

"Of course, Your Ladyship. When?"

"Tonight. I'll be dressed and down in just a bit."

"Tonight, then. I shall relieve her of kitchen duty for the evening. She'll enjoy the chance to watch the Descent herself. Excuse me."

It had gone exceptionally well, even if Mertle rushed to the bucket the moment Verti was out of the room.

"Is there a special event tonight?" Vergil asked. He was ensconced by the window, watching the night traffic flow by. "There's a lot of people out there."

Sil moved a curtain aside and watched the other side of the Meadow's trench. People flocked to the tavern in twos and threes, sometimes even larger groups.

"Yes. The Descent. Gods come down and incarnate. Lots of drinking generally follows. Fire shows and the like," she said as she surveyed the scene. "People start drinking here, keep going in the Agora. These aren't revelers, though." Soldiers dressed in common garb was her guess. Right enough, there were patterns in the movements, in the way they entered the buildings opposite them, in how they stopped and smoked and chatted at convenient knots in the alleys.

"I see five crossbowmen," Mertle said over her shoulder. She swilled some water and spat it out in her sick bucket. "They're covering from the rooftops. More went in that building over there."

"How can you . . ." Vergil muttered. "Oh, right, I see them. Two more on the right, over there." The snowfall hid them well, but not enough.

Something changed in the flow as what had been a flood started thinning to a trickle. Sil recognized a perimeter being set up. She couldn't know how wide it was but recognized the tactic. She wondered if there were any casters coming in or if they were the second wave.

Whoever ran the operation was doing it precisely by the book. They had the element of surprise and advance knowledge of their target. The first step, always, was to limit and control the movement of the quarry.

"We're being boxed in," she noted as she pulled on her shawl. "If we're doing this, we need to do it now before they move in. We need to be more proactive than them."

Mertle rolled her shoulders, shook her hands, and cracked her knuckles. She would either hold together or not, but they couldn't take Iliaya's Staff out with them. Their survival rested squarely on her shoulders.

Sil didn't have the heart to suggest she run away. She knew it wouldn't work. Instead, she packed Vergil's helmet and the staff in a small rend. She couldn't open an entire room like Tallah could, but a pocket was all she ever needed for essentials.

"Do or die," Mertle finally said as she stepped out into the corridor. "I'd kiss you for luck, but it feels wrong to do it with this face."

"Later, when we're clear," Sil replied. She squeezed the elendine's hand so hard that it almost hurt to let it go. "Do or die. Tallah would be proud."

CHAPTER TWENTY

Do or Die

No other time can serve you quite as well as the now.

Tallah couldn't remember who had taught her that, but she'd been teaching it forward her entire life. She watched the scurry of activity below, huddled up against the great belfry on the corner of the Guild Hall. It really never ceased, this endlessly agitated life that Valen lived and breathed. Adventurers flowed in and out of the great building like the tides of the sea, merchants dressed in fine fur clothes brought in requests, recruiters wove through the crowd looking for their next candidates. It really didn't matter that they were less than a bell's strike away from a Descent.

Showed how much truck most adventurers and merchants held with the divine. She'd laugh if not for the gnawing worry that He might actually show. And it'd be all she could do to not piss herself in abject terror of His presence.

Wind whipped her hair to and fro, and her mask stung against her fevered skin. Bianca's anchors kept her in place on the frozen precipice, stuck tight against the corner of the belfry.

She listened to the rhythmic *tick-tick-tick* of the mechanisms within the tower as it wound down to the moment of the bell's strike. A great hammer hung above, poised for the blow, silver veins on blackened forged steel shining in the light coming from beneath.

'If my timing's right for the boy, they should all be at the Meadow right now,' Bianca informed her. 'We should make our move in fifty heartbeats to take advantage of the bell's tolling.'

Tallah counted. Her target would be the archives of the Guild. Impenetrable under normal circumstances, an attack there would throw the Guard onto a million guesses as to what her plans were.

Bianca's suggestion was, indeed, safer than a direct attack on the Fortress. Adventurers ran if there were no profits to be gained, and it would take some time for the Storm Guard to rally to her. She could cause enough damage to make an impact and be seen.

'We've made poor decisions this winter,' Christina whispered. 'Let's hope this is not another.'

Her inner furnace burned steadily now. Fear gnawed on the edges of her resolve, but its insistence only served to infuriate. She'd need her anger burning bright.

If Ort did come down, she'd bloody him. Revenge be bent, she would bloody the bastard even if she had to set fire to Valen a second time. Christina's silent encouragement and support helped her bear down on her fears, smother them under the heel of her will.

She willed herself back to the matter at hand. How would she have prepared the attack if she had to capture someone like herself?

I'd set up a firebreak and get bodies around her that would make it hard to move about. Control and deny her escape routes. Have mage killers manning the front line, the rank and file behind, and as many archers and crossbowmen as I can gather to pin her. Force her out of hiding and into the open, where I could box her in with a healer and Egia. Decisive first strike if possible. Devourer even, if she's dangerous enough.

She grinned at the thought. She was dangerous enough to warrant a devourer used within the walls. Falor wouldn't hesitate.

Sil and the others would need to bluff their way through a waiting army that thought they were deadly dangerous. Mertle would probably handle the talking all right, but it fell to Tallah to ensure their arguments were believable.

Twenty.

She breathed in deep, letting the freezing air stab at her chest. Power coursed in with the cold and stoked the furnace. She drank the vial of aerum that she kept on her belt at all times and reveled in the rush that came with it. Every breath was crisper and richer, life-giving. She could hold her breath through a blazing inferno if need be.

Thirty.

'I feel like we'll come to regret this nonetheless.' Christina sounded uncharacteristically pensive. 'Even so, I want a crack at the princeling if you face him.'

"Pride will see us dead, Christi."

'Curiosity, not pride. I want to see what the empress has made. I want to have the measure of him for when we come back for his head. The last time you clashed, I was too indisposed to pay attention.'

Tallah laughed as she watched the great hammer above ponderously swing into striking position. A mechanism had whirred to life somewhere in the wall. The great lump of metal moved up with glacier slowness and equal inevitability.

She got to her feet and stretched out the kinks in her muscles and joints.

Forty.

With a snap of her fingers, she was wreathed in constellations of flitting fireflies. With a sigh of pleasure, she allowed herself to rise up and take charge of the power at her disposal. After all, she didn't need subtlety tonight. Only firepower. Christina and Bianca surrendered themselves to the guidance of her hand. Their powers sang in her blood.

Fifty.

Tallah slipped into Cinder's old skin, walked to the edge and ignited her fire lances. She stepped off and fell with the hammer.

Mertle couldn't remember the last time she'd felt so naked. When she'd worn masks, once upon a time, she had control. Now, with every step, she felt her control slipping. This wasn't her skin, and it wasn't her face, and those weren't her eyes taking it all in. When she spoke, it wasn't her voice she heard.

She hid under the cowl of a borrowed cloak and hung on Vergil's arm. Sil ushered them through the raucous crowd. Miria waited for them by the exit, her insurance and potential hostage.

Mertle had walked into the Meadow, and she had made herself abundantly visible to every soldier watching the entrances. She had not walked out. Miria was of similar build and height. With a shawl on and her horns hidden, she would be an acceptable match at a glance. If they were concerned only of Tallah, she would pass by without much scrutiny.

The cold shocked her back into herself. Tianna wore things only a pyromancer would feel comfortable in.

"How can she dress like this?" she gasped out to Sil. "These aren't clothes. This is a sack with holes in it." Her teeth chattered, and she drew tighter against Vergil. The boy shivered worse than she did, though she was convinced it wasn't the cold that bothered him. Still, he walked forward with admirable determination. Tummy's eye for people was seldom wrong.

Sil said nothing and only offered a grim smile in return.

She shook the snow from her cowl and looked at the darkened alleys ahead. Sprite light shimmered and twinkled as snow kept falling implacably. Tension was almost electric in the air, a far cry from what the Night of Descent normally offered. Furtive glances from patrons and from passers-by, shadows drawing back into doorways, windows clicking shut. Frozen snow crunched underfoot.

Her skin itched and her bones hurt, but her heart was calmer than her head. Her mouth talked about nothing at all, filling the silence as she waited for the strike from the dark.

"I know her."

"Pardon?"

Vergil had spoken low and hadn't stopped walking. He threw a sideways glance, and she followed it to a doorway where a woman was talking to a man under the low rim of a slanted roof, hidden from the weather. Mertle caught the glint of dark eyes under a heavy hood for the fraction of a moment before they casually turned back to the man. It was enough.

"She's the one I met," Vergil whispered. He had stiffened on her arm and walked with the stricken gait of seeing the gallows rise.

Mertle let out a slow breath that misted white in the air and let go.

"You, there!" She whirled on her heels and strode to the two people talking, holding her dress up so she wouldn't fall. "Just how long are you intent on harassing me, Storm Guard?"

Now Tianna was armor, and her voice became her blade. Mertle understood blades very well, and by the look that flashed over the woman's face, her opening strike had gone straight between the right ribs.

"A good evening to you, Mistress of Aieni Holding," the woman replied, voice as unperturbed as marble. Her eyes took in the group with calculating coldness.

Miria had stopped somewhat further down the road and waited patiently. Vergil waited with her.

There was a shuffle further in the alley, the soft crunch of heavy boots scrambling through snow drifts, and the oil-slick sound of blades drawn. She felt the gaze of a crossbow aimed at her back.

Tianna's boiling fury took over. She'd seen Tallah's anger enough times to know what it should taste like on her tongue and how it should burrow into the gut. Her blade unsheathed and stabbed out again.

"Don't you dare spout pleasantries at me. I demand an explanation! What is the meaning of this?"

Sil moved closer and opened her mouth for an apology—

"Save it, Silestra," she snarled without taking her eyes off the woman. "We've put up with all of this for long enough. I shall not be threatened any longer."

Again, the woman's eyes flickered away. They widened slightly when rested on Sil and on her wooden staff. A moment of confusion and reassertion. The man she had been talking to moved his hand on the pommel of his sword, trying and failing to look calm and politely confused. Eyes of a killer stared from beneath his hood, intently locked on her.

"I'll admit this is not how I expected things to go," the woman said. "Are you coming willingly?"

Mertle bristled up with the fury of the storm.

"Coming willingly?! Are you bloody daft, woman? I am asking you to cease your harassment."

She had moved closer, a step too far. The sword came out and leveled at her throat. She recoiled and stared from it to the woman.

"You threaten me? Do you know who I am?"

"We do," said the woman with infuriating calm. "If this is the charade you mean to play, know that a hostage will not change matters."

So far, so good. She leaned harder into the anger, like a cornered animal snapping.

"Charade? Hostage?!" Mertle screamed at the woman. Echoes of her voice bounced off the frozen walls. Her face felt flush with the abject anger of one mistreated. "Your men have been following me around Valen all winter. Your *special* liaison came and threatened me out of the blue. For what? What did I ever do to any of you?"

The point of the sword wavered for a moment, and she pushed it aside with the flat of her hand as if it weren't worth consideration. She could have it down the soldier's throat in less than a heartbeat. She could have it in her hands and shove it through the prissy cunt's flint eyes in three.

She moved closer again, heedless of the men gathering close with weapons drawn. Snow fell off roofs as crossbowmen rushed into position. No space to run or hide.

"Is this how the Enlightened Empire treats its allies and subjects?" Sil spoke up for the first time. Her voice trembled with fear. "Knives in the dark coming for innocents? This is your idea of enlightenment? On the holy Night of Descent?"

She took Mertle's hand in her own, squeezing it. It was hard to say if her fearful shivers were her playing the part or if it was all real. There were a lot of armed men closing in. Out of the corner of her eye, she could see two of them readying a metal net. Mage killers, but not well-trained ones. Well-trained ones wouldn't have needed confirmation from their superior.

Answer, woman, blast you. I need you to answer. I need you to talk.

A small hand signal from the woman. More men in position. The circle tightened. Soldiers with heavy pointed shields came to the front and formed a lance head that closed up the narrow passages, perfect to take the brunt of a sorceress's opening salvo.

Mertle felt her insides turn to water as she tried to stare down the woman. It was like trying to intimidate a slab of onyx. If this one thought she was facing Tallah, how could she be so calm about it?

There was a tightness on top of her head, and she felt ragged points of pain on her forehead, her horns trying to push out through her borrowed skin.

Mine, not borrowed. She forced her fear to shift focus, to take the shape of anger.

"I would appreciate if you would surrender yourself without further theatrics. I don't know what you're trying to achieve, but I'm not buying it. I wasn't born today."

A rustling jingle of the heavy net being raised. The sound of crossbows clinking against armored shoulders. Boots in the snow shuffling closer.

An explosion rocked the fragile stillness of the moment. Above it, the spire bell rang out thrice. Another explosion sounded in the distance, followed by a rising cacophony of high-pitched whistles in the night. They made a pattern that repeated with frantic urgency.

"Captain?" the man with the sword asked uncertainly.

The woman hadn't taken her eyes off her, but a flash of reluctance played across her face. She bit her lower lip, but her eyes were still and cold as a snake's.

A flash of light across the sky turned night to day for a moment and threw off long black shadows against the walls.

"Captain," one of the soldiers on the rooftop called out, "the Guild's on fire. A bolt of lightning's just struck there." He moved further up the roof, slipping in the snow. It fell in sheets all around. "I think the commander's there."

There was a sound like thunder, and more explosions bothered the night. Lights lit up in windows, and Mertle could see more of the crossbowmen on perches atop the roofs. There were enough of them to fight a small war. They hadn't lowered their weapons.

Again, the whistles in patterns. Some Mertle recognized. Fire. Not an exercise. Danger to the city.

"I . . . believe we've made a mistake," the woman said and signaled to the soldiers. Weapons were lowered and hidden from view, disguises redrawn. They dispersed at a hurried trot, ghosts disappearing in the night. "You have my apologies."

She also turned to leave, but Mertle seized her by her cloak, yanking her back.

"I demand an explanation. Who are you? What was this about?"

The man with the sword came forward, but the captain waved him back.

"Gather the men, Vial. I can take nine others with me. Lowest ranks to form fire brigades. Quickly. With the commander in play, we need to shelter the civilians. Make it a priority."

She turned her flint-black eyes to Mertle and pressed her hand over hers.

"My name is Quistis Iluna, Mistress of Aieni Holding. I am acting captain of the Storm Guard cell of Valen, second to Commander Falor Merchal." She licked her bit lip. "And I must apologize on behalf of the Eternal Enlightened Empire. We seem to have made a grave error and mistreated you."

Mertle gave a slow, nervous laugh. She allowed a manic tremor in her voice. "I'd say. What is happening, Captain Quistis? What have I done to warrant this?"

Quistis pulled Mertle's hand away and held it for a moment. She looked down at it with a raised eyebrow, her touch fire-warm to Mertle's shivering skin.

"Unless you plan on assaulting me, you are innocent and free to go. I will personally write an apology for this unfortunate misunderstanding."

"Don't bother. I aim to leave Valen. My father will hear of all of this." She gave a scornful smile. "I had higher hopes for the Storm Guard."

Quistis held her gaze for a moment longer, then she looked over the others. Vergil had drawn closer to Miria, shielding her from the retreating soldiers. Sil was pale with terror but held herself up with an aelir's wounded pride.

The captain stared at Sil for a long time.

Vial gathered up a group of men, and they all clustered around Quistis.

"Again, I apologize profoundly for all of this," the woman said, and there was no malice in her voice. She released her hand and gave a short nod to the men.

Vial put a hand on her shoulder, and the others did the same to one another, forming a connected line. Quistis reached into her robe and pulled out a bundle wrapped in cloth that hung on a chain around her neck. When she unwrapped it, the shard inside flooded the alley in blue light.

She closed a fist around it, and they all disappeared with a pop of inrushing air.

Mertle allowed herself a shuddering breath. Sil did too. They looked at one another and embraced with the sudden ecstasy of criminals suddenly spared the noose.

"You were amazing," Sil whispered, elation in every word. "You were absolutely amazing, my love."

She hadn't been amazing. She could have handled the encounter in a million better ways. It had been such a near thing. Quistis Iluna hadn't been afraid of her in the least. And it wasn't the simple stoicism of a well-trained soldier. No, this was absolute confidence that she had everything perfectly in hand.

Had she decided on more caution, they'd all be in chains.

She shouldn't have touched the woman.

"We need to go," she whispered. "It's slipping." Already the long dress felt too large for her, too empty, much too cold. Bone ground on bone, anxious to twist back into proper size and shape.

Sil turned to Miria. "I am so sorry you were caught up in this."

Mertle harrumphed behind her, all wounded dignity and appearance of control.

"Yes, I apologize, Miria. They seem to have had me confused for someone else. I've been harassed endlessly since I came back." She adjusted her cowl and shook snow off her cloak. Her nose wrinkled. "Tonight, they came with murder on their minds. Bloody ridiculous! I'll understand if you'd rather not come on this errand anymore."

"No, Your Ladyship. I trusted that you had things well in hand," Miria replied with a slight bow. "It is done. I worry more about what's happening at the Guild. Those did not sound like celebrations."

More voices rose in the night. People came out and muttered about an attack. Some scaled the roofs and called down about the fires spreading. Fire brigades formed and organized to intervene. Valen had a long memory. It had not forgotten the great fire that had almost ended it. Drunken stupor gave way to hard-edged determination.

"We'd best get indoors before things get more serious." Mertle strode down the narrow streets even as they were packing up with the curious and the fretful alike. Tallah's idea of a distraction went beyond reckless. Soon half of Valen would turn up for the spectacle.

"I'll need to run off the moment we get inside the shop," Sil whispered by her ear. "I'll leave the girl in your care." A packet passed between their hands, a sleeping concoction to knock Miria out and fuzz up the night. "You know more about these things than I do."

She did. Away from the danger, she felt a kind of manic elation, a longing ache in her fingers that craved more than the thrill of a disguise. Wisdom warned against her enjoying the moment too much. She'd never been very good at listening to wisdom.

"I'll handle her, don't worry. Tummy's got supplies for you to grab." Elation turned into an ugly, leaden lump as she realized Sil was going to go to Tallah and into real danger. "I'll handle the rest. You'll owe me answers when you come back." She leaned into the healer and poked her in the ribs, pretending to slip on the ice. "No more secrets, not from you."

"No more secrets," Sil agreed, voice tight. "If we survive the night."

Thunder clapped above, and a bolt of lightning streaked the sky again. It shattered the night into day for an ear-splitting moment.

"Soul of the Goddess . . ." Sil's voice was tiny in the silence that settled like snow. "She's roused him."

CHAPTER TWENTY-ONE

Night of Descent

I thought he'd be taller,' Bianca said.

"And I thought we'd have more time," Tallah growled.

It had gone as expected until it hadn't. The Guild Plaza emptied the moment the first trio of fireballs flew and detonated. Aside from the guards protecting the sliver of the Ascendi, the other adventurers had turned tail and fled. She glided in through the chaos and unleashed her fireflies, turning the offices and tents inside the great Guild to smoldering ruins. The great tapestries adorning the walls fell in ragged scraps and caught fire. It wasn't long before she heard her old moniker being shouted by the guards, and soon after, the whistles started.

Then, the strangest thing.

The guards fled. They simply abandoned their posts and melted out with the rest of the scrambling, panicking population. Heavy gates that separated the plaza from the rest of the Quarter, gates that never shut as a symbol of Valen's unending pulse, ground and moaned on great hinges. With titanic weight, they closed and shut her inside.

'Fancy that. They've learned,' Christina said. 'How many times do you think they've practiced this?'

Tallah felt her hair stand on end. The air crackled and buzzed with electricity. Even the breath of the storm seemed to catch in its throat. Aside from the fire devouring the Guild Hall, everything settled into a pregnant, waiting stillness.

Falor was there in a flash from the dark, as if come down from the sky itself like the snow. Thunder clapped a fraction of a moment later, and the Guild building shook.

"He's learned new tricks." Tallah would have been impressed by the entrance if not for the look on his face.

His head was bare and his hair wild in the gathering wind. He pinned her with a liquid-black gaze, taking in her measure, spelling out her sentence in his silence. A great warhammer was clutched in his hands, and he wasted no time swinging it.

Another flash, and lightning snaked through the air like a crack through ice. Bianca pushed her out of the way at a thought. She glided back through the courtyard, lithe and quick as a feather on the wind, and fired back an incinerating lance in answer to the opening steps of their dance. He stopped and strangled it out with a gauntleted hand, his eyes never wavering from her. Runes shone on the gauntlet.

In the mask's vision, he was a storm, a violent whirlpool of raging illum that outshone even the Ascendi shard spinning in midair, oblivious of their contest of strength.

She had expected recriminations. An acknowledgement of her survival. Maybe questions? But he had nothing to say, just the mission to carry out.

'You've learned some new tricks too,' Christina whispered, a strange fascination tinging every sensation she let off. 'Let's impress on him that killing us is not going to come cheap.'

She moved her hand in an arc, and white-hot fire burst at Falor's feet. He swung his hammer down and blasted the flames away. Another crack of blue-white lightning tore across the ground, and she ran from it. The air stank of ozone and of misting water, of burnt expensive fabrics and paper.

Fire and lightning chased each other across the Guild's courtyard. Tallah tried to keep the Ascendi shard between them, but Falor was having none of it. His bolts crashed from above and burst from under her, testing her, prodding at the way she defended. If he was surprised by a pyromancer moving with the skills of a manipulator, he didn't show it.

She was dimly aware, through Christina's whispers, of soldiers gathering on the walls around the courtyard, swarming among the covers of the battlements. Crossbows leveled at her through slits and gaps in the wall. Steady hands tracked her, waiting for a signal.

Falor was only intent on her. In his shining white armor, trimmed with accents of azure blue, he was every bit his mother's son. Tallah's blood curdled at the sight of him.

She threw three fireballs, then three more. They scattered and flew wild, heading for the soldiers on the walls. Screams followed as they detonated and showers of masonry rained down.

Falor came at her with avenging fury, his warhammer swinging in a wide, bone-crushing arc. Bianca pulled her into his swing, tethered to the hammer, swinging with it in a tightening spiral. Her hand touched Falor's chest and wreathed him in fire.

A fist shot out and caught her across the face before she could draw away, and sent her reeling back. A blast of power scattered her flames like smoke. That blasted gauntlet absorbed her flames again.

She tasted blood, and the splinters of a tooth stung where they lodged in her cheek.

Soldiers dragged their wounded from the walls. Crossbowmen moved into new position.

The moment she was paces away from a still-smoking Falor, they all loosed on her.

Bianca picked the quarrels from the air and aimed them right back. Some screamed as they were hit, most dodged away. Falor gave an inarticulate roar of anger and signaled his men back.

Tallah reacted. She reached out to the men and held them in invisible grasps. She yanked, and men fell from the walls, screaming.

She could have yanked the hearts from their chests, and he knew it. A momentary flash of worry on his face as bodies thumped into the high snow.

'We've been seen enough. It's time we run. Hit him.'

Tallah's feet touched down on solid ground, Bianca's power fading back and Christina's coming to the fore. She drew her sword and imbued it with heat. Flakes sizzled on the edge as she aimed it at the princeling's heart. It earned her a raised eyebrow.

'Keep up,' Christina said, and electricity hummed in her chest. Like a swarm of summer wasps, she was abuzz with stored power.

She ran at the prince, jumped, and Christina sent her bursting through the air at the speed of thought. She covered the span of the courtyard in the blink of an eye, and there he was, straight in her reach, his throat rushing to the sword's keen edge.

'Yes!'

One moment. One slash. One cut. If she took his head right there, right then—

A dark-haired boy ran through her mind, five or six summers old, yanking on her cloak as she made her report to his mother. Black eyes smiled up at her. Small hands groped for hers. Joyful laughter that she was back from her mission, and that she was safe.

A moment of distraction. Her blade whistled through falling snow, and she missed. She also missed her feet and landed awkwardly, set off balance by the speed.

Falor smashed her in the ribs with enough force to break her in two. It happened in a frozen moment in time, in less than a heartbeat. Bianca cushioned the hammer blow as best she could, but the force of star ore meeting soft flesh sent her tumbling head over heels.

'*Coward!*' Christina spat in her mind.

Air exploded out of her in a blinding instant of shattering pain. At least three ribs splintered.

It wouldn't have worked, she lied to herself through the haze of agony. He was moving before she had even launched her attack. He knew something was coming, and just as she'd taught him, was meeting and countering it. Tallah had transferred straight to him, something she shouldn't have been able to do without Christina. It should have been a killing blow, her secret weapon, the one that she hoped would behead an empire.

He'd been ready for it. She was dead certain of it.

Pain knifed in her side as she struggled to draw breath. Soldiers cheered on the walls and hissed at her. Falor simply watched her struggling to her feet, hammer held loose at his side. His breaths came in small white puffs that blew away on the wind.

'This is an execution, Tallah,' Bianca realized. 'He is only playing with us.'

"I know," she wheezed out between bloodied lips. Air rattled inside. Something had shattered. A sharp jut of bone poked something tender, and she felt sick. If not for the aerum, she would have fainted.

Curse the memory of the boy he'd been . . .

"Get up," Falor said. His voice was cold and detached. "Make sure and die this time."

"So your mother hasn't cut your tongue out, boy?" Tallah had to force the words out.

He didn't reply. Instead, he dropped his hammer and pointed two fingers at her.

She stared down her death. Lightning struck Falor from above and dispersed in circles of power around him. Again, faster. He shone like a miniature star as he readied a devourer, all for her. If she could have found the strength to laugh, she would have.

'This was a stupid plan,' Bianca whined. Tallah refused her nudges to run and pull away. She couldn't outrun a Titan's Punishment any more than she could outrun the morning light. 'We are going to die . . .'

Falor unleashed his devourer. It surged through the air, a blinding rush of power that was going to render her down to scattered atoms to fully erase her from existence.

'*Now!*'

She raised her hands against the blinding flare, and Christina reached out from her prison, ghostly hands doubling Tallah's own.

The devourer hit her with the power of an unleashed storm. She allowed it in. It burned in her veins. It rattled her teeth, singed her sinews, almost melted her from the inside out. Her mind burned!

She raised her hands, and Christina flung the power back outward, into the walls, into the snow, anywhere it would go. Screams rose as soldiers were caught in the blast. A part of the courtyard wall exploded outward in a cascade of stone and mortar, the blast taking out neighboring buildings.

'Blood and teeth and bones of my sisters!' Christina's voice was a croak of anguish. 'I can't do that again. Run, Tallah.'

If she had the strength, she would have flung the Punishment back at Falor. Pity that she had only barely survived it.

Bianca anchored a tether to a point outside the wall and launched her into the air as Falor ran to his screaming men and the collapsing walls. She set everything she had into escaping, angling her flight away from the plaza and towards the Alchemists Quarter. Trying to use the shard that close to the Ascendi could see her smashed against it, so she needed distance.

Pain nearly blinded her, and she couldn't focus on keeping her hearth lit. The cold cut through and chilled her down into the marrow, a constricting grip on her battered chest. Winds buffeted her path and shook her as violently as Falor himself.

She flew in a dizzying, headlong rush, only barely aware of the rushing buildings, all sense lost to the buffeting black storm. Bianca kept her down, hidden between buildings, rushing dangerously through narrow gaps and over the heads of people putting out fires.

Tallah lost consciousness and woke when she hit the cobbles below. A gasp for air. A chill in her hands, spreading through her chest. Blood running down her chin.

Bianca lifted her again and launched upward, fighting for height against the wind.

'Don't faint. Don't faint. Don't faint. Don't—'

Tallah did. A jolt woke her again, the sense of falling a dangerously long way. Christina screaming at her.

Bianca's lines of power caught on a gargoyle somewhere, and Tallah stopped in the air between two nearly invisible buildings, lost and shaken, bones rattling inside her chest. Panic rose in her gut. Had she gone too far from the

Agora? Somewhere close to the Alchemists? It was hard and getting harder to think. Her vision dimmed again on the edges.

'*Do not dare faint! I cannot do this if you go unconscious.*' Bianca yanked on her tether and moved with a certainty Tallah didn't feel.

"I'm still alive. Keep going. He won't fol—"

A bolt of lightning struck the roof she aimed to land on. Snow and shingles exploded, and she crashed through, falling to the street below. Impact drove all air from her again. Something in her arm snapped with a wet crunch.

In another flash, Falor was on top of her, hammer coming down wreathed in light.

Tallah kicked out against his legs and pushed away. Cobbles, snow, and black ice exploded. She fought to find her feet, but Falor came again. Another crash of the hammer, a hair's breadth escape. She rolled and crawled and gasped in agony. Blood oozed from her mouth as she climbed to her feet and dizzily stumbled away from the monster as he came for her.

"You could have died easy back there," he growled. Fury and a manic determination coated his words. "I offered you an easy death. I offered you an execution. Please, just die."

Odd turn of phrase. She'd consider using it later if she managed to refuse him.

"That was you being kind?" She couldn't resist the taunt, even if she barely whispered the words out. "And here I thought you'd have outgrown childish sentiment by now."

She struggled to think, to stall for time.

He wouldn't risk another Punishment, not so deep in the city, surrounded by innocents in their homes, not with her able to push it back. He showed that he could chase her down. It was more than enough to finish her.

Another blast of lightning. It hit her square in the chest. Christina screamed as she dispersed the power, but she faded with the effort. Music flooded into the space the ghost left.

"That would be Christina Cythra's power, I assume," Falor said, a dark twist to his face. "And you've been running with Bianca Vel's. That's two murders finally solved. Are you holding Anna Theala's abilities in reserve to surprise me? It won't work."

She had to give his investigation credit. Someone on their side was very good at seeing a larger picture. She'd bet a griffon it was Rumi Belli.

"I haven't absorbed her yet. No tools here." She leaned on a wall to keep her feet. The pain in her side throbbed and promised a fatal conclusion.

He grunted, his anger smoldering beneath the obsidian intensity of his gaze. He was resolved to kill her.

"Why?" he asked, voice tightly controlled.

Why what?

Why run? Why kill her old friends? Why betray the empire? Why . . . why?

Thoughts gelled in her head. Bianca whimpered for guidance, torn between defending them and protecting her soul from the ghastly music pouring past Christina's absence. Falor had grown exponentially in the six years since their last clash, and he still held so much back.

"It was necessary." She straightened and pulled in illum. He wasn't taking her seriously. That couldn't bloody stand. Fear melted down into anger, and that distilled into rage. This had been a mistake, but she refused to let him murder her in a dark alley like some helpless urchin.

There was still work to be done.

"Soul theft is an immediate death sentence." He had noticed her building power again. "Even if you do escape me here, there won't be a single place on Vas that will harbor you. We'll send word to Aztroa. Anywhere you go, you'll be hunted. Your crimes exposed. No allies would shelter you again."

She laughed wetly, choking on a glob of blood halfway through.

"I'm already hunted, boy. Your mother's made sure of it. Do you think she didn't know I was alive?" She took a step towards him, her hands flashing into fire and lighting her up, paling in comparison to his luminescence. "And why? Don't you know why?! Doesn't she trust you enough even for that?"

Her words stung. She saw it in the stoop of his shoulders and in the tightness of his jaw. But he was talking. Something held him back, and she couldn't be sure why.

Her illum built up inside. Maybe enough for one Disintegration.

"You murdered your cell. You betrayed the trust of your men and of the empire. You poisoned Valen and nearly burned it to the ground. Need I go on?" He held his hammer two-handed, and lightning coiled around the jagged head. "And soul theft, the sin." His grip tightened with a grind of metal on metal. "Why all of it?"

He'd asked that before, those six winters prior. She had refused to answer him then.

They were three, maybe four, steps apart. Whistles echoed, calls to action, screams of the panicked. His lightning buzzed and crackled across his weapon.

'Just tell him. He's hesitating. Maybe . . .' Even Bianca couldn't finish that thought. Falor wouldn't believe the truth.

"I didn't kill my cell. I never betrayed the empire. And I am not doing what you think I am." Her fury grew, and she spat more blood to the side. "I never betrayed anyone that didn't stab me first. Do you know what happened to all those that I hunted down for your mother?"

"Locked in Drak's Perch. Some of them blanked." He sounded affronted. He believed the lies. "It's better than they deserve."

Tallah chuckled grimly. "Drak's Perch is empty, Falor. Go see for yourself if you won't believe it, once you've dealt with me. There's nobody there. Empty walls. Silent cells. Nothing."

He didn't dismiss the notion straight out of hand. Still as a statue, he waited for her answers, hammer abuzz with his fury.

"They're all under Aztroa's Crown, out in the Expanse. Tortured. Dead. All of them emptied out and buried as husks. I saw the graves. I dug two of those myself." One for Rhine's corpse. One for herself. She squeezed down on the pain of that memory and added it to the fuel of her furnace. His black eyes were unreadable. "I confronted your mother. She didn't take it well. And here we are."

A frown creased the impeccable line of his forehead.

Tallah felt Christina's whimpering in the back of her mind. Good, she hadn't been burned out of her. In that electric, quiet moment, she couldn't afford the grief.

She breathed in and sought for the right words when something crashed into Falor, howling from above. A figure had bounded off a roof and leapt down with two weapons in hand, toppling the prince. They went down in a sprawl of limbs, sparks, and flashes of electricity. Tallah got the impression of a horned helmet and two axes glinting in the firelight.

"Vergil?" she asked, incredulous, unable to believe her eyes.

Vergil howled with glee as Falor threw him off. He rolled through the snow, landed on all fours, and bounded back against the prince like a wild animal. An axe in each hand, he closed the distance again before Falor could bring his hammer to bear. Dull clangs of metal sounded as Vergil smashed aside the hammer head, hooked it with an axe's beard, and almost yanked it out of his enemy's hands.

Falor moved with the pull and smashed into his opponent, armored shoulder to armored chest. Vergil drew back and slammed his helmet down on Falor's exposed forehead, drawing blood. The prince caught him by the arm, released his hammer, and blasted him with a bolt of lightning.

Tallah rushed to help the boy.

She didn't see the blade. It came from the shadows for her throat.

Both she and it slammed into an invisible hair-thin barrier that stopped the killing blow. The figure holding the curved sword cursed, and Tallah recognized him. Barlo. The Miscreant had caught up with Falor and had waited for his moment.

"Pay attention, Tallah. Vergil can handle himself."

That was Sil. The healer called down to her from a perch way on high on a rooftop.

"There are soldiers coming. Move."

Barlo slammed two gauntleted fists into the barrier, and Sil yelped above. Cracks formed in the air. Tallah was unarmed and hurt. Her sword was lost somewhere. She couldn't fight the mage killer then and there.

Vergil, smoking and steaming from Falor's hit, howled and launched himself again at the princeling. Another blast of lightning, and the boy moved with incredible grace around it, just like she'd taught him to. That this was Horvath fighting got stowed away for later digesting.

He came at the prince with such fury that it got Barlo's attention off her. Before the vanadal could rush in to help, Sil dropped the barrier, and Tallah blasted him into the wall with a kinesis push. Vergil's axes clanged against Falor's hammer, a flurry of blows that managed to push the star ore head away. The commander defended with his bare gauntlet and barely pulled back from a strike that would've buried an axe in his forehead. He was forced to drop his weapon.

Vergil leapt at Falor with murderous intent.

Tallah grabbed him midair with Bianca's power, and with a twist, launched him skyward towards Sil, saving him from a lightning strike from above. It shattered cobbles and raised another cloud of dust and steam. She launched herself as well before Falor refocused on her. She couldn't run from him.

But she didn't need to.

Sil arrested Vergil's flight with a barrier, and he cursed in ancient Dwarven at her, screaming and kicking for the fight he was being denied. Tallah reached them, pulled them both close, and used the shard hung on a string at her neck.

The world and the night and the snow all lurched sideways, and they dropped awkwardly through nothing.

Momentum carried them through the teleportation. Wherever the other shard spat them out, they kept moving until they slammed into a wall.

Vergil was the first up on his feet, growling, axes held out.

Tallah followed, stumbling from pain and exhaustion. Her left arm was shattered and the pain maddening.

Soldiers surrounded them on all sides, some of them more surprised than others. It had been a trap!

No. Details resolved in her vision. An old bookcase. Another. Dust and discarded scrolls. Overloaded work desks and alchemical compounds strewn about.

They were in Ludwig's home. There, at the other end of the room, held at knife point, was the old bastard himself, white-faced with fear and terror.

Rumi Belli held his hand in her own, and two soldiers held his arm. Three fingers were bent at wrong angles. One was missing.

Tallah lashed out with Bianca's kinesis, grabbed a soldier that had drawn his sword, and launched him bodily at the mind-skinner. She dodged out of the way, and the flying body hit another. Ludwig stood there, frozen to the spot, frightened stupid.

"Move, old man," she called out as she flung another man through his home, knocking over bookshelves. An explosion of paper and dust choked the air. Vergil was already moving, cutting with his axes. He took an arm off someone and kicked another with enough force that Tallah heard the sickening snap of bone. "Sil, move. Get to him."

A soldier had come out behind her, sword raised. She turned and smashed him with a flung piece of furniture. It looked like the old man's favorite armchair. It shattered to splinters, springs, and cascading stuffing.

Men cursed and rallied. Crossbows were drawn, pulled back, and loaded. Bolts flew but smashed into invisible walls. Sil moved towards the stricken Ludwig, pinning people in place with her barriers. In the melee, Tallah had lost track of Rumi Belli. She turned to scan the room and was met by Vergil, who swung his axe at her. Bianca yanked her sideways, and she heard the clang of weapons meeting.

A man wearing loose black clothes, looking like one of the Guild's handlers, had snuck up behind her. He held a twisted three-bladed knife almost as long as her arm. She'd seen him somewhere before but couldn't place that plain face.

The man dropped his knife and moved in, chest-to-chest with Vergil. Even the mad ghost couldn't keep up with the storm of fists, elbows, and knees that the warrior unleashed. Vergil spat blood through his visor slit as an elbow drove into the side of his neck and snapped his head sideways. Another fist to the stomach scythed the strength in his legs, and he dropped to his knees, gasping for breath.

Tallah intervened with a kinesis burst. The man avoided it, pulled back, and disappeared in the chaos, lithe and graceful as a dancer. A strange glint in the way he looked at her triggered some ancient instinct, and she moved sideways just in time to avoid a knife to the small of her back from Rumi Belli. The hammer strike's echo slammed her, and she nearly blacked out with the effort of staying upright. The aerum had run out, and she was dizzy with effort. Every breath was a fight. Vergil's axe swing chased off another attempt from Rumi Belli.

Thunder rumbled above, and the wind whistled inside through the shattered window. A flash of white. Another crack of thunder that seemed to cover the world. And Falor was out there.

"We need to go," Tallah called to Sil. The healer had locked down most of the soldiers and helped Ludwig stand. "Go to her, bucket-head. Go, go." She didn't bother grabbing at Rumi and the warrior in black. She focused whatever reserves Bianca still had and heaved forward.

Ludwig's front wall exploded out into the night, dropping heavily over Falor. Twin fireballs set the entire ruin alight in a burst of embers and glass.

Tallah rushed over the detritus to Sil and Vergil. The boy stood awkwardly, like a doll held up by strings. No time to worry about him.

"I hope you have a way out, old man. Now's the time to use it." She was panicking and could hear the bursts of lightning that threw away the wreckage of the building. It was all about to come down on top of them.

Ludwig fumbled awkwardly with one hand to his neck and shakily drew out a shard dressed in cloth.

"My supplies a-a-are up-upst—"

"We don't need them." Tallah reached out and grabbed the shard in her fist.

Sil grabbed Vergil by the back of his collar and wrapped a hand around Tallah's.

Falor flew at them through the crumbling ruin of the door, singed and smoking, hair matted by blood, his hammer already swinging. His eyes met hers for a brief instant. Maybe . . . maybe she thought she saw hesitation there.

Probably just imagined it.

Pity it had come to this. She had regretted it six years prior, and she regretted it now. She would have wanted to know if he believed her, if without Vergil's intervention they could have—

Too late for regrets, much too late. She siphoned illum into the shard, and Valen dropped away.

CHAPTER TWENTY-TWO

Visit from the Empress

Quistis waited in the cold and watched the gate as it slowly completed its final revolution. Symbols in a language she couldn't decipher glowed around the circumference of the great star-ore portal. In the chill morning air, she sweated.

Falor wasn't back yet, still helping with the fires. Barlo helped dig out those caught in the blast at the Guild. Rumi and Aidan were sifting through the ruins of Angledeer's home.

That only left her to face the great gate. She would rather have faced Cinder. But Cinder had managed to escape and had sent the entire Valen council into an absolute tizzy. She didn't even want to imagine facing High Lord Diogron that morning, or on any other day for the rest of winter.

And, of course, there had been no Descent yet that night, and it was nearing dawn. The mood around Valen was as sour as pickled lemons. Some hopefuls still hung around the podium raised at the Fortress, doggedly determined to wait until the first sliver of light for a god to show.

She'd been awake for so long already that her vision swam and her legs felt as if made of jelly. As the gate glowed to life and its circle filled up with the tar-like substance that allowed transference, she found herself scratching insistently at her throat, where the sword had . . . cut her?

"Bugger." That image and the feeling attached to it would take some time to fade. She pulled her collar up and hid away the freezing line of blood. A draft would take care of it later.

A woman stepped through the portal, walking with a steady, confident gait down the frozen slope. She was bareheaded, with a crown of loose ashen-gray hair blowing in the early-morning breeze, and a tiny, frail circlet of spun silver sitting atop her head. Eyes the color of distant glaciers found hers and bore through to the back of her head, as if aiming to read her mind. Of what she knew of Empress Catharina's abilities, that might have been the case.

She wore the Storm Guard uniform, white and blue, and a short sword hung at her belt.

Another woman, dressed in furs, trailed shortly behind and struggled to not slip. Quistis could only see bespectacled green eyes shining from the narrow gap between the face covering and the cloak's fur-lined cowl.

"Good morning, Your Majesty," she said to the first, trying to sound cheerful, and saluted.

How the empress had found out so quickly of the night's events, she couldn't begin to imagine. But when the runner found her in the Guild's ruined courtyard and told her that the gate was calling in, she had known who would be visiting.

"Where's my son?" the empress asked with barely a glance at her disheveled state. "I want to talk to him."

"He's helping put out fires."

"Fetch him. I'll be in his office." Her voice was as calm and calculated as if this were just an informal visit.

Quistis found herself dismissed as the empress strode past her. The woman following gave her a short friendly wave of the hand as she followed her liege. No bodyguards came through the gate, no advisers or courtiers. It shut down with a hiss of steam escaping from somewhere within the great construction.

The empress and her adjunct were in Valen. Diogron would be livid, and she'd need to deal with it after they left. Cinder had come calling and had escaped. Falor had nearly blown up half of the Alchemists Quarter. Again. And the two most dangerous women in the empire had come by gate at the crack of dawn, straight into Valen's heart. May as well have made a declaration of war while they were at it, to top off a smashing night.

Quistis wanted to curl up in a dark, quiet corner somewhere, eat a bagful of burn-leaf, and put herself to sleep through what was going to be a couple of absolutely buggering days.

She found Falor supervising the digs through Angledeer's ruined abode. When Cinder had disappeared to wherever she had gone, the entire place had come down around those trapped inside. Naturally, it also caught fire, and it had spread to the buildings tightly clustered around. Smoke hung in the air. People shouted and worked to dig out their homes.

Falor stood amid the sooty wreckage, hands and uniform stained black from the work, cuts and bruises clear on whatever skin wasn't dirtied. His hammer was leaned against a wall nearby, discarded.

He'd refused her healing earlier and sent her to deal with the other wounded. His head wound had dried, and his forehead was grimy where he'd tried to wipe away fresh blood.

"Your mother's going to have kittens if she sees you like this," she said by way of greeting.

"She's going to have kittens any way she sees me. Is she here?"

"Waiting in your office. Came alone with the adjunct. Can't remember the name."

Falor gave a short grunt and a nod. He washed his hands in the snow and went to pick up his hammer. Didn't even need telling that the empress wanted him.

Rumi and Aidan huddled together over some pieces of the wreckage, carefully extracting some tomes from underneath the rubble. Two soldiers held up a tarp over them to hold off the snow.

"Report as soon as you have anything interesting," Falor called to the two. "I want to know where they've gone. And I want that shard. Keep digging until you find it."

"Aye, sir," Aidan replied without looking up from his work. Rumi just waved a hand in acknowledgement.

Quistis followed up behind him, running to catch up to his long strides. "Let me heal you at least. Please."

He didn't respond, just kept walking. He wasn't even angry, not really. She recognized his anger in all its forms, and this wasn't it. Something else ate at him, but he'd bring it up when he was good and ready. All in all, Cinder hadn't done as much damage as feared. Either she'd held back or she'd been careful for some reason, but her destruction had been tame compared to six years prior.

Most of the damage was from Falor himself, a fact that would not escape Valen's council and their lengthy complaints.

"Do you know why she was trying to get into the archives?" she ventured as they climbed the stairs to the Fortress.

Their soldiers guarded the entrances and were all standing ramrod straight. The empress had passed that way, it seemed, if their steely-eyed, terrified expressions were anything to go by.

"I haven't the bloodiest, Quis. Wish I knew at least that so the night wouldn't have been a total loss." He sighed heavily and looked over his shoulder. Clouds of smoke were dispersing in the clear morning light. The snowfall had eased up, and they could see across the entirety of Valen.

"We were so certain of the Aieni connection," Quistis said. She also sighed.

"We harassed an innocent woman. Runner came back saying Lady Aieni refused my apology. Slammed the door in his face."

Falor let out a slow, grim chuckle as he braced to push open the door to his office.

"Pyromancers . . ."

The door swung open from the inside, and the short, thin woman from the gate welcomed them into their own office. Her name . . . was Lya? Laya? Quistis was pretty certain it wasn't.

"Good morning, Leea," Falor said as he passed by.

Empress Catharina was seated behind his desk, ruffling through the papers that he was supposed to get to after the Cinder operation was complete. Reports, mostly. Guard routines. Troublesome elements in Valen. Mage killers and their training. Nothing of immediate concern. The look of absolute boredom on the empress's face said as much.

"So, she's not dead?" she asked, looking up at him over the rim of her tiny reading glasses.

Falor shrugged and dropped his hammer with a dull thud on the floor.

"You're in my seat, Mother," he replied instead. "Find another."

They stared at one another, and the atmosphere charged with electricity. Leea sidled up to Quistis and whispered, "Would you like me to bring you a mug of coffee, Captain Quistis?" She even gave her a bright, dimpled smile that was simply not fit for the state of that morning.

Adjunct Leea outranked her so severely that Quistis froze for a moment, mulling over the ridiculousness of the offer.

"Yes, please," she whispered back, finding her voice. "And one for him. Strong as you can make it. It'll mellow him out."

"Like mother, like son." Leea melted out of the room as soundlessly as a ghost.

"You look like death. Did she really take so much out of you?" The empress looked Falor up and down with a critical eyebrow raised. "I'm frankly disappointed in you and Cinder." Her eyes snapped to Quistis. "Why haven't you healed him? I can see the blood from here."

Quistis felt her spine grow cold under that electric gaze.

"He won't let me." Her voice squeaked, and she felt a blush going up to the tips of her ears.

"Typical." She sighed and rubbed under her glasses. "Sit down, Falor, somewhere. I'm not angry. I just have questions."

Leea returned with a tray of steaming mugs and handed them out before taking her place behind the empress. The fresh aroma of dark-roasted coffee filled the small office. They all sipped their drinks in silence for a few moments before Falor spoke up.

"She's not dead because she had shards ready. Two sets of them, even." He grimaced at the idea. "That's egg on my face. I'm already checking our reserves of shards in the vaults, testing every one. Everything seems accounted for."

He sat heavily in Quistis's chair and groaned as some ache of the night found him. "Fortunately, I'm sure that she's not picked up the twin of the one she first used. We should have it soon."

The empress raised a finger to Leea, and the adjunct quickly wrote down something in a small ragged notebook.

"We'll check ours in Aztroa Magnor, and the ones in Solstice, though I doubt it came from any of the known stocks. Did you relay my message to her?"

"Hadn't the chance."

"Quite. I heard you came in swinging the gavel." She glared at him, glasses steaming as she sipped more coffee, though she said nothing more on the subject. "Do you know who's been helping her?"

Falor looked to Quistis.

"We believe she's got two permanent associates," she said carefully. "One's a healer, unidentified. The other's a warrior, unidentified as well. This was assumed from the flesh doll memories and confirmed last night. As she has Iliaya's Staff, we can't identify by face, but we'll run a recognition campaign all the same once the dust settles."

"They were also helped by one Ludwig Angledeer," Falor went on, cracking his finger joints one by one. "Scholarly type. Seems to have been a teacher back in Cinder's days at Hoarfrost. No trouble caused in Valen before. Traveled about and came back here to roost." He rubbed at his forehead and let out a groan but waved Quistis away when she moved to see about his clearly concussed skull.

"Stop that," both Quistis and the empress snapped at him as he started on the other hand's fingers.

"And just let the girl heal you, you overgrown child. Stop sulking. Your head bleeding won't suddenly end Cinder, wherever she's gone." The empress looked up and over her shoulder. "Leea, why does Angledeer sound familiar to me? Did I ever commend this person for anything?"

Leea thought for a moment before replying. "Yes, Your Majesty. He is person number three on your list for immediate execution if ever found within a hundred leagues of Aztroa Magnor. He is to be beheaded and, to quote Your Majesty, fed to the dogs in itty-bitty-tiny pieces. Boiled, preferably." She smiled apologetically, as if she'd said something rude.

The empress snapped her fingers. "Oh, right, I remember him. Goboid of a man. Surprised he's still alive." She leaned back in Falor's chair, closed her eyes, and drained the rest of her mug. "He's finally found someone to take his insanity seriously. Only took him a century or so."

Quistis finally got her hands in Falor's hair and felt about. It hadn't been a concussion, but close enough. She whispered her prayer to the Goddess and healed him. It made her feel better, if not him.

"Do you know where they've gone?" Falor asked.

Quistis could see his knuckles turn white as he squeezed the cup. She took it away from him before it shattered and he cut himself.

"Oh, yes," the empress replied. "I know exactly where they've gone if they went along with that basket case. If you do find that shard, don't use it."

"Tell me. I'll have her dead within the week."

"You'll have yourself dead within the day, and me very cross. No, I—"

Vial burst into the room and nearly toppled Quistis. "Captain, you need to see this." He froze when he saw the empress looking at him, eyebrow raised. He made to kneel, but Falor gestured for him to be at ease.

"What's happened?" he asked urgently. "More fires?"

"No, Commander. There's been a Descent." He looked from Falor to Quistis, red-faced now that everyone was staring at him. "Uh, you need to come see."

"Well, that'll give Diogron something to preen over," the empress said as she rose and strode past. "Can't imagine Lord Ort's come down, so I don't see why all the excitement."

They could hear voices rising in hymns and cheers as they neared an exit to a balcony. A chill blasted in when soldiers opened the wide doors. The noise was louder now, and some confusion mingled into the cheering.

A crowd gathered in the courtyard. People surged in through the thrown-open gateways as word spread out into the city. Men and women still sooty from fighting the fires came in droves to see who'd come to bless Valen's thaw and summer.

Diogron was there, on his knees, resplendent in his best robes. Sprite light made him twinkle as he raised his hands to the figures on the podium.

On one side of the marble podium was a woman of incredible height, like a tower of rippling muscles, with auburn hair cascading down her shoulders. Her skin was the color of burnished gold and seemed to reflect the sprite light. She wore the most intricate dress Quistis had ever seen, adorned with jewels of rainbow colors, fragile chains of gold and silver, and armor plates that floated gently atop the rest.

Three enormous swords orbited around her, each of a different make and style. A thin, straight rapier like the gentry of Valen, Drack, and Aztroa favored, encrusted with sapphires and blood rubies. A broad black bastard sword favored by the daemon-forged warriors of the Twins, the blade of blackest obsidian. And an ugly curved scimitar of the simplest steel. Barlo would be insufferable for this clear show of favor from Cassandra herself.

But even the Goddess Cassandra stared in utter confusion at the second figure.

"Who is that?" Falor asked what Quistis and the crowd were thinking.

She'd been to Nights of Descent with her sister when they were girls, and then as part of the prince's retinue once out of the School of Healing. Quistis had never felt compelled to kneel.

She did so automatically now.

The second figure was small and so white, as if made of chalk. She was also completely naked. She marched along the edges of the podium and stared over the crowd, her gaze swiveling as if searching intensely for something.

Gasps from the crowd had Quistis raising her eyes. The figure had jumped down among the people and elbowed her way through the crowd, still searching. Everyone parted for her.

She reached the edge of the courtyard, stopping at the gate atop the great stairs coming up from the Inner Plaza. After a long time looking across the city, she stamped down her foot in frustration and vanished without a word.

The empress whistled and then confirmed what Quistis knew within herself.

"Now that's peculiar," she said with a tinge of amusement. "That, boy, was Panacea. Haven't seen her in over two centuries. Wonder what's dragged her out from under her rock."

CHAPTER TWENTY-THREE

Into the Dark Below

Lightning preceded a deafening crack of thunder that made Tallah's teeth vibrate. The cold here had a steel bite to it. In spite of her best efforts not to, she shivered.

"Sit. Still!"

Sil bit off the words and the suturing thread.

Pain flashed white-hot in her already battered side as the healer worked on her, poking and prodding. Normally, Sil would have offered at least something to dull the pain. Not today. Anger made her cruel.

Mercifully, Tallah blacked out for a few heartbeats while Sil started working on one of her other cuts. If she had anything left in her stomach, it would've probably ended up on the cave's stone floor.

She probably also deserved the misery.

Sil grumbled as she worked. "Stubborn fool. You and her both. Why did you have to drag her into our mess?"

"She offered," Tallah wheezed out in a gasp of agony.

Sil tugged on a suturing thread to break it off, mercilessly careless.

"You don't accept offers like that. Not from *them*. It was bad enough that Tummy trained the boy. Now this." Sil's anger was a near furnace blast on the back of Tallah's head. She avoided turning to meet that accusatory glare. "You and I had an understanding. One simple rule."

Tallah expected some kind of violence to her tender side and braced for it. Instead, Sil draped some fabrics over her head.

"You don't deserve these, but here. She had them ready for you."

She pulled down a fresh black coat and an undershirt. Mertle's handiwork was as clear as Sil's fury. Gloves and a leather jerkin thudded by her side.

"Get dressed and don't infuse. Heat's going to make the pain worse. Vergil's coming to. I'll heal your arm later if the accelerant doesn't take." Sil's footsteps moved away before another crack of thunder filled the small alcove with screaming echoes. Only the howl of the wind outside drowned them out.

Tallah fingered her side and Sil's sutures. Her entire chest felt tender and bruised. Her left arm hung painfully in a sling, limp, swollen, and useless. Someone had gotten a knife in her at some point, though for the life of her she couldn't remember the cut. "Not life-threatening" had been Sil's opinion before sewing her up.

She remembered Falor's hammer like the tolling of a death bell. Her ribs would remember its caress for a long time to come.

'Lovely cock-up, ladies,' Christina's voice mewled in her head, as quiet as a rustle of paper. 'Let's try to remember what our arrogance buys.'

'Our arrogance, Christi? I opposed this madness, you might remember.' Bianca, but lacking her usual bite. If Tallah knew her at all, she was relieved that Christi was speaking.

An accusation hung in the air. Christina did not voice it, nor did she voice her disappointment for sparing the prince. No amount of justification on Tallah's side could convince her that the attack was doomed to fail even had she not hesitated.

"Lovely cock-up, yes," Tallah groaned as she forced herself to move and stretch out the kinks in her muscles. Bruised and cracked ribs told a tale she'd not forget soon. Sil withholding her healing drafts *for the time being* was a way of ensuring just that.

It took a few labored attempts to get the jerkin on one-armed. Tears welled up when she tried to tighten the straps. Ultimately, she asked for Bianca's help. Wasn't as snug a fit as her usual carapace, but it'd have to do. The rest of her gear was just as difficult to pull on. She avoided calling for Sil's aid.

The boy had taken his own savage beating even with the ghost possessing him. Who that dark-skinned bastard had been she couldn't fathom. Very likely a Claw, or a Claw's shadow. Rumi Belli's? Likely a Rian. Well trained and adept at dealing with people like her. To knock the dwarf on his arse made him dangerous enough to look out for.

She'd need to remember him the next time she clashed with that particular cell. That, or risk another knife in her back. Blind luck and nothing else had seen her surviving the night.

Sloppy, sloppy work. Good lesson to remember for the future. Falor had defi-nitely remembered his and surrounded himself with competent aides. They were nothing like the lackeys she'd fought on her way out of the vault raid.

"Easy, lad. Don't move too much. Sip this."

She ambled over to where Ludwig was trying to get a very confused Vergil to drink out of a flask. The boy's eyes were glassy and unfocused, his hand groping weakly for something. She toed his helmet forward until his fingers touched it.

That seemed to bring him around.

"Where are we?" Vergil asked as he finally drank.

Sil crouched next to him and brought her sprite about. He shied away from the light. An ugly black bruise marred the side of his jaw and neck, and his nose looked to have been badly broken. He was missing at least a tooth, from what Tallah could see.

She let Sil work on him. The healer was, at least, being kinder to him than she had been to her. Kindness on Sil's part still had thorns around it, so Vergil's cries echoed over the storm more than a few times.

"Where are we, old man?" Tallah asked Ludwig when he joined her by the cave's entrance. Ice already rimmed the narrow gap they'd burned to get inside and, by nighttime, it would probably seal completely. Not that there was much light coming through the stormy veil.

"Deep in the Crags. If you know your maps, this would be Marrow's Gulch."

'How wonderful. We survived the hammer so we could commit suicide.' Bianca let out a weary mental sigh. 'Nobody will ever see our bones at least. Death by stupidity in complete anonymity.'

Tallah's feelings echoed perfectly.

"I can't imagine how you've gotten this far in here. Even the map's just assumption for the most part."

"Shards, girl. Shards and months of the Sisters' ministrations." He chuck-led as Vergil's pained cry sent echoes dancing around them. "We got as far as we could before we got sick. Buried a shard and then went back and got treated by the Sisters. Repeat until here."

Tallah's eyebrows rose. "Must've taken whole seasons," she said, impressed in spite of herself.

"Two full years, actually. Mind you, we did not brave this place in winter. Can't imagine it possible at all without the Sisters."

Determined bastard for sure. She eyed him a bit more carefully, looking for some sign of that dogged determination in his bent and weary form. Before leaving, it seemed he'd had the foresight of stowing a necessities pack in his own rend. The Guard had invaded his home while he was in the middle of preparations.

"He'll be fine," Sil said as she joined them. "Had to pull out a tooth from the inside of his cheek, and straighten his nose before I healed him. Bugger of a time getting his shoulder back into place." She handed Tallah two glass vials without looking at her. "First the green. Then the draft. You've got the Goddess's own luck to be standing."

"Can't say I feel lucky."

"You've got six cracked ribs and your arm's shattered into three pieces. One more kiss from that hammer and I expect I would've had to dig you a grave."

Tallah uncorked the antidote and swallowed it without further comment. The following healing draft made all of her flare up in agony. At least it came and went quickly. Bones knit painfully back together. Whatever was making her wheeze finally shut up. Sutures tightened and the cuts closed up. It wouldn't take much to reopen them. She would need to allow herself some time to heal properly.

"I drank so much of this green stuff already that I should be immune to anything anyone tries to poison me with."

"Not how it works." Sil reached inside her rend and rummaged about. The dark portal fizzed around the edges as she retrieved four more vials from inside. They shone silver in sprite light.

She handed one to each. "These you drink in exactly one swallow. Keep it down whatever you do. If it works as I hope it does, you won't be shitting blood from whatever's floating on the air here."

"I've heard of these. Blood of the Hearth, was it called?" Ludwig asked. "Never knew someone to have actually brewed this concoction." He held the vial up to the sprite, the liquid inside shining like quicksilver. "Did the Sisters really give you sap to make them? Or did you use a substitute?"

"No such thing as a substitute for the sap." Sil drank, licked her lips and smiled smugly. "And no such thing as the Sisters giving it away."

Tallah could already see the staff's effects waning. Sil stooped somewhat and the color of her hair, under the thick shawl Mertle had gifted her, had begun fading. The smudged edges of old scars showed faintly on her face and neck, discolored lines getting more pronounced by the moment.

"Amazing." Ludwig also drank but seemed to have a bit of trouble with the aftertaste.

"Sweet?" Tallah asked. It's how Sil brewed all her alchemical composites. If they didn't make your teeth want to be somewhere else, they weren't quite right by her standards.

"A . . . unique taste, yes," Ludwig confirmed with a twist of his mouth.

"Keep other comments to yourself. She gets touchy about this stuff."

Sil shot Tallah a murderous glare. The healer's eyes were becoming mismatched in color as the large acid-burn on her face became pronounced. It spread down her face and neck, all the way to beneath her clothes.

"You're lucky I have a full store ready," Sil warned. "Without this, we'd be dead out here in days. Only have two vials of it left over. Let's make sure we don't need to be here long enough to need them."

"Did you hear where we are?" Tallah asked.

"I did. I have no idea where *Marrow's Whatever* is but I doubt it's a stone throw's distance from safety. It's the Crags. Don't need to know more."

"You could say that." Tallah finally drank and nearly brought it back up. "Lovely. As always."

"Not a word, Your Ladyship. You brought us here and got—" Sil clamped up, looking angrily at Ludwig. "You kicked the hornet's nest. We can't go back to Valen yet. So this trip had better be worth the risk."

She strode away towards where Vergil was trying to get to his feet.

Tallah followed, arm resting in a sling against her chest. She had to force down the oily, too-sweet liquid. Her stomach threatened rebellion.

Tummy had equipped the boy with the axes she had asked him for, and the ghost had done great work with them. Now Vergil was looking at them awkwardly, unsure what to do next.

"Good work in Valen." She took an axe and showed him how to fasten it to his belt. "Amazing timing."

Sil sniffed in annoyance. "I ran the soul out of me," she complained in a huff. "Horvath led us. Don't ask me how."

Vergil grimaced as he stretched, looking at the battered state of his helmet. The Rian had caved the faceplate in. Probably would have taken Vergil's head off if not for it.

He grimaced in pain. "How much did I run? I'm sore all over."

"I'm amazed you weren't spitting out lungs," Sil said. "How the ghost tracked whatever this idiot was doing, I haven't a clue."

"I remember flashes of lightning. I think I was following those."

"'Where there's lightning, thunder can't be far behind,'" Tallah intoned one of the oldest maxims about Metal Minds. Another flash of Falor's eyes on hers got chased from imagination by Christina's annoyance. "If he weren't hopping mad, we could learn some things from the dwarf."

"I don't think he's quite as insane as you think he is," Vergil said, a sheepish note in his voice. "Don't ask how I know. Just . . . gut feeling?"

That's worrying. She filed it away for later. Not the time or place to deal with the boy getting attached to his parasite ghost.

"What's next?" she asked Ludwig, itching to move and put Valen farther behind them. Too much to think about and kick herself for.

She desperately needed rest, but Sil's agitation seeped into her own mood. The only way back to Valen would be by shard, and Falor would have the Ascendi under watch with the entire city primed for her return. A single sign of activation so soon after the night's events, and every soldier, adventurer, and commoner in Valen would be braying for her head.

Nothing for it but to move forward on the old man's fool quest.

"We are a day's march away from my ingress point into the underground," Ludwig said, squatting and pulling out a battered old map. He summoned a sprite of his own and illuminated a mess of scribbles upon the ancient paper.

"Beyond the gulch, there's an entrance into a deep fissure. We need to make for that and from there the path's a straight line to Grefe's entrance."

Grefe. The name sparked recognition somewhere in Tallah's memories. Ancient history. Mythology. Never-been. Faer land and all that.

Little wonder Ludwig had been cagey about his misadventure. She would have laughed him right out of Valen and off of Vas itself. Now she bit her tongue.

"Grefe? Is that the city you were on about?" Sil asked, looking at his map. "Nasty trip to there," she mused as she checked his annotations.

Ludwig's eyes sparked in the sprite light. "Yes, Miss Silestra." A gnarled finger stabbed at the map. "History. Right here. There is nothing like it anywhere on Edana. Nothing as old. Nothing as terrible."

"Or so you think," Tallah mused, quietly. Any place old enough could be *the oldest* if there was little surviving proof to say otherwise.

But Grefe was part of faer stories. Even in those, the name was rare, a place of hidden magic, unattainable, unexplored. One that wasn't real. Both she and Christina had enough respect for Ludwig's work as a scholar not to point this out. Curiosity got the better of them now they understood the lengths to which the man had gone to reach this place. One doesn't brave the Crags and their poison only on the promises of children's stories.

Whatever it actually was, that anything had ever lived in the Crags and had grown themselves a civilization tickled her scholastic fancy.

"Half of these passes will be closed off." Sil traced a finger across some of the routes on the map. "I'd suggest we wait out the storm, but I doubt it ever quiets down around here. Can you handle the crossing?"

The question was aimed at Tallah and her wounds, but Ludwig answered instead, "I shall guide us through. Have no worry of that." Ice could melt in his fervor.

Sil shared a look with Tallah. She shrugged. *Your mess*, the look said in Sil's usual resigned way that deferred to her in matters of danger.

"Why does this taste like coolant fluid?" Vergil asked as he handed over his empty vial.

"Why do you know what coolant fluid tastes like?" Sil replied.

"How do you know what coolant fluid is?"

"I don't. It simply doesn't sound like something you should have been drinking."

Vergil stretched and set his helmet atop his head without pulling it down.

"If I understand all of you," he said with a slight lisp, "we're in a bad place, we'll die if we stay too long, and we need to go somewhere worse. Is that about it?"

"Pretty much," Tallah confirmed.

He stuck his tongue through the gap where his incisor had been. "Cool. Best get on with it?"

"What are you staring at?"

Vergil looked away immediately, whipped, making Sil regret her tone.

Of course the boy would stare. He'd never seen her without the glamour and there was quite a bit to notice. She resisted touching her face to feel the acid scar, trace its outline and think on how she'd earned that one.

It'd only give her a headache.

"Sorry," he said as they ate a small meal.

"No, Vergil. I am. Shouldn't snap at you. It's not you I'm angry with."

That was for Tallah's ears and got back a satisfying, poorly concealed wince. The sorceress avoided her glare and blushed all the way up to the tip of her ears. Good. Sil felt partially vindicated. A few more prods like that and she might consider being civil again.

She dipped inside Tallah's rend and took stock of their provisions. Jars upon jars of preserves, pickles, and odd assortments of vegetable spreads. A barrel of fresh water. Some wine? She spied a couple bottles of rose petal wine. Ruby Red, good vintage, clearly hand-picked. It was as good of an apology as she'd ever get out of the mule-headed creature. The thought was nice, though.

There was smoked and dried meat, of course. Some sausage that smelled awful even in the rend's peculiarly thin air. And, for some reason, salted pork rinds.

"What did you raid? The entire Agora?" she asked when back out in the frigid cold of the cave. It was actually colder than the rend, if such a thing were possible.

"That drackir place next to the Sizzling Boar," Tallah said. She was chewing on a rind.

The sight of it turned Sil's stomach after the night's excitement. Vergil worrying on another piece made it worse.

"The one with the . . . that weird sign up front? That weird bugger that likes to scare off children that come for the candied fruits?"

"That one."

To her raised eyebrow, Tallah continued, "I paid for all of it. My conscience insisted."

At least the food would be good quality and slow to spoil. If anything, they wouldn't starve to death out in that wasteland.

Ludwig had been quiet by the cave's mouth, his beard crusted with ice as he waited for them to be ready. Wind whipped his cloak, but the old man seemed too excited to eat or drink, or pay attention that snow went up to his knees.

"I'll put you under," she told Vergil as they packed up. "I don't doubt you'd make the effort, but I need the dwarf's strength for this part."

"By all means. Just please don't let him get me punched again." He grinned gap-toothed and pushed down the helmet. "I don't know how many more times you can set my face right. I'm rather fond of it."

Sil felt herself smiling as she siphoned illum to him. Vergil's boyish grin melted away into an ear-piercing howl as he sprang forward, hands to his axe, eyes wild behind the visor slit.

"Enough of that," she said. "There's only snow to fight. Be my guest to try."

They'd seen the ghost often enough by now that its theatrics had run their course. Horvath understood what was being said to him, but never replied in anything more than grunts or screams. Sil felt mocked more than anything. He disregarded her and stared past, to Tallah. His fists clenched over the hafts of the axes but a glare from the sorceress had him wincing back and growling a stream of what were definitely curses.

He seemed to remember his first meeting with Tallah well enough to back off before she got him under heel again.

That Sil had been wearing the helmet at the time did not make for a pleasant memory. She sympathized somewhat with the dead dwarf.

"Get out of the cave and wait," Sil instructed. "I need you to plow our way through the snow. Stop grinning. That's not remotely what I mean. Do you understand what I'm asking of you?"

No answer, unintelligible or otherwise. He walked by her and shouldered Ludwig aside as he stepped into the gray light of the storm.

"Shall we?" she asked as Tallah joined her.

"No better moment."

Ludwig already waded out into the snow, a hand covering his face against the ice shards the wind whipped up. For as decrepit as he was, the old man moved with a sureness of foot that should have been beyond his age.

Wind slammed into Sil with enough force that it stole the breath from her lips. She pulled up the thick scarf until only her eyes remained exposed. Tears froze in their corners.

She focused on Horvath and pictured walls around him. Two of them, angled together, harnessed to him. A complex bit of weaving that she rarely had a chance to practice. In spite of the cold, she was glad for the chance to test her skills.

Horvath stumbled back as the force of the storm slammed into the invisible snowplow she conjured. Sil groaned at the illum draw.

Maybe this wasn't such a good idea.

The dwarf's spirit pushed Vergil upright after some time, adjusted his stance, and walked forward as if to spite the tempest. She rethought the proportions of the plow until he walked nearly unhindered.

They had arrived into the blizzard in a mad, panicked rush that had nearly seen them scattered had it not been for Tallah leashing them together. Ludwig had opened up the cave for them, though only the gods knew how he'd spied it.

I hadn't realized the place was so dire. Sil dared a look upward into the milky-white light filtering through the high cloud cover, and the sight chilled her.

Cliffs rose high into the snowy mist, jagged and unwelcoming, their crests impossible to discern. Lower down, scattered, were the bones of some ancient creature, rising to claw against the walls of the fissure, their size dwarfing some of the highest spires of Valen.

Gorges intersected there and the wind assailed them from every side, sometimes aiding, most other hindering their progress. Ludwig walked behind Vergil, a hand on his shoulder to guide the way forward. It was all Sil could do to keep her eyes open against the cold. Tallah walked by her side, one arm wrapped around her waist, keeping them close behind the two men.

No words could be shared without screaming over the echoing howls of the many tunnels and fissures where the wind voiced its complaints at their intrusion. In some odd way, it was nearly musical.

Valen's gentle settling into winter's embrace had dulled her expectations and muted the memories of trudging through the high snows of Solstice. The Crags reminded her the season had fangs.

Sil had a miserable time of it.

In a bell's time, the strain of the barrier and of Horvath together began wearing on her. After another, she needed ink nettle dust. She lost a packet to the storm and cursed quietly as she fumbled for another. Her stock was good, but the dust was rare enough to buy. Tallah offered her cloak as a windbreak while Sil forced herself to inhale the fine powder. Frigid air stung her nose and lungs.

Horvath's ditch offered next to no protection against the elements, and she was already too weary to make any more barriers. With each passing bell, she became convinced of the folly of their attempt, and irrationally resented the old bastard his obsession.

Tallah walked bareheaded, her ponytail flapping in the wind, defiant against the chill. Sil wanted to strangle her.

"We're almost through," Ludwig screamed over his shoulder at them as they restarted their slow advance.

Through to where, though? Shadows pooled through the deep crevices they doggedly tried to pass. Cold seeped through her boots and up her legs. Each step forward, a small agony.

In places, Tallah took point ahead and blasted the ice blockage rather than allow Ludwig to turn them around to explore a different way forward. She seemed as annoyed and unnerved by the place as Sil was.

Gradually, the storm quieted. Cliffs slowly met above and the gorge tightened and shrank, strangling the breath out of the blizzard. First to a whistle, then an eerie huff, finally to nearly nothing.

Ludwig halted them next to a narrow fissure. How he had spied it in the gloom only spoke of how intimately he knew their route. He stopped Tallah from blasting a larger hole for their ingress. Instead, they were made to slither in through a gap that squeezed the breath out of Sil. She also had to dismiss the construct off Vergil for him to attempt the crawl.

It opened into a room that had them all stooping, packed tightly together, breath misting white as Ludwig created a sprite. Further on, a crack through stone, wide enough only to be traversed sideways in single file, and barely even so, marked the only exit aside from the entrance. Black ice covered the walls. Maybe it would be wider come thaw, but Sil very much doubted it.

"Do not use your fire here," Ludwig warned as Tallah studied the frozen slit. "Vapors leak out of the stone in warm seasons and get trapped in the ice of winter. I doubt even you would survive the kind of explosion a careless spark would cause."

"Yes, Tallah, maybe try to not do anything else too stupid." Sil couldn't resist the opportunity for a barb. She was coming to dislike the place with ferocious intensity and it, in turn, made no efforts of gaining her sympathy.

The sorceress said nothing in her defense. She looked slightly distracted for some reason. Sil dismissed the helmet's possession so Vergil could also hear the explanations.

"It opens up in some spans," Ludwig went on. "It will be a tight crawl for a time."

If not stiff from the cold and keeping the weave going, Sil would have laughed. Nothing could assure her that the narrow crawl had anything worth waiting for on the other side. *Who would come this way if sane?*

"Please follow close." The old man stowed his pack in a rend as he talked. "There are some diverging paths. Some open into sumps. Some of those won't be frozen over and the drop can be fatal. Best not lose the way."

"What's happening?" Vergil asked from the back of the group, head shaking away the cobwebs of possession. "Are we there yet?"

"We're squeezing through that," Sil said, breathing easier without the siphon. She felt a nosebleed dripping into her scarf, quickly freezing over and sticking the fabric to her skin. "If you're not up for it, I'll get the ghost back."

Vergil looked past her to where Ludwig was wedging himself through, and shrugged.

"Looks cold," he said enthusiastically.

"Probably is."

"I'll be fine. Can I be last?"

"Suit yourself."

Cold did not begin to describe it. Ice at her back. Ice at her fingertips. Every breath more frigid than the last. All of it wrapped in tight misery as they made their excruciatingly slow way forward, one shuffling step at a time.

"A tremor would see us into paste," Tallah mused ahead of her, breaking her strange silence.

"Thank you for that." Sil gritted her teeth and closed her eyes, trying not to mistake her own shivering for the rock's.

Ludwig's sprite floated ahead of them, its light coming and fading as the crack turned and twisted. It was beginning to slope downward. Gently at first, then more pronounced until it was only the tightness of the squeeze that kept them from sliding.

She did slip. More than once. She gained a different bruise and knock each time.

Vergil struggled and muttered incessantly. "Not the cage" sounded often. And slow, quiet sobs that were impossible to hide in that narrow crevice. He struggled but kept up, and Sil found it kinder not to say anything.

She walked straight into Tallah's elbow. In the pitch, the flash of fire in the sorceress's hands came blindingly.

"Go. Away." Tallah growled at something Sil couldn't see.

Ice misted to vapor where Tallah touched the walls, and the sudden heat threatened to smother them. Sil couldn't see her friend's face but saw the rest of her recoil from something ahead.

"I can't go anywhere." Sil choked on the overheated air. "Put that out. You'll kill us all."

"Go away," Tallah repeated, louder now, a manic edge creeping into her voice. "You're not real." She tried pulling back and pushed against Sil. Her hands burned on the ice wall, the flames turning blue.

Oh no. Tallah was chatting with a ghost, and not one of her two.

Sil tried to retreat from the heat but Vergil was there, crowding her, as stuck as she was. They slipped on the ice underfoot and nearly toppled. Vapors from the flash-melted ice stung her eyes and she smelled rotten eggs. Desperately, she kicked out low and caught the sorceress on the shin with enough force that it staggered her.

Fire fizzed out and the cold rushed back in mercilessly. It took long moments for Tallah to move again, and for Vergil to help Sil regain her footing.

Tallah said nothing as she began edging forward.

Vergil made a sound like the beginning of a question. Sil shushed him.

"Not the time. Not the place. Nothing happened," she said resolutely. They followed two paces behind Tallah to the sounds of ice cracking where the sludge froze back over.

Their path angled dangerously downward now. Each step was an effort of maintaining balance and grip against the ever tightening embrace of ice. It hurt to breathe. It hurt to keep going. Cold seeped into Sil's bones, past layers of cloth and padding, to torment and slowly murder her.

How is the old man moving so fast in this? She could see his sprite light sometimes, still ahead. Still moving forward. She envied whatever fire kept him going while she struggled not to succumb to weariness and the biting chill.

Tallah brooded in silence, moving mechanically forward as if indeed nothing had happened. That worried Sil worse than the near absence of any feeling in her toes.

It was suddenly over. She took another step forward and nearly toppled forward into a gaping maw of darkness. Tallah caught her neatly by the arm and pulled her from the fissure. The sprite was there, but she couldn't see anything ahead of them.

The wall was at their back, a lone, material thing in the dark. They stood on a narrow shelf of stone, the ledge barely wider than an arm's span.

Tallah released her once sure she had her feet, then reached into the fissure and guided Vergil just the same.

"Have we arrived?" he asked.

"I'm afraid not," Ludwig replied. He sat on the edge of the narrow shelf with feet dangling over the black abyss. "You could say the journey's just now beginning." He gestured dramatically to the side, to where the path disappeared into the underground night. "We can rest here for a time."

Sil looked around. If there was a far wall, and there had to be one, the light of a sprite could not reach it. She summoned her own and sent it out. It reached beyond her range without finding the far side of the chasm.

The ledge snaked away into the distance. It hugged the wall tight and remained only wide enough for them to travel in single file.

And it was all so dreadfully quiet. Not a whisper of wind or an echo of the mad storm above. Nothing but the quiet sounds of their rest, the shuffling of boots on stone, the rustle of Vergil's armor and the clang of his helmet when he set it down beside him.

Nobody had anything to say.

She grabbed Tallah's arm and marched her forward down the path, aware of the two men looking after them. She walked until out of the light around a narrow bend of the path. Any further could be suicide, and she resisted the urge for light.

"What was that?" Sil bit the words off in a whispered snarl. "What were you seeing?"

"Rhine. She was there," Tallah replied, her voice quiet and distant. She answered quick and sharp, almost eager to have the words out. "Should have known better than to react. I'm sorry."

"Are you hallucinating? Fever? Did you breathe something in?"

She had her hand on Tallah's arm but felt nothing but the gentle heat of her infusion. A slight tremble told of a head shake.

"No," came the spoken reply. "She's gone now. Was just a careless moment."

"You're a piss-poor liar, and we both know it. Why . . ."

Tallah normally saw her dead sister in one particular situation.

"Is it waxing? Is the draw strong this late in winter?" she asked, trying not to sound too panicked by the implications.

Again a shake of the head answered. "Falor nearly burned Christina out of me. I was exposed for a time. May have lost some . . . parts."

Sil let out a slow, shuddering breath and closed her eyes. Her grip tightened on Tallah's arm.

"What did it take?" she asked. Anger and worry mingled in her voice.

More time passed before Tallah replied. "Rhine. The . . ." She swallowed and her voice frayed around the edge. "I can't picture her face. From before the mountain. I can't call it to mind at all. It's all gone from me. I can only remember what became of her."

A shudder and a slow exhalation in the dark. A sniff of annoyance. Tallah pulled her arm away and took a step farther, mindless of the danger. "I'm fine," she said, but Sil knew better.

"You've got a portrait hung in Solstice. That may help."

She knew better than to push further. Tallah would deal with this in her own way and she'd speak her worries when ready. Unlike other times this had happened in the past, moments where the power of the soul trap had flared, she seemed to be taking the new development much better than expected.

Another reason to worry, then.

"You'll tell me before you blow your top off, right? Not like in Garet?"

It was a light enough jab, but Tallah refused the bait. Another sniff of annoyance. "I'm fine," she repeated.

"Good. Now come and make a fireball for me." She tried to force herself to a kind of calm she didn't feel. "I think this time I may have lost some of my toes."

She turned and headed back towards the light.

Some time later, Tallah followed.

CHAPTER TWENTY-FOUR

Passage

The thing leered from beyond the flickering edge of sprite light.

She ignored it. Acknowledging it would only allow more of the music to seep in, and it was stronger now that it had lodged another hook in her soul.

'We need Anna,' Christina said in a distant, barely there whisper of a thought. 'I may not be of much use for a time.'

Tallah nodded, not really listening to Ludwig's long-winded explanation of how he'd come to discover such an out-of-the-way route to an ancient wonder. Bastil priests featured in there, somewhere, but she hadn't been listening since before he opened his mouth.

She should have been on her way to Solstice. Her tools were there, all the apparatus she needed to spin the soul thread to bind Anna's spirit. And then would come the long healing process, the battle of wills, the negotiation and the bargains.

The prospect of it all made her teeth itch.

Christina had been a willing sacrifice and, even so, it had been an unconscious contest for control between them. Bianca hadn't consented—hard to do when being beaten to death with a ledger—and it took months before she listened to the plan and her interest was piqued.

Anna . . . Anna was monstrous in all possible ways. To bind her to the cause, to get her to accept the bargain, what would Tallah need to promise? She dreaded even imagining it.

'Her power would gain us years.'

Christina was right, but what would the cost be? What could Tallah promise to get that vengeful monster's support?

There was no way to reach Solstice, not from the Crags. Even in fair weather, even with her disguise, it would take at least until summer to travel the span of Vas.

Marestra. Drack. Valen. Bastra.

Solstice.

Each a challenge. All under Aztroa Magnor's watchful eye, all of them now aware that she lived and practiced the highest heresy.

Someone hit her in the shoulder.

"What?" she asked, more to show she was present.

"Next time I aim for the sutures." Sil waved a piece of dried meat in her face. "Eat a bite. Drink some water. We need to make for a wider shelf before we get some sleep."

She snatched the piece of meat and bit into it hard enough that her teeth hurt.

"I heard. I was listening."

"No, you weren't. You were sulking over how the prince beat you like the drum of Aztroa's Court. Again."

She felt her cheeks flush and opened her mouth to protest. The look in Sil's eyes made her choke instead.

'She's giving you space to sulk.' A momentary wave of warmth emanated from Christina. 'Once in forever, the hen can be shockingly accommodating to your moods.'

Sil was on her feet and giving her a calculated look of frustrated impatience. Vergil and Ludwig were already a few steps farther down the path, waiting, the sprite bobbing in the air above them.

Oh. She'd been out in her head for quite a while. She ate as she walked, not really tasting the salted meat. The shelf twisted and turned as the cavern wall did, narrowed and widened unexpectedly in places, went up and then dipped sharply. She held up a fireball to allow herself more light as the sprites kept disappearing beyond twists in the path, in and out of crevices that led nowhere.

What a miserable expedition this must've been, once upon a time. She knew there was a destination to reach, but what would those accompanying the professor have known? Just miserably marching into the unknown on the heels of a zealous madman. Oddly, she gained a measure of respect for Ludwig for the temerity of braving that impenetrable dark and leading people down a path that could see them dead at the merest hint of a quake, on a quest to find a place that had likely never existed.

'Maybe this will be worth our trouble,' Christina whispered. 'Maybe they did know something we don't. This at least has the feel of heading somewhere hidden.'

Hopeful thinking. Tallah had gone chasing that particular squirrel before. It was how they'd ended up with the cursed helmet. To accept again the hope of a different way than the one they followed was folly, and she refused its temptation.

And the wraith followed on dead-silent feet outside the lick of her fireball's light. It made the back of her neck itch.

'She's not there.'

She knew that. On every conscious level, she knew that. Thinking too much about it would see her walk straight off the edge so, instead, she moved closer to Sil.

"I'll take watch when we rest," she said.

"No," the healer replied curtly. "You're not taking any watches until I say so. What's there to watch for?"

"Vergil twitching himself off the path?"

It had been meant as a joke, but Sil remained grim-faced.

"I'm going to give you burn-leaf, and you will take it without comment. I'm exhausted and I haven't done half of the things you did. Haven't been half as stupid either."

Sil's glamour had all faded away now. Tallah was by her scarred side and a side-glance from her discolored eye was enough to silence any protest. Even if she now towered over the healer in height, Sil's presence more than made up the difference. It was probably wisest not to tempt her temper just then.

"How long until your secret city, old man?" she called to Ludwig as they slowed for a particularly narrow shelf.

"Days. Three, if we make good time. Four or five if we tarry." He seemed to be enjoying himself.

"We rest and sleep on the first wider portion," Sil ordered. "I'll have no discussion on that."

They did. And Sil did exactly as promised, having Tallah drink the tea she'd grown accustomed to in Valen. Even as she drank the foul thing, she saw lidless eyes in the dark and the impression of an outstretched hand.

It called her beyond the path's edge.

'It's not real,' Christina reassured her. It did little to quiet the gallop of her heart. 'I am trying to banish the figment. Bear with it a while more.'

Christina would rebuild her strength in time, but until then her promises carried little weight. Bianca had gone quiet, doing the work of two in stanching the bleeding wound left behind by Christina's humbling.

Tallah forced her eyes to Ludwig and Vergil as they sat one next to the other, leaned against the wall, quietly chatting while Sil fussed over them all.

"Don't look down into the abyss, lad," the old man was saying. "It will call to you and it might be hard to resist taking the fatal step."

"I'm fine." Vergil grinned at him. "I'm more accustomed to this than you'd believe."

Deep lines of exhaustion showed on his face, and Tallah was reminded that he'd not slept, nor even rested since before heading into the blizzard in Valen. Through it all, he'd not complained once, nor lagged behind. He'd pushed himself harder than she had any right to demand of him. Whatever she thought she knew of the boy needed revising.

When up in the gibbet, he'd raised his hand to ward her away. She remembered the moment with frightening clarity. Desiccated, starved, and more than half mad, he had tried to warn her of danger. And she had nearly ended him.

Who dragged you into my path? Why?

Sleep overtook her before she twisted herself into a ball of anxious, guilty suspicion. Chance was a dangerous thing to trust, especially given who its patron deity was.

Burn-leaf took out the dreams from her sleep. But she'd had it too often, for too long, and now black peaks rose from the depths of memory. She slipped beneath consciousness and Christina's waning protection.

High storms above. The lash of freezing rain. Wind moaning through crevices and the dray on their heels howling their echoing cries.

The mountain rose around her, its jagged cliffs murderous in the split-moment flashes of lightning. She was bleeding. Stumbling nearly blind down a breakneck path. Death stalked their footsteps, its hand outstretched in every chasm and out of every shadow.

She fell, the pain too much to endure. Music thrummed inside her chest, writhed and squirmed through the deepest recesses of her head, and sank deep, barbed hooks into her soul.

And it yanked so hard she couldn't breathe for the pain.

Freezing hands dragged her up and she leaned into the other, stumbling barefoot down the treacherous incline. Oblivion claimed her. She woke to hands on her. Pressure on her wounds. Sheltered? A cave. Echoing boom of thunder filling the world as she pitched forward. Desperately tried to get up.

"Sit. Down. Let me work."

She stared up into wild ice-blue eyes, pools of light in the darkness.

"Press here. Don't pass out."

Again she tried to rise and was pushed back. Her hands guided to the wound and the compress, made to apply pain to stanch the flow.

"I can't heal you. I've tried. I can't. I'm dressing your wounds best I can with what I have."

What was her name? She couldn't remember it. Her torturer . . .

Not the moment to think on that. She needed this one, at least until safety. A jolt of agony dulling into pressure on her leg as the healer tied her makeshift tourniquet. She was cutting her shirt to make bandages.

"Don't pass out. I can't carry you on my own."

Tallah slipped away and was jolted awake when dragged up to her feet, pain lancing up her leg. The cave swam before her eyes. She took a step forward. Nearly fell. Stumbled over a corpse, but the healer held her.

"They're close. We can't wait any more," the woman said by her side. "I got the drop on this one. Broke my knife in his collar bone. I don't know if others heard him die."

And they were out in the freezing rain, the wet cold another shock to her senses. Bloodred eyes waited for them in the early dawn light, surrounding the cave's mouth. Dark animal shapes crowded their path. Silver fangs reflected the sprites of handlers further back. Whistles echoed.

"No . . ."

The closest dray leapt—

Tallah woke with a jolt and a hand covering her mouth to drown her cry. She nearly fired off a flame lance before seeing the eyes staring down at her.

Sil had a finger to her lips, shushing her, unperturbed by the heat hovering near her chest. One blue eye, one gray and scarred. Their gazes remained locked until Tallah's breathing eased and her heart calmed.

"Just a nightmare. You're safe," Sil whispered as she took her hand away and inspected where Tallah had bitten her. "I got lucky. Any harder and you'd have taken a finger."

"Sorry."

"It's fine."

She shook her head to clear the clinging cobwebs of memory and gratefully accepted a canteen of water. In the black underground night, her traitorous imagination filled the silence with distant, howling echoes.

"How long was I asleep?" she asked.

"Not long enough. You've barely been out a bell."

Vergil and Ludwig were each huddled against the wall, turned away from Sil's sprite, fast asleep.

Tallah lowered her voice. "Rest. I'll watch."

"No."

"I'm fine."

"No."

May be for the best. Away from the light, the wraith lingered, and she couldn't trust herself not to confront it if left to her own devices.

Sil noticed easily where her gaze went. A sharp, frightfully well-aimed kick to the shin snapped Tallah's attention right back to her.

"Sil!" she hissed.

"Eyes on me, ash eater." Flat tone. Flat, unimpressed stare. Calculated insult.

"Are you trying to annoy me?"

"Is it working?"

'I believe she'd have quite enough time to figure that out if we push her off,' came Christina's muttered annoyance. Tallah hardly resisted a smile.

"I heard you, ghost," Sil lied.

Tension eased out of Tallah, her shoulders relaxing. She breathed in. Held. it. Breathed out. The familiar felt good. They were all safe, albeit their circumstances required a broad definition of the word.

If she'd allow Christina to voice off her grievances with Sil, they'd peck one another to bloody tatters. There was reassurance in their mundane dislike for one another. She took another swig of water, rinsed her mouth, and spat over the edge.

They sat together some paces away from the men, feet dipped into the chasm. A soft scrape announced Sil putting up a barrier.

"Vergil," she explained to Tallah's questioning look. "Even exhausted, he tosses. I kicked him back in place twice so far. Was going to kick him in the head next, but you started making noise."

"You were nicer as a blonde," Tallah commented and ducked a cuff to the ear. It was her turn to be an annoying twat.

"Shush. I'm all sunshine and bloody rainbows."

It was the scar, Tallah realized. It twisted Sil's face into a perpetual, dead-eyed glare that no sort of smile could make look serene. Both of them were scarred, and both refused to be healed by Aliana. A good pair in a tight spot.

"Do we go all the way?" Sil blew out her cheeks and rubbed her fists in her eyes. "We should be dealing with your condition if your ghosts are having trouble. That monstrosity from storage would help, I think."

"Christina was suggesting the same thing. Can't say I look forward to having her in my head."

"I agree fully. Who'd want Christina in their head? Even she didn't want herself."

'Push her off. Do this and you will never hear another peep from me. I give you my oath.'

"I heard that. I love her too." Sil gave a shit-eating grin and pursed her lips.

Tallah stuffed a fist in her mouth and yawned. Tears stung the corners of her eyes. "We go all the way with the old man. What other choice is there?"

"We could portal out. Make for Solstice." The healer shrugged. "It'd be rough, but not impossible."

Tallah shook her head. "We'd either end up in Marestra, or right in Aztroa from here. Hardly good places to visit in our current condition."

The rest didn't need mentioning. Without their disguises, they'd travel by back roads or straight through open country. In winter, it was as good as suicide.

"Besides," Tallah went on, "we might find something that could help in the old man's faer city." She managed to keep a straight face through it.

Sil looked back to where Vergil clutched his helmet. She snorted.

"I'm not touching anything we find." Some levity crept into her voice. "Learned my lesson."

"Your artistic contribution to it hasn't washed off. I've seen him try to clean it."

"We could call him unicorn-boy. Seems fitting."

It felt good to laugh, even muffled to not wake the others. It purged away some of the doubt festering in Tallah's gut. Christina propped up her spirits with her own feelings of wounded pride. It led to a heady mix of despairing energy that needed a focus.

"What's the most important step?" Tallah asked with a smile. It had been one of their main topics of conversation for many years back when their plans were still in their infancy.

"The next," Sil answered by rote. "Always the next. Feeling better?"

"Wretched. But self-pity won't get us where we need to be. May as well be civil with myself." She spat again into the abyss. "I'm sorry for dragging Mertle into this. I really am. I wasn't quite myself in a panic."

Sil had every right to be upset. Tallah hadn't been blind to her efforts of keeping Mertle safe and separate from their own circumstances. Always sneaking about to be with the elendine, always taking several precautions more than reasonable, always just so careful.

And Tallah had pissed on it all in a moment of panic.

Sil stabbed a finger in her side. "I am going to take it out on your hide if anything happens to her. We're clear on that, yes?"

"Crystal."

The healer scooted closer and rested her head on Tallah's shoulder. "Good. Because if I go much longer without sleep, I'll be the one who starts biting. I will take fingers."

Tallah wrapped an arm around her waist, pulled her closer, and they sat in silence for a while longer. She wished she could tell Sil about Mertle, all the things the elendine had kept private, even from her lover.

It wasn't Tallah's story to tell. She'd been sworn to silence from the first moment. Instead, she kept quiet and accepted the guilt.

"If this place could be fouler, I'm having a hard time imagining it," Sil complained as she made her way back to the group. "Squatting over the chasm to pee is an entirely new flavor of terror."

Tallah ignored her.

The path had been descending for two days now, though time felt syrupy in the underground. How deep, she couldn't say, but it kept on going, sliding ever deeper beneath the surface. The air was grave-stale and smelled faintly of some hidden decay. Mold? A long-dead corpse? Maybe both. A draft would catch Tallah's attention every so often but even these were rare now.

How deep could it go?

Over it all, she felt awash in a kind of power that seeped into her skin and burrowed through her veins to corrupt her stores of illum. The power roiled inside her veins, gurgled and whispered noise. If not for Sil's concoction, she felt certain she'd be violently sick.

She'd never visited the wastelands of the Crags before. Why would she? There was nothing here but death and leagues upon leagues of shattered earth. If something did survive this place, she wasn't certain it was wise to bother it.

Even the flow of illum behaved strangely. In places, she felt it stagnating into pools through which she had to wade. In others, it was a torrent that slammed into her in waves. The Crags lived up to their miserable reputation thus far.

If Sil felt it, she said nothing.

"This can't be the way into a city," Vergil said from the back of the column. "It seems absurd, doesn't it?"

She agreed.

"You'll see when we reach our destination," Ludwig assured him. "I believe this was once part of something very different, cast asunder by some manner of catastrophe."

"I'm honestly curious of where this leads to," Sil admitted. "If it's a few rocks arranged in some fashion that merely suggests a settlement, I will punch you, old man. My disappointment would be boundless."

That last part was sarcasm. Ludwig either didn't notice it, or ignored it. "I assure you, Miss Silestra, that you will be amazed," he said. Tallah envied his certainty. "Grefe is a magnificent place. My words would do it no justice. You need to see it with your own eyes to believe me when I say there is no wonder built by man that can match its glory."

"Fancy words, professor," Tallah said as she slowed them down for a narrow strip of path.

Something looked to have ripped off the wall there to leave behind a narrow shelf, barely a palm's width wide. They would need to hug the wall to advance.

"Bugger," Sil sighed as she approached and took in the sight. "You must be joking."

All bags went into rends and four sprites rose into the air to illuminate the way. Tallah was first, to care for Ludwig if he fell. Sil remained last, to watch over Vergil.

"Can you make a barrier bridge?" Tallah asked.

"Yes. Want me to?"

"No. Save your illum for an emergency. I feel we can pass this on foot."

It was slow, quiet going. The whole length of the passage may have been several dozen yards in all, but it felt like much more. The dark below sucked at her feet as she took one sideways shuffling step after the next. Every breath was shallow. Every footfall tested before lending it her weight.

"Don't look down. Don't rush," she said early on. It was hard listening to her own advice, what with there being little more than a heel's support underfoot.

It must've taken them a bell to finish the crossing.

Once past and on a wider platform again, she helped the rest pass over.

"I've always thought you had a knack for waxing poetic," Tallah continued once they were all past, needing the levity. "It made your abominable lectures that much harder to stomach."

Ludwig laughed nervously. His teeth chattered after the crossing. "I do remember you saying that at one point. If memory serves well, I believe your exact words were that if you plugged up my mouth, excrement would erupt from my ears."

'You did say that,' Christina noted. 'He wasn't quite so amused back then.'

Tallah grinned. "And I remember you petitioning old witch Zakovia to have me, and any who laughed at my observation, lashed for it. Has hindsight let you finally admit I was right?"

"Does *lashed* mean exactly what it sounds like?" Vergil interrupted.

"Oh yes," Tallah went on. "Get stripped to the waist, tied to a pole, and whipped with a cat o' nine tails for as many times as needed to satisfy the ego of whichever imbecile demanded it."

"Sounds cruel and painful."

"I wouldn't know." Tallah chuckled softly. "When they came for me, we threatened we'd burn the Academy to the ground and salt the earth if they so much as laid a finger on any of us."

"Us? Who's *us?*" Vergil asked.

"Tallah was part of one of the most powerful cliques that ever formed at Hoarfrost. Cythra led them," Ludwig provided several heartbeats later, when she didn't elaborate. "It was believed amongst us faculty members that they were more than capable of making good on the threat. We chose the wiser course and I dropped my claim for satisfaction."

In as much as anyone could lead a gaggle of power-lusted sorceresses, Christina did make a good attempt at it. Tallah smiled as the vague flash of arrogance emanated off her back.

A slight tremor on the tips of her fingers. It passed quickly, almost unfelt, like a rock rolling somewhere in the distance. No change in the dark around. No sounds. No echoes of their words. They all stopped and waited.

The world shuddered again and immediately stilled.

"I really don't like how that felt." Sil remained close to the wall. If she could grip it in hand, she likely would.

"You get these tremors here," Ludwig assured them. "It's nothing to worry about. Distant echoes of the Salmek disaster. Nothing more."

Salmek's illum hearth had detonated more than five hundred years earlier, effectively ending the aelir assault of Vas by instantly wiping out more than half of their fleet and decimating their foot soldiers. Millions of humans had died then, wiped out in a flash. As violent an event as that had been, Tallah doubted it was to blame for this.

They began walking again. Slow progress. Sil kept close to the wall, and Vergil to her back. Ludwig had failed to calm even them.

It started as a vibration in her chest. A distant rumble growing to a roar in the span of a heartbeat. Her ears popped.

She opened her mouth to call out the quake. Too late. The world roared. She turned too slow to grab hold of Sil's hand. Didn't reach in time.

Like a great beast trying to shake them off, the shelf under their feet bucked and twisted. She groped for a handhold in the wall but a second shock slammed them and she found herself pitching into the black, the entire world shaking with an ear-splitting groan of cracking stone and shifting walls.

She reached for Bianca, needed her tethers to save everyone, but the ghost was buried deep in the work of keeping her soul attached to her mortal coil. A gasp behind her and a thunder crack spoke of the path fracturing and the others falling.

"To me," Sil called out.

Tallah fell sideways and slammed bodily into something hard that swayed beneath her. Pain screamed in her sutured side. Pure, heady mix of fear and adrenaline got her back up to stand on empty air. Around, Vergil and Ludwig were similarly suspended, slow to find their feet, a sprite hovering just above all three.

"Don't gawk! I can't do this for long," Sil called again, her voice strained with the effort. "All of you to me. Now, or I drop you."

Tallah took a cautious step on the invisible platform, found that it held, then rushed forward towards Vergil. He lay still on all fours, locked in place by terror. She hadn't time in Valen to teach him much about Sil's skills.

Where she was sure she'd step into nothing, another platform would take her weight, the one behind crumbling as soon as she was off. She grabbed the boy by the arm and hauled him to his feet, dragging him along. He held on to her arm and followed in exactly her footsteps. Ludwig joined next to Sil.

Their path was gone, shaken clear off the wall. Sharp pieces of rock remained in places, puncturing the chasm.

"How much longer to the bottom?" Tallah asked Ludwig as she got an arm around Sil's waist.

"A few bell strikes." The old man stared at the ruins of the path. "We were nearly where we needed to be."

"Sil?"

Sil swayed in place, eyes wild as she looked at the ruins of the path. They could see now the aftershocks hitting, the path rumbling and swaying while they remained safe.

Tallah knew they weren't simply floating. To hold anything aloft like that, there needed to exist an entire support structure anchored somewhere—which meant Sil was now at the center of a terribly complex system of anchors, supports, and invisible walls. It was a gargantuan effort on the healer's part to keep them from plummeting to their deaths, and steady to not be shaken off by the earthquake.

"I can walk or I can focus. Not both at once," Sil said, voice shaking. "Thigh pouch. Nettle. Have on hand."

Tallah extracted the tightly tied bags and pocketed them for later.

"I can carry you, Sil," Vergil said.

"You can't," Tallah replied. She grabbed him by one of the helmet's horns. "But Horvath can. I can't make a tether like she can, but I can power you by direct contact. I can't make this any clearer: You *need* to keep him restrained. Am I clear?"

"Yes, Tallah. Count on me."

"I am."

She moved her grip to his shoulder, focused, and in a heartbeat the mad dwarf was in control. He twitched, made to rip away from her, and suddenly stilled, head swiveling as he took in the situation. He spat.

"You know what you need to do?" she asked, fearing the worst. For that moment alone, she wished she shared in Vergil's gut feeling, that the ghost wasn't as insane as he appeared.

Of course, no reply but he picked Sil up in his arms and waited. For a heartbeat, Tallah half expected him to throw the healer into the abyss just to spite them all. Maybe, for a heartbeat, the ghost had considered it, for he turned a ghastly grin her way.

Sil raised a hand and pointed towards the wall. They were yards away and swayed in the air. The quake had quieted, its violence lost in the depths of the earth. Some stones fell from somewhere above, missing them by less than ten paces. They'd been lucky.

"Take me closer. Easier that way."

Vergil took a step forward and Tallah followed, her grip on him white-knuckled. Ludwig held on to her sleeve. His terror, at least, sufficed for them all.

Sil built their path as they went. Where the shelf was gone, she erected steps that hooked into crevices and held on to the remains of the old path. Slow, blind work. Tallah called out suitable anchor points as Ludwig's sprites fanned out to light the way. Each step forward, a small victory.

They had been spared the worst of it. Further on, a whole portion of the wall had detached, leaving behind a wound large enough to obstruct the far side. This would be the old man's last trip to his fabled city, unless he'd somehow master the flight of a manipulator.

Sil's nose bled after long, sustained effort, her illum cost climbing higher and higher. Tallah had already fed her half of the ink nettle dust stock to help her replenish.

The black remained bottomless and hungry.

"I can't." Sil whimpered as another of her constructs shattered when she tried raising it, its support too thin or misaligned. "Tallah, I can't. I need . . . I need to rest." Blood flowed down her chin, bubbled against her lips with every word.

"Just a little more. We must be near something. There must be a bottom to this." She tried to sound reassuring, but her own anxiety prickled the words. "Go as slow as you need."

Bianca remained quiet, deep in the work within Tallah. Christina was still too weakened to help or take over, but doing her best to keep the wraith away. The last thing they all needed now was Rhine distracting Tallah's focus on providing illum to the helmet.

Sil teetered on the precipice of burnout. Already the built shelves were only narrow enough for them to cluster together, the effort too large for anything wider.

"It can't be far now, Miss Silestra. You've nearly gotten us there." Ludwig spoke through his terror, failing to keep it out of his voice. "The gate should be near now."

Sil was silent. She drew in a shuddering breath. Her face twisted in agony as she concentrated still.

"Forward," she urged.

Five steps forward. Another break. Another bag of ink nettle. Five more steps forward. The constructs swayed and shuddered under their weight.

Horvath's draw on Tallah hurt now, the familiar pressure between the eyes growing while the strain mounted. She could use some of the ink nettle to replenish herself, but it seemed a dangerous gamble.

The next step did not find solid surface.

They pitched forward as the support underfoot shattered. And hit the bottom of the chasm two panic-strewn moments later. Impact knocked the wind out of Tallah and she lost her hold on Vergil.

She came to her feet immediately, panic flaring that they were about to drop off the world. But no, there was black rock underfoot, and a cloud of fine dust lifted into the air by their fall. She scrambled over to Sil, to where Vergil had dropped her. The boy was slow to rise, still confused by Horvath's sudden departure.

"I couldn't hold us anymore," Sil said, bloody tears streaking her face. "I couldn't. Was too much." Her breathing was fast and ragged.

"It's all right, Sil. We're on the ground. It was enough."

"I could've killed us!"

"You got us down. It's enough." She kneeled by the healer and cradled her head in her lap. She wiped away the drying red streaks. "Breathe slower. Easy. We're all fine. You can relax now."

Vergil came up, shuffling and raising a cloud of dust behind him. He had his helmet in his hands and looked flushed. In the end, even the ghost had strained with the effort of carrying the healer.

"We're still alive," he said, half-amazed and half-relieved. "Did I do good? I tried to fight him for control, but I'm not sure what exactly I managed. It all gets weird when I'm under."

"He behaved," Tallah confirmed. "If that was you, or if it was him not being suicidal, I can't say."

It seemed to satisfy Vergil.

Sil had drifted off to exhausted sleep and her breathing eased into deep sighs.

"Drench a cloth in water and give it to me," Tallah instructed, her voice low.

She gently wiped off the residue of ink nettle mixed with drying blood.

Sil had fallen face-first into whatever that fine powder was, but Tallah didn't dare go through her vials for some preventative mixture. Only Sil knew her mixtures and would get murderous if they were disturbed.

"Is this ash?" Vergil asked as he ran a hand through the dust. "Smells like ash."

"There will be more ahead," Ludwig confirmed by his side. "We're some distance shy of our mark, but at least we're here."

"Vergil, help me lift her."

With the boy's aid, Sil ended up slung over Tallah's shoulders in the fashion of a soldier's carry. Tummy would thrash her if he saw how her knees wobbled even under Sil's nothing weight.

Eat some meat. Do the exercises. You will always have your muscles on you, but what good will they be if you ignore them? She grimaced and felt the poke of his rough finger against her chest.

"Are you sure?" Vergil asked.

Tallah shifted Sil's unconscious form until she could stand unassisted. Had to stumble twice before she could properly carry the healer.

"You've done your part. It's my turn," she said as she took the first step towards Ludwig. "Let's get to this blasted gate of yours, old man. I expect we can rest more easily there."

Ash rose with every step, drifted lazily in the sprite light, and quietly settled to cover their tracks once they were past. It was knee-high in places, but soft as if it had just freshly settled. Like dunes, it spread across the bottom of the chasm to form an endless black desert. Its only visible edge was the rock wall and Tallah kept them close to it lest they lose whatever sense of way they still had.

From the freezing cold, to this desert of fine, sticky powder. It swallowed up the sounds of their steps as they advanced. No whisper of dunes shifted. No crackle like that of snow underfoot.

Just endless silence.

Ruins rose from the ash. The remains of dwellings littered the dunes, their walls tumbled and shattered into unidentifiable chunks of crumbling masonry. A settlement had once occupied those depths, its remains stretching away as far as the light would touch. Shadows twisted and danced with their passing.

Illum pooled here, as it did in most places where death had come suddenly and violently. She avoided drawing it in. Like in an open field after a battle, the stench of death and rot hung suspended on the tides of power, gagging to anyone sensitive enough to it.

Ludwig had been optimistic in his assessment of distance. It took what felt like two bells more of walking before Tallah stumbled onto the first stone steps rising out of the ash. She would've dropped Sil if not for Vergil on her elbow catching both of them from stumbling. Her back and legs burned with the effort, but she refused his aid.

Their initial stone path had fallen and cratered the ash dune around the raised platform. The only way back would be by portal. At some point they'd need to face that particular risk and hope for the best.

"Do you know . . . how much . . . I hate . . . being carried like this?" Sil groaned as Tallah jolted her with each slow step. "Put me down . . . I'm going to be . . . sick."

"Swallow it until we're up these bloody stairs. You're heavier than you think, and these are slippery."

If Sil had any more indignant responses ready, she didn't get to voice them. They reached the top another half-bell later, and Tallah stepped onto empty air where she had expected one more step underfoot. This time Vergil wasn't quick enough as she and Sil spilled onto the smooth stone floor.

"Ow," Sil groaned.

Tallah echoed the sentiment and accepted Vergil's hand to get back up.

"Not one word, bucket-head," she warned.

Vergil swallowed whatever he was about to say and went to help Sil stand. She wobbled as she rose but pushed away his help, casting a bleary gaze around at their new surroundings.

"So, it's actually a city," she said, looking at the shadow-clad ruins on the edge of the sprite light. "Fancy that. Still, smaller than I expected."

Vergil caught her when her knees gave out. This time she didn't refuse his help.

Double stone doors were cut into the rock ahead at the end of the platform. Taller than Valen's Citadel Gate, and again as wide, they were carved with intricate patterns so life-like that it seemed to Tallah as if their entire surface moved and slithered when light touched it. Winged beings crowded the stone and rose in ranks towards a distant sky filled with stars and floating cities.

There was something human about the depictions, and also something not-quite. The scene of ascension filled her with an odd sense of longing that confused both her and Christina enough that Tallah looked away from the carvings.

One door was ajar just enough to allow one person to slip through the gap.

"Twenty men dragged at that," Ludwig said. "Twenty and we barely managed to move it so much in days." He had the smuggest grin on his face, the look of a man that had proven his doubters absolutely wrong.

Tallah walked away before he had the chance to croon.

It wasn't the size of it or the old man's recollection that drew Tallah closer to the gate. Again, the sense of poisoned power, but stronger here, cloying to her senses. If she focused, she could see a kind of vapor quietly emanating from behind the opened door, carrying with it a faint, almost imagined stench of blood and rotting offal. No, not quite. *Mold more like, and something aged beyond putrefaction.*

With a shudder, she took a step closer to peer beyond.

"It's whispering," Sil said as she came within paces of the door. "Or is that just me?"

"Sounds like static to me," Vergil said.

It was whispering, but not in words, not as such. More a background hum, an insect-like insistent noise. Tallah's skin crawled with the sensation of flies trying to dig into her ears.

"Faer place," she murmured in spite of herself.

'The professor may not have been exaggerating.' Christina's wonder was subdued, her tone reverential.

Ludwig answered with a low chuckle. "It does seem that way, doesn't it? And yet, the real wonder still waits beyond. We're merely on the threshold. Halfway there, as it were."

A ripple in the illum flow. A sense of bottomless, desperate hunger. Anger. Despairing loneliness. Tallah drew sharply back from the entrance and Sil rushed behind her.

"Our host stirs," Ludwig said, unperturbed. "Be not alarmed. It doesn't go beyond the gate."

Vergil's hands were on his axes, eyes wide at the door. Yes, even his instincts reacted to the presence waiting beyond. Sil, still wobbling, came to stand at Tallah's back, peering over her shoulder.

Something moved on the other side. Vapor roiled out of the opening and then ceased to flow as the passage beyond was blocked. A low, angry growl thrummed in the air and made the ash rise in clouds. Hot breath roiled out carrying a cadaverous stench, wet with the promise of violence.

Tallah straightened and stiffened her back, and counted ten quick heart-beats before the creature slunk away from the doors. Had it seen them? Or was it simply patrolling its territory? A sense of wrongness washed across her, diminishing the beast's departure.

"I assume that is what you need my help with?" Tallah said, finding her voice just a shade uncertain.

"Oh, no. Not with it, no," Ludwig replied. The old git even chuckled.

Even without the Ikosmenia Mask to see the illum shape of the creature, she had felt the sheer bulk of power that wreathed it. An illum leviathan in the truest sense of the words, it beggared even Falor's display of strength from the Night of Descent. How she'd deal with it she couldn't fathom. Christina remained pensive, turning over the captured sensations of that instant of contact.

'Something very wrong with that beast,' the ghost said. 'I need information before I make up my mind on it.'

"The guardian is a nuisance, for sure," Ludwig went on once the rumble in the air died away. "It is the crossing that is the real danger. Beyond the gate there is poison in the air that kills in the most horrifying fashion I've ever had the misfortune of witnessing. Your mask will guide us through. *It* is what I truly need from you. If the guardian were my issue and it could be killed, I expect I would have worn it down in a century."

Tallah scrunched up her nose in displeasure. She wasn't keen on hiding from the thing while traversing a road as dangerous as what the old man described. But the truth of her feeling couldn't be denied: The creature would not be easy to kill.

"And it won't bother us?" Sil asked, still reeling from the assault on her senses.

"It will, if we are foolish enough to channel. It smells it. And if it gets a whiff of that, we will all die."

"Lovely."

Vergil set down his pack and rummaged loudly in it. "Well, since we're going to die, let's at least have a decent last meal. I, for one, am starving. Nothing like near-death to whet an appetite."

"Get me wine," Sil said without taking her eyes away from the doors. "May be my last meal. I aim to enjoy it."

CHAPTER TWENTY-FIVE

Chance Meeting

Y ou've got her scowl down; I can tell you that much."

Lady Aliana was likely trying to be encouraging, but Mertle only felt a growing sense of terror. She dared a look in the tiny mirror hidden among the priestesses' bottles of tinctures and ointments. The face that glared back was alien and the sight of it knifed deep through the center of her forehead.

"I'd avoid mirrors if I were you. You're not ready for that just yet," the priestess said.

Aliana wrapped up tight the silver staff and hid it once again in the secret hollow of the root passing through what would charitably be called an office. Mertle thought of the place as some kind of mad laboratory of a deranged witch. An elend healer wouldn't have half of the things on display, and would never stoop to some of the ingredients she'd seen Aliana mixing. Wax root? Crow's tongue? Mint? Repulsive!

"I'm not unraveling, am I?" She massaged her hornless temples. No bone ridges poked out. A minor victory in that.

"Not at all, you're just flustered. Drink this."

"I don't need a drink, Lady Aliana. I need—"

She threw up her hands and bit her lip. The words got lost somewhere along the way. She needed Sil to tell her how far she should go with the Tianna masquerade. She had accepted to help during the first night and had hoped to disappear into the dark to somewhere she wouldn't be followed. That had been the plan.

It had worked. In many ways, it had worked too well, except for that crucial final part.

Tallah got what she needed. *Her* own plans remained safe for the time being. Tianna, for better or worse, had escaped the Storm Guard's immediate attention and remained a free woman.

But things were changing.

Mertle found herself constantly followed. The moment she showed up as Tianna anywhere, there were eyes on her. Always watching. Always bloody probing for a mistake. People constantly came to the Meadow seeking audiences that Verti had been instructed to turn away, but she could only hide for so long before suspicion would dawn.

She couldn't make Tianna disappear. And she couldn't make a mistake in being Tianna. The cage around her couldn't have been tighter if it had actual bars.

"What you need is a drink," Lady Aliana insisted. "And to stop pacing before you wear a trench in my floor."

She took the proffered glass and downed it without thinking. Not bad, as human spirits went, but did little to quiet down her thoughts. Aliana replenished the glass. It went down just as easily, warmed her up well, enough that she could feel her hands and face again.

"Thank you. I'm sorry. Just . . . I wish they'd left me with some more instructions." She sat down heavily on the one free chair in the room and pressed fists into her eyes. "I was supposed to preserve this disguise and then get *Lady Tianna* out of the city. But they're always *there*. I feel that if I'd gone with the caravan, at least one of the Guard would've come with."

Then she would've needed to kill whoever that was and she really didn't want to kill anyone. Not unless her back was truly to the wall. It wasn't a pleasant prospect. She hadn't killed any humans yet.

"We do this until the sorceress gets back. She'll call in when she does." In her Sisters' gown, leaning against an overladen desk, Lady Aliana looked every bit her imposing station. Of course, she was immune to anything the Storm Guards could muster, so Mertle's worries likely did not impress anything on her. "Fail or quit, and she might return to a waiting trap. You heard what the princeling did to her?"

Mertle nodded. Even with the surprising appearance of the Goddess of Healing that very night, the whole of Valen was talking about Cinder getting destroyed in fair combat by the lord commander of the Storm Guard. They'd been toasting to Lord Falor's health nightly at the Gooseberry. She could hear them from across the Agora.

If that monster got the drop on Tallah the next time, she might not survive the encounter. Mertle's part to play pressed down on her with the weight of a lodestone.

"Here. This should help you." Aliana drew her out of her own head.

Mertle caught the object thrown at her and studied it. A silver armlet engraved with a smattering of runes she'd never seen before. Sil's work, sure enough. She recognized the style at a glance, even if not the runes themselves.

Something off that wand she'd been studying?

"What's this?"

"I had one of my girls follow the instructions your lover sent over. We finished the engraving."

"This is half of a twin." Mertle followed the logic of the runes, feeling herself settling better into her disguise. A blush crept up her cheeks at Aliana's mention of her *lover*. Touching the silver provided something, though she couldn't quite say what.

Skin-contact-activated. Not an immediately obvious effect, so likely a passive engraving. Yes, this rune arrangement would achieve that.

"It's got a complex effect," she surmised.

"Good eye. Second part is on the staff. Your disguise should take a longer time to dispel now. Silestra wasn't very clear on the inner workings of the enchantment, but it seems to do what she said it would."

It fit her arm snugly and the glamour stopped fighting her. It settled in her bones like a content lulled beast.

"How far can I be from the staff before it starts waning?"

"Test and find out. Feels better?"

"Much." It really did. She wouldn't brave the mirror, of course, but it no longer felt as if she had to hang on to the staff's effect by tooth and nail. The glamour became a snug, comfortable fit.

"Good. Now get out. I do have other business to tend to."

Sil had asked her to trust the priestess of the Dryad. She hadn't asked for Mertle to like the woman, and the feeling seemed mutual. Still, she'd tarried for long enough and time was short.

Back straight. Chin up. Expression like an itch somewhere unpleasant. She walked out of the small office daring any of those waiting in line to challenge her preferential treatment. None did.

Her handlers would find her soon after walking out. They usually did. After the Descent confrontation with that captain woman, the Guard had stopped watching her as overtly as Sil had described. There weren't any soldiers watching the Meadow, but there didn't need to be. They watched the gates and the Guild. Sometimes they started after her when she passed, and sometimes ignored her.

Miserable bastards and their human games. Some days she could almost believe that it was all in her head, imagining patterns where there weren't any. But long service to her aelir'matar's crop had taught her much about patterns, enough that a lifetime away from Nen couldn't erase.

She adjusted the brim of her hat, tightened her cloak, and stepped out into cold midday light. There would be some more storms left to this winter, but not on this day. Cares was high up and the sky a perfect blue, stretching to the inky shadows of the mountains and beyond them. From up high on the steps of the Sisters of Mercy, she could see beyond Valen's walls to the snow-capped ridges of the Valen-Drack range, and all the dotting villages up to there. Dark lines of caravans braved the high snows to reach some of these places and deliver food and medicine where it would be most needed.

They always help one another in hardship times. The aelir had only cared for themselves. If their thralls froze to death in winter, there would only be fewer mouths to feed come thaw. This human gentleness, even after five years living among them, still struck her as unimaginably odd.

"Lady Aieni?"

She froze halfway down the steps, recognizing the voice with terrible certainty. Terror, white-hot, ignited in the pit of her stomach. Swinging her gaze from the mountains back to her path showed her exactly who she dreaded worse. Lost in thought, she hadn't noticed Captain Quistis Iluna just off the side of the path leading down from the hospital. She was talking to a one-armed beggar woman huddled into a nook in the side of the building. The Sisters rarely minded beggars by their steps, but the city's council did not approve of the practice. There was a whole cluster of them gathered around the Storm Guard.

"I'm sorry. I will be back soon," the captain said to the woman, then passed her a small pouch before rushing in Mertle's direction. She nearly slipped in the late-winter sludge of ice, mud, and salt.

Mertle wondered for the briefest moment if her surprise was as etched on her face as the shock in her soul. She had gone to great lengths to discourage this woman from seeking her out. She had slammed the door in the face of every runner and envoy of peace the captain had sent, and told each and every one of them where the guard lady could shove her apologies.

And, now, here the woman was, dressed in the civilian garb of a healer, rushing through the muddy snow to greet Mertle.

For a heartbeat, she considered fleeing. It would've been easy to turn her back on the woman, quicken her pace, and shoulder away through the crowd.

Captain Quistis reached the bottom of the stairs before Mertle's mind was made up, and smiled up at her in just such a way that negated any hope of getting away from at least acknowledging her presence.

"Captain Quistis," Mertle returned the greeting, carefully constructing her tone into a mixture of suspicion, cold displeasure, and heartfelt loathing. "I'd say it's a pleasure seeing you again, but you might try to arrest me for lying to your face." She made the words cold enough to sting, yet it seemed there wasn't much effect.

"You make it terribly hard to reach you," Captain Quistis said, still barring her way with that infuriating smile. "Can I please, now, offer my apology? I don't want to resort to battering down your door for it."

"I don't want or care for your apology. I need you and your men to leave me alone."

She tried to move past but couldn't. The woman stepped in time with her to bar the way. Any closer and they'd be chest-to-chest.

"Then allow me to treat you. Coffee and sweets. Please. At least that for all the discomfort I've caused you?"

Mertle stared, caught halfway between baffled incredulity and suspicion. Was this a joke? The woman nearly had her turned into an arrow-ridden pin cushion, and now she was offering her apology . . . in pastries?!

"There—there's a very nice place close by, just by the Guild," she went on. "I know you like to sample the finer things. I can guarantee you haven't been to this place yet. It's my treat. No strings. Nothing." She tapped her breast where the usual insignia of the fist wreathed in lightning would be emblazoned. "I'm off duty, and it was pure chance to run into you. My honest word for it."

"I . . . err . . . Fine?" Hard to say no, politely or impolitely, to an invitation like that. Tianna did have a ravenous sweet tooth, and the woman was clearly informed about her habits and preferences. "Lead the way, then. Maybe after this you might just leave me be."

If Quistis turned her back, maybe Mertle could slip away into the crowd. But the woman never did. Infuriatingly, she led the way in perfect sync her own steps, making sure the crowd had no chance of separating them. At times, she even touched her arm to guide her around some particularly stubborn layabouts.

Chance meeting, my arse, captain, she thought sullenly as the two of them approached the Guild's gate, and took a sharp turn towards the Daylight Wall.

It was, as Quistis had promised, a very nice, out-of-the-way café, hidden in a narrow gap between two shops selling healing herbs and alchemical compounds. Far enough from the Guild and the Sisters to not be treated to the noise, but easily within walking distance to both and the elevator into the Lower City.

Once past the heavy nondescript door, Mertle found herself in a cozy, candle-lit place with separated narrow booths and two-person tables. The cushions were all velvet and there was pipe smoke in the air, sweetened with scents of fruit. String music drifted in from somewhere, though she could see no musician in attendance.

Privacy was the coin of trade here. No windows. No sprites in the air. Only flickering candlelight and the warmth they produced. Patrons were nearly faceless in the cozy gloom, their voices lost in the hum.

A faint breeze wafted the smoke about and made the flames shimmer and shiver.

Mertle took it all in upon first step, and loved it. Not so much the company she was forced to endure, but even that couldn't dampen the charm of the café. Slightly disgusted with herself, she moved inside, following close behind her unwelcome date.

A serving girl took their cloaks and greeted Captain Quistis with the ease of long familiarity. She led them among the labyrinthine arrangements of tables, down a short flight of stairs, and into an unexpectedly private booth.

"If I worried of your intentions, Captain Quistis, I would think you were leading me into a dungeon," Mertle said as she seated herself on feather-soft cushions. "The Guard must pay spectacularly well for one to be intimate with a place such as this."

"Please, just Quistis is fine, Lady Tianna. I'm out of uniform and this is really just a personal invitation."

There was a lie in there, somewhere. Mertle could read it on her face, though she couldn't figure exactly what she was being lied to about. She nodded and picked a menu plaque from the wall.

"Quistis, then," she said, softening her tone to hide her shock at the prices on the plaque.

Two bloody lions for a cup of coffee?! In the Agora, two lions would buy her and Tummy an entire meal and leave over some eagles for a couple mugs of Valen beer. Pastries and cake *slices* were even more absurd. She looked over the edge of the plaque at Quistis and raised an eyebrow.

"I don't come here by myself. And I never get to pay," Quistis said and there was a slight, very human blush on her cheeks as she said so. "Serving in the Guard does not pay quite that well, I'm afraid. And, anyway, most of it goes home to my parents."

Stowing her shock, Mertle ordered coffee—sweetened, of course—and five different cake slices of the most expensive varieties. Three of them had *decadent* as a descriptor. She only stopped after the fifth when she saw a momentary flash of panic on Quistis's face.

One more cupcake, for good measure. Petty revenge for that terrifying night, true, but it relaxed her to see the Captain sweating and touching her money pouch.

"You offered. I accepted. Or did you believe my company would come cheap?"

"I'm just surprised, really." Quistis looked at her with raised eyebrows. "Did not expect your sweet tooth to be quite so ravenous. I've never seen anyone, except maybe an elend, stomach two of these sugar monstrosities. My date normally can't even finish his." She only ordered a coffee for herself. Black. No sugar needed. "It'll be a tale for the barracks and no doubt."

Mertle cursed inwardly and pretended to look at the menu for one more item. There was no attack in the captain's words. Ultimately, she shrugged and replaced the plaque on the wall.

"I'm eating out of frustration, if you must know. And I hold you personally accountable for it."

"Me? Whatever for?" Quistis drew back from Mertle's pointed finger, her ignorance almost comical.

She leveled her best, most loathing glare at Quistis, the kind she only reserved for the obnoxious customers come to haggle back at the shop. It usually got them blubbering.

"You scared my friends away."

Quistis blinked in confusion, mouth halfway opened. It took several heartbeats for her to answer. "Pardon?"

"Your foul shenanigans and that ghastly threat of violence on my person, the things you're trying to bribe my anger away for? After all that, my companions disappeared into the night. Thank you so bloody much, *Quistis.*" She added a slight hiss to the name, for effect.

An excellent opportunity had just presented itself, to deal with the one detail that could hinder her. Tummy couldn't become Vergil—too tall, too large, and too single-minded for the staff to work—and Aliana couldn't turn into Sil—the reasons too many to count. Tianna losing her constant companions would be an impossible to ignore detail for whoever had been bright enough to suspect her as Tallah in the first place.

"I did wonder at that," Quistis replied quietly. "You don't mean quite literally disappeared into the night, right?"

"Absolutely literally. The moment your lot disappeared from sight, so did they. That elend girl with us fainted of fright—again, thank you for that embarrassment. I rushed her indoors. Silestra and Vergil remained behind outside." She made a *poof* gesture with her hands. "And they were gone. Not so much as a word. Simply gone. Bloody incredible. I blame you entirely."

Quistis regarded her with an interesting mixture of emotions as the serving girl brought in their order on two trays. A tiny bowl of honey was set next to her coffee, after the southern style from Calabran. Mertle cooed over the detail, her anger seemingly overshadowed by this touch of home. The further north one traveled, the rarer honey got.

Since Tallah's departure, she'd had Tummy read to her about the southern cities, as she'd only spent little time in the ports of Vas. Amazing how much humans wrote of their homes and customs. She considered dictating some things to him about Beril.

"Did y—"

Mertle shushed Quistis as the serving girl set down her cakes. Chocolate. *So much chocolate!* Three slices were, indeed, *decadent* in how they were decorated with intricate leaves and flowers made of some brightly colored sugar paste. They were almost too beautiful to eat.

The fourth was a slice of something called *First Snow*, and it had the look of a tiny, miniature mountain peak capped with the most delicate snow Mertle had ever witnessed. It was cream, she realized, and it sent her mouth watering.

And the last had vibrant glazed fruit slices atop it. Lemon slices! It was impossible to distinguish between what was real fruit, and what was finely sculpted icing.

She bit her lip to suppress a soft moan of pleasure at the sight. Oh, what she wouldn't give to have Sil there, at that very moment!

Quistis coughed politely before speaking again. "Did you have any word from your friends since?" Her gaze had unfocused and she scratched at her neck, beneath the collar of her robe, a gesture completely at odds with her overall bearing.

"You'll cut yourself if you keep doing that," Mertle noted and took a bite out of the first cake. Rich, velvety chocolate! She took some time to savor it before responding. "Not a peep."

"Have you had any valuables go missing?"

"I couldn't say. Silestra took care of that stuff, and she did the packing for our planned trip to Solstice. We were supposed to leave on the Vulniu caravan, but then you showed up and buggered my plans." She tasted each cake. Every slice was so different and each so wonderfully prepared. She desperately wanted to come back here and have Sil try these as well.

"What were your plans, Lady Tianna? Why were you planning to leave?" Quistis's interest had changed. The way she held her hand curled on her mug, one finger tracing the outline of its lip. How she leaned forward slightly and her eyes focused intently on hers. No longer out of uniform it seemed.

Tallah and Sil hadn't had the chance to set their plans into motion properly, chased out of the city as they'd been. All Mertle knew was that it involved the south, Ria especially. Sil had talked to Lucian at the Guild, and several other caravan masters. The trail was there. With Mertle stuck in Tianna's role, with no real way to disappear into the night, she could at least smooth over the details.

To Quistis she shrugged dismissively, as if the matter did not warrant consideration. Her attention was on the sweets and her wonderfully sweetened coffee.

"I've tired of Valen and its gloom. Especially, I've tired of the stench of smoke everywhere. I was heading for Solstice, and from there down to one of the southern cities. I miss the sight of the Divide. It's been too long since I've felt the ocean breeze on my face." Safe answer. From Solstice, it was an easy trek down to Calabran, home, and from there she could head to Vas's opposite coast.

"Why were you at the Sisters of Mercy earlier? Looking for news of your two?"

"This is turning into an interrogation, Quistis," Mertle said. She'd finished one slice of cake and moved on to the next. Yes, she would finish all five, but the cupcake would need to come home with her or she'd waddle. "One normally uses hard drink to get answers, not cake. Bold strategy."

"I apologize. Just . . ." Quistis floundered for a moment and then reached inside her robe and took out a scroll. "I can have people looking into your companions," she said, voice lowered to a conspiratorial whisper, as if hiding her preferential treatment. Not that she needed to. There was nobody around on this lower level. "Or . . . Look. There are two people of interest, a healer and a warrior, that have come to our attention at pretty much the same time you say your companions disappeared. Given some of the circumstances that led us to mistakenly accuse you, what you're saying now is difficult to ignore."

Even by flickering candlelight, it was entirely too easy to recognize who was sketched out on Quistis's proffered scroll. Mertle's heart skipped at least two beats when she looked.

"Who's that?" she asked, spoon resting against her lower lip to hide any emotion.

"Do you recognize this woman at all? Have you ever seen her around any of the places you were at? Please, think very well on this."

The background hum of the café and the soft music died away as she pulled the image closer and stared down into Sil's charcoal eyes. It was a very good rendering of her likeness, right down to the twist of her mouth in anger and the shawl Mertle had gifted her. Someone had gotten a very good look, probably in the commotion Tallah had stirred.

She swallowed her cake and took another bite before pushing the paper back.

"Looks a bit like a younger you, if I'm honest," she replied. A stupid but true answer, after a fashion. If she hadn't known Sil to be an only child, she could see Quistis as her older sister from the resemblance. Nose and eyes were very similar. "But otherwise she doesn't strike me as familiar."

The scroll stood between them for a while longer as Quistis sipped her coffee. "More's the pity, I guess. Would've given me something to go on." She rolled back Sil's image into a tight cylinder and stowed it away. "We'll be circulating plaques of this person and hope for the best."

Mertle choked on a lump of cake, gripped her coffee and tried to wash down the lump of chocolate. It made it worse.

We were seen out together!

In more than one place and in less than platonic circumstances. They'd never made it any kind of secret while out and about, enjoying the kind of freedom only a human city could afford an elendine. Several of her Agora neighbors had remarked on how cute of a couple they were.

Lady Rosa had gifted her a late-bloom rose for her *very special friend*. And there were so many others that had seen them together. Sil drew attention wherever she walked.

Quistis rose to help her. Mertle waved her back as she tried to compose herself.

"Went down the wrong way," she wheezed out as she emptied her coffee mug. It all tasted like dust now and she felt a sudden stab of pain through her forehead. The armlet felt hot to the touch and she struggled to breathe. Cold sweat drenched her back and plastered the dress to her skin.

"Most people pale when choking. You've gone quite red in the face," Quistis noted with some worry.

"I'm fine. I'm fine." She breathed out, coughed, closed her eyes, forced herself to calm. *Nothing has yet happened,* a distant voice whispered in her ear. *This meeting is a blessing in disguise. Without it, you wouldn't have had advance warning of what was to come.* There would be time for panic later.

"Did not expect it to be quite so hard to push down."

A wintry smile, a signal to the serving girl, and two more Valen lions marched out of Quistis's pouch.

"Bugger me, that was embarrassing." Mertle sipped her fresh coffee and burned the roof of her mouth without feeling it. "So tell me, who was that on the scroll?"

"I can't say. I'm sorry. But I can have my people on the lookout for your two missing companions."

"You don't need to do that."

"It's the least I can do. I'd like to ask about them if you don't mind."

"I do mind." Mertle moved on to the next slice and brandished a spoonful of it at Quistis. "This is excellent cake, Captain, and this is my first real moment of joy since the Night of Descent. I'll be much more favorably inclined towards you if you'll just let me enjoy it without more interrogation."

Quistis sat back and cupped her mug in both hands. She had the grace to look abashed. "I apologize."

"No need. Consider my anger somewhat abated. You delivered as promised, and I got to see you sweat. I think we might be near to even. Now have your men leave me alone and I will truly be satisfied. I'm tired of always being followed about. It was flattering for a time, but now it borders on obnoxious."

"Pardon? I don't have anyone on you at the moment. I called back surveillance after the Descent."

That brought Mertle short, especially as there was no lie in the words. "I can recognize soldiers, Quistis. I can recognize when they're following me. The same sort of people that have been dogging me all winter. Your men." She leaned forward and licked her lips. "I'm sorry to say, they are not that good at their job if the point was to remain unseen."

It was Quistis's turn to frown and hide it behind the coffee mug. "My men are hand-picked, one and all. If your stalkers answered to me, then you wouldn't have noticed them." She sounded offended. Downright pouted.

Maybe if I was what you thought I am, Mertle thought with relish. Of course, she'd had very different training and could see an imperial tail from the other side of Valen. This was going into self-indulgence already. Maybe these watchers were simply of the Aieni Holding, keeping tabs on the prodigal daughter. It made some sense, but . . . what if not?

Tummy had prepared some of her old blades, honed and laid them out for her. She would start carrying one, just in case. It wasn't *going back to bad habits,* as Tummy had put it, if she just chose to not be defenseless.

"As you say," she conceded with a pout of her own. "Must be my imagination, then." A hint of malice slipped in, just enough to sting Quistis's pride again. "Don't look so goggle-eyed. Is there something on my face?" She wiped the corner of her mouth with the heel of her palm, a definitely unladylike gesture, to declaw her previous words.

"You've finished four of them . . ." Quistis looked a bit green at the sight of four empty plates, her mouth twisted in a mixture of awe and disgust. "How are you not sick? Will you be able to walk?"

"Because they're excellent. Have you tried this one? Puts to shame Verti's girls, and they're elend."

"My teeth hurt only thinking about one of those."

Mertle took entirely too much pleasure out of Quistis wincing when she took the next spoonful. "As for walking." She closed her eyes in pleasure at the taste of distant lemons. "I'll waddle."

It was worth it.

CHAPTER TWENTY-SIX

Labyrinth

Tallah stretched and grimaced at the way her back popped. If she missed one thing about Iliaya's Staff, it was the flexibility of her own joints.

Age was a terrible thing to experience again.

Ludwig was arranging supplies in his rend, talking all the while. "The beast devours illum. I saw it drain a pyromancer to a husk and then eat him. Poor Morgyas. I can hear his screams still, echoing here."

"Poetic. Are enchantments safe at least?"

"It draws it closer, but not like illum does. If we don't stop in place, it will not find us easily."

"Lovely." She was far from reassured. "Light? Sound?"

"Doesn't seem to notice either. Certainly not torches."

Tallah scanned the swirling mist oozing from the passage. She'd seen no other sign of whatever waited beyond the gates, nor felt its terrifying presence, but weariness had already set in from first contact. They were rested, fed, and, once Sil finished rummaging about her rend, they would go forward. Her fingers idly toyed with the mask.

"How long does your concoction last?" she asked the healer as she emerged.

"If you shit out blood, it's probably expired. I haven't had a chance to field test it before."

Lovely answer, as befit her lovely companion. "You said you had more?"

"Not enough for everyone." Sil shrugged as she haphazardly tossed some bundle back into the rend. "You try to get sap from Aliana next time and let me know how it goes. Like bleeding a stone."

Lovelier and lovelier still.

"Here, hold these." Sil doled out three vials of a tar-like substance to each of them. "I'm not lugging twelve of these around. Care for your own share."

"What's this?" Vergil asked as he set the vials in the loops of his belt.

"What coffee would be if you managed to distill it down to its soul." Sil made her rend smaller and reached deep inside to pull out five different flasks. "This should be everything I need," she mused, checking her satchel. "Here, take this into Tallah's."

Vergil no longer hesitated before lugging the bags inside the larger rend. For this part of the journey, the decision was to travel lighter. They aimed for a three-day march across the maze. There would be little time to rest. Best to stow excess baggage.

"Grab torches while you're in there," Tallah called to the boy. If she couldn't blast the guardian, a club on fire would be the next best thing.

"Incredible capacity for volume, Tallah," Ludwig said as he circled the dark portal. "How much do you carry in there?"

"Enough for my needs."

He stopped and regarded her more closely, as if weighing her. Her glare at his interest did little to dissuade him.

"My guess is that you need about six limiters, Garet variety, to maintain full coherence. Good estimate?"

Christina let out a scoff in the back of her mind. 'Six limiters were the pinnacle of strength back in his day. Poor comparison. The world's moved on. Full coherence? Ha!'

Sil chuckled. "Waste of money, those. Their formulae were ancient and outclassed when the empress was still a girl."

"Still, am I close?" Ludwig accepted a torch and lit it with a small fire bolt.

"Six would be about half of what I need to maintain *directed control.*" Tallah scoffed at the idea of *full coherence.* Nobody spoke of that anymore, the term as ancient as Ludwig. "I use five limiters made by Sil."

Ludwig whistled appreciatively. "Pure silver?"

Sil laughed. "She melts those in two days just meditating. I've been using electrum for her. Expensive as sin, but it does the job."

Ludwig's eyes looked ready to blow out of their sockets. "Not many have a claim on such raw power. I am in awe."

"Blow it out your arse." Tallah prickled at his fool praise. If she were as powerful as she needed to be, she wouldn't be using limiters at all. Falor and Catharina hadn't needed any and she'd been taught the painful lesson of the gulf separating them.

She donned the mask and, for the thousandth time, envied the true Egia.

Illum raged around them and gently resolved into lines of power rushing through the gateway ahead.

"That's odd," she mused.

"What do you see?" Ludwig had asked to try on the mask and she'd refused him. Now he hovered close to her elbow, relentlessly wringing his hands, his gaze swiveling back and forth between her and the way forward. "Gods help us, I pray this works."

"The gate was a seal that you broke open," she said. "Illum doesn't flow through the material. It goes around, like water going around a rock. Something was sealed inside. Maybe the creature." She splayed her fingers through a stream of power, drew it in, found it bitter, released it. "Maybe something worse."

Normally she would see veins of bright blue in an undisturbed flow of illum. Here, furious reds and purples colored her vision and sparked the first sign of a headache in the space behind her eyes. It was hard to tear her attention away from the chaos.

In the dead center of the maelstrom there was a sliver of calm, of gentle flow. The blue she normally knew, flowing through like a guiding light in a storm.

"I see the path," she called to the others. "I need you all to stay close. It's narrow."

Passing through the narrow gap gave an odd feeling of walking through veils of gossamer-thin silk, its ghostly touch verging on the edge of physical sensation. It lasted for a brief heartbeat and then they were through.

The sight forward sent a cold shiver down Tallah's back. Vergil behind her gasped in wonder. She had to grab his arm or he'd wander forward past her, gaping like a fool.

Ludwig swung his torch to look around. "Been so long since I dared this place. Gods . . ."

"If you're going to get misty-eyed on me, I'm leaving you behind," Tallah snapped. She raised her torch and set to the path.

A cavern awaited beyond the entrance tunnel. Ruins snaked through the fine mist, dressed in riot illum colors. She dared a look without the mask. Light from the torches barely illuminated ten paces ahead, swallowed by the roiling, churning cloud-like swathes of mist. Fire sputtered and hissed, shrinking back from the dark.

Another ruined city or some kind of outpost. Like the ash-covered remains outside, this too had been cast down to near nothing, the ground beneath it cracked and shattered, twisted in ways that could not be natural or intended. Pathways wove among the wreckage of time, going up and down, sideways and back into themselves.

Through the Ikosmenia, the path was a clear tunnel through the mad haze of power. It swayed and shifted, shrank and enlarged in uneven intervals. Safety fleeted. Like the mist, the flow of illum moved unpredictably and couldn't be relied on for long.

"Lovely place, old man," Tallah mocked as they advanced. "May the wonders on the other side be as impressive as this pit of despair."

She set the pace at a steady march, following a path bordering the bottomless depths where the rock had shattered. Their lifeline swayed on invisible tides.

"Did you learn what happened here?" Sil asked from the back.

"I'm afraid not," Ludwig said. "Our time was too short to learn much of real value."

"And yet you brought back plunder. Greed somehow works out."

Nearly a bell's worth later, Tallah had to backtrack as the path she'd followed plunged into the chasm. Soon after, she withdrew them from the lip of another precipice, already atop what had felt like an endless flight of uneven stairs. Her lifeline became a distant guiding light that she sought out rather than followed. Safe passage often seemed chaotic. The best way forward was not the obvious.

"Your sense of direction is as great as ever," Sil grumbled. She and Tallah had to squeeze by one another in the narrow gap between two ancient walls, now leaned on one another and slowly crumbling to nothing.

"Would you like to lead, Sil?" Tallah shot back in her most honeyed tone. "I'm more than happy to pass you the mask."

"Sure. Give it over. We can take breaks while I puke every few steps." Her tone dripped honey.

"Then can it," Tallah ordered. Her temper already frayed and they were barely past the threshold. "This place is mad enough as it is."

"Charitable assessment, I'd say."

"I have often had nightmares of this part of the journey," Ludwig said. He and Vergil brought up the rear. "We tried mapping the place. The poison moves."

"I can see that. What I'm surprised is that you've not been getting nightmares of your own shadow." On and on the old man went. Terror this. Horror that. Nightmares and woes. He and the accursed place wore on her patience. She could push him off the path and be done with the bleating at least.

'Temper, Tallah,' Christina whispered. 'You're drawing in power. Release it.'

She did so. Hairs pricked on the back of her neck and her gloved hands sweated. Danger hung in the air like the mist, ever-present and oppressive. She didn't need to invite more of it closer.

'I believe something stalks us. I can feel it out there, out of the light.'

Tallah ignored this. It wouldn't do to become paranoid. Creeping across the narrow sliver of stone was effort enough without worrying of the fall or the beast. It took enough focus not to see the wraith that followed on the edge, always wreathed in the underground poison, ever silent.

"It's so quiet here," Vergil said. "I can hear my heart in my ears."

That, at least, was an understatement worthy of a village idiot. The mist sucked in every sound. Even Sil's terse reply came to her ears as a muffled whisper, unintelligible to Tallah, and she was barely five steps ahead of the healer. No echo to their steps. No sound of pebbles grinding underfoot. No swish of cloth on cloth or rattle of sword in its scabbard.

Just silence, unbroken. She forced herself to release more of the power she'd been drawing in.

"Hold. Shush." She raised her fist in warning.

Something slithered ahead. Tallah saw it as a mess of illum erupting from the chasm. A massive shape hauled itself from the depths, settling with a tremor on a rock outcropping. She risked a glance from under the mask and saw the impression of a massive head moving side to side, mist clinging to it on the edge of torchlight. What manner of creature it was, she couldn't say. Her gaze slid off it, as if it wasn't quite there, yet very real at the same time.

It sniffed the air and grumbled, the vibrations of its heavy growl throbbing through the soles of their feet, yet as soundless as the mist itself. It advanced, sniffed, growled, swung the great head around. Confused. Angry?

Hungry.

"What is it doing?" Sil's voice squeaked behind Tallah. The healer's hand grasped her own and squeezed.

"Searching."

Again, the creature growled and turned in place, lumbering back whence it came, heaving into the dark depths. Its vibrations took a long time to settle.

Tallah saw the poison following him and swallowed the lump in her throat. Fear locked her in place, growing into bone-deep terror. The illum shape of the monster trailed it like a ghostly afterimage.

"Why are you stopping?" Sil asked from behind. "We should be getting as far from it as possible."

Only after the impression of power faded did she lead them forward. It was only a few steps before the next hurdle revealed itself.

Tallah stared into the maelstrom of poisonous power roiling beneath their feet. The impression of a sea at storm came to her. Among the crashing waves of reds and purples, the blue line of safety shimmered and descended, straight in the wake of the beast.

Uneven steps led down into the leviathan's domain. They needed to follow it. Had it known? Had it felt them and waited now in ambush?

'Don't be absurd,' Christina chided. 'It's an animal. It probably senses we're here, but if it can't see us, it can't hunt us. Keep tight rein on your illum store, and I believe we will be fine.'

"You can't be serious." Sil's tiny, muffled voice echoed every drop of terror Tallah felt as she took the first step down. "There's no other way?"

Tallah called a halt just in time for Sil to feel her knees buckle with exhaustion. They'd been going relentlessly for so long that she could barely still keep upright. Up and down endless flights of broken stairs, in and around ancient structures, back and forth through the mist.

The creature's specter was there, always out of torchlight, though Tallah had said nothing about it since the first sighting.

My imagination will be the death of me, Sil admonished herself as she leaned against a wall and pulled out the tonic. To the others, she said, "Drink the first vial. It will ease the fatigue."

"Distinctive taste, Miss Silestra." Ludwig grimaced and turned slightly green around the gills as he swilled the tonic in his mouth.

"Very different from your usual, Sil." Vergil coughed twice, forcing himself to down his portion in as few gulps as possible.

"Are you poisoning us? This is disgusting." Tallah . . . reacted as expected.

"Bugger you all," Sil spat. "Don't drink it, then. See if I care when you stumble off the path in exhaustion."

Yes, the tonic tasted like fermented elkana milk. Charitably. And it looked like she'd scraped it off the sidewalk beneath some street vendor's food cart. Again, charitably. Sil was keenly aware of her work's shortcomings.

But that's how the mixture came together. She'd tried to make it more palatable, but then it turned into a sort of laxative and that defeated the purpose of something meant to keep you on your feet for a week.

"Sil, my tongue's gone numb. Is that normal?"

"It's normal. It's only bad if you can't feel when you bite it."

"Ow."

That dash of pettiness helped alleviate the gnawing fear that squirmed in her guts. They hadn't seen the beast again and it'd been near a day since that first time, if Tallah's timekeeping was to be believed, but Sil could swear she felt the tremors of its presence. Her traitorous imagination filled the silence with too many otherworldly sounds. She took a moment to recite a healer's mantra under her breath.

The tonic filled her with restless energy as the others struggled to get it down. Tallah's guidance had them following the creature's trail, though it hadn't made another appearance since the first. They rested now at some kind of temple—she assumed it a temple, for there were statues rising through the mist, depicting some kind of winged beings surrounding a central platform too featureless now to guess at its purpose. Her legs ached but she couldn't sit. Every scrape of boot on rock, swish of cloth, clang of armor sent her heart into flutters. She envied how easily Vergil rested on the edge of the chasm, feet swinging idly over the emptiness.

So she busied herself making a study of the statues and the vague remnants of mosaic paintings on what remained of the walls. Humanoid torsos. Two-armed. No idea on the legs. Winged. Above, the cupola of the building was opened, as if to peer at the sky. It made very little sense.

"Worshipping winged beings underground? What kind of idiocy is this?" She lifted her torch trying to get a better view of the heads of the statues. Most were shattered, smashed clean off by some weapon, ages before. Mist clung to them in ghostly wisps.

"Makes you wonder what's happened here. Have a look through this," Tallah said. She approached and handed over the Ikosmenia. "Have a look at this."

Sil could only take a few heartbeats of the maddening swirls before she had to hand back the mask. Already she felt her head swimming.

"How are you not clawing our eyes out," she asked, though she didn't expect an answer.

Tallah offered her arm for support until the dizzy spell subsided.

"I've never seen illum behaving like this. I could swear it's bouncing off of something at times. In some places it pools." Tallah finished the last of her tonic and grimaced. "Same as before? Two of these per day?"

"One. It's concentrated. Reason for the taste. Figured it'd be less traumatic to only drink one that's a bit fouler."

"Admirable sentiment." She burped and hiccuped, pressed a fist to her mouth and swallowed. "Not sure about the trauma part. Come on. Illum's shifting. I don't want to backtrack again."

They set back on the tortuous slow trek forward. From the temple out into an open street, among wrecked hovels that hung shattered, stone bones tumbling across chasms. Tallah led them across some of these walls turned bridges, picking their way onward, testing each step.

"If the guardian senses magic," Vergil said from behind her. "Shouldn't it feel the mask and follow it right to us?"

"Enchantments are a different form of *magic*, as you call it, lad," Ludwig replied. "They hold very little illum. It does leak, but not as strongly as a channeler's weaving. Some people have spent lifetimes developing ways to scry an assessment of an enchantment by touch. Some bastil Shadow Priests can do it at a glance. But it's a rare gift even for them."

"I don't know what a bastil is. Is that another species?"

"Odd. You should at least know of the seven, lad. Were you taught to read but not this?"

"I grew up in the sticks before coming to Valen."

Sil grinned at Vergil's poor lie. Yes, that's what they'd told him to say if anyone asked about his incongruities. But, like Tallah, he was an embarrassingly bad liar when put on the spot. He said the words with the same cadence of a child reciting his letters.

"What are the seven?" Vergil went on.

"Human. Aelir. Elend. Vanadal. Bastil. Drackir. Dwarf. Though that last one's mostly died out unfortunately."

"I don't think I've ever laid eyes on a bastil, myself," Sil said. "Aren't they beastly?"

"Miss Silestra!" Ludwig sounded affronted by the very idea of it. "That is base human centrism! The bastil are a noble people with a rich culture that have much to teach all of Edana, if there weren't so few of them. Yes, they have fur, but that hardly makes anyone *beastly*. I've visited their homeland. It is a marvel."

Sil wanted to answer this, but stepped in a crack and lost her balance. She grabbed on to Vergil's arm and they both toppled into a pile with a short, muted cry. The torch rolled away into the chasm, its light swallowed in less than a heartbeat.

"Watch where you step," Tallah called back, stopping long enough for Ludwig to help them back to their feet.

The path fragmented and loosened underfoot.

They climbed atop the crumbling remains of what Sil assumed to have been some kind of aqueduct. It shifted with each step, every sway sideways sending her heart high in her throat. Fine dust, like ash, covered it, marking the passage of their footfalls.

"Are you sure this is the way?" Vergil swung his torch over the abyss.

Sil cringed at the utter emptiness surrounding their chosen route.

"I haven't the foggiest." Tallah sounded far too sanguine for the situation. "It's safe. I think we're in a kind of illum funnel. If I'm right, there's a clear flow of power that goes from the entrance to the exit."

"You can't know that," Sil protested.

"No better explanation, at least for now. Best guess as any."

"I haven't seen that many kinds of people in Valen," Vergil said, picking up the earlier conversation. Sil silently thanked him for the distraction. "I've met elends and aelirs, but that's about it."

"You forget there's a dwarf ghost in your helmet," she provided helpfully.

"Does it count? He just screams all the time. Could as well be a bear for all we know."

"Very dwarfish behavior," Ludwig remarked.

"Now who's being human-centric?" Vergil cut back at him.

"It is well documented, and commonly known, that dwarves were a belligerent society that valued strength of arm above most anything else. If they weren't fighting, they were building, often with the intent of going to war. A quiet dwarf was an abnormality."

"So is a quiet human," Tallah said.

"Well, yes, true. But we don't fight ourselves out of existence."

"The aelir might have something to say on that subject. And the empress herself."

That shut him up. Two centuries of near-endless civil war. The aelir's slaughter of ancient human empires, all to stop relentless human expansion, paled in comparison to what the empress had wrought. Only the gods knew what her goals were, but the amount of blood she'd already shed could drown cities.

"You've also met a vanadal, Vergil," Tallah said without looking back. "In the snow storm. The one with the Storm Guard captain."

"Seemed an odd fellow."

"Be happy you've met him like that and not in a fight. Barlo's one of the meanest mage killers in the entire empire. He was trained by the adjunct's personal guard."

"Even odder is that he's on Vas," Ludwig mused. "Vanadals don't often leave Nen. They're beholden to the aelir."

"Not the ones from the steppes."

"Long way from there to here."

"I've met a drackir once," Sil said to keep herself from imagining more shapes in the listless movement of mist, especially with the road swaying underfoot. "Back when I was still at school. Hard to stomach. Tentacles and all that. Was an all right person, though. Liked bees a lot."

"Never knew them to be the healing sort. Most drackir I've served with were keen on disemboweling."

"Pretty much. They did like the autopsies best."

Vergil gave a loud belch and immediately clamped a hand over his mouth. "I'm sorry," he said softly. "The tonic—"

"It'll do that, don't worry," Sil assured him and stifled her own noisome belch. "It's made to keep you going, not to do it in a nice way."

"Can't you work out the taste to be less gross?" Vergil asked. "I don't think I've ever tasted anything worse. Tastes like rotten meat smells."

Sil turned to him and brandished her torch. She gave him a wide grin.

"Would you like me to tell you what I ground up and put in them, bucket-head?"

"I'd rather you didn't."

"I'm glad you want to know! You see, I take the legs off of this blue-bellied roach and then grind it down to—"

"I had to deal with a roach infestation once," Vergil interrupted her. He grinned right back. "I'm glad you mentioned how you're making us drink insect bits."

No! He wouldn't dare.

The boy kept going with entirely too much enthusiasm. "I was supposed to burn out these shiny silver roaches but found that they were really quite tasty. Spent a few days just eating myself into a stupor wherever I found a nest. They'd do this cute squirm whenever you bit into one." He wiggled his fingers for emphasis.

It stunned Sil into silence. How could one boy be this disgusting?!

"Finally had to set them alight. I couldn't eat enough of them, fast enough, to stop their spread. They made this little sad pop when they caught fire and burst."

Sil turned away and dry heaved over the edge to no success. She had brewed the tonic to be nigh impossible to regurgitate.

"A lot of the things that clogged up the vents were surprisingly edible," Vergil went on, in a cheerful tone. "I did change colors a couple of times. My stool—"

"I swear I will push you off this ledge," Sil said without turning back to him, gesturing instead with the flaming end of her torch over the emptiness. "You are the most disgusting creature I've ever met."

Vergil dodged the flame before it smacked him right in the face. "Well, you insisted on telling us what you're putting in the bloody tonics. I'm still more palatable than those."

Tallah gave him a slow, gloved clap, without even turning to look at their little argument.

"How do you discover, by accident, mind you, that a roach is tasty? Asking out of academic curiosity, naturally," Ludwig said. He grinned, gap-toothed, in Sil's direction.

"Yes, Vergil, do tell us. I bet Sil could grind up some of those into an even more disgusting version of this drink," Tallah said.

If Sil could slap her, she would've. The last stretch of the aqueduct lay tumbled, broken to pieces onto which they had to climb. What waited at the bottom was something resembling solid ground again. She offered a silent prayer of thanks to the Goddess for this small mercy.

Tallah stopped them. She reached out a hand to the side and withdrew it quickly. "Path's getting real narrow ahead. The nasty illum's closing in on us." Her head swiveled around, tracking something in the dark. "The creature's close. Keep your wits about you."

Sil peered over her shoulder and saw the narrow slit into which the path led. Two dwellings lay crashed against one another, walls forming the narrowest passage since the ice squeeze. Something caressed her cheek, burning her skin like the kiss of acid. She recoiled, swinging her torch around, heart threatening to jump out of her throat.

"Don't move about," Tallah warned. "The poison stings even at a touch. I expect it'll be worse if we breathe it in. Deep breath while we still have air."

She turned sideways and slid inside the gap, torch held forward. Sil and Ludwig extinguished theirs and followed inside.

"Dark, cramped, and dangerous places; story of my life," Vergil groaned as he brought up the rear.

It wasn't a long passage, but it squeezed them tight and kept them quiet as they made their way along it. Rough stone scratched at her cheek. Her heart drummed a melody of panic in her ears. Would this even lead somewhere forward? She wanted to ask Ludwig but breathing was enough of an effort.

"Deep breath. Hold until I say so," Tallah called back, words strained. "Don't panic. It will hurt, but I expect it will hurt a lot more if you gasp in the stuff."

Sil inhaled just in time for the first stinging caress on her face. It kissed her skin like drops of acid. She groaned. Pain washed across her, faded, came back again, like waves lapping at the shore.

How would it be to die to this? To be stuck in the sea of pain, with no way to know where safety lay, forced to breathe in the agony—

Vibrations in the wall stopped her spiraling imagination. Pressure on it, like something tremendously heavy leaning on the other side. Breath wheezed out between her teeth as she felt crushed and dissolved at the same time. Stuck fast, the wave of poison enveloping her in a stinging embrace, the creature on the far side sniffling about. Its heartbeat—it had a heartbeat!—thundered rhythmically against the stone, in and through her.

One heartbeat. Two. Three. Four. She counted and her own sped in a panic. Her chest . . . her chest burned. Too frozen in fear to draw anything, even if she could. The corrupt touch of the place washed over her, needling a scream in the back of her throat.

Not like this. Vision blurred in tears. She shut her eyes tight against the constricting pain.

It moved away, thump by blessed thump. Pain fled with its departure.

Tallah grabbed her hand and yanked her forward, out of the passage's grip. "Breathe," she said. She reached inside again to pull Ludwig forward. Then Vergil. "Don't dawdle. I don't know how far it's gone but it's pulled some of the poison after it." She was already moving forward, stepping around something only she could see, urging them to follow.

Sil tried to keep up and gasped for breath, still feeling the touch of corruption on her skin, fearing she might inhale whatever it had been. She stumbled. Ludwig helped her to her feet and they kept up with Tallah's long strides, never looking back.

Torchlight drowned in the mist. Tallah swung it around and raised her mask, massaging her eyes.

"Rest a moment." She relented. "I don't feel we've seen the last of that thing."

In the unsettling quiet, the beast roared. It was a long moan of anguish, an animal sound that spoke of hunger and terrible frustration.

"Well, bugger you too," Tallah said to the dark.

By the eve of a third day of walking, crawling, and slithering through gaps, moods had begun to sour. Tallah found herself snapping to anger at the slightest provocation, especially as their bursts of progress became shorter and shorter.

"Aren't we going in circles?" Sil asked, for the hundredth time, it seemed. "It feels like we're going in circles."

"How would you even tell? Do you have the mask on?" Tallah asked, more tersely than she intended. Everything hurt and her eyes stung with sweat.

Sil didn't reply. She sullenly drank from the vile tonic and huffed.

The farther in they got, the greater the evident devastation. It wasn't even ruins that surrounded them anymore, but an expanse of bottomless chasms dotted here and there with the vestiges of buildings. And everywhere the mist. Endless and fathomless and frustrating.

Stairways up or down into nothing. Dead ends she needed to backtrack from. Narrow squeezes ending in blocked passages. A thousands ways of losing valuable time, each a reason to stoke her anger.

And always Rhine. Everywhere she looked, the wraith stared back and grinned.

"Is the fog getting to you?" Tallah asked Sil, trying to hold back the red tide of her own annoyances.

She got a rant in answer. "It's not even fog, Tallah! Fog has volume. It has class. This is just a piss-thin curtain of vapor. Bloody right, it's getting on my last nerve!"

Under her mask, Tallah raised an eyebrow.

"It's a good thing the creature guarding this place is deaf. They must have heard you over in Valen just now."

In spite of Ludwig's age, it was Sil that was having the hardest time keeping up. The healer had shed some of her layers and wore her undershirt tied at her waist. The temperature kept dropping and increasing, and she'd taken to complaining incessantly. Granted, it filled the grating silence.

"I think we're coming up on something," Tallah mused.

"How so?"

She scraped the floor with the heel of her boot. "Mosaic tiles here. I think I saw some parts of walls in the dark. The poison flows around them. And the waves are coming in faster now, like they're bouncing off something, like at the entrance." She shrugged, almost speaking to herself. "If we're not close to an exit, then I'm stumped."

Sil looked to the old man as he rested with Vergil, talking quietly with the boy. "How do you figure the old man made it through? With twenty men in tow?"

"Slowly." Tallah ducked a cuff to the back of the head. "I'm serious."

"And I seriously want to hit you for that one. I'm in no mood."

Sil's Terrible and Healthy Tonic, as Vergil had dubbed it, was fast losing its effectiveness. Weariness set bone-deep and every step forward took effort of will. It showed on everyone.

Miserable experience with no end in sight. She could only glance at the blue line lately, always just on a different path than them. It was probably why Sil felt they were going in circles. *More a spiral*, Tallah realized as she looked to her guiding light, trying to discern it better. If she'd paid more attention to it . . .

'It is a spiral,' Christina said. 'Thought you'd noticed at some point. We've been going lower and lower for a full day now. If Bianca weren't immersed in the work, she could tell you more.'

"You know what's odd?" Vergil asked as he and Ludwig came down the path.

Tallah gave him a flat look, gesturing with the sputtering torch in a wide arc.

"Argia's been trying to connect to something since we got in here," he said, oblivious to the irony. "It keeps pinging something and waiting for replies. Every few seconds. I think it's finally going bad."

"Have it join Sil. She's going nutty too, the poor biddy."

Sil belched and showed a rude gesture.

"We should be coming up on the end of this," Ludwig said, a hint of hope in his voice.

"How do you figure, old man?" Tallah drew the mask back onto her eyes and stretched the kinks out of her back.

"I remember the fractured path. It should be close to the end."

"Well, that's encouraging, at least. How'd the girl manage this trip? It couldn't have been easy on a child."

Ludwig sputtered, "Oh, she handled it better than any of us. Wonderfully resilient child. She put to shame grown men. Hardened veterans of a dozen war fronts."

"And one grown healer, I might add." Tallah gave the healer a grin, just to draw her into the routine. Too much sulking, and Sil was likely to get bitey again.

Sil refused the bait. Rather, she stared at them, open-mouthed, eyes wide. Stared through them. Tallah looked over her shoulder and met the beast's gaze.

How it had snuck so close, she could only imagine and marvel at. Christina had been watching for it out of the back of Tallah's skull. They'd both been on alert since the last unwelcome meeting but had sensed nothing of the creature. No disturbance in the illum. No errant sound. Not even a whiff of rot!

But it was there, on the path closest to them, close enough it could reach over and grab any one of them. Great bat-like wings folded around a serpentine body. It propped itself on two massive, multi-jointed and clawed limbs.

She could see no eyes on it.

It was there and not wholly there. It breathed in the poisonous mist and exhaled it twofold.

And it stared right at Vergil, who stupidly stared back.

"Connection achieved," he said, fixed in place like a seamstress's dummy, eyes unfocused. "Why?!"

A great maw of teeth opened and cadaverous stink filled the air. Spikes bristled and it hunched forward, long tongue lashing about, searching.

Tallah grabbed Sil and Vergil by the arms and hauled them along. Ludwig could follow or be eaten. The creature lurched forward, its massive jaws snapping at the space where the boy had been with a crunch of uneven fangs gnashing together.

"To your senses, you two," Tallah growled. "No time to go deaf and dumb. Run now. Lose your minds later."

"That never happened before," Ludwig squeaked behind her. "It's never come for someone without provocation."

"It did now. Shut up. Move."

Vergil managed on his own, snapped out of his stupor. Sil kept trying to look behind. She needed dragging and shoving before snapping back to a semblance of clarity.

"It's coming, Tallah," the healer squeaked. "It's behind us."

Tallah didn't look. "Stop gawking at it. Run. We'll lose it in the ruins ahead. Vergil, if it's your bloody thing that's drawn it, shut it off."

"I can't. I don't—it lost connection. Trying again. Shock me. Do something."

"Just run."

The path vibrated, rumbled, was still, as if something massive had fallen off it. Or taken to the air. Her imagination provided the sound of leathery wings beating against the vapor-choked air and the world darkening just a little as a shadow passed overhead. *Silly woman*, she chided herself. There was no light to cast a shadow.

Rubble and ruin blocked the way forward, a dead end of masonry that spilled into the chasm and rose to unseen heights. She urged them to scrabble over it. No time to go back or around. A near avalanche followed, noise swallowed by the fog.

Tallah reached the top first and looked out to the immediate surroundings. Rhine's wraith had become a kind of beacon for danger. The wraith was absent. Beyond, down the ragged slope, twenty paces away, the fog swirled out like raging through a funnel. The end in sight.

Sil fell. Broken masonry shifted underfoot and she tumbled back with it, too far from either Tallah and Vergil to reach out. With a thud, she landed on empty air. A barrier bloomed underneath her.

Damn the woman's reflexes!

A triumphant roar filled the air and fog swirled above.

Tallah reached inside, found Bianca, yanked her to the surface. "Wake up. I need you." She braced for the flood of music, but she barely felt it in the panic of the moment.

'What do you think you're doing?' Bianca asked irately. 'What in the bloody throne is that?' she added as Tallah's eyes rested on the surging beast.

"Tell you later. It eats illum."

She reached out, grabbed Sil and pulled hard. No sense in concealing their illum now. Bianca provided the anchors. The healer flew through the air just as the creature crashed into the ruins. Its jaws crushed rocks as it rose and bellowed. Dust exploded off it in a cloud.

"Run to the exit," Tallah called to the others. "Don't stop until you're out."

'What do we do?' Bianca overcame her panic easily, and Tallah felt herself grow lighter than air.

The beast came up the slope with thunderous roars of anger, great maw snapping for prey it knew was there. The others slid and tumbled down the other side. Tallah drew in power and launched herself over the creature, and back down the path they'd come from.

Lead it back to the chasm, make it take flight, outmaneuver it. That's about my entire plan.

'Context, please.' Bianca wasn't nearly as spent as Tallah expected her to be. Normally, when only one of the ghosts did the work of both, they would be spent within bells. The store of illum the ghost brought to bear was nearly intact.

"It sees illum. It eats it. I expect I can't fight it. If we go off the safe passage, we die. That enough context for you?"

'Plenty.'

It came upon her like a murderous tempest. Fog wreathed it and it was suddenly there, fully real, no longer an uncertain conjuration of the ruins. A swipe of its tail would've broken her in two as easily as she would a twig. Talons as long as her arm swiped after her, but Bianca whirled her sideways. She sailed down the shifting passage and the beast charged after her like lightning.

Her fireball slid off its bristled hide like water. It only made it roar, a feeling of excited pleasure emanating from it as clear as if it was . . . human? In the rush of the moment, Tallah could swear it felt something human from it, and yet horribly wrong.

It snapped and clawed for her. She dove and slid under its great bulk. Bianca tried anchoring her to it but the power slid off. She fell through the chasm, dipped feet into the poison, rushed back over in a sailing arc. Drew her sword.

If the weave fails, maybe steel?

"The wing," she urged the ghost.

'No,' came Bianca reply as she pulled her away. 'It's not really flying. Can't you see it?'

With an effort to focus, Tallah could see it: the same kind of weave she was using. The beast channeled its own tethers to keep that great bulk aloft. A moment after realization hit, the beast opened its mouth and fire belched out. Bianca yanked her sideways and the heat merely blistered rather than consumed. Another furnace blast followed, and it was all the ghost could do to keep ahead of the flames.

A glance back. She was no longer leading in the chase. The creature dove from above. Talons reached out to enclose her. Bianca pulled down with such force it snapped Tallah's head back. Blood filled her vision as she rode the breakneck dive.

'Brace,' the ghost commanded. She did, shut her eyes tight. Her flight lurched sideways, avoiding another swipe of the creature. The others should have had enough time to get away. She couldn't run for much longer. Poison caressed her skin, burning with all the pain the flame breath promised.

'Open your eyes. I need to see through the mask.'

It followed unbelievably fast.

'Don't pass out. Don't pass out. Don't pass out.'

"I won't." Tallah gritted her teeth and urged Bianca for more. The beast kept up too easily, unhindered by its tremendous bulk, much more intelligent than she would have expected of it. It saw through every move and maneuver, matched Bianca's skill, and cut off their options.

Tallah loosed another blast of fire to no result, not even slowing it down.

Panic began to sizzle and bubble. As fast as Bianca could pull her, the creature was simply faster and bloodlust frenzied. It flew straight through walls she needed to avoid, snapping and swiping after her like a storm of knives. One talon grazed her leg, knee to ankle. Pain blossomed, red-hot. She drew her sword and awkwardly parried the claws. The strength of the swipe sent her sideways, tumbling through the mist, into the poison. Pain sharpened her focus.

A flash of light. One heartbeat away from disaster. She drew sideways and the furnace blast flashed by, so close her skin blistered.

Pull me back, hard as you can. Any more of this chase and we'll be trapped. It's herding us.

Bianca acknowledged only by obeying.

They swirled together through the roiling mist, dipping painfully in and out of the thing. It pushed her back inwards, away from safety and the exit, cutting off her retreat.

Bianca set a tether atop a statue jutting out of the mist and swung them around in a wide, accelerating arc.

'Be ready. You'll probably see red. Don't panic.' If they couldn't run from it, they'd run *at* it. The exit was right behind the monster.

Tallah drew in a last gasp of burning air before it happened.

No amount of bracing could have prepared her. Bianca didn't just accelerate. She launched them back like a stone out of a catapult. Tallah's eyeballs pooled in the back of their sockets, vision turned bloody.

It was in front of her, meeting her, jaws open, teeth bared, still coming at incredible speed. She couldn't and didn't dare try to blink.

An arm's reach away from its center mass. Claws flashed to rip into her.

Bianca's tether pulled hard sideways and down, and she felt her bones ready to rip out through her skin, every joint distended, prepared to snap. Sil's sutures, barely healed, burst to release a cascade of pain down her side.

They flew under the claws' killing sweep by a hairbreadth. A palm's width separated them from the creature's brutish torso.

And they were past its tail, away through the painful mist.

'Blast its bones, it's fast,' Bianca warned and dove her downward in time to avoid a blast of fire.

If she turned her head to look, her neck would've snapped.

Too slow. Too clumsy. It was on her, flying in from the side, jaws coming down to snap her in two.

It smashed into something invisible with the force of an earthquake. Tallah heard Sil calling out and, through the red haze of burst capillaries, saw the healer atop the mountain of refuse, leaning heavily on her staff. Tallah's flight brought her near in a heartbeat.

She caught Sil as she flew by, one arm around her belly, tethers binding them together. Sil's head smashed against Tallah's shoulder. The healer went rigid, then completely boneless—likely fainted—with the sudden motion as Bianca raced them to the exit.

The creature's roar of frustration made the whole cavern vibrate. Tallah didn't care. She flew through the barely opened doorway, Sil in arms, at blinding speed and only slowed far down the following tunnel. She wasn't quite certain if she'd passed Vergil and Ludwig but was happy to feel solid ground underfoot again. Her leg couldn't hold her weight, and she toppled forward over the healer, gasping for air, feeling sick.

In the rush, she hadn't had the time or strength to breathe.

"Are you two all right?" Vergil ran in from the back of the tunnel. A crash followed him as the monster smashed into the gateway and bellowed out its anger.

"Alive," Tallah gasped as she rolled off Sil's unconscious form. "See to her."

But Sil was already stirring. She groaned in pain. "I can't believe that worked. I can't believe it."

"Agreed."

The why and the how of it barely mattered. Nothing else had even slowed the thing. She was thankful they'd both made it out alive.

Vergil brought Sil her satchel as she forced herself into a sitting position to rummage about. She threw Tallah the usual healing draft.

"Well near broke my back when you grabbed me," she complained as she tried to get up and winced.

"Either that or leave you to get eaten. You're still walking. You're fine."

"How did . . . how did you do that, Tallah?" Ludwig broke his silence. He stared at her, the first inkling of doubt crossing his face. "How could you do that?"

Even if he hadn't seen her taking on the beast, he had seen her fly through. Pyromancers rarely flew, and it was generally in pieces.

"Practice, old man. It does wonders. Are we safe out here?"

He remained unconvinced. Sil trudged over and asked to inspect the cut leg. It had healed, yes, but it still hurt like crazy. All of her did, mercilessly.

"Nearly cut the bone in two," Sil noted. "Drink this too. I think you painted the path red."

"We're safe, yes," Ludwig finally said, weighing every word while he eyed her suspiciously. His gaze swiveled from her to Vergil. "This never happened the first time. What are you, boy?"

"Lost," Vergil answered with characteristic honesty. He shrugged. "And as confused as everyone else."

"He's a long story," Tallah cut in. "Leave him be. I got you past the horrid place. Be happy with that. You've only waited a lifetime for the moment."

"And you'll all wait a few bells more," Sil said, definite. "Line up. I want to have a good look at each of you. We rest and sleep, or next we'll be seeing things that aren't there."

'There's no music here,' Christina whispered in her ear while the men did as ordered. Ludwig had given her one final look and then seemed to reach the right decision and dropped his questions. 'There's no draw at all.'

'There was,' Bianca said. 'But it got quieter as we moved in there. Was waiting to see if it went away completely when you pulled me out.'

'It has. Not a peep. Not a bit of a draw. Whatever this place is, you're shielded now.' Christina let out a mental sigh. 'We can all rest, for once.'

For once, her soul would stay attached to her mortal coil without Bianca and Christina clawing at it. If her heart hadn't been bursting out of her in the labyrinth, she would have noticed how much easier it was to breathe now, how much more settled she felt in her own bones.

It had been such a long time since she'd felt this free. There was here, after all, some solution to her dilemma.

"Fancy that," Tallah said. She looked back up the tunnel at the half-opened doors and thought back to the near-human feeling that had washed off the beast. "Wonder what we've gotten ourselves into."

CHAPTER TWENTY-SEVEN

Crepuscular

Quistis could still hear the reveling as she slunk back into their cell's office. It'd been . . . what? She counted seven days since the Night of Descent but probably longer. She'd had precious little time to relax between then and now, and the days had a way of blending together if one slept too little.

A half-empty mug of cold coffee perched on the edge of her desk. She hadn't even tasted it before being called out to look at whatever Rumi had found in the Angledeer home.

Not much of interest at a glance. Books in a myriad of languages miraculously saved from destruction by sheer bulk. Schematics for some rather strange implements. Some boxes of foul-smelling tea.

Odd, that one.

Everything had been dug out, written down, and painstakingly carted back to the Citadel. A lifetime of refuse gathered in a hovel in Valen by a man with an edict on his head. Wonders never ceased.

Falor slumped in a chair by the fire, gripping a cup of coffee. His also looked to have gone cold. For a moment, as she hung up her cloak to dry, she thought he slept.

"Welcome back."

Quistis jumped at the sudden noise.

Falor opened his eyes, stared into the fire and lifted his mug to his lips. "Anything of interest?" he asked, voice low.

On his other hand, he wore his white gauntlet. Fine black cracks spread across the fingers, clear even in dim firelight. He formed a fist and the whole thing creaked, shards flaking off.

"Why aren't you in bed?" She took note of the dark circles pooling beneath his eyes. "Put down the coffee and go rest. You've done more than enough."

And he had. After Cinder's escape and throughout the following days, he'd helped with clearing the rubble, putting out the fires, and quieting the unrest. And after that he'd supervised the Illum Ascendi, hammer in hand, in case the sorceress tried sneaking back in the same way she'd left.

Valen's people hailed him as a hero. "*For the lord commander's health, may long and strong be the arm of his law!*" was a toast in every tavern from the Upper City to the Lower. Much to Diogron's displeasure, but that was a worry she put away for whenever she'd miss a headache.

"Don't even think about it," she warned as he raised the cup to his lips again. "Sleep. Or the next time you spar, I'll let you bleed into unconsciousness."

He listened and let out a slow breath, setting the mug down on the floor.

"You know . . ." He turned a black gaze upon her. His hand went to his neck and massaged slowly, like feeling around for an invisible cut. "She could have killed me. Did anyone report that? She could have taken my head clean off, and there was nothing I could've done to prevent it." His tongue licked across his upper teeth. "Nothing at all."

"You can't know that." It was an effort not to flinch and look over her shoulder at the spot he was staring at.

He smiled grimly and rolled his shoulders. She heard every pop and creak.

"I assumed she had hidden strength or else she wouldn't have come out of hiding like that. I was braced for it. But that burst?" He shook his head slowly, sucking in breath between his teeth. "Even Mother can't do it that cleanly. I was utterly unprepared for it. And this . . ."

He raised his gauntlet and it crumbled like porcelain, parts of it dropping to shatter on the floor.

Quistis felt a surge of pity to see it in such a state. It was a work of art, constructed and enchanted by some of the finest artisans of Aztroa Magnor. A gift from the empress herself, back when their cell had been sent as peacekeepers to Valen.

The enchantment, as Quistis had seen it working countless times, was made to break weaves. Granted, it had a limit as any enchantment did, but she'd never seen anyone, save Falor himself, even strain the piece.

"You finally broke it?" she asked, forcing levity into her voice.

Falor was in one of his rare black moods, and she wasn't certain where it was springing out of. She took a step towards him and hesitated, unsure if he wanted the company. He didn't seem to notice.

"*She* broke the enchantment. Overloaded it. It was . . ." He licked cracked lips while studying the damage. "Some lances and a few fireballs? Not even a devourer. Can you imagine how powerful her output is? If she had stood her ground for a head-on, the night might have ended quite differently."

So that preyed on him. She'd read the reports. Everyone celebrated how the commander had defeated Cinder's assassination attempt—that's what they were calling it, anyway—and how wildly outclassed the sorceress had been throughout the engagement. Nobody seemed to understand how close they'd been to disaster.

"Maybe she's not as good as you give her credit for," Quistis said, feeling like she had a handle on the situation now.

The commander could be a sore loser now and again. He was only human, same as anyone.

"You're wrong," Falor protested.

"And you're dead on your feet. Go rest."

No answer for long enough that she had a chance to consider her coffee. The mountain of paperwork on her desk loomed and it was definitely much too late in the night to deal with. As Quistis lifted the mug, she considered her own advice.

Besides, cold coffee was disgusting.

"Why do you think she hesitated?" Falor turned back to the dying fire, gauntlet set down by the cool mug. "You think she tried to scare me? Make a point of some sort?"

She couldn't answer that. Falor knew Cinder much better than she ever would. Pupil and mentor. If he wondered at her motives, Quistis couldn't even begin to guess.

"I wouldn't know. But you need rest, commander. No point in dwelling on what the mad do."

"She's not mad, Quis. I guarantee that. No more than you or I."

Sounds of the citywide celebration carried through an open window somewhere down the hall. It was winding down after all, compared to previous nights, some of the revelers peeling away, their whistles and cheers dying out in the distance.

"You fought her off, and everyone in Valen is celebrating," she tried. "Wouldn't do for their hero to sulk himself sick."

Not even a chuckle. Just the same black, exhausted stare.

"They're celebrating the Descent, not me. I failed to bring her to heel. Hesitated on the killing blow. Do you know what my mother asked me when we were alone? Before she left?"

Quistis hadn't been listening in on that. Rather, she'd been busy keeping

Diogron away from the gate while the empress exchanged some parting words with her son.

"*What did you do to Cinder?* That's all. Didn't even bat an eye when I described her spitting my devourer back at me." He shook his head again, eyes unfocused. "I don't understand what she meant by that. I've hurt Cinder, but that answer didn't satisfy Mother. She just . . . grunted and turned away. I just don't understand."

Falor plunged into darker waters. Quistis recognized that spiraling mood and decided on a change of tack. Her work wouldn't get done on its own, but it would keep for a few more bells. She set her staff on its pegs and made her way to his chair. They were alone in the entire wing of the Citadel, the rest of their cell engaged in the city or sleeping off daytime celebrations.

She put her hands on the back of his neck, thumbs pressed on his knotted muscles. A gentle upward pressure made him shudder.

"We know she's using shards," she said. Her fingers began a slow massage, thumb over thumb as her mother had taught her. "She's not coming back into the city that way. The gates are watched. Rumi and Aidan are training the guardsmen for what to watch for. Vial's seeing to getting the plaques made for the other two associates of hers. Barlo's drilling the city guard on what to do for the next time she shows up. All is firmly in hand."

Her fingers slid under the collar of his uniform, massaging the coiled ropes of his muscles. If Falor were any stiffer, he'd match the actual statue of him that some wished erected.

"You are wonderfully efficient, as ever." He looked up at her and shifted in the chair. His shoulders began to relax under her touch. "What would I do without you?"

"Overwork yourself into an early coffin, I believe." She leaned forward and whispered in his ear, "I'll make you a deal, commander. You go to bed, and I will join you. We could both do with a good night's sleep. Or what may remain of it, anyway."

After interminable silence, Quistis was almost certain he'd fallen asleep right there and then. Almost certain and more than a little disappointed.

"I'd like that," he said with a deep inhale of breath. In one swift movement, he rose from the chair and stretched. "The crises of tomorrow can wait until morning, I suppose. Let's."

Quistis lingered for a bit longer, emptying cups of coffee over dying embers and cracking open a window. Echoes of the night bells carried over the soft whispers of late-winter wind. Three of them, the cusp of midnight. She set a paperweight on her mountain of work and cursed herself for the diligence. *I should leave you to be blown into the night.*

She shook her head, ascending the staircase into Falor's chamber.

Echoes of the night bells chased some of the dream cobwebs as Quistis woke groggily in the dark of deep night. Five bells? Maybe six? Hard to say and harder to understand what had woken her so early. Heavy drapes covered the windows with barely a slit between them. The room was bathed in pitch. Not even a sliver of light penetrated from the outside.

She tried stretching but her legs and abdomen protested the idea. *Right, that's going to take a day and a warm bath*, she thought as she withdrew from Falor's back and cringed at the aches of her muscles.

He stirred under the quilt as her arms slipped free. A sliver of cold air goose-pricked her skin at the loss of contact.

Had she heard something?

Clearer vision came to her dimly, along with a rough understanding that there would be some more bells tolling before dawn. These were the uneven, quiet times spanning midnight to sunrise, the no man's land of living where bakers lit their ovens and criminals retreated into their lairs.

Falor's armor hung on its support, undisturbed and still soot-stained by Cinder's attack. His star-ore hammer rested next to it, a dull spot of gray in the night. Stacks of books on the floor. A pyramid of scrolls on his desk. The smell of weapon oil and sweat. All familiar and grounding to her as she resisted the temptation of sleep stinging her eyes.

Something felt off . . . yet nothing was disturbed.

Falor's room was small and cramped, a place of storage rather than living. His bed was almost as narrow as the one in her quarters, barely fitting two people embraced. She tried not to move too much and wake him. His even breathing was synced with hers even as her unease grew into spreading, irrational panic.

Shadows. More than there should be. Black on the deep blue of night. Darkness seethed across the room. Alien. She masked the agitation with a yawn as she resettled herself beneath the comforting weight of the quilt.

Someone was in the room with them. She knew it with the powerful certainty of a knife in the back. And she was suddenly and terribly aware of how naked they both were. How far they lay from their weapons. Her staff hung on its pegs in the office, two floors below. Falor's maul was two arm spans from the foot of the bed. The closest thing to a weapon was a long-tailed broom leaned against the wall by her side.

There was no movement around the bed. No sound. Not even an errant draft whispered aside from the revelries outside the walls.

A tremor where her leg touched Falor's, the barest hint of power buildup.

Good. He was awake and aware. If she could feel the oddness, he would have as well.

Six people would be dead or incapacitated for anyone to gain access to this room, four of them Storm Guards, loyal beyond question. Her blood ran cold at the prospect of senseless murder.

Falor shifted position, the rustle of cloth hiding the draw and buzz of power. Any moment—

Pure black erupted from the farthest corner of the room. In a heartbeat, they leapt clear of the bed, the cover thrown into the encroaching dark. Quistis made for the broom, eyes held tightly shut, ready for Falor's opening strike. A flash of lightning blasted away the night and turned the world bright red. Glass and wood crashed and splintered to the floor in a cacophony. Wind rushed in on frigid wings with a sandblast of dust.

Quistis snatched the broom and cast it in a wide arc. Nothing connected. She swung again, the wall at her back, and tried to blink away blots of colors.

Another thunder-clap from Falor and more waves of cold rushed into the shattered room. No one assailed her.

She built walls around herself and summoned a sprite above to take measure of what had happened.

A hole yawned into the cold Valen night. Falor peered out of it, one arm wreathed in pulsing, arcing lightning. The window was gone and so was nearly a quarter of the room. What survived of the curtain flapped in the breeze. In the far distance of a cloudless night, light crested over the mountain horizon.

Falor clambered from the wreckage and dug out his clothes from the debris. He threw Quistis her tattered robes.

"They ran. Crepuscular channeler. See to the guards," he ordered, pulling on trousers.

His hair was matted down by dust but there was no blood on him. What sort of assassin would have given them such an easy time? Quistis instinctively looked about the wreckage.

"Falor," she called.

Her sprite rose to the ceiling to reveal a message left to them.

Falor spared the sight but a glance before turning away. "See to the guards." He launched himself into the faltering night. Thunder followed as he blasted across the Citadel's rooftops. His maul flew by her head a moment later, trailing its wrathful master.

Down below, in the courtyard, shouts and whistles resounded. The Citadel came alive with alarms.

Quistis stood still and read the words over again.

"The sins of the mother taint the son," was written above their bed in what was certainly blood.

The cold bit into her naked skin and her wits slotted home. She hurriedly drew on robes and ran down the stairs towards the first guard post.

Their next crisis, it seemed, hadn't even been able to wait for morning to break properly.

About the Author

C. M. Antal is the author of the Tallah series, originally released on Royal Road. He was raised on fantasy and sci-fi books, video games, and just enough sunlight. Antal was born too early to traverse new worlds and has resigned himself to building his own and letting his characters explore (and explode) them. Antal lives in Romania and is a dad to one human boy, a dog, a cat, and two chinchillas.

RESPAWN YOUR CURIOSITY

follow us on our socials

 podiumentertainment.com

 @podiumentertainment

 /podiumentertainment

 @podium_ent

 @podiumentertainment